Moon Gold

AURIANO CURSE SERIES
BOOK 4

PATRICIA BARLETTA
www.patriciabarletta.com

Published Internationally by Patricia Barletta

Boston, MA
Copyright © 2022 Patricia Barletta
patriciabarletta.com

Exclusive cover © 2022 inputux.com
Interior design by Tamara Cribley www.deliberatepage.com

PRINT ISBN 978-1-7355994-3-4
EBOOK ISBN 978-1-7355994-2-7

Editor: Joanna D'Angelo

Copy Editor: Amy Sharp

This is a work of fiction. Names, characters, places and incidents are either the
product of the author's imagination or are used fictitiously, and any resemblance
to any person or persons, living or dead, events or locales is entirely coincidental.

Acknowledgments

Finishing the last book in a series is a bit like sending a child off to college. You're happy to see that child go out into the world, but sad they won't be permanently living under your roof any longer. I've lived with *The Auriano Curse Series* for many years, since I first conceived of the idea of a Venetian family living under a terrible curse. I'm glad that it's complete, but I'll miss the members of the House of Auriano. And like that child in their last year of high school before heading off to college and beyond, writing this book has had its highs and lows, times of smooth sailing and times of angst-ridden hair-pulling. Cheering me on through it all has been my editor/production manager/troubleshooter, Joanna D'Angelo, without whom I might have lost my way and never typed THE END. My gratitude next goes to Steve Coppola, who designed the gorgeous covers for the complete series. Each one is more striking than the last. Amy Sharp, my proofreader, caught all those grammatical and punctuation mistakes with her eagle eye. And Tamara Cribley at The Deliberate Page once again created beautiful inside pages. This book would not have been complete without all of you. Thank you.

The journey of Raphael and Sydney through the austere beauty of the Moroccan desert and the country's colorful cities might not have been as authentic if I had not traveled there with the Woodleigh Wanderers, led by the intrepid Bob and Katy S. I am so blessed to have been included in their travels and to count them as dear friends. Our tour director, Rosa, made sure we were steeped in the culture of the country, its people, and its history. The trip was an amazing experience, and I thank each and every one who traveled with me.

As always, my thanks go to my children for their support and enthusiasm for my writing career throughout the years, and to my grandchildren who never fail to give me joy.

Besides my own experience in the country of Morocco, I relied on many resources, most notably the ones below:

In Morocco, by Edith Wharton

"I Joined a Sahara Salt Caravan," *National Geographic,* November, 1965, by Victor Englebert

"Trek by Mule Among Morocco's Berbers," *National Geographic,* June, 1968, by Victor Englebert

"Drought Threatens the Tuareg World," *National Geographic,* April, 1974, by Victor Englebert

The Auriano Curse Series is dedicated to my late husband, Ken, who fought the curse of fronto-temporal dementia (FTD). In the course of the disease, he became a shadow of his former self, the inspiration for the curse on the House of Auriano. I'm sure he didn't mind, for he was tremendously supportive of my writing. Unfortunately, no magical Sphere of Astarte exists to combat FTD. My hope is that someday, a cure will be found, and the cursed disease will be banished.

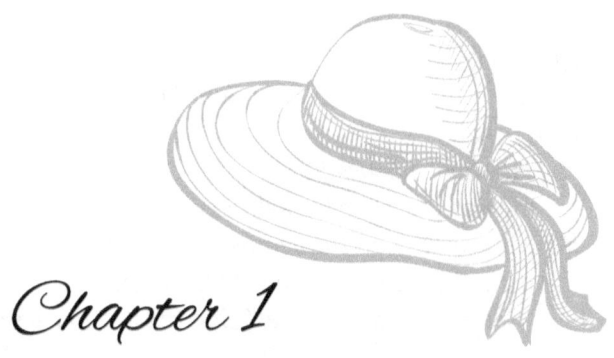

Chapter 1

1799, Somewhere in the Sahara Desert

"Give it to me."

The words swirled inside his head like hypnotic smoke. He wanted to give her what she desired, whatever it was. Part of him knew if he did, his life would end. But even that tempted. He watched her walk toward him with a sensual seduction that brought to mind the slide of skin on skin, the taste of arousal. Her tongue licked across her bottom lip. Immediately, heat pooled in his groin.

She was beautiful. Her black hair hung in a satiny fall well past her hips. Her dark eyes lured with the promise of unbelievable pleasure. The red dress draped on her lush form like a lover.

"Give it to me."

Her words, this time, were a soft whisper, an enticement. He was rock hard, aroused to the point of pain, but he knew there would be no release until he gave her what she wanted. Even then, the threat of pain balanced equally with pleasure. She swayed closer. Her ruby lips smiled. His arms jerked, either to draw her near or push her away, he couldn't be sure, but that movement made him aware he was chained, cold metal links wrapped around his arms and legs.

"Give it to me."

Her words pouted, as if she were wheedling a worthless trinket out of his pocket. She drew her nails down his bare chest, the sensation of plea-sure-pain making him gasp a breath.

"Give. It. To. Me."

Each word pounded into his head with such force that bright, white, excruciating light knifed into his brain, splintering his mind into jagged *edges. He knew then that she would torture him until he gave her what she wanted. For that reason, and for another he could not quite remember, he refused.*

He shook his head.

Her smile turned cruel. Her expression turned ugly. The coldness in her eyes came from the depths of Hell. Her hand at his chest became a claw, the nails digging, ripping into his flesh.

"You will give it to me." She twisted her hand, clutched his heart and squeezed.

"No-o-o-o!" he screamed.

He shot up, sucking for air, sweat running down his body as if he stood in the rain. Wildly, he looked around, trying to equate what he had seen in his nightmare and what was before him—the dim interior of the large tent, his rumpled pallet, the low tables, plump cushions, the thick carpet beneath his feet. His hand clutched hard on the hilt of a sword.

"Raphael."

He swung toward the voice and crouched into a defensive position, the sword held to ward off attack.

"Raphael. *Akhi.* You are safe."

The familiar, calm voice that called him brother broke through the terror-filled fog. He blinked at the indistinct form standing before him as his sight cleared. The figure solidified, turned into Zayed, his friend, his bodyguard, his brother through adversity.

Raphael straightened, lowered his sword.

"The dream demons had you in their grasp," Zayed said.

"Yes." Raphael wiped the sweat from his eyes with his forearm and filled his lungs with air.

"They are coming harder, more frequent." Zayed remained standing, still and calm.

Turning away, Raphael slipped his sword back into its scabbard. "No worse than before."

"Hm." Zayed's wordless comment said he did not believe his friend. He turned to light a lamp. "I have heated water for your morning tea."

A glance to the edges of the flap covering the tent entrance told Raphael that dawn was approaching. Barely perceptible light seeped in. Beyond, a murmur, the scrape of a metal pot on stone, a single dog barking told him the Tuareg village of many camel-skin tents, camped where the oasis met the desert, was beginning to stir.

The sudden complaint of goats, excited voices, barking dogs, the music of a camel bell approaching on the other side of the village broke the quiet. Running feet, a shouted challenge, and the unmistakable cocking of many rifles came to his ears. He grabbed the hilt of the sword once more and turned a questioning glance to Zayed.

"I will discover the source of this commotion," Zayed said.

As his friend strode toward the entrance, they heard a scratch from the outside. Zayed pulled the flap aside, held a short conversation with the man beyond, then turned back to Raphael.

"A woman wishes to speak with you," Zayed said.

Puzzled at the odd request, Raphael frowned.

Zayed explained. "It appears an English woman has traveled very far to find the man called Al Qarsan, the Pirate."

Raphael grinned. "Then I shouldn't disappoint her."

Sydney stood outside the tent and drew a breath. The man who had led her here waited in silence to her left. Intimated by his impassive gaze above the dark blue cloth covering the bottom half of his face, she refused to show how nervous she was. Her friend and companion, Mrs. Foster—Lucy—remained on the other side of the camp with their guide, barred from accompanying her by the men who had greeted them. Sydney had been told she would have to visit this man's tent alone. She disliked the order, and Lucy had fussed, but no amount of persuasion or arguing changed any minds.

With another breath, she ducked beneath the flap covering the entrance to the sprawling tent, which the man held open for her. As soon as she stepped through, he let the flap fall closed behind her. She blinked as her eyes adjusted to the dim interior. Inside, the air was warm compared to the chill of the desert night. Lamps hanging from wooden supports lit the space. She was surprised by the comfortable furnishings—two pallets at right angles to each other at one side, low tables of dark, carved wood, a screen of painted silk at the back, a plush carpet of vibrant colors and intricate design beneath her feet. Yet what drew her attention was the figure sitting in leisurely ease on cushions across from her — a man dressed in the traditional robes of the desert nomad, his head wrapped in the distinctive dark blue turban of the Tuareg with the end pulled across the lower part of his face, like the man who had led her here. Only his eyes were visible. Those eyes were beautiful, the color of old gold, and framed in luxurious dark lashes. She had learned that the Tuareg men veiled their faces, while their women went unveiled, opposite the rest of the Arab world. Slightly behind and to one side of him stood another man, tall, unveiled, his skin darker and marked by small, dotted tattoos swirling across each cheekbone. A sword hung from his belt.

"Welcome, *lalla*," the veiled man said. "May I offer you tea?" He motioned to the low table before him, set with a small brass pot and two glasses. His accent was unlike anything she had ever heard. It seemed to be a combination of several accents and quite pleasant to the ear, almost musical.

Although he had addressed her politely as "miss," Sydney was put out that he did not rise to greet her. If, in fact, the man before her was the one she sought, she had heard reports that he was charming, besides being ruthless. But then, she could not expect drawing-room manners from a brigand.

She remained only a few paces inside the tent and pointedly did not accept his offer of refreshment. Perhaps she violated a code of desert courtesy by being so abrupt, but her need to find this man was deep-seated and compelling. She could not waste her time on niceties. Besides, she felt safer with distance between them.

"I am looking for the man who calls himself Al Qarsan — the Pirate," she said.

The veiled man remained silent for a moment. His eyes gave nothing away. "Do not pirates sail the seas?" he asked, his head tilted in curiosity. Amusement rippled beneath his question. "We are far from the ocean, *lalla*."

Aware that she was alone in a tent with two men, both of whom could turn violent at any moment, Sydney contained her annoyance at his mocking tone. Taking a breath, she reminded herself, *don't provoke him.* "I was told this man lives in the desert."

He drew up a knee and rested his arm on it. She had the sense he was indulging her. That he was toying with her.

"Qarsan. Pirate," he mused. "An odd name for a man living in the desert. Are you sure you haven't lost your way?"

Raising her chin in response to his ridicule, she said, "I am not lost. This is the Oasis of El Balah Akbar, is it not? The Oasis of the Biggest Dates?"

The veiled man nodded. "It is."

"I was told this man, Al Qarsan, pitches his tent here, and I was given very detailed instructions about where I might find him."

"By whom?" Although he sounded merely curious, she sensed something much darker beneath his words.

"That is information I am not at liberty to share." She was not about to reveal that her sources were members of the Legion of Baal, the secret organization headed by her father — her late father.

The veiled man said nothing, but she felt his penetrating gaze studying her as if he could see into her mind.

Sydney forced herself to remain still under his scrutiny, but she would not tolerate his insolence any longer than necessary. "If you cannot help me, then I'll not bother you further." She turned to leave, disappointed that she had come so far for nothing, relieved at the same time to escape this dangerous man's presence.

"It is very poor manners to refuse refreshment in the desert, *lalla.*" His words, although spoken quietly, held a hint of warning beneath them.

She turned back to him. He had not moved, but something in his posture — the contraction of a muscle, the pause of a breath — transmitted that she had placed herself in serious peril. His eyes glittered in the reflected light of the lamps, like a lion of the desert. Or a pirate who realized he had stumbled upon a cache of treasure. Apprehension trickled through her.

She reminded herself that she was not dealing with an excruciatingly polite English gentleman, but rather a brigand in the middle of the desert who adhered to a different code of behavior. The hilt of a dagger at his hip glinted menacingly in the lamplight. She was a lone woman inside this man's tent. The other man—his body-guard, perhaps?—looked lethal and capable of quick and extreme violence. Between the two of them, they could easily commit whatever mayhem they wished. Lucy and the guide Sydney had hired at the last camp where they had stopped two days earlier comprised her only allies, and she could not be sure of the guide. Lucy, a bit timid, would be more likely to scream and faint. Sydney decided placating this man might be a wise choice.

Tightening one shaking hand into a fist and hiding the other trembling hand in the folds of her skirt, she forced a smile. "I would never wish to be accused of poor manners."

He inclined his head, accepting her indirect apology, and gestured to a pile of cushions to one side of the low table. "Please."

As she settled herself, he poured tea into a small, plain glass with a flourish, then nudged it toward her. She eyed the glass with apprehension. Was it merely tea? Or did it contain something dangerous, perhaps lethal?

She peeked at him from beneath the wide brim of her hat. His gaze on her was steady and cool, but she had the feeling if she refused to drink, she would cause offense. What would be the result of that insult? She'd rather not discover that. She took a sip. The tea was quite hot, but not scalding, very strong and very sweet. The traditional mint tea of the area. After riding a camel for miles during the last few hours of the chilly night, she found it reviving and invigorating.

But the veiled man did not drink. He merely watched her with those disconcerting golden eyes. Were her suspicions correct? Did the tea contain a dangerous substance?

Raphael watched her, this woman who had traveled so far from England. He was curious why a lady would travel such a distance to find Al Qarsan. She was either brave or foolhardy. She wore a wide-brimmed hat draped with a heavy veil, obviously protection from the harsh elements of the desert. Her plain skirt and tightly fitted jacket of canvas showed signs of hard use. With the veil of her hat turned back, she used the wide brim expertly to hide or reveal her face.

Her alabaster skin was tinged with a light tan from days in the desert. Not even that heavy veil could totally protect her. A delightful sprinkling of freckles crossed her nose. Her eyes were neither blue nor green, but somewhere in between and shaded by thick lashes. The lamplight picked up an intriguing hint of auburn in the dark slashes of her brows, He found he wanted to see her hair, completely covered by her hat and veil. She was quite lovely.

The hand she used to take up the glass of tea was small and delicate, and he suspected if he held that hand, he would discover that it was soft and cool, the hand of a lady. That tiny hand shook ever so slightly. She was afraid yet forged on despite her fear. Was she desperate, perhaps? Her long journey to find him suggested she was.

"Now tell me, *lalla,* why are you looking for the man called the Pirate?" he asked.

She stared at her tea and ran her index finger up and down the glass. A gold band, intricately wrought, decorated that delicate finger. When she looked up, she met his gaze and answered his question. "I need him to help me find someone," she said.

Raphael kept his gaze locked on hers. Why him? He rarely searched for people. Smuggle, yes. Raid, occasionally. Guard caravans, most certainly. Thieve, when the prize was worth the effort. Although his curiosity itched, he would discourage this woman. Searching for those who were lost was not his favorite sport. The hunt usually ended in tragedy, especially here in the desert.

"I do not think the Pirate is in the business of searching for missing souls," he said. "Surely, there are others who could help you."

She gave her head a little shake. "This person I am searching for is not missing. I believe he is hiding, most likely in plain sight."

"You search for a man," he observed, then huffed a laugh. "Are there no men in England you deem worthy?"

A faint blush colored her cheeks at his barb, and she made a sound of impatience. "Do not mock me. I am not looking for a husband or a lover. I have come a far distance and expended a great deal of time, energy, and coin to get here."

He bowed his head, smiling behind his veil. "My apologies, *lalla*. Please, tell me about this man you seek."

"I need him…" Her voice trailed off. She glanced away, around the tent, then back at him. "I need him to kill someone for me."

Surprising. Interesting. Beneath the beautiful exterior, this woman hid a ruthless soul of violence. Raising a brow, he said, "Surely, you could hire an assassin closer to home."

She frowned. "Of course, I could. But this man has…special abilities."

"Ah. Special abilities." He knew about special abilities, for he had his own. He sensed Zayed's interest spark behind him.

Anger turned the soft blush of her cheeks into bright spots of color and caused those eyes to snap green. "You mock me again."

He was charmed. And intrigued. "I would never mock a beautiful woman," he said, although that is precisely what he had done. He wanted to see how brave she truly was, to learn how far she would go to get what she wanted. And he was curious about this assassin for whom she searched. "What special abilities does this man have?"

She shook her head. "No. That is something you don't need to know."

Her reticence made him probe further. "Why do you need an assassin of special abilities?"

"That is my business and would not be part of any agreement between us, *Mr. Pirate*."

His gazed thinned. "Are you certain that is who I am?"

"If you aren't, then I am wasting your time and mine." She paused, tipped her head so the lamplight slipped beneath the brim of her hat. A tiny smile teased her lips. "If you aren't, then I'm sure you can get a message to him."

That tiny smile made up his mind for him. Allah, God, Yahweh, or any other name of the Almighty, help him. He nodded once. "I could, perhaps, do that."

Zayed shifted ever so slightly. His friend was not pleased.

"Good," she said briskly. "Then we have an agreement."

A woman who took control. He would end that now, for he would be under no one's control, especially this slip of a woman. His life depended on it. "We have no arrangement, *lalla*. You have not heard the terms." He leaned forward and refilled her glass. "The man you call Pirate has severe terms."

"I will pay anything he wants." She reached for her tea, then stopped, her fingers not quite wrapped around the glass. Glancing up at him, she added, "Within reason, of course."

"Of course," he murmured, knowing full well that what he would demand was far beyond reason. He mentioned an amount, an outrageous sum.

She nodded. "Agreed."

Her quick response told him she was wealthy, but he was not interested in her wealth. He had enough of his own. "That is not all, *lalla*," he said.

She frowned, the glass halfway to her lips, then replaced it on the table. "I think the amount I agreed to is quite enough."

"If the man known as Al Qarsan — the Pirate — decides to take on this quest, you will follow his orders without question." He made his words stern.

As she opened her mouth to protest, his hand cut through the air. "He tolerates no argument on this. It may mean the difference between life and death." He did not mention whose.

He watched her rethink her position. Her lashes swept down, and she nodded. "All right," she said quietly. "Yes."

"There is more."

Her head came up. "What more could there be?"

"Your name." His demand was quiet, yet unyielding.

She stared at him a moment, then her eyes narrowed. "Only if you tell me yours."

Ah, the woman was wily as well as beautiful. "You already have it," he said.

"'Pirate' or 'Qarsan' isn't your true name." She challenged him with her eyes as well as her words.

He shrugged. "It's all you need to know. Your name, *lalla*," he prompted.

Drawing herself up, she stated primly, "Miss Whelton."

He held in his smile at her prissy answer. Goading her, he said, "You must agree to one last term, Miss Whelton." He emphasized her name, turning it into a gentle jibe.

"What term?" Her tone contained a tinge of impatience.

"Take off your hat. Let down your hair." At Raphael's demands, Zayed made a sound, a barely audible expel of breath that only Raphael could hear. His friend was vexed.

Miss Whelton's eyes widened. "I will do no such thing."

"Then we have no agreement." Raphael turned away as if uninterested. "You will have to find this man with special abilities on your own."

She sat absolutely still. He waited, wondering how much she wanted to find this mysterious man. Finally, the rustle of clothing signaled movement. Her hat landed with a soft plop on the table. He did not look, but remained staring into the space to his left. The click of hairpins hitting the table reached his ears. When the sound stopped, he turned to look at her.

Her hair, unbound, fell in waves across her shoulders almost to her waist. It was dark, but the lamplight picked out fiery highlights in its depths. He imagined in the sunlight it would burn with its own flame. He wanted to touch it, to feel the contradiction of its appearance of heat with its coolness. Perhaps in the future he would find that chance. Perhaps, he would arrange events so chance had nothing to do with it.

Her eyes transmitted their own heat. "Have I met all your demands, Mr. Pirate?" she snapped.

He smiled. "Quite."

"Then we have an agreement?"

He nodded once. "We do. I have only one other question."

She stood, gathered her hairpins and dumped them into the upside-down crown of her hat. The veil trailed onto the floor. She balled it up into a clump. "I have answered all the questions I intend."

He settled deeper into his cushions as he gazed up at her guilelessly. "You might wish to answer this one," he murmured.

Her mouth tightened into a line, but she waited.

"In what direction do you seek this man?" he asked mildly.

She puffed out a breath of irritation. "East. In the east, Mr. Pirate. I hear he is in Egypt with the French general, Napoleon."

"Very well." He leaned forward and took up his glass of tea. "Then we will leave two hours before dawn. Your guide will remain behind. He is not needed."

Without another word, she rose and stalked across the tent. At the entrance, she stopped without turning. "Thank you." Her quiet words floated back to him.

You are welcome, he replied silently, and let his response brush lightly across her mind.

Her back stiffened and her head snapped up.

Before she bolted, he added silently, *A woman should keep her head covered in the desert, especially a woman with hair such as yours.* Without moving a muscle, he flipped one of her curls into the air and let it fall.

She gasped, dumped her hairpins onto the floor, plonked her hat on her head and threw her veil over it. Her movements were jerky, and even from where he sat, he could see the tremor in her hands. Her attempt to cover her heavy mass of hair was unsuccessful, for ends curled beyond the edges of the veil. Leaving it as is, she ducked beneath the flap and let it drop behind her as if she were escaping a haunted ruin.

Entertained, Raphael pulled the veil from his face and took a sip of tea. "An interesting woman, Zayed," he commented.

Zayed moved from behind him and sat on the cushions the woman had vacated. "A dangerous woman," he said.

Raphael chuckled. "Have you ever met one who wasn't?"

Zayed picked up the woman's glass and finished her tea, the habit of not wasting water in the desert ingrained. "This search of hers is peculiar."

"The man she searches for is peculiar." Raphael fingered the talisman he wore on a leather cord beneath his tunic. The piece had been with him his whole life. It was the only connection to his childhood.

Zayed did not miss the gesture. "You think this search might provide you with information." Zayed's questions were often couched in statements.

Raphael looked at his friend. "What if it does, Zayed?"

Zayed sat back against the cushions. "You race to conclusions that have no logic."

"Something …" Raphael flattened his hand against his chest, pressing the talisman into his skin. He had felt it warm when the woman appeared, then again when she mentioned the assassin.

"What if this woman and the man she seeks hold the key to my identity?"

Zayed shook his head. "Not 'what if,' my friend. You are what you are. What you were before does not matter." Zayed poured himself more tea. "*Inshallah.*" In the hands of Allah. He took a sip. "But that does not mean you should not be careful. Something about this woman disturbs me, like a stone beneath my blanket on the desert sand."

Raphael also took a sip of tea. "Then I should discover more about her. I think I will pay a visit to her tonight before the moon rises." He set down his glass and pulled the talisman from beneath his tunic. "Shadows are always less visible in the darkest hours."

Zayed frowned. "This woman is not so important that you should taunt evil. Wait until tomorrow when you can speak as we journey."

Raphael glanced at the tent flap where the woman had recently stood. "I do not think she will reveal a great deal. She seems to keep her thoughts close."

Zayed sighed and a shade of sorrow crossed his eyes. "Then I will kill a lamb and roast it, and once again beg women slaves from Hareem Sheik for your pleasure when you return."

"Only those who are willing," Raphael warned.

His friend looked offended. "Of course."

Placing a hand on the other man's shoulder, Raphael said, "You are a true friend, Zayed. An older brother to me. I wish I could repay you in kind."

With him since childhood, Zayed understood the dark cravings Raphael endured when he returned from his dark form. The first few times, Raphael's attempt to deny the urges that burned through him sparked violence neither man anticipated. When the violence turned inward, Raphael's body had weakened, flashing between human and the darkness until he was near death. He had only been saved when Zayed had instinctively known what would cure him — feeding his appetites.

Zayed stood. "You will repay me when the curse is lifted, when you no longer need the talisman to keep you human. You will repay me by your happiness." Turning, he walked across the tent and ducked beneath the flap. As he did, sunlight streaked in and was extinguished when the flap closed.

Raphael was left in the shadows, a condition with which he was very familiar.

Sydney quickly wended her way among the tents of the Tuareg village. Elation bubbled through her countered by a heavy dose of unease. Al Qarsan — the Pirate — had agreed to help her find the man with the Crystal Dagger. But the Pirate had to be the most unsettling man she had ever met.

Of course, he would be unsettling. He was dangerous. Those golden eyes seemed to see everything, much too much. Even though he had been sitting, his presence dominated the tent. She blew out a breath. How would she endure weeks in the desert with him? Besides that, his taunting was insufferable. What gentleman would force a lady to remove her hat and take down her hair? But then, he was a brigand of the desert. He most likely thought nothing of his request.

As she rounded the last tent in the village, she was relieved that she felt no ill effects from the tea. She had been foolish to drink it, but then, she'd had little choice. If she had refused…. A tiny shiver trickled down her spine at the possible consequences.

She saw Lucy pacing before their tent and the sight of her friend reassured her. The small canvas structure appeared insignificant beside the sprawling, camel-skin tents of the Tuareg, but it had been home for many weeks since she and Lucy had landed in Ouarhran on the northern coast of Africa. The caravan leader who had allowed them to join him on his journey south had laughed at their puny tent. Why use such a thing when they had the stars and sky as a roof? Bowing to the inevitable, they had rarely used it, for the guide-interpreter they had hired grumbled whenever they asked him to pitch it for them. They realized how impractical it was after it blew down in high winds. But upon their arrival at the village, they had insisted, wishing for a bit of privacy.

Lucy rushed to meet Sydney. "Oh, my goodness, I was so worried!" She linked her arm with Sydney's as they returned to the tent. "Did you find Al Qarsan? Did you speak with him? What did he say?"

Sydney grinned at her friend. "I met him. He will do it, Luce. He'll help me find the man with the Crystal Dagger."

Lucy halted, gasped and covered her mouth in astonishment. Her eyes gleamed. "That's wonderful news! After all this time, you'll finally get justice for the death of your father."

And for her mother, Carolyn, who had wasted away with a mysterious disease that began the same night the strange-looking man had come to her mother's gaming hell. Sydney glanced down at the gold ring that had been her mother's, remembering. First, black veins had appeared on her mother's hand. The next day, they had crawled up her arm. Then her neck, and down over her chest, eventually covering her whole body. The physicians had whispered *poison* and hurried away. She suffered for three endless days before dying. Sydney suspected witchcraft had infected her mother and believed she knew who had used the craft in such a malignant manner.

That was a month before her father's death. He had been sympathetic and solicitous when her mother died, and had spent more time with her, instructing her in more of the secrets of the Legion of Baal. He had invited her to watch a ceremony at Stonehenge from afar. When she had stolen closer, she had been warned away by a shadow figure that appeared concerned for her safety. Fearful of the apparition and afraid of discovery, she had run, only turning back when the ceremony erupted into chaos. Curiosity drew her closer, but she saw only confusion. Until Nulkana, the evil sorceress, appeared, standing atop one of the stone plinths. Sydney had been frightened, but unable to look away. This was her father's enemy, whom he had been trying to eliminate for as long as she could remember. When the sorceress attacked the Legion, Sydney fled, terrified by the immense power of the combatants. Only much later had she crept back and discovered her father dead with a large, blackened hole in his chest.

In the two years that followed, she had grieved the deaths of her mother and father, prepared for this trip, and made her way to the desert. Guilt had brought her to seek out the Pirate. While she could not have prevented her mother's death, she could have stayed to help her father battle Nulkana that night at Stonehenge. But she had been too cowardly. So, after months of living with guilt, she shuttered the gaming hell and convinced Lucy to travel with her. Compassionate, timid Lucy, who agreed to journey through foreign countries and across hostile lands to help her find the man called Al Qarsan.

Relieved to be away from the presence of the dangerous man she had just met, Sydney sank to the sand beside the remains of their campfire. "I wish my mother were still alive so I could tell her what I've accomplished."

Lucy sat beside her. "She was so proud of you. And I'm very glad you asked me to come with you on this journey."

"How could I leave my best friend behind?" Sydney wrapped her fingers around Lucy's hand.

She and Lucy had been friends since Lucy had appeared, bedraggled and begging for a job, at the back door of the gaming hell five years ago. Lucy's father, a wealthy squire, had arranged for her to wed an elderly, dissipated viscount, who needed an influx of cash. Instead of marrying someone who repulsed her, she had run away. Sydney had convinced her mother to allow Lucy to work in the kitchen, and then had discovered that Lucy was a marvelous cook. The two girls had bonded immediately.

Sydney smiled. "I've found Al Qarsan, the man called the Pirate, and he's going to help us find the man with the Crystal Dagger. Then we will kill the sorceress who murdered my father." And most likely her mother. Her lips thinned into a determined line.

"You're so brave, Sydney," Lucy said.

Sydney smiled. What Lucy called bravery she knew as something else—guilt, compelling her onward. She also felt a responsibility to continue her father's quest to rid the earth of the evil sorceress. Sydney loved her father for he had indulged her with gifts, taught her things women did not usually learn. He shared secrets with her he shared with no one else. He made her feel special.

He visited every few weeks, for her parents were not married. Her mother was her father's mistress. Sydney was illegitimate, a fact she accepted because that was what she knew. Despite that, her mother raised her like any gently bred young lady with dancing classes, lessons on the pianoforte, and instruction on proper manners. Her father made sure she could defend herself with knife, sword and pistol, and provided her with tutors who taught her numbers, history, and geography. He even made her read the classics in Latin.

She didn't question her parents' relationship, despite its unconventional nature, but she never sensed any tenderness between them. To Sydney, their bond felt like a business arrangement. Her mother passed along gossip and tidbits of information she overheard at her gaming hell, while her father protected the illegal house from anything that might harm the business. Even though her mother never admitted it, Sydney suspected that if her mother stopped providing information, that protection would cease. When she questioned her mother about the arrangement, her mother told her that relationships between men and women always had degrees of give and take, no matter what form that relationship took. But Sydney never liked it.

Long ago she decided that she would allow no man to have such power over her. She might never marry, for she had witnessed how some men treated women in the gaming hell. And she knew a married woman had little freedom in determining her own fate if her husband was a tyrant. Lucy had been very brave to run from that arranged marriage.

Her thoughts strayed to Al Qarsan. She had seen no signs of a woman's presence in his tent, wife or mistress, and she wondered what sort of husband he might be. Then she immediately quashed the thought. She had come all this way to hire him as a guide to find the assassin who could kill Nulkana, not to consider his worthiness as a husband. He was a brigand. She had trembled in his presence. His golden eyes seemed to see into her soul. His words had whispered into her mind.

She pondered that ability as she suggested to Lucy that they eat something. She remembered another who had spoken to her in the same way on the night of her father's murder. But the whisperer wasn't human, merely Shadow, beautiful and eerily exotic. Surely that Shadow couldn't be connected to Al Qarsan. Coincidence, she decided. Al Qarsan's ability was merely a parlor trick.

Sydney helped her friend rummage in their baggage for their food. Perhaps on the journey to come, she could convince Mr. Pirate to teach her how to speak silently into someone's mind.

In the starlit night, Raphael stood in the lee of a sand dune and looked back at the camp settled at the edge of the oasis. He knew he could not be seen, but he practiced caution, a habit that had saved him many times. No danger came from the camp. Its inhabitants were his allies, one or two perhaps his friends, but he kept his secrets to himself. No one in the camp needed to know what he did on this night.

He had removed the talisman from his neck. Now he was darkness, a shadow with no sense of taste, smell or touch. The condition — the curse — had been with him since his youth. Sometimes, as now, it proved helpful. Most of the time, it was a burden. Always, when he replaced the talisman about his neck, he returned to flesh and bone. Then he endured an overwhelming need to feed all his senses when they came rushing back. During those hours, he was barely human. After it passed, when he felt sated and exhausted, he thanked the universe for sending him Zayed, for his friend kept him from madness.

The moon had not yet risen and the stars, sprinkled in abundance across the night sky, provided his only source of light. He did not need more to see. The fires in the camp had died down. The camels had settled. No one moved among the tents. The village slept.

At the far edge of the clustered tents stood one other, set a bit apart. Its small size and simplicity marked it as the shelter of the English woman. In front, a small cooking fire dancing in the light breeze lit a slender woman curled on the ground in sleep. Miss Whelton. He smiled, remembering their exchange that morning. This journey he would take with her would be interesting, both for its purpose and his traveling companion. But before they set out, he wanted a bit more information. Thus, his transformation into darkness.

He approached the tent from behind, keeping the shadow of the dunes behind him, and stole around to the front corner of the canvas shelter. Miss Whelton reclined, asleep on a blanket, her back resting against a camel saddle near the fire. An open book and pencil lay on her lap. Noiselessly, he stepped closer and peered across her prone form at the book. A journal. She had been recording observations of her journey. Curious, he read her last entry. It was about him.

I have met the one called Al Qarsan, the Pirate, and he has agreed to help me find the man with the Crystal Dagger. Al Qarsan is mysterious, quite arrogant, and infuriating. His golden eyes seem to see everything and made me quake despite their beauty. He is a dangerous brigand and is taking far more in payment for his services than I expected. Why, he demanded I unpin my hair as one of the conditions to our agreement! The rogue!

My hope is that this exorbitant expense will be worth it. Given my first meeting with him, I shall no doubt find him insufferable as a fellow traveler, but his reprehensible reputation recommends him as the only one who can act as guide and help me accomplish my task. We leave in the morning, two hours before dawn.

Raphael grinned. The woman had no idea how insufferable he could be. With a flick of his fingers, he flipped to the pages at the front of her journal. Those entries merely spoke of her preparations for her journey and the sights she encountered as she traveled. Nothing more about the mystery man she sought who possessed a useless dagger made of crystal. However, inside the front cover, she had written her full name: Sydney Charlotte Whelton. An unusual name for an unusual woman.

She stirred, rubbed her eyes, and sat up.

Raphael crouched before her.

Her eyes widened, her lips parted, and she sucked in a breath.

Before she could scream, he placed his finger across her lips.

Sh, he said in her head.

His silent admonishment caused her to go absolutely still. Although relieved he had muted her scream, he was disconcerted by the sensation of his finger against her lips. In his dark form, he usually felt nothing, for his sense of touch vanished. But beneath his finger across her lips, he felt a tingly heat. His gaze dropped to her mouth, and he rubbed his finger against her lips ever so slightly back and forth. He had not been mistaken. A tingling warmth penetrated the numbness he usually endured while darkness. Who was this woman who could make him *feel*?

His eyes snapped up to meet hers.

She stared back, frozen.

He could drown in those eyes. In the dark of the night, he could not see their color, but he knew they were glorious. Blinking, he forced himself to focus on why he was here. He could not think of her eyes, nor that tingle he felt when he touched her skin. He would explore the connection another time.

Will you scream? he asked.

Her eyes widened even more. She shook her head.

Slowly, he lowered his finger, missing that sensation of tingly warmth.

She pressed her lips together and scooted back.

Are you afraid? he asked.

"No," she whispered with another shake of her head.

You may change your mind when we're finished, he taunted.

"I can defend myself." Her hand came up, gripping a knife. The dying embers of the fire reflected on its blade.

Raphael hopped back from the sharp edge and laughed. *I'm glad to hear that. You never know when you might meet a dangerous brigand in the desert.*

Her eyes narrowed. "You read my journal."

It was there in plain sight. You were sleeping. He shrugged. *How could I resist?*

"An honorable man would not have looked." She sniffed her disapproval.

Grinning, he said, *Unfortunately, I'm not honorable. And, at the moment, hardly a man.*

Her gaze turned speculative. "I've seen another like you," she said.

Shock tore through him. He took a moment to absorb her revelation. *Another?* he asked. The word echoed in his head. Someone else turned from human to darkness? He thought he was the only one so cursed.

"Yes, another." She studied him. "The other is quite beautiful, like you."

"You think I am beautiful?" His question was part taunt, part preen.

19

Ignoring it, she reached toward him, then stopped. "May I touch you?"

Raphael shot to his feet and stepped back. The revelation that there was another like him, along with the disconcerting sense of tingly warmth when he touched her, made him wary. He needed to process this new information.

Perhaps another time. Perhaps when we become lovers, he said, baiting her.

Lovers?! Sydney snatched back her hand and felt the heat in her cheeks. Asking to touch him was outrageous. And dangerous. And much too intimate. What had possessed her? If she were home in England, she would never have asked such a thing of a man, not even in her mother's gaming hell. But he was not a man. He was a dark shadow. But beautiful, seductive. His suggestion intrigued her. Oh, good heavens, no!

"We will never become lovers," she snapped.

He laughed. *Are you so sure?*

She drew herself up. "Of course, I'm sure. I do not consort with...." Words failed her. What should she call him?

He tipped his head. *You do not consort with desert nomads? Or men of darkness?* He shook his head. *You might find that difficult, since desert nomads are the only people who inhabit this area, along with myself, of course.*

"I did not mean—" she began, wishing she could take back her words.

Of course, you did. He took another step back, and his words became cool and proper. *I'm afraid you'll have to reorder your thinking. Life in the desert can be unpredictable.* He swept her a bow as elegant as if he were in a formal drawing room. *Until we meet again. Sydney.* Her name whispered through her mind like warm honey.

Dumbfounded at the bow, she stared as he took another step back, and another. Each step made his form less distinct. He was dazzling, a mass of darkness punctuated by a pair of eyes like molten gold. In the shifting light from the fire, she could see the faint outline of features and muscle. He was perfectly formed, and if he had been human, would have rivaled the beauty of a statue by Michelangelo. Slowly, with a grin, he disappeared into the dark of the desert night.

Sydney remained staring, even though he was gone. Despite her instinctive refusal to his suggestion of being lovers, the thought of being this creature's lover intrigued her. What would he be like? His touch across her lips had created a heat on her skin unlike anything she had ever experienced. His voice in her head sounded like black velvet.

Reality came rushing back. What was she thinking? He was a shadow. Ethereal. Mysterious. Unreal. Possibly dangerous. She would never become his lover. The idea was ludicrous. Besides, she was in the desert to find the man with the Crystal Dagger, not to frolic or flirt with a creature of the dark. And she would probably never see him again. Glancing down, she saw her journal was still open. He had read it. And discovered her name. Heat bloomed in her cheeks. She slammed the book shut, gathered it up along with her pencil and blanket, then strode toward the tent where Lucy was already asleep.

She had other things to think about instead of silly fantasies about lovers. Like the man called Al Qarsan, who forced her to take down her hair in payment for his services. The rogue. She would have to watch him carefully to be sure he did not rob her blind. Or worse. He could easily slit her throat while she slept. She must keep her wits about her. She could not be foolishly daydreaming about a shadow creature.

But before she ducked through the tent opening, she glanced back at the dune where the creature had disappeared. At its summit, she thought she saw a silhouette outlined against the night sky. Were those two eyes of molten gold, or only stars? She blinked. It was gone. Foolish girl. It was only her imagination.

But she knew she had not imagined his heated, tingly touch, or the frisson of awareness when he crouched so close.

21

Chapter 2

"We'll stop here," Raphael said the next day when the sun reached its zenith.

They had set out two hours before dawn, as he had directed the day before. He'd been mildly surprised that Miss Whelton and her companion, Mrs. Foster, were packed up and ready to leave on time.

As he slid from his camel's back, he heard Miss Whelton let out a tired sigh. He glanced at her, but she studiously avoided looking at him. Instead, she gazed around. Her shoulders slumped in dismay at the surroundings.

The well where they stopped was nothing more than a hole in the earth that someone had marked with a single ring of stones. A lone acacia tree stood like a sentinel several yards away. Sand and rocks stretched for miles in all directions, the same scenery they had traveled through for hours. Far in the distance, a ridge created a dark line between earth and sky. In between, mirages shimmered, beckoning with a false vision of cool water.

Throughout the morning, Miss Whelton had kept her back straight and eyes focused forward. Now, she wilted as she stared longingly at the only shelter from the sun, the spindly acacia tree. A small patch of shade lay at its base, but even that was pierced by spots of sunlight. The devil rose up in him and he hid a grin. He wondered how much he could rile Miss Whelton before she lost her temper. He wanted to see her lose her composure very much.

She ordered her camel to kneel and slid from its back. When she landed on her feet, she swayed a bit and braced herself against the beast. Despite his intent to torment her, Raphael's first instinct was to reach out and steady her, but he refrained.

Beside him, Zayed's camel knelt, and his friend stepped to the ground. "I will fill the water bags," he offered.

Raphael turned to him. "Let the woman fill her own."

Zayed's brows drew together.

"She must be able to take care of herself," Raphael said. "You know that."

Zayed's quick glance to the woman indicated his doubt she could. "You will be helping her before this journey is done."

Raphael started to deny, but he was interrupted by Miss Whelton's companion straggling up. Mrs. Foster had difficulty managing her camel. The beast took every opportunity to complain, spit and nip. Contrary to his opinion of Miss Whelton's self-sufficiency, Raphael felt obliged to help the other woman. He wondered what had prompted her to agree to accompany Miss Whelton on such a rigorous journey, for she did not seem the least bit adventurous. She appeared more suited to sitting in a corner and reading a book while she ignored the chatter of others around her.

He marveled that her husband allowed her to undertake such a journey as the one she was on. While Miss Whelton's traveling clothes were practical, they still flattered her delightful figure. Mrs. Foster was swathed in layers of scarves and veils that made her appear like a rumpled pillow. Spectacles, slightly askew, perched on her nose.

His musings scattered as Mrs. Foster's camel appeared ready to bolt. He quickly grabbed the camel's lead, forced it to its knees, then held out a hand to the woman. As she landed on the ground, her legs buckled beneath her. Raphael caught her by the elbow.

"I will fill your water bag," he said.

She pushed her glasses back up her nose and peered at him. Relief made her shoulders sag. "Oh, thank you, sir. You are so kind."

He was about to tell her he was not kind in the least, and certainly not a *sir*, but she ducked her head and scurried away. With a mental shrug, he unhooked the water bag from her saddle and headed toward the well. As he neared Miss Whelton, she held out her water bag. Raphael stopped, all thoughts of Mrs. Foster evaporating before Miss Whelton's striking green-blue eyes.

"Is there a problem with your water bag?" he asked.

"No, I thought...." Confusion created a tiny line between her brows.

Raphael nodded toward the well where his friend was drawing up water. "When Zayed has finished filling our bags, you may fill your own."

Color bloomed in her cheeks and her mouth flattened. Her bag dropped to her side. "Of course," she said in a clipped tone.

He handed her Mrs. Foster's bag. "Your companion needs to rest," he said. "In the desert, we all bear responsibilities equally."

At his reprimand, she snatched the water bag from him. The blush in her cheeks flowed across her face. He suspected it tinged her neck and shoulders, probably even lower. Her eyes turned the color of pine trees he had seen in the forests of Russia. Intrigued by the beguiling Miss Whelton, he forced himself to turn away. As he strolled to his own camel to unpack the supplies for their meal, he could feel her gaze pierce his back like a razor-edged spear. He grinned. If nothing else, he decided this journey would not be boring.

Sydney could have kicked herself silly for expecting any sort of chivalry from the man called the Pirate. He was insufferable, as she first thought. Although his statement about sharing responsibilities made perfect sense, she had the feeling he was using that excuse to be contrary and provoke her. She refused to be provoked. If he wanted her to fill her water bag as well as Lucy's, she would, and she would perform any other chores that needed to be done as well. With a smile. She was as capable as he was.

She helped Lucy unpack a small meal while she waited for Zayed to fill his water bags. That impossible man, Mr. Pirate, spread a rug beneath the acacia tree, then spread himself out on top of it in the only available shade. Throwing his arm across his eyes, crossing his ankles, he appeared to go to sleep, while Zayed set out food. Hmph! Evidently, *he* didn't need to share responsibilities equally, the cad.

Despite her unfavorable opinion of him, Sydney had to admit he was an impressive figure stretched out on the ground with his robes fanned out around him. He had changed from the blue turban and dark robe of the Tuareg to pure white turban, white tunic and pantaloons under a white robe trimmed with intricate red embroidery. His pantaloons were tucked into soft, knee-high boots. He was quite tall. She still had not seen his face, for he kept it veiled, but those eyes the color of old gold and surrounded by thick lashes were quite stunning. And quite disconcerting. She felt their glance like a physical touch. He walked as if he owned the earth, like a true prince of the desert — or a pirate on the deck of his ship.

But no matter how striking his appearance, his arrogance irritated her. The reports she had heard of his pleasant manner and courtesy were obviously complete falsehoods. He was rude and insolent. Insufferable, as she surmised.

Zayed had finished at the well, so Sydney took her turn to fill the water bags. As she drew up the bucket, Zayed murmured something to the Pirate. Then she heard the jangle of harness bells and the muffled swish of camels moving across sand. A group of riders appeared several hundred yards from the well. She watched them approach, and a smile crept across her lips.

At Zayed's warning, Raphael rolled to his feet. He was annoyed at the interruption of his rest. He had not slept at all last night, having spent part of the night as darkness and indulging his curiosity by visiting Miss Whelton, and part in satisfying the dark cravings he endured when he returned to human form. Since they had left two hours before dawn, the remainder of the night had been spent traveling to reach this spot.

Like the others, he watched the riders approach. His irritation escalated when he recognized the leader. Al Jabbar. A mercenary like himself. The man had named himself "The Mighty," which sounded better than thief or murderer. What the devil was he doing here?

He exchanged a glance with Zayed. Together, they stepped forward to the edge of their little camp and stood with legs braced apart.

Clearly, his friend shared his wariness about Al Jabbar's appearance. In tandem, their hands hovered near the hilts of their swords.

The group of five riders halted.

"*Salaam aleikum,*" Al Jabbar greeted them. *Peace be with you.*

Raphael returned the greeting.

"May we approach?"

Raphael gave a curt nod. In the desert, everyone was welcome at a well.

Al Jabbar dismounted from his camel and stepped forward. His gaze went beyond Raphael and landed on the woman standing at the well. He bowed and touched his fingers to his heart, his mouth, his forehead. "*Salaam aleikum,* lady," he said.

Raphael swiveled to see Miss Whelton smile and nod a greeting. "Good day to you, Al Jabbar."

He hid his surprise at her response and cast a suspicious glance at Al Jabbar. "You know this woman?" he asked.

Al Jabbar gave a nod. "We came to an arrangement some weeks past."

Miss Whelton stepped up beside Raphael and offered her hand to Al Jabbar. "I'm so glad you were able to find me quickly," she said.

Al Jabbar took her hand and bent over it as if he were greeting a duchess in her English manor. "I was drawn by your beauty, dear lady." The man's blue eyes twinkled.

Raphael scowled at her swift change in demeanor. Miss Whelton was actually smiling and blushing like a young girl. He stepped between them. "What sort of arrangement do you have?" he ground out.

Al Jabbar laughed lightly. "She engaged us to protect her on her journey to the east. She evidently did not trust you to keep her safe from raiders or ruffians or wild animals in the desert." He placed his hand to his chest. "I myself would never trust a man called Al Qarsan."

"And I would not trust a man who claims direct descent from Mohammed but wears the eyes of an infidel." Raphael crossed his arms.

Al Jabbar grinned, his blue eyes dancing. "Allah is capable of many miracles." His gaze went past Raphael's shoulder. "I see Zayed

27

has begun to make tea. Will you invite us to share with you, or will I have to cut your throat?"

"The tea is made with goat piss. The bread is made from camel dung." Raphael did not budge.

"Sounds delightful if one is born of a demon and raised by a scorpion," Al Jabbar remarked.

"Better than being born of an asp and raised by Satan," Raphael shot back.

They glared at each other for five heartbeats. Finally, Al Jabbar said quietly, "It's good to see you, my friend."

"I have not called you 'friend' for a very long time." Raphael's tone chilled the air between them.

"You know each other?" Miss Whelton exclaimed.

Al Jabbar turned those twinkling blue eyes to the Englishwoman. "Alas, dear lady, our acquaintance is long."

Raphael frowned at her. "You have hired a blackguard to protect you from a pirate, Miss Whelton."

Miss Whelton's gaze traveled from Raphael to Al Jabbar and back again. Drawing herself up, she said sternly, "You both came well-recommended. I will rely upon your mutual honor to refrain from slitting each other's throats while we travel together." She spun on her heel and stalked back to the well.

Al Jabbar watched her, then murmured, "A formidable force in such a small package."

"Indeed," Raphael agreed, as his gaze followed her. He turned back to Al Jabbar. "I would suggest you stay away from her."

"Have you marked her as your own already, Raphael?" Al Jabbar raised a questioning brow.

"She doesn't belong to me, nor will she be yours, Robert." Raphael's hand rested on the hilt of his sword. "Miss Whelton's idea of honor is not mine."

Al Jabbar, known also as Robert Thurgood, gave a nod. "A contest then. To the winner go the spoils and life."

Raphael sighed. "Don't make me kill you, Robert. I may hate you for what you did, but I don't want you dead."

Al Jabbar's eyes lost their twinkle. "That's quite odd, Raphael, because I am looking for an excuse to send you to your just reward."

"You have never needed an excuse to kill before," Raphael observed.

"I'm making an exception in your case." The twinkle returned to Al Jabbar's eyes.

"Then I'll watch my back." Turning on his heel, Raphael sauntered to the patch of shade where he resumed his prone position. Although he appeared to be resting, every muscle and nerve ending in his body was alert. The arrival of Robert Thurgood complicated this journey. Not only did he have to contend with two women who knew little about traveling in the desert, he now had to deal with the man who had betrayed him and wanted him dead.

The desert held enough dangers without having a viper as a traveling companion. He would rectify the travel arrangements before the snake attacked.

As Sydney drew water from the well, she watched the two men she needed to complete her quest. Besides the unfriendly words they had exchanged, their postures suggested they might draw weapons and cut each other to ribbons at any moment. When Al Qarsan retreated once more to the spot of shade and Al Jabbar motioned to his men to dismount their camels, she breathed a sigh of relief.

She had first learned of the Pirate from a man who had come to the gambling hell in London. He had served with British forces fighting Napoleon in Egypt and told tales of the desert and its inhabitants. Because of the British blockade of Egypt, Sydney couldn't sail directly there to contact the man with the Crystal Dagger, so she had devised the plan to enter Egypt from the desert. Al Qarsan had seemed the perfect man to guide her. When she had arrived in Ouarhan on the northern coast of Africa, she made inquiries to discover where to find him.

Since she knew nothing about him, she thought she should have some protection, so she hired Al Jabbar as well. He was a member of the Legion of Baal, the secret organization that her father had led, and could provide protection against any threat from Al Qarsan. But she also needed him to help complete her final task. She wasn't sure why she needed him, for her father had been vague on that point, but quite adamant about it. Perhaps her father hadn't completely trusted her to complete the task on her own. That irritated.

Her father had told her little about the members of the Legion other than they were men who were powerful in some way. Their common goal was to kill the evil sorceress Nulkana. Despite the members living in far-flung places on the globe, finding and contacting Al Jabbar had been relatively easy, since the members of the Legion corresponded regularly with each other.

She'd had no idea that Al Qarsan and Al Jabbar were acquainted — and seemed to dislike each other intensely. That made this trip more complicated, and possibly more dangerous. As if it weren't already dangerous enough. She would have to keep her wits about her. And use every trick she had to keep Lucy and herself safe. With a sigh, she tossed the goatskin bucket back down the well.

Late that afternoon as the sun began to slide down the sky, Raphael rousted everyone from their naps in the shade of their camels, and they set out again. They were strung out in two horizontal lines — Zayed, Raphael, Miss Whelton and Mrs. Foster side by side in front, Al Jabbar and his men behind. Two pack camels, which Raphael and Zayed led, separated the two groups.

Raphael was uneasy with Al Jabbar at his back. Rather than reveal his disquiet, he said nothing and remained alert. Yet he was curious about the connection between the prim Miss Whelton and the man who slit throats with a twinkle in his eyes. He turned to the woman beside him.

"You seem to have unusual connections for a gently reared Englishwoman, Miss Whelton," he said.

That wide-brimmed, veiled hat turned in his direction. The veil shielded her face, but he could feel her cool gaze on him. "Perhaps I am not what I appear, Mr. Pirate," she said. "Appearances can be deceiving. For instance, when I first met you, I believed you to be one of the Tuareg, for you dressed and lived as one of them, but your accents and your physical characteristics belie that. Perhaps, Mr. Pirate, I should question your origins, beginning with your true name."

He smiled, enjoying the irony of her statement. If only he knew his origins. Instead of answering her, he said, "If Al Jabbar is to be on this journey with us, I would like to know how you found him. He does not frequent areas that would be safe for proper English ladies."

Miss Whelton faced forward again. "I found him the same way I found you, *Mr. Pirate*." She emphasized his name, indicating her displeasure with his refusal to tell her his true name.

"You never satisfied my curiosity on that matter," he said.

The hat swung back in his direction. "And you will remain unsatisfied as long as I wish you to be. You also have not satisfied my desire for another name to call you."

He grinned. "Since you hired me, Miss Whelton, my only goal is to satisfy all your desires."

She sniffed at his taunt and faced forward. "I would also like to know why we are heading west, when I told you that the man we seek is in the east, specifically in Egypt. That is hardly satisfying my desire."

He was surprised she had noticed, but then, he supposed she had been traveling long enough to know the sun rose in the east and set in the west. Raising a mocking brow, he asked, "Did you think I could conjure him out of thin air? Or perhaps you thought I might commune with the desert sands and discover him. We are traveling to the city so I might inquire if anyone knows of this man. Please allow me to do what you hired me to do."

At his reprimand she ducked her head and shifted in her saddle. He had embarrassed her, and he felt an unfamiliar twinge of remorse. Annoyed with himself, he focused on the stretch of wasteland before them. He should not have such feelings about a woman who paid for his services, despite his attraction to her.

A soft plop distracted him from his thoughts, and Miss Whelton emitted a tiny sound of exasperation. He saw that she had dislodged a small valise and it had fallen to the sand. She halted her camel.

"I'll get that," Raphael said, quashing the sense that he was making up for his rebuke. He offered merely to avoid halting the group, to allow her to dismount, retrieve the valise, and then mount again.

Smoothly, he slipped from his camel's back while it still plodded forward and strode back to retrieve the valise. It had popped open, and a pool of black satin embroidered in purple lay on the sand. Why had she brought such a frivolous, useless garment on a trek through the desert?

Irritated, he bent down to stuff the satin back inside the bag. As soon as his hand touched the material, the talisman he wore on a cord around his neck tingled and grew warm. The desert faded away, and he found himself standing in the cool air of the north, the dark sky littered with unfamiliar stars, green grass beneath his feet. Monolithic stones created a large circle. A ring of robed, hooded figures, each carrying a torch, stood widely spaced in its center. At the apex of the ring was a man wearing a black satin robe embroidered with the purple glyph of a frog. Deep within his cowl, his face was covered by a gold mask. Facing the man was a woman, crouched before him. A purple robe draped across her shoulders. It was torn, revealing an ugly scrape down her arm. A bruise darkened one cheek. Her lip bled. Her hair fell in tangled curls around her shoulders and down her back. Next to her knelt a man, disheveled, as if he had been mauled. But something in his manner suggested he wanted to protect the woman. Vicious tension hung in the air. Danger. The threat of death. Raphael wanted to jump in to protect the woman, but he could not move. She turned her head and met Raphael's gaze.

He sucked in a breath. She had golden eyes — eyes that bore an uncanny resemblance to the ones he saw reflected back to him when he bent over the water hole at an oasis. Who was this woman?

He snatched his hand away from the black satin and blinked. The circle of stones vanished. Sand and stones stretched for miles in all directions. The sun was making its descent in the sky. Turning his head, he saw the two lines of camels with their riders slowly plodding away from him, only a few yards beyond where he had left his camel. Barely any time had passed, but he felt as if he had been gone for much longer. What had happened?

He looked down at the swath of black spilling from the valise. Purple stitching peeked from between its folds. It was the same black satin the golden-masked man in the vision wore. He turned again to the small figure of Miss Whelton in her wide-brimmed hat as she swayed to the rhythm of the camel's gait. What was the connection between her and the woman in the circle and the other people in his vision? And what was *his* connection to all of them? Was Miss Whelton a danger? Or was she a key to his identity?

Crouching over the valise, he tentatively touched the black satin. The talisman resting against his chest remained quiet. The earth beneath his feet remained sand. He stuffed the material back into the bag, snatched it up and loped back to the camels. After handing it to Miss Whelton, he grabbed his camel's hide and one ear and sprang back into his saddle. Bemused, he watched her fuss with the bag as she attached it again to her saddle.

The vision disturbed him, and the questions it raised swirled inside his head. The black satin robe was obviously imbued with magic. Did that mean the lady who carried it in her valise was also magical? He decided that he would keep the mysterious Miss Whelton very close for the remainder of the journey, and perhaps beyond that until he found his answers.

Later that night, Sydney awoke with a start. A hand covered her mouth. Her eyes flew open. Something blocked out the dark, star-studded sky. The moon had not yet risen, but through a trick of light, she caught a gleam of golden eyes.

"Do not cry out," the Pirate whispered next to her ear, more breath than sound, "or I will have to tie and gag you. Or knock you unconscious." He raised his head and stared down at her. "Will you do as I say?"

Shocked at his threat, still groggy from sleep, Sydney nodded. Even if she wanted to fuss, she could not draw breath enough, for his other hand laid heavy on her chest and pinned her to the ground. She could feel his leg against her hip, his hard muscles bunched and tensed even through the layers of clothes and the light blanket over her. Uncomfortable in such intimate proximity with the man, she tried to shrink into the ground beneath her.

Her squirming brought her into tighter contact with him. Although his face was deep in shadow, she sensed his amusement. She stilled immediately.

When he removed his hand from her mouth, Sydney blinked and drew in a breath. What was he about? He rose fluidly to his feet and held out his hand to her. With his warning still whispering in her head, she put her hand in his. He pulled her up to stand next to him.

Leaning toward her, he whispered in her ear, "We are going to the camels. You will come with me. Not a sound, or I will not hesitate to carry out my threat if you alert the others."

Frightened, Sydney nodded her agreement. Without dropping her hand, he turned and led her away from their camp. His grasp on her was firm, and much to her dismay, she found their hands fit together much too perfectly. His skin was warm against her chilled fingers. She was reminded suddenly of that shadow man who had visited her — was it only the night before? — and the tingly heat generated from his touch. Why had she remembered that? Embarrassed at her thoughts, she tried to wriggle out of his hold. His grip tightened, and he shot a warning glance back at her. She caught the glint of a dagger in his other hand.

As he led her away from their camp, she turned to look back. In the starlight, the others who were still sleeping looked like dark, indistinct mounds of clothing scattered across the sand. A snore here and there broke the silence of the desert night. One of the forms on the ground rose up and crept to where Lucy slept. Zayed. She watched as Lucy was awakened, then followed Zayed to the opposite side of the camp, where the two blended into the night. Her friend would be frantic at her disappearance and frightened at being forced to follow Zayed alone into the desert night. Would Al Jabbar follow? He slept at the far side of the group. She wanted to call out to him, alert him to what the Pirate was doing, but she dared not with that dagger in her kidnapper's hand. Part of the reason she had hired Al Jabbar and his men, besides needing him to help kill the evil sorceress, was for this reason, to protect her and Lucy from rogues who would drag them into the dark wilderness. Evidently, that had been money wasted. She would have to protect herself. And she hoped Lucy would be able to do the same.

When they reached the camels, she saw that two were already saddled and kneeling, waiting to be mounted. The Pirate took her by the waist, lifted her as if she weighed nothing, and plopped her onto one of the animals. He mounted his own animal, took her camel's rope, urged the camels to their feet with a quiet command, and set off into the desert.

Sydney remained silent, but she worried about Lucy's safety. Her friend was a gentle soul. Would she ever see Lucy again? She had to escape and get back to her friend.

When they had traveled well away from their camp and she was sure that no noise would travel back to those they had left sleeping, she urged her camel forward to match its strides with Al Qarsan's.

"Mr. Pirate," she began.

He turned to her. His brow quirked up. "Were you about to berate me, Miss Whelton?"

His eyes caught the starlight, and something about them reminded her of the shadow man who had visited her — his teasing words and tingly touch. But how was that possible? The Shadow had looked like a fantasy, something dredged from dreams and mist. This man on the camel beside her was solid male.

Dismissing her wayward thoughts, she straightened her back. "I would like to know the meaning of this abduction. I do not appreciate being awakened with a hand over my mouth, nor with threats of violence whispered in my ear."

Turning to face front, he said, "Whispering threats of violence in a woman's ear is not my usual habit. I would have much preferred whispering sweet endearments in your ear. But I saw no other way to keep you silent."

Incensed at what he implied, she snapped, "So those threats were empty? You did not mean them?"

He cocked an eyebrow.

Although a bit intimidated by that brow, frustration at his refusal to answer made her press. "Why, pray, did we need to be silent?" Sydney ignored his comment about endearments.

"Because I was abducting you." His words held a grin hidden behind his veil.

She sniffed. "I am not entertained, Mr. Pirate. And I am sure my companion, Mrs. Foster, is likewise not entertained by her abduction. She is most likely frightened to death. You will return me immediately to our camp, and you will fetch Mrs. Foster back from wherever your friend has taken her."

"No, I will not." He leaned toward her. His gaze turned serious. "And you will not try to escape, or I will carry out my threat to tie you up and gag you."

A finger of fear traced its way down her back. But as long as she had him talking, she decided she would take advantage.

"You could at least tell me why you felt the need to abduct me and Mrs. Foster."

Although she demanded an answer, she was not sure she wanted to know what it was. This man, more knowledgeable of the desert, more physically powerful than she was, could easily do whatever he wished with her. A man known as the Pirate must have performed many contemptible deeds. The rumors about him certainly implied that he had.

He studied her a moment before he answered. Finally, he said, "What if I told you I abducted you because I find you beautiful?"

She frowned at his blatant flattery. "Then I would say that the desert sun has ruined your eyesight."

"And I would say that you have not looked in a glass recently." He turned away, presenting her with his profile. "Why do you *think* I abducted you, Miss Whelton?"

Sydney decided that since she was already in danger from this man, the truth would not put her any further into jeopardy. "I can only think of one reason, sir, and that reason frightens me to my very soul. Your intentions are dishonorable, and if I had been aware that you were such a man, then I certainly would not have hired you."

"You believe that I'm dishonorable?" He huffed a laugh. "Miss Whelton, in comparison to Al Jabbar, I am a saint. He and his men would rob you blind, take your camels and your gear, then leave you stranded in the desert, if he decided not to slit your throat, most likely after he had his way with your person."

Anger overrode her fear. "And kidnapping me and Mrs. Foster is the act of an honorable man?" she snapped. "I am alone with you in the desert, so you could slit my throat as well, not to mention that…other thing. And we left everything behind. If Al Jabbar is the villain you say he is, you have given him what he would have stolen."

"Your valuables and your money pouch are in the bag hanging from your saddle," he said, as if relating something as commonplace as the sun rising tomorrow. "Zayed will be meeting us in a day or two with your companion, unharmed, and the rest of your gear. All of it. Every last bag and valise."

Dumbfounded, Sydney gaped. "You collected all that while I slept?"

He nodded. "While you slept, Miss Whelton."

She searched for words. All she could find were two. "Thank you."

The Pirate cast a speculative glance at her. "Don't be too grateful, Miss Whelton. You are still quite alone with me, and we have many miles to travel before we meet with Zayed and Mrs. Foster. I may still take it into my head to be dishonorable."

Bending down, she slipped a knife from her boot, and waved it at the Pirate. "If you come near me, I assure you that my blade will score your skin." Once again, the image of the shadow man came to mind, of her flashing a blade at him as well. What was it about those two that had her reacting in the same way?

The Pirate's gaze dropped to the knife, then snapped back up. He threw back his head and laughed. Urging his camel into a faster pace, he called back to her, "You have no idea how much I like a challenge, Miss Whelton."

Sydney's hand tightened on the hilt of her knife. The urge to fling it end over end into the Pirate's back nearly overcame her good sense. But she was alone at night in the middle of the desert. She could not be sure she could find her way back to their camp. He was her only defense against certain death. Grinding her teeth in frustration, she stuck the knife back into her boot and urged her camel forward as well.

If she had known how insufferable he would be, she would never have hired him. She had been told he was the best man for the job, and perhaps he was, but as soon as she saw the chance, she would put as much distance as she could between herself and the man known as the Pirate.

Chapter 3

They had been traveling for hours. The only light came from the stars and a sliver of moon that had finally decided to poke its head above the horizon. Even so, Sydney could barely see in the black of the desert night. The monotonous swish of the camels' feet against the sand and their rolling gait made her drowsy. She had vowed she would keep a close watch on the man who led her through the wilderness. She had no idea where he was taking her, and the reason he gave for spiriting her away in the middle of the night, to keep her safe from Al Jabbar, seemed fabricated. But even if his reason were true, she felt as if she had gone from one fire into another. At least at the camp she had the comfort of Lucy's presence, even though her friend was not much help with defense against brigands.

Sydney's thoughts circled inside her head. This journey to find the man with special abilities was foolhardy. But she felt compelled to finish what she had set out to do. After her mother died, her father had made her promise in a small secret ceremony that she would search out the evil sorceress if he were killed. At the time, she wondered at the strange request, for her father seemed invincible. She had felt special that he had given her this task, that he had wanted her to do this for him. But now, the longer she journeyed, the more she felt the danger inherent in his request. Whenever she faltered in her determination, the urge to carry on drove her, as if she could not help herself. Besides that, she carried the guilt of not helping him when the evil sorceress had attacked him. She wanted — no, needed — to avenge his death. But she had accomplished the first step in seeking revenge in her father's name. She had found the man, Al Qarsan — the Pirate — who could help her find the man with the Crystal Dagger.

She contemplated his back as he rode before her. His loose clothing hid his form, but she had felt his hard muscles when he had abducted her. His body was powerful, honed, no doubt, from his years of living in the desert. Apprehension assailed her. What if he was taking her someplace to ravish her? On the other hand, what if he was right and Al Jabbar was as treacherous as a snake? How could she trust either one of them?

She strained to see the expanse stretching away on all sides. All she saw was a bit of rocky sand beneath her camel's feet and beyond that, darkness that swallowed up the distant miles. No fires signaled civilization. She felt as if she and the Pirate were the only two inhabitants on the earth. For now, she had to rely on his goodwill. Her gaze landed on his back again, a straight and broad-shouldered form in the black night. He swayed gracefully with his camel's gait.

Why was he so damned attractive? And why did she feel so drawn to him when she should be completely uninterested? In fact, she should feel repelled, for he was a blackguard. Overbearing, arrogant, and rude.

She needed to keep her wits about her, but watching the rhythmic roll of his shoulders was hypnotic. Her eyes grew heavy. She was so tired. The journey to this desert land had been grueling. She wanted to sleep. She'd rest her eyes for a moment....

She jerked awake. Annoyed at herself for dozing off, she straightened her spine. She would not fall asleep and slip off her camel. She had to keep her guard up at all times. The man called the Pirate could attack her at any moment, especially now that they were out in the middle of this wasteland and far from the others. Uneasy, she glanced around, then loosened the knife stuck into her boot. That kept her alert for a few minutes, but then the continuous sway of the camel made her eyes droop again.

Raphael knew the woman fought against sleep. He heard her quick intake of breath every time she jerked awake, and then the rustle of her clothes as she shifted on her seat. She had drifted off twice and was in danger of falling off her camel. He glanced over his shoulder. Her head bobbed and her eyes were closed. He halted the animals, slid from his camel's back and reached her as she toppled sideways. She landed perfectly in his arms.

Her eyes popped open, she gasped, and wriggled. "Put me down this instant! How dare you!"

Raphael grinned. "I dare, *lalla*, because you would have encountered the ground, and perhaps broken a bone or two in that lovely body of yours."

That lovely body wriggled again. He found the experience very enjoyable.

She drew an indignant breath. "You are too forward, Mr. Pirate. A gentleman does not speak of a lady's —" Her voice strangled the last word.

"Body?" He offered and sniggered. "What would you call it?"

She held herself as far away from him as possible, a neat trick since he had her snugged up against him. Her lips compressed and she glanced away. When she turned back, her gaze was as cool as starlight. "Please put me down."

"No."

Those changeable eyes widened. "No? *No?* Why you —!" She squirmed in his arms like a puppy.

Raphael tightened his hold. "No, Miss Whelton, I will not put you down, for I do not wish to repair any broken bones you might incur from falling off your camel again, nor do I wish to waste the time tending to those broken bones."

Preventing her from hurting herself had been his first reason for catching Miss Whelton as she slid from her camel, but it had become an insignificant second after he had experienced the enticing feel of her soft curves against his chest, despite her attempt to keep space between them. As she squirmed, he discovered she wore no corset beneath those utilitarian clothes, which was a wise decision while traveling in the desert, but a surprising one, considering her priggishness. His hands itched to explore her delightful shape, but he forced them to behave. She smelled like lilies with a touch of spice, and he wanted to breathe in her scent until he became drunk on it. Dismayed at his intense reaction, he strode the few steps to his camel

41

and set her at the front of his saddle. Before she could argue, he had his camel kneel. She sputtered her protest as she was forced to hold on, first being thrown frontwards as the camel went down on its front knees, then back as the camel folded its back legs.

He mounted the beast behind her, then had it stand. Her bottom slid delightfully back against his crotch when the camel rose to its front feet, but sadly slid away again when the camel stood on all four. As she settled that lovely bottom more firmly in the saddle, she grazed his thighs. He forced himself not to clamp them closed around her. This woman was delicious, and he would enjoy every minute with her.

"You will ride with me," he announced, as he captured the lead for her camel.

"I'll do no such thing." She tried to wriggle away.

Ignoring that wriggle between his thighs, he wrapped his arm around her small waist and pulled her against him, for her safety, but enjoyed the delectable feel of her bottom between his thighs. "I believe you have no choice, Miss Whelton," he said as he urged his animal forward. "You are here on my camel, and we are moving on."

She loudly voiced her objections to his arrogant manhandling, her abduction, the forced journey in the middle of the night, leaving Al Jabbar behind, and abandoning her companion. As she berated him, she squirmed to get comfortable. He clamped his teeth together, steeling himself against the dangerous allure of her soft body nestled between his legs. Perhaps he had made a mistake by putting her before him on his camel.

Sydney was furious. After she had run out of complaints, she sat bolt upright in front of the Pirate and as far away as his iron-like arm about her waist would allow — which was not far at all. The heat from his body seared her back, and the scent of him filled her nose. He smelled of sun-heated skin, a wisp of sandalwood, and warm male. The combination was a heady perfume that made her want to inhale forever without ever exhaling. And that desire infuriated her even more.

"I'll have you know, Mr. Pirate, that I made my way from England to the desert without once needing to be saved by an overbearing man," she said, speaking to the space between the camel's ears.

"Mm." His wordless comment was neither admiration nor condemnation.

"I demand that you allow me to ride my own camel." She used her most authoritative tone.

"And let you fall off again?" He snugged her back against his chest. "I think we've already had this discussion, Miss Whelton. Go to sleep."

Sydney ground her teeth. If she had known how impossible he was, she never would have sought him out. His arm about her waist was as heavy as an iron chain and nearly as strong. His chest against her back felt as solid as oak. He was powerful and hard. Dangerous.

Fear insinuated itself into the heat of her anger. A chill ran through her that did not come from the cold air of the night desert. While he'd done nothing to harm her so far, still, he had abducted her, and she was alone with him. She knew nothing about him except what she had heard from others. With his arm about her waist, she could not reach her knife stuck into her boot. In her long journey from England, traveling by coach and cart and horse and ship and camel, this was the first time she was truly afraid, not merely apprehensive or wary. The man sitting so close behind her could do anything he wished—ravage her, sell her at the slave markets, kill her—and no one would be the wiser. Her mother had taught her never to show fear because that was when men would take advantage. So, when she had crossed paths with other dangerous men on her journey, she had bluffed and charmed, hiding her apprehension. But the Pirate unnerved her, threatened her equilibrium, unlike those others. What was she to do?

"I will not harm you, Miss Whelton." His voice, smooth as honey, murmured in her ear.

She twitched, startled out of her thoughts. Could he read her mind?

"Go to sleep." His command was a soft rasp.

"I will not. I will remain awake as long as you remain awake."

She attempted to sit up straighter.

That steely, muscled arm prevented it.

A rumble erupted from his chest that sounded suspiciously like a chuckle.

She wanted to throttle him.

And then he began to hum.

The sound was so incongruous coming from such a dangerous man that she was riveted. It was a sweet tune and sounded like an Arabic lullaby. The melody soothed, rising and falling in the night air. Despite her declaration of remaining alert, she felt her muscles relax. She was lulled into closing her eyes. His chest, instead of being stiff and hard, offered a comfortable support. Perhaps she would rest for a few minutes.

Sydney's eyes popped open. Stark sunlight blinded her. She winced and shut her eyes against the glare. She was lying on the ground, comfortably padded by several blankets beneath her, and her head was propped on the camel saddle. She did not remember how or when she had transferred from the Pirate's camel to the ground. How could she have forgotten stopping to make camp, laying out her blankets, stretching out on the ground and going to sleep? The last thing she remembered was the Pirate's humming.

That made her eyes pop open again. Where was he? Had he abandoned her? Or was he watching like a hungry predator, waiting for her to awaken so he could pounce? Cautiously, she sat up and glanced around. The camels lay contentedly a short distance away, chewing their cud. The ashes of a small fire smoldered at her feet. And there, across from her, the long form of the Pirate was stretched out on the ground. He lay on his back, his arms crossed at his chest, his legs crossed at the ankles, his eyes closed. He was sleeping.

Sydney took the opportunity to study him. He was certainly well-formed. His soft clothing draped over muscular arms and legs and across his broad chest and shoulders. A curved dagger rested at his hip. He wore the end of his turban still pulled across the lower part of his face. He had never lowered it in the time she had been traveling with him, not even to eat or drink. Instead, he had grace-fully slipped his food beneath it. When he drank, he always had his back to her as he held the goatskin bag aloft, tipped back his head, and allowed the stream of water to arrow between his lips.

Curiosity made Sydney bold and rash. She desperately wanted to see the features that went with those hypnotic golden eyes. She knew Tuareg men kept their faces veiled, but she suspected he was not a member of their tribe. The gossip and rumors she had heard hinted that he was from someplace else, possibly the Near East, maybe even Europe or the Americas. Perhaps he was malformed, and that was why he hid his face.

Carefully, as quietly as possible, she crept across the rocky sand that separated them. When she reached his side, she sat back on her heels and watched to see if he would awaken. He didn't move. His breath came quiet and regular in his sleep. Slowly, she reached out and lifted the edge of the veil from his face.

A strong jaw covered in dark stubble, the curve of a chin, and the corner of full lips. Intrigued, she lifted the veil a bit more. She saw more of his mouth, then watched as his lips compressed in his sleep. She wondered fleetingly what he was dreaming about. And then a hand snapped around her wrist like a hunter's trap. With a gasp, her gaze flew up and met those golden eyes, not hypnotic at all, but cold and suspicious. She froze.

"Do you assault all the men you travel with, Miss Whelton?" His chilly tone underscored how aggravated he was.

Sydney allowed the corner of his veil to slip from her fingers and tried to scoot back, but his grip was too tight. "I'm sorry. I did not mean…that is…I was not…" Her words trailed off at his stony expression. Mortified at being caught, she turned her head to hide the violent heat in her cheeks. Whatever had she been thinking? The sun must have addled her brain.

"You were not what, Miss Whelton?" he asked, sounding only mildly curious. "About to slit my throat? Stab me through the heart?" He paused. "Kiss me?"

Sydney choked. "Absolutely not."

"Then what, Miss Whelton, were you about to do?" His grip tightened fractionally, threatening.

Sydney stared into those lion eyes, so beautiful and so deadly. They would see if she lied. She swallowed. In a very small voice, she said, "I wanted to see your face."

A heartbeat passed. Then his gaze softened.

"Ah," he said. "Well, then. You realize, of course, that if I reveal my face, you will have to reveal a part of your body." He put a slight emphasis on the last word.

Sydney's eyes widened. "I beg your pardon?" She shook her head. "No."

His head tipped. "Fair is fair, Miss Whelton. One revelation for another."

How much did she wish to see his face? Very much. But the idea of revealing herself, even the tiniest bit, made her tremble. When she had taken her hair down for him in his tent, her stomach had clenched with embarrassment. But she would never allow this man to see her weakness.

"I will not," she said and ripped her wrist from his grasp.

His eyes narrowed fractionally. "As you wish," he said, and rolled to his feet.

Sitting on the ground, gazing up at him, Sydney felt as tiny as a mouse, as if she had failed some test and disappointed him. As he stepped away, she said, "Perhaps later."

He halted and faced her. "Why would I wish to reveal myself later?"

She had no answer, so she shrugged helplessly. But as he turned away again, she said, "You can't hide forever, Mr. Pirate."

He gave a mirthless chuckle. "Neither can you, Miss Whelton."

She watched him saunter beyond the camels into the desert where he stopped to relieve himself. Quickly, she averted her gaze, and noted the faint pink band on her wrist that marked where he had held her. Absently, she rubbed it. While she had been alarmed at his fierce response to her invasion, she had been aware that his grip had not hurt her. His fingers had been firm but gentle, even when he tightened his hold. She thought she had sensed a tiny tingle where their skin connected. When she jerked away, she felt as if she had lost something.

She raised her head and saw he had returned to their little camp and was checking on the camels. The physical distance reminded her that he was merely a guide to her final destination, provided, of course, that his kidnapping did not lead to her eventual demise. She had to remember he was dangerous, that she could not relax her guard. No matter how attractive or compelling he was.

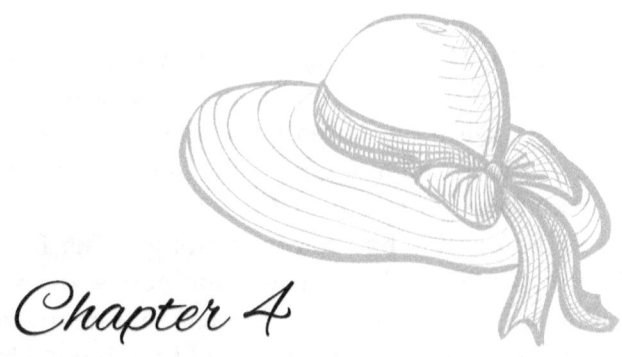

Chapter 4

They had been traveling all morning, the Pirate ahead and Sydney trailing. Her bottom ached from being in the saddle, so she decided to walk, leading her camel. The Pirate, however, still rode, not slowing his pace in the least and completely ignoring her. For a man who had kidnapped her and dragged her, alone, into the desert wasteland, he was curiously inattentive. For some reason, she had envisioned having to constantly fend off his advances. Except for the previous night when he had taken her onto his camel, he had been quite proper. Rather, he seemed to enjoy tormenting her with his aloofness, his silence, and the dogged rate of travel.

Sydney's feet hurt. Her bottom hurt. Her head hurt. And she was thirsty. She needed to rest for a bit.

"Excuse me, Mr. Pirate," she called. "Could we stop for a while?"

"Not yet, Miss Whelton," he replied without turning.

"I would like a drink of water," she said. He had the only water skin, for she had drunk all of hers.

He unhooked the goatskin from his saddle and held it out. When she did not take it immediately, he let it drop to the ground and continued on. Sydney hurried forward and snatched it up. She gulped down the goaty-tasting water. When she lowered the goatskin, she saw that the Pirate was quite a distance away. Aggravation made her grit her teeth. The man was as inconsiderate as a bear, not that she had ever met a bear, but she assumed bears would have no manners. She hung the water skin on her saddle and tugged on the lead to make her camel hurry along. The animal let out a bleat of resistance and refused to move. By the time she had her camel moving, the Pirate was even farther away than before. She rushed to catch up and muttered every vile curse she could think of. He'd had the audacity to kidnap her, and now he would leave her in the desert. Didn't he care that he might lose her? Or perhaps, that was his purpose all along, to bring her into the wasteland, abandon her, and leave her to die.

Before she had another thought, her foot fell into an animal's burrow. Her ankle twisted, and pain shot through the joint and up her leg. With a cry, she landed in a heap on the rocky sand. She lay for a moment, stunned and breathless. Her ankle throbbed as if someone was pounding it with a hammer. Her palms stung where they had broken her fall. Her entire side ached. She dragged herself to a seated position and glanced around for her camel. She thought she might use it to leverage herself upright. It was plodding slowly away in the direction the Pirate had taken. Stupid animal.

Pushing to her feet, she took a tentative step. Intense pain shot through her ankle, and she collapsed to her hands and knees. A sob escaped her. Her head drooped. She was going to die. Alone. In the desert. She had come on a fool's errand. She wished every horrible thing to rain down on the Pirate's head.

She heard the soft swish of a camel moving across sand. Thank the Heavens, her camel came back. It stopped within arm's reach. She was saved. And then, as she raised her head, she saw the Pirate's booted foot hanging at the camel's side.

As if she were merely strolling along a Hyde Park path in London, he asked, "May I offer you a ride, Miss Whelton?"

She glared up at him. He was an extremely obtuse and unsympathetic man. But what could she expect from someone who called himself the Pirate? And that thought made her rethink her first impulse to berate him. She could not afford to make him angry, not here, with an injury and alone with him in the wilderness.

"I've hurt my ankle," she said, forcing her tone to mildness. "I'm not sure I can walk on it."

He tipped his head and studied her a moment. His glance dropped to the injured joint, then he slipped from his camel's back. Squatting before her, he cupped her heel in one hand. That minor movement caused pain to shoot up her leg, and she gasped.

"We'll have to remove your boot, Miss Whelton," he said.

Sydney bit her lip and shook her head. Besides the fact that taking off her boot would hurt like blazes, she was not about to bare anything before this man. Then she remembered their earlier conversation.

She boldly met his gaze. "If I remove my boot, you will have to reveal yourself," she said.

A single brow quirked up. "And if I refuse? What then? Will you endure the pain without complaint? What if your ankle is broken? If it heals without being set, it will be malformed. How will you dance a gavotte or a quadrille with a limp?"

She was surprised at his knowledge of English dances, but his challenge annoyed her, despite its good sense. Her chin tilted up.

"I'll manage," she sniffed.

He stared for a moment, those golden eyes penetrating, then he gave a short nod. "Very well." He dropped her foot and stood.

Her foot, barely off the ground, made a tiny impact when it hit the sand. Still, shards of pain shot up her leg and black spots danced before her eyes. As her vision cleared, practicality overcame her reticence and her obstinance. He had proved his point.

"Yes," she said quietly.

"What was that, Miss Whelton? Did you say something?" he asked, his tone innocent.

He was being an ass. She ground her teeth.

"Yes," she snapped. Then said calmly, "I believe we should remove my boot. Please, will you help?"

Humor flashed through those golden eyes as he hunkered down again. He gently lifted her foot and loosened the laces on her boot. Then in a swift, deft move, he pulled it off. She felt a sharp twinge but nothing more. He gently probed her ankle, around the arch of her foot, across the instep, and a few inches up her leg. The touch of his fingers soothed, a most delightful sensation. Around and around, his fingers stroked, calming the pain. She closed her eyes and drifted, mesmerized. She wanted his ministrations to go on forever.

"Nothing is broken, Miss Whelton. You have merely sprained it."

Her eyes snapped open. Annoyed at allowing herself to fall under his spell, she straightened her spine. "Thank you for your diagnosis."

She tried to pull her foot from his grasp, but his fingers tightened, refusing to release her.

"It should be bound," he said. "You will be more comfortable."

Sitting crossed-legged before her, he placed her foot in his lap without waiting for her consent. He ripped a long strip from the bottom of his thin kaftan and wrapped it snugly around her foot and ankle. Despite her aggravation at his autocratic manner, she found that her ankle felt much better after his ministrations.

"Thank you," she said. "But fair is fair, Mr. Pirate. I have revealed a part of me, therefore you need to reveal a part of you."

His eyes glinted mischievously. "As you wish, Miss Whelton." With a sweep of his hand, he pushed one loose sleeve up to his elbow.

She tsked. "I have already seen your arm. Your sleeve falls away whenever you reach for something." She did not mention that every peek at that arm fascinated her.

He studied her a moment. Those golden eyes seemed to probe beneath her skin and made her cheeks hot. Then, with a deliberate movement, he pulled the veil from his face.

Sydney stared. The glimpse she'd had before had not prepared her for what she now saw. The man was beautiful. Straight nose, defined cheekbones, sculpted mouth. And those eyes that reminded her of a lion. But a thin, pale scar slashed across his left cheek. It disappeared into the dark scruff that covered his jaw. What caused that disfigurement? She should have expected something, for he named himself Pirate. He must have been in countless sword or knife fights and could not have escaped them all unscathed. But instead of disapproval for his wicked ways, she felt a sympathetic sadness that he was so marred. Without thinking, she reached out to touch the scar.

He flinched away and a growl rumbled in his throat. His gaze turned hard.

She froze, her hand hovering above the corner of his mouth. "I'm sorry. I did not mean…" Her words died away, and her hand dropped.

He stared a moment. Then, as if the last few moments had never happened, he removed her foot from his lap and rose to his feet. Bending, he lifted her as if she weighed nothing and placed her on her camel.

Sydney had no time to protest, for he quickly mounted his own camel, grabbed the lead to hers, and they started off, the animals side by side. Baffled by his contradictory moods, she sat in silence for a moment, then her good manners kicked in.

"Thank you," she said.

He gave a small nod of acknowledgment. Their camels plodded forward a few steps.

"Robert Thurgood," he said.

"I beg your pardon?" Puzzled at his response, she turned to him.

Without looking at her, he repeated, "Robert Thurgood. The man you know as Al Jabbar gave me the scar."

The revelation stunned her into silence. Again. The man was a mystery loaded with surprises.

She swallowed as she tried to absorb both his information and the fact that he had disclosed something about himself. "I'm so sorry. Is that why you hate him so?"

His inscrutable gaze landed on her. "No." Then he turned away and urged his camel into a faster gait.

Sydney was forced to follow. Her emotions were a mix of sympathy and aggravation. While he had given her some explanation, it was as clear as a London fog. She was wildly curious about the story behind that scar and the reason for the animosity between the two men. From Al Jabbar's comments when he met them at the well, she surmised that he and the Pirate had a long acquaintance and once had been friends. What had turned them into them enemies?

She had been told that Al Jabbar could be counted on as a reputable guard. She had also been told that the Pirate was the best man to help in her search. How could she trust either of them if they were enemies? They might fall on each other with knife or sword and kill one another. Then what would she do? Perhaps she should forget her quest and return to England. But the compulsion placed on her by her father urged her on. That, and her guilt.

She glanced around. The desert stretched away in every direction. Her gaze landed on the back of the man riding in front of her. She was alone in this wasteland with him. She had no idea where they were. Perhaps she would never get back to England. Perhaps her life would end in this vast, untamed land. Self-pity engulfed her and tears threatened.

Then she heard his low, melodic voice. He was humming again. It was beautiful. His hum turned into a song, a strange tune that could only have come from this wild country. How could a man with such a voice be evil?

Raphael finished his song and lapsed into thoughtful silence. Singing calmed him, and at that moment, he found himself in need of calm. He had disconcerted the woman with his admission. He had disconcerted himself. He never shared anything about his past because it meant nothing. The past was a jumble of memories, most of which were unpleasant and painful, none of which he wanted to share with anyone. No one needed to know how wretched most of his life had been. But for some reason, that tidbit of information about his scar had fallen from his lips before he could stop it. That made him uneasy, and he shifted his seat on the camel's back.

He examined the possible reason for his lapse. Perhaps he wanted the woman to know how treacherous Al Jabbar could be. Although he could not understand why he cared. But he couldn't think of any other reason. Surely, he had no interest in whether she found Robert more attractive. His interest went only so far as the rest of the fee she would pay him when he found the man with a useless crystal dagger. This journey was merely a diversion. *She* was a diversion, for he enjoyed poking at her proper manners and baiting her to see the color rise in her cheeks.

If he were truthful with himself, another reason presented itself. He sensed she held some answers to his past, answers that were connected to the talisman around his neck. It had warmed against his skin when she entered his tent, and that had never happened before when he was awake. It only happened in his dreams — his nightmares — and only when that evil woman appeared. What connection did Miss Whelton have to his origins? He needed to find the answers, and the only way to do that was to keep her close. Making her fearful of Al Jabbar drew her closer. And having her close was definitely pleasant. Besides, Al Jabbar was the deadliest man he had ever encountered, and he did not want Miss Whelton falling into the man's clutches.

Raphael was also curious about the vision he'd had when he touched the black satin garment that had fallen from her valise. What was the significance of the vision? Who was the woman with golden eyes like his? Who was the man beside her who looked like he would die for her? And who was the man in the gold mask? Where were they? Was it a vision from the past or the future? And why did Miss Whelton have such a garment?

The questions swirled in his head. But out of the chaos, one thought was perfectly clear. He would keep Miss Whelton with him for as long as it took to get answers.

Chapter 5

They had been traveling for two days when the mountains became a distinct feature on the horizon. Sydney had watched them appear as the sun rose, for they journeyed at night before the heat of the sun baked the earth. Surely, they were not going to try to cross them.

Her traveling companion had become very quiet after the revelation about his scar. The only conversation he indulged in was to inform her when they would be stopping to rest, and when they would be moving on. Their last conversation had occurred some time ago just after dawn. The sun was now nearly at its zenith. They had stopped to rest and were both stretched out in the shade of their camels to get some sleep before setting off again when temperatures would be cooler.

Sydney lay on her back and tried not to move because any movement in the heat made perspiration break out all over her body. Then dust would cling to her, and that was very uncomfortable, not to mention how appalling she looked, nor how disgusting she smelled. She wanted a bath. Badly. These things had not bothered her when she was traveling with Lucy but traveling with the Pirate made her self-conscious and put her on edge.

She carefully rolled to her side. Tiny rocks dug into her, but she tried to ignore them. She needed to sleep so she would not fall off her camel again. But sleep eluded her. Not far away, the Pirate was stretched out and slumbering peacefully. He had not bothered to cover his face again, so she was able to study him. Asleep, he looked more approachable, not so fierce and dangerous. She wondered what had made him so.

She rolled to her back again and closed her eyes. As she began to drift off, she heard him muttering and mumbling. Annoyed, she covered her ears. He had never talked in his sleep before. Why did he have to start as she was falling asleep? She opened one eye and peeked at him. He seemed quite agitated. Perhaps she should wake him.

She watched another moment. He flung out his arm, and a low groan escaped him as if he were in pain. He grimaced. That decided her. Quietly, so she did not startle him, she crept to his side. She placed her hand on his shoulder and shook him gently.

"Mr. Pirate," she whispered.

"No," he mumbled, and lines of pain deepened around his mouth.

She shook him again. "Mr. Pirate, wake up, please."

He gasped a breath and his eyes snapped open. They were dark, glazed, and not at all like his normal, beautiful eyes. He stared at her, and seemed not to see her but something else, something that riveted him, something that terrified him. Before she could think, he grabbed her arms, pulled her down and kissed her.

In shock, Sydney froze. She thought she felt the touch of some-thing dark and malevolent in her mind, but it was gone before she could focus on it. Instead, several things ran through her head. His fingers around her upper arms were warm and firm. His chest beneath her was hard muscle. His lips and tongue were softer than she imagined, making her feel extraordinary sensations, like nothing she had ever felt. Tingly. Wanting more. She should push him away. She really did not want to do that. But she really should.

Gathering her willpower, she jerked back. Her eyes locked on his. They had returned to their usual gorgeous golden color. And they were looking back at her in bewilderment that slowly turned to amusement. The corner of his mouth tipped up.

"I've never been awakened in such a pleasant manner, Miss Whelton," he said.

Flustered, Sydney shook her head. "I didn't…I never…" She swallowed. "You seemed to be distressed."

His gaze turned thoughtful. "Distressed," he murmured. "Perhaps I was. Dreams can sometimes be distressing." Then he smiled. "But it was only a dream, and you have chased away the dream demons."

His smile caught her by surprise. She had never seen him smile. He certainly had never been approachable, and now he was charming. That charm caught her off-guard. She nearly smiled back, but a sudden suspicion reared in the back of her mind. His dream had distressed him terribly. Beads of sweat speckled his brow. Before this, heat never seemed to affect him. He never perspired, not even when they traveled as the sun baked them and she thought she might melt. But now, after that dream, droplets of perspiration sparkled at his temples. Whatever he had seen as he slept had terrified him, and he was pretending it had been nothing. He could be dissembling as any man might who did not wish to reveal a weakness, or he could be hiding something dangerous. She suspected the latter.

She pulled away and landed hard on the rocky sand. "You are lying."

His smile died and his eyes snapped into slits. "Were you present in my dream, Miss Whelton? Or perhaps you can read minds?" he growled.

Sydney wanted to scoot away from his anger, but she refused to be intimidated. Raising her chin, she said, "No, neither of those. But I can interpret dreams. I might be able to help with yours and chase away those—ah—sleep demons."

Slowly, he rose to a seated position, pulled up one knee and rested his arm across it. He studied her a moment. "I have heard of those who can interpret dreams," he said finally. "They are usually old hags and crumbly old men." He tipped his head. "You look like neither one. Unless you are a sorceress who can change her appearance. So, tell me, Miss Whelton, beneath that lovely exterior, are you ragged and wrinkled?"

Her mouth dropped open. Did he truly think her attractive? He had told her he thought so once before. Perhaps he did. The thought made heat rush to her cheeks. Then rationality prevailed. No, he was using charm to learn her secrets. She had made a terrible mistake. She never should have offered to help him in his distress. She could not let him know what she was. Feigning insult and misunderstanding, she stood.

"If I am ragged and wrinkled, it is because you forced me to travel through the desert without the help of my companion. I pride myself on my toilette, Mr. Pirate," she said with a haughty tone. "I do the best I can with little baggage and less water." She turned and took a step toward the shade of her camel, then swung back to him. "And I will not offer my aid again when demons invade your dreams." She stalked to her blanket, plopped down, and turned her back to him.

After a moment, a snigger reached her ears, and she heard him settle back on his own blanket.

"Pleasant dreams, *ya helo*," he murmured.

Sydney's breath caught at his tone. She had no idea what those foreign words meant. Were they complimentary or an insult? She couldn't be sure, but when he had uttered them, they sounded a bit seductive. Perhaps she had misunderstood, and he was merely being amiable. Charming, even. But she refused to be charmed. Her mother had warned her of the treachery that people would use to learn her secrets. The Pirate, with his beguiling golden eyes and silver tongue, might be the most treacherous of all.

Raphael lay on his blanket and thought about the woman lying on the far side of the cold embers. When she had first entered his tent, he sensed that she was different from other women. The warmth emitted by the talisman resting against his skin had told him that. When he had visited her in his shadow form and touched her, the tingles in his skin where he normally would have felt nothing revealed that she held some secret about his curse. Besides that, his talisman had warmed again when they had kissed. Surely that indicated some connection between them. Her offer to interpret his dream indicated she was more than ordinary. Few possessed that skill. The combination of all those things convinced him that she was the key to discovering who he was and why he was cursed.

More than that, her kiss had been delicious. When she had awakened him, he had been in the thrall of the devil sorceress who regularly invaded his dreams and demanded he give her something, whatever that was. The demon woman both aroused and repelled him, attempting to draw him into her black seduction where he knew he shouldn't go. Seeing Miss Whelton leaning above him broke through the malignant murk of his nightmare. She was a pure, shining light.

He was unable to control the craving to have her, to drink her in as a panacea to the evil that clawed at his soul. If Miss Whelton had not broken away, he wasn't sure that all he would have done was kiss her. If he had gone further, he wouldn't have been able to live with himself, for despite his misdeeds and transgressions, he had never forced a woman to lay with him. Even that tiny kiss made remorse twist through him, despite how splendid it was.

He listened to her toss and turn as she searched for a comfortable spot on her bed of rocky sand. When he had made arrangements with Zayed to separate and abscond with Miss Whelton, his main reason had been to split from Al Jabbar. Raphael wanted nothing to do with the man he had once called a friend. Besides, he knew he could find the man with the dagger of crystal without Al Jabbar's help. His pride had been stung when he learned that Miss Whelton had hired another in her search. Even though he knew little about her, he suspected she knew even less about the villain she had hired to protect her. So, for her safety and for his peace of mind, he had wanted to put as much distance as he could between them and Al Jabbar.

Miss Whelton had finally fallen asleep. The woman who wanted his help to find a man with an unusual dagger held many secrets. Now that he was alone with her in the desert, he planned to discover every one. They would be traveling many days together, so he had plenty of time. The thought made him smile. Unearthing Miss Whelton's secrets would be a delightful diversion on their journey.

Far beneath the lagoon that protected the city of Venice from the sea, in a cavernous chamber of black marble, of huge pillars disappearing into the darkness, of torches set in golden brackets, and many corridors branching into mysterious spaces, Nulkana, the ancient sorceress, screeched in rage. With a swipe of her arm, she sent bottles and vials and clay vessels crashing to the floor. Liquids and powders of poisonous purple, putrid green, and noxious yellow spread and swirled in an evil rainbow.

"I can't find him, Kek," she yelled. "He defies me. Each time I get close, he pushes me back. I can't find him!"

Kek, his skeletal features set in an expression of sympathy, stepped forward out of the gloom. "You will find him, mistress. You will find him and take what is yours."

She growled in frustration. "He is strong, this one. Stronger than the others. And I can't find him."

"It is only because you haven't healed completely, mistress," Kek soothed.

Nulkana rubbed her chest with a withered hand, spotted and bony with age. "It shouldn't take this long," she snapped. "That Auriano bitch found a Druid to help her. A Druid!" She pulled at the neck of her black, shapeless garment and revealed scabbed skin on her chest, oozing green pus and black blood. "Look what he did, Kek! If I don't find that piece, I will die."

"No, no, mistress, you won't die. You are strong yet. Remember what you did to that one who called himself the Lord High. You killed him like a bug."

Nulkana's eyes lit with vicious satisfaction. "I did, didn't I? The wretched insect." She swayed and leaned heavily on the table next to her. "Kek," she whined. "I'm dying."

"No, no, mistress. You need to feed." Kek snapped his fingers at a hooded figure deep in the shadows. "Your mistress needs to feed, worm."

The hooded figure stood unmoving for a long moment. When Kek snapped his fingers again, the figure moved off with slow, silent steps into one of the long corridors and was swallowed up in the darkness.

The ancient sorceress watched him go. "My worm is becoming more resistant. I shall have to use another binding spell." She glanced up at the ceiling far above her head. Faint cracks of magic sizzled in the black marble, then died. "I must repair that," she mused.

Turning back to the table where broken fragments of glass and clay lay scattered after her outburst, she gazed into an irregularly shaped red crystal. She caressed its surface like a lover. In response, it glowed softly.

"He has a woman with him, Kek," she said. "A woman who pulled him away from me. I almost had him." She held up her gnarled hand

and slowly closed her fingers into a fist. "I will get him. This woman is nothing. I will get rid of her. Destroy her."

"Yes, mistress. Of course," Kek crooned.

The screams of frightened young women echoed from one of the passages.

"Your meal is coming, mistress," Kek said. "You will feel stronger after you feed."

Nulkana nodded, but she was not thinking of her forthcoming meal. The woman who interfered consumed her thoughts. Something about the woman intrigued her, angered her. Something about her was familiar. She should not have been able to pull him so easily out of his dream. Nulkana's hand tightened on the red crystal. She would discover this woman's weakness and swat her like an irritating gnat. Or perhaps, she could turn the woman to her will. She pondered that possibility. Whichever way she decided, the woman would cease to interfere. Then she, Nulkana, ancient and powerful, would find him and take what was hers. As soon as she healed. As soon as she regained her strength.

Raising her head, she bellowed, "Where is my meal, worm?"

Chapter 6

Shortly before sunset the next day, Raphael and Sydney entered a small village at the foot of the mountains. It huddled in an oasis that was fed by a stream gushing from the slopes. Sydney had never been so glad to see rushing water. Now she could finally bathe.

The flat-roofed houses were made of mud bricks of a yellowish tan color that blended with the dirt and climbed up the slope of the mountain. Most appeared only big enough to be single rooms, although some had been expanded and looked like a child had cobbled together building blocks. A few goats wandered among the houses, and chickens scratched at the ground. Green terraces planted with crops stepped down along one side of the houses. Date palms created a backdrop to the village where they grew along the streambed. Except for the palms and terraces, the sparse, low vegetation was a muted grayish green color. Young children played in the dirt, and older ones helped with chores.

At their entrance into the village, people gathered around them. An elderly man emerged from one of the houses. The Pirate dismounted and murmured to Sydney to remain with the camels, then stepped forward. He greeted the villager with a bow, and a touch to his heart, lips, and forehead. The elder returned the greeting. As the two men held a short conversation, some of the younger children gathered around Sydney. One of the youngest, barely a toddler, ran to keep up. She tripped, went sprawling, and began to cry. Without a thought, Sydney scooped her up, brushed her off, and tried to comfort her. The little girl was inconsolable. And adorable with her huge dark eyes and wavy dark hair. The mother rushed up and took her little girl with a jumble of words and several bows. Then she returned to the crowd and disappeared among them.

The Pirate returned to Sydney's side. "These people cherish their children," he said. "That was considerate of you."

Her cheeks heated at the compliment. "The little girl fell. Anyone would have done the same."

"Not anyone," he murmured, his golden eyes warm with approval.

She could have fallen into those eyes. Instead, she turned to fidget with the ropes that tied some of her baggage.

"We'll stay here for the night and wait for Zayed and Mrs. Foster," he said. "You'll be staying with the headman's sister and her daughter." He indicated an old woman who bobbed a bow and showed a toothless smile, and a younger woman who bowed with her.

Sydney nodded her agreement. "When will Zayed arrive with Mrs. Foster?" She worried for her friend's safety.

"When Zayed can evade Al Jabbar." His abrupt response implied that she should have understood that.

Disconcerted by his swift change from compliment to reproof, she huffed. "I am concerned for Mrs. Foster. I do not truly know you, Mr. Pirate, nor do I know your friend, Zayed. How can I be sure he has not murdered her and buried her body in the desert?"

His brows drew together. "Why would he do that?"

"Because he wanted to," she snapped.

He drew an aggrieved breath. "Miss Whelton. Have I given you any reason to think that either of us is a murderer?"

She crossed her arms. "None. Except that your reputation names you as ruthless. You spirited me away in the middle of the night from my friend."

He crossed his arms as well. "I spirited you away from the man who would have murdered you and buried you in the desert. You are here, safe, and I have provided you with sleeping arrangements. Doesn't that prove that I am trustworthy?"

Sydney grudgingly conceded the point and felt even worse for impugning his honor. But she still worried about Lucy. "Perhaps you plan to leave me here so you may meet up with Zayed somewhere in the mountains."

He raised his eyes to the heavens and muttered, "Allah, give me strength."

Before Sydney could argue further, the headman said something. The Pirate responded, then turned to her.

"The headman wants to know if your accommodations are unsuitable. He thinks you are displeased because of our argument," he said. "If you don't bow or at least smile at him, he'll be insulted."

Ashamed that she had been rude, she ducked her head. She didn't want to insult the man who had graciously offered them a place to sleep. She turned to the headman with a smile. "Thank you for the accommodations," she said. "You are very kind."

The Pirate translated for her. The headman beamed, and the villagers appeared pleased as they dispersed to return to their chores. With a small bow, the headman's sister indicated the way to her house. Sydney followed.

She would see about that bath, but she would remain vigilant. She was not about to allow the Pirate to abandon her. Although, she had to concede that the Pirate had done nothing threatening beyond stealing her away in the middle of the night. In fact, he had helped when she turned her ankle. If his intent had been to abandon her, that would have been the perfect opportunity. Instead, he had torn a strip from his kaftan and wrapped her joint. The recollection of his gentle touch made her swallow against the warmth that flooded her. Pushing the memory away, she resolutely followed the headman's sister. All she could do was wait and see if Zayed appeared with Lucy, safe and sound. Besides, she very much wanted to bathe in that stream.

The men had finished the long meal with a great deal of storytelling and music when Raphael had finally excused himself. The sun had descended while he had been inside, but the moon had not yet risen. The stream beckoned him. He looked forward to a dunk in the chilly water as he strolled down the narrow path. He had enjoyed his time among the men, but in the middle of a conversation he found himself wondering about Miss Whelton. What was she doing? Was she comfortable among the women? Had she eaten? Was she sleeping?

Annoyed with himself for allowing his thoughts to dwell on a woman who seemed to dislike and mistrust him, he decided he would banish all thoughts of her as he bathed. He knew of a small pool where the water was calm at the edge of the stream. It was protected by rocks on two sides and scrubby bushes on the third. The women used it to launder clothes and for bathing during the day. He doubted anyone would be there now in the darkness between twilight and moonrise.

As he wended his way down the palm-lined path, his thoughts were on the problem of Al Jabbar and the very good possibility the man was tracking them, despite spiriting Miss Whelton away and having Zayed lay a false trail with Mrs. Foster. The outlaw was cunning and imbued with prodigious tenacity. Anxious to continue the journey, Raphael hoped Zayed would arrive soon.

When he neared the pool, he heard splashing that disrupted the sound of the rushing stream. Perhaps an animal had come looking for a drink. Cautiously, he crept closer. He was not about to share the stream with a lion or leopard. As he reached the rocks, he saw a figure in the water, but it was not feline. The moon chose that moment to peek above the trees, and the water reflected a splinter of light. With a jolt, he realized that Miss Whelton was bathing, her pale skin luminous in the night. His gaze stuck. She was sleek, like a lithe desert cat. He was mesmerized. He should look away, turn back and return later after she had finished. But for some reason, he couldn't seem to make his feet move. He remained silent, perfectly still. Entranced.

He watched as she scooped up water and let it spill down over her hair. In the dark, against her skin, her hair appeared black, but he knew that it held a fire in its depths. With her arms raised, her breasts rose pertly, accenting the flat of her stomach. Her narrow waist flared out to gently rounded hips and smooth thighs with a dark triangle between. Did that triangle of hair, like the tresses that flowed across her shoulders and down her back, hold hidden fire as well? If he touched her there, would she explode into flames of passion? He swallowed down his thoughts. The rest of her disappeared in the stream. She was a water nymph, a spirit come to entice him.

Abruptly, she swung in his direction. Had she heard him, some-how felt his presence? He sensed her shock, then her outrage. Miss Whelton's hand flew up, palm out, and she mumbled a few words. A flash, and something punched him in the chest. He flew backward through the air and landed with a thud on his back in the middle of the path. The breath whooshed out of him.

Dazed, he blinked as he dragged air into his lungs. What had happened? The palm trees above his head were dead still. No *haboob*, no wild sandstorm with its dry, driving wind had swept him off his feet. What, then, had it been? He heard the woman scrambling from the stream and the patter of her feet on the path. The dark outline of a head bent over him and blocked out the scattering of stars blinking through the palm fronds.

As he gazed up at her, the realization at what she had done flashed through his brain. "You're a witch," he growled. He scram-bled to his feet. Miss Whelton fell back several steps. "You're a witch!" he shouted.

"You were watching me, spying on me!" she accused. "How dare you!"

Disconcerted, Raphael yelled back, "I was not!"

That short moment when he saw her in the stream couldn't be called spying. But then, he had been so entranced by Miss Whelton's luscious form that he had no idea how long he stood rooted, watch-ing. He dismissed his unease at what he might have done with the dawning knowledge that the beguiling Miss Whelton had secret abilities. He scowled and rubbed his chest where the magical blast had hit him. He'd have a bruise there in the morning.

Miss Whelton studied him with pursed lips. Quietly, she said, "Are you all right? I'm sorry if I hurt you."

The moon shed enough light that he could see the pale oval of her face, the glint of her eyes, the dusky shape of her mouth. In spite of what she had done, Raphael wanted to kiss her. He wanted to trace the outline of those lips with his tongue. He wanted to feel their softness, nip the bottom plump lip with his teeth. He wanted to have those lips part beneath his and invite him in. He wanted to cover those pert breasts with his hands, massage them, roll the tight nipple between his fingers until she gasped in pleasure. The impulse made him think he might be going mad. Or perhaps he might be under some spell. He knew about witches. The evil sorceress who regularly visited his dreams was malevolent and vicious. He should not want to kiss this woman before him. Because she was a witch. And weren't all witches wicked?

She tipped her head, and her brows drew together. "Are you all right?" she asked again.

Raphael realized he hadn't answered her, and his hand still pressed against his chest as if he stood before her as a supplicant. Or some weakling who could not endure a little pain. He also realized she had apologized. What sort of witch did that after inflicting harm? And what sort of woman did that after accusing him of harboring malevolent thoughts?

Dropping his hand, he straightened his shoulders and gave a short nod. "Yes. I'm fine."

Her brow cleared. "Good. I did not mean to hurt you."

Blindsided by her admission, he heard a sideways apology tumbling from his mouth. "I did not mean to stare."

Her lips twitched. "Yes. Well." She glanced away, then back, earnest, and serious now. "Please, you must not tell anyone."

Irritated that he had not guessed her secret, he raised an eyebrow and challenged, "Why should I keep my silence? You accused me of planning some mischief against you. You deceived me. You made me believe you were merely a woman searching for someone when you clearly have power beyond the ordinary. When you are perfectly able to protect yourself from any mischief I might concoct. The headman of this village might be very interested to know he has a witch amidst his people."

Her eyes widened. "Please, don't tell him. I promise not to do anything like that again."

"Another bargain, Miss Whelton? Like revealing one body part for another?" Blatantly ignoring the fact that he'd seen nearly all her body parts, he wondered what she would offer in return for his silence. The possibilities intrigued him. *She* intrigued him. Despite being a witch.

She swallowed. Then her chin went up and, even in the dark, he could see the blaze of her eyes. "You've just seen everything," she accused.

He shrugged. "It's very dark."

"I could incinerate you," she said with a scowl.

"Yes, you could," he agreed solemnly. Then his mouth tipped up. "But you won't because you need me to find this man with the strange dagger."

She waved away his argument. "I can have Al Jabbar guide me."

His eyes narrowed as he wondered if the witch and his enemy had some way to communicate secretly. "If he can guide you, why did you hire me?"

She glanced away. "Because I was told you were the best at finding things. I already told you that I hired Al Jabbar for protection. He'll probably catch up to us eventually despite your kidnapping me and leaving him behind."

Confident in his own abilities, Raphael smiled. "No, he won't." Then the devil made him provoke, "Perhaps I'll take you into the mountains and abandon you."

She gasped. "You wouldn't!"

"Why not?" he prodded. "You don't trust me. You think I might inflict some harm on your person when I have given you no reason to think that. So why not do as you expect me to do? Besides that, you have made a bargain with my enemy. And you haven't yet paid me the rest of my fee. You have given me no reason why I should keep my silence about what you are."

"But—but I thought...." Her words died. She gnawed her bottom lip, a very luscious lip, then said, "I told you I would pay the rest of your fee when we found the man I'm looking for."

He noticed she did not mention his silence about her being a witch, so he crossed his arms and looked away as if he were bored.

She drew a breath and let it out. "Very well. Please, if you keep silent, I will tell you how I came to engage Al Jabbar in this quest."

Surprised at her offer but very much interested, he pretended indifference. "I'm not sure that's an even bargain, Miss Whelton."

"I have nothing else to offer." She sounded a bit desperate.

"I think you have much more to offer," he murmured. Before she could process his seductive implication, he said, "But I'll accept that for now. I might decide to renegotiate later."

Her tension released in a tiny whoosh. "Thank you." A heartbeat passed, she glanced away, then she said, "I believe I'll retire now."

"Of course." He waited for her to leave.

She remained where she was.

He wondered why she did not move.

She gestured at the path behind him. "Ah, if you don't mind…?"

Glancing right and left, he realized he was blocking the path. "My apologies." He grinned and stepped to the side with a mocking bow.

As she glided past him, she murmured, "Good night, Mr. Pirate."

Raphael watched her disappear into the dark night, then he turned and descended to the stream. With his brain in a muddle, he stripped and entered the icy water, but he didn't notice the cold. He focused instead on what he had learned about the woman who had hired him to find a man with a crystal dagger. She was the most confounding woman he had ever encountered. She was the most entrancing creature he had ever met. She was a witch.

He wanted to kiss her until she could not think.

He wanted to kiss her until *he* could not think.

She was a witch.

What was he going to do about her?

He should leave her in the village, disappear into the desert, and wipe her from his mind. But that idea chafed. He felt drawn to her. But this was not like the compulsion he felt in his nightmares with the sorceress. This was different. This compulsion was in his chest, approximately in the same place where her magical power had hit him. Absently, he rubbed the spot. The ache of the bruise made him wince. She had apologized. Once again, he wondered at a witch who did that.

As he climbed out of the stream, he decided he needed to learn more about her, if only for his own protection. As he had discovered, a witch could be unpredictable. But she was also considerate. He had witnessed her interaction with the child at the village. A kind woman who wanted to hire an assassin. Perhaps not such a kind woman. A complex woman. Intriguing.

He remembered the day she had first entered his tent when the talisman he wore around his neck had warmed. She was a witch, but perhaps she was a witch who could help him discover who he was and where he came from. Perhaps, his first instinct to help her in her search had arisen from something deep within him. This search might prove more of an adventure than he anticipated.

He pressed his hand against his chest again and felt the lump of the talisman beneath his kaftan. It was chilly from the stream. No warmth there now. But perhaps at some point in their journey, it would warm again, and he might gain some insight into his origins.

Pacing up the path back to the village, he felt a tiny spark of hope. Along with that, he looked forward to learning more about Miss Whelton and her entrancing lips.

The next day, Raphael was sharing a meal with the village elders when a commotion erupted at the edge of the village. Amidst barking dogs, braying camels and excited voices, he watched Zayed arrive with Mrs. Foster and their two pack camels. As Zayed slid from his animal, he sent Raphael a glance loaded with meaning. Zayed exchanged greetings with the village elders while Mrs. Foster reunited with Miss Whelton. Raphael watched the two women embrace as if they had been separated for months instead of a few days. Mrs. Foster drooped against her friend, and Raphael wondered again at the reason why the woman would undertake such an arduous journey, for she didn't seem to be suited for adventures. The two women disappeared into one of the houses and the commotion died down. Zayed pulled him aside to have a quiet word.

Zayed's eyes were hard as he said, "Al Jabbar followed us across the desert. We could not lose him."

"Son of a dog!" Raphael spat. "He's like a jackal on the scent of a kill." He crossed his arms and stared at his boots as he thought over the problem. "Why do you suppose he wants my death now, after all these years?"

"I think he wants more than your death," Zayed said. "I think he wants what Miss Whelton wants."

Raphael's brows rose in skepticism. "This man with a foolish crystal dagger?"

Zayed nodded. "Perhaps this dagger is not so foolish. Strange circumstances surround this quest, my friend. Miss Whelton traveled far to find you without Al Jabbar's protection. Why would she need it now when she has found you?"

Raphael grinned. "Because I am known as such a dangerous man."

"You have never hurt a woman," Zayed said dismissively, ignoring Raphael's attempt at humor. He shook his head. "I feel they have some connection they hide from our eyes. I feel forces gathering that we cannot see. Miss Whelton makes me uneasy."

Raphael opened his mouth to tell his friend what he had discovered about Miss Whelton, then closed it again. Zayed would want to abandon the two women and give up the search, but Raphael was not ready to do that. Miss Whelton concealed many more secrets than the one he had learned, secrets that might lead him to knowledge of his past and his identity. He thought back to the warmth of the talisman against his skin when she first entered his tent, and the strange vision he had when he touched that black satin garment in her valise. He remembered the tingle in his finger when he touched her lips in his shadowy form. These instances were all unusual. He suspected that Zayed's uneasiness might be grounded in a truth they were yet to discover about the woman, beyond her being a witch. But he was not yet prepared to abandon her. Besides, he was intrigued by this crystal dagger and the man with special abilities who carried it. He ignored the fact that Miss Whelton also intrigued him.

"I think," he said finally, "that we need to prevent Miss Whelton and Al Jabbar from meeting again. Something about their connection troubles me, as well. How far behind is he?"

"Perhaps a half day, perhaps a bit longer."

That knowledge made Raphael wary. "We should leave now."

Zayed shook his head. "Mrs. Foster needs to rest. She could barely keep her seat on her camel."

Raphael's lips compressed in frustration, then he gave a short nod. "We'll let her have a meal and rest, then set out an hour after the moon rises." He turned back toward the headman's house. "Come. We'll plan while you eat."

As he ducked through the door, he tried to decide if he wanted to evade Al Jabbar completely or lure him into a trap and end their feud forever.

Sydney dashed from the hut where she had spent the night when she heard Zayed and Lucy arrive in the village. After greeting her friend with a hug, she walked Lucy toward the hut, then paused outside.

"I'm so glad you're safe," she said, giving her friend another hug.

"And I am so glad to see you," Lucy sniffled. "I was so worried, but Zayed kept saying that you would be all right."

"He did not do anything untoward?" Sydney asked.

Lucy turned serious eyes on her. "He's a good man, Sydney. But, you know I fretted about you being alone with that man, the Pirate." She shivered. "He frightens me. You are safe, aren't you?" Lucy stared into Sydney's eyes as if she could detect any injuries.

Sydney laughed as she endured her friend's examination. Lucy could detect if someone were lying or suffering in some way. "Yes, I'm fine. But are you unharmed? I was worried for you, as well."

Lucy nodded. "Al Jabbar followed us the whole way. Zayed and I were far ahead, but we could see his fire at night across the desert. Are you sure you need him? He gives me a bad feeling. I don't like him."

With a sympathetic hand on Lucy's arm, Sydney said, "Yes. I'm sorry you don't like him, Lucy, but I do need him."

Lucy gave a tight-lipped nod, then glanced around. "Is there anything to eat here? I'm famished."

Sydney smiled, looped her arm through Lucy's. "I'm sure we can find something for you."

The two village women welcomed Lucy into their home with smiles and made sure she was comfortable on several cushions before they served her the traditional *tagine,* a stew made from meat and vegetables, then cooked over the fire for hours in a dish with a cone-shaped cover. After Lucy scraped her bowl clean, the two women retired to a corner to allow Sydney and Lucy time to chat.

Lucy sighed in contentment. "That was delicious. It tasted like my first decent meal in years."

Sydney chuckled. "It's only been about a week since we left the Tuareg camp. I am so glad to see you safe," she said again for the third or fourth time. "Are you sure you're all right?"

Lucy's head bobbed, and she waved away Sydney's concern. "Yes, yes, I'm fine. Zayed was a perfect gentleman." Then her voice dropped to a whisper. "I looked into Zayed's soul. He is an honorable man, Sydney." She giggled. "He always called me 'madam,' as if I were some snooty, old matron. He even showed me some of the exotic spices he uses when he cooks. And he saved me from a huge scorpion."

She grabbed Sydney's hand and her eyes behind the spectacles grew large. "It crawled right toward me. I was so frightened, I ran out into the desert screaming. But Zayed stabbed it through with his dagger." She bowed her head and twined her fingers together. "I'm such a ninny. I don't know why you ever brought me along."

"Oh, Lucy," Sydney said and wrapped her arm around her friend's shoulders. "I brought you because you are my friend, and I think you are very brave." She had convinced Lucy to accompany her because her friend had nowhere else to go.

Leaning close, Lucy whispered, "How was your journey with the Pirate? I saw he has uncovered his face. He looks quite ferocious." She shivered and her gaze swept over Sydney. "Are you sure you're unharmed?"

"You know I am. He was a perfect gentleman," Sydney said a bit too quickly. She didn't think he looked ferocious at all, but rather a bit haunted. And the handsomest man she had ever seen.

Her friend's brow creased in disbelief. "A gentleman? You called him a rogue and insufferable."

Sydney huffed a little laugh. "Well, he is insufferable. But I am here in one piece, sitting before you. He never bothered me. He even bound my ankle when I twisted it."

"You showed him your ankle?" Lucy gasped, horrified.

"Well, I couldn't do it myself. It was quite painful." She was not about to tell her friend of the bargain she made in exchange for allowing him that one little liberty. Nor was she going to tell her about that kiss, frightening and delicious, that he stole at the end of his nightmare. And the fact that he had a marvelous singing voice. Lucy might discover that for herself. But she did need to confess one thing. "He knows I'm a witch," she whispered.

Lucy's eyes widened and her hand flew to her mouth, but before she could comment, a knock came at the door. The younger woman of the house rose to answer it, then turned to Sydney and beckoned her forward. The Pirate stood in the opening.

He nodded a greeting. "We will be leaving here an hour after moonrise."

"But Mrs. Foster needs to rest," she declared.

"She can rest now, until we leave." His tone said he would allow no argument.

Sydney argued anyway. "You can't make us leave. I hired you. So, we will leave when I am ready."

A muscle twitched in his jaw. "Miss Whelton, you hired me to help you find the man with the silly crystal dagger. I intend to do that. I also intend to stay alive, and to keep you alive as well. You have the choice of leaving with me, or staying here and finding your way by yourself, in which case my services end here."

Her chin rose defiantly. "I see no threat to us in this village. I believe you are being overly cautious and overbearing."

His eyes snapped to slits. "You see no threat because you are not looking. The threat is close." His jaw clenched again, and he snapped out, "One hour after moonrise. Be ready." He spun on his heel and strode away.

"What threat, Mr. Pirate?" she called.

"Al Jabbar," he flung over his shoulder, and disappeared into the dark.

"Well!" Sydney wanted to stomp her foot at the man's rudeness and domineering attitude. She would have gone after him to argue again, but she could feel three sets of eyes on her. She would not cause a scene for the women who lived in the house, and she did not want to upset Lucy. But inside she seethed. The Pirate was spiriting her away again from the protection for which she had hired Al Jabbar. But she could do nothing. If she wanted to find the man with the Crystal Dagger, she knew she must rely on the impossible Pirate who set her teeth on edge and made her stomach flip-flop with his kiss.

"Sydney?" Lucy inquired from where she sat.

Resigned, she turned to her friend. "You should get some rest," she said. "We'll be setting out again in a few hours."

As they settled together on a pallet, Lucy whispered, "What did Mr. Pirate do when he learned that you are…special?"

77

"Nothing. It was of no consequence," Sydney whispered back and wished she had never mentioned it. Now Lucy would worry. "Go to sleep. You need to rest."

She soon heard Lucy's even breathing as she slept, but Sydney lay wide awake. What would the Pirate do with the knowledge that she was a witch? Now that he knew, would he abandon her in the mountains as he said? He had seen to her safety so far, but that was before he had learned her secret. Apprehension slid down her spine. She must be even more vigilant. As sleep overcame her, she wondered how she ever could have decided the Pirate was perfect for the job.

Chapter 7

They traveled endless days in the mountains. Sydney hated the mountains. At first, the slopes rolled benignly up and down. Low vegetation gave the impression of cushioning the hard ground. Then, the gentle slopes turned rocky and steep, and bare patches appeared where nothing grew. She had the sensation that at any time she might fly off into the air. Sometimes they came upon a plateau where the ground was flat, and the mountains rose around them. Lulled into a sense of trekking across level ground, Sydney breathed easier. She told no one about her fear of heights. Not even Lucy knew, for Sydney was much too embarrassed.

Before they left the village, they had exchanged their camels for mules, sure-footed animals that seemed comfortable with the height and rough terrain. Occasionally, they came across a Berber village hugging a windswept slope. The houses, like in the village where they had stopped before, were made of the same type of mud bricks, but rather than the tan of the lower slopes, these matched the red-or-ange soil of the higher altitudes.

They stopped at a few villages for the night or to replenish their supplies, but they made their own camp on the outskirts so they didn't impose on the villagers. Some of the settlements were sur-rounded by terraces of flourishing gardens of vegetables or grains. Others appeared dusty and barren, as if the people barely had enough to survive. Everyone greeted them warmly, but they looked curiously at the two Englishwomen accompanied only by two men of the desert.

Most of the time, they traipsed up and up, sometimes dipping down between slopes only to climb higher farther on. They had left the foothills behind several days ago, and now trekked through mountainous peaks that were rounded by the elements over many eons. The trail they followed was rough and rocky, switching back on itself as it skirted a deep valley. It hugged the steep slope, where a glance to one side showed a head-spinning drop into a tangle of brush that hid rough sand and rocks. In several stretches, the path balanced precariously on the spine of the mountain with a perilous drop-off on either side. A wrong step and one of them could plunge to a horrible death.

Only an occasional tree poked up from the low brush, which was dense and a dull gray green. This was not the lush green of the English countryside, nor the arid sand of the desert spotted with ground-hugging plants thirsty for water. This area was peppered with tough shrubs used to the harsh, mountain climate. In between the bushes were stretches of rock, knife-edged and forbidding. Sydney felt as if danger threatened from everything around her. She might become irrevocably tangled in the bushes, or sliced to shreds by the rocks, or fall off the edge and get dashed to pieces.

She stoically covered her terror by keeping her eyes on the path in front of her and pretending everything was fine. When they stopped for the night to huddle around a fire under an overhanging rock or on a flatter stretch of ground, she chatted with Lucy as if nothing was amiss. But when the time came for sleep, Sydney curled into the tightest ball she could, afraid that she would somehow roll off into thin air. In the morning when she awoke, her stiff fingers clutched the blanket around her, and she carefully checked to be sure she was not near the edge. After seeing the surrounding thicket and the tip of the cliff too far away to grab her and fling her off, she took a breath and gingerly climbed to her feet. Then she pasted a smile on her face as if nothing were wrong as they set out for another day.

They traveled in a line, the Pirate in front, then Sydney, Lucy, and Zayed in the rear. Sydney was impressed at how well Lucy handled her mule, for her friend's first experience with riding any animal had been on this journey. Sydney's mule was not as docile as the others. The Pirate had offered to switch animals with her, but despite her surprise at the man's generous suggestion, her pride made her decline.

On this day, they were leading their mules, for the trail was barely wide enough to accommodate the animals with their packs. On one side was the mountain sloping up and away far above them. On the other was a sheer cliff that dropped off sharply. Occasionally, as they walked the narrow ledge, rocks and dirt became dislodged and scattered down the rugged edge into the ravine far below. Sydney dared not look. The height made her dizzy.

The trail curved sharply around a huge boulder that jutted out from the side of the mountain. She watched the Pirate navigate the treacherous track and disappear from view, his mule following tamely behind. From where she stood, the path looked as if it disappeared into thin air, as if the Pirate had simply vanished. Logically, she knew that was merely an illusion, that he was perfectly safe on the other side of the rock. But for some reason, she couldn't send that message to her body. She began to shake, and she halted, frozen to the spot. Nothing usually unsettled her. She had traveled all the way from England with only Lucy as her companion. She had obtained cabins on ships, procured guides for various legs of the journey, and had found the man called the Pirate. She had bargained and bartered with some of the most disreputable-looking characters she'd ever met. But being in the mountains unnerved her, and the sight of the empty space beyond the boulder glued her feet to the ground.

Lucy called to her from behind. "Sydney, are you all right?"

Sydney forced an answer. "Yes." The single word emerged on a thin breath and sounded more like a squeak.

She had to move. The others couldn't discover her terror. Besides, remaining in this spot was not an option. She was on a quest to find the man with the Crystal Dagger, and he obviously was not hanging from the side of a mountain for her to pluck off. But her fear made her want to sink to the ground and clutch at the earth.

She stepped forward, one foot, then the other. As she edged around the boulder, she expected her mule to follow. Instead, it balked, pulling back on the lead. She lost her footing and slipped on the shale. Her equilibrium fled. She couldn't focus. The trail beneath her feet seemed to undulate, and the edge of the cliff seemed to disappear. All she could see was empty space. She had nothing to grab onto. Her arms wind-milled, and she jerked the mule's lead. It brayed as its back hoof slid on the edge. She was going to plummet through the air to shatter on the earth far below. She was going to die.

A hand grabbed her wrist from beyond the boulder. It swung her around the huge stone and plastered her against a wall of rock and dirt. She pressed her back into the mountain as she tried to get as far away from the edge as possible. The tips of her fingers clawed for something to grip, dislodging pebbles that bounced and trickled over the edge. Her lungs felt frozen. Heat, then cold spilled through her. She didn't want to die.

As she fought her panic, one part of her brain registered that the Pirate yanked on her mule's lead and pulled it back from toppling into the valley. At the same time, his hip pushed her against the rock face, his big body blocking her in, making her feel secure and grounded. After the mule landed on her side of the boulder, the Pirate barricaded her in with his arm. She grabbed it. The muscle beneath her fingers was as solid as the mountain at her back. His chest blocked the view of empty air.

She was safe.

Her mule was safe.

She found the courage to take a tiny breath.

She would not fall off the mountain.

With that realization, she became brave enough to glance around. Her mule complained loudly with fright and shook itself. The movement dislodged the small valise hanging from the saddle. It bounced once on the edge, and then fell into the void. She watched, appalled, as it hit an outcropping and broke open. The black robe with its purple embroidery escaped from its confines and unfolded like a huge bird taking flight. As it floated down, it burst into flames in a puff. An urgency, a strange compulsion enveloped her. She wanted to run, to chase down the Crystal Dagger and use it — violently, viciously. Her father's voice came to her as if on the wind. *Find it. Kill her.* Sydney sucked in a breath. Within seconds, the robe incinerated into nothing. Not even bits of ash remained in the air.

Sydney watched in stupefied silence. *How did that happen?* The compulsion drained away, leaving her confused and shaken.

The Pirate, riveted on the extraordinary event, stiffened. Slowly, he turned back to her.

"What was that?" he demanded in a low growl.

In shock, she blinked up at him. The man who made her feel so protected a moment before crowded her, overwhelmed her with his strength. His heat contrasted sharply with the chilly mountain at her back. Despite that warmth, she trembled. She couldn't breathe. From fear of falling to her death? Or the robe bursting into flame? Or the sound of her father's voice? Or the vexed question from the man before her? Or all of those?

Forcing in a breath, her wits began to unscramble. She couldn't tell him about the compulsion, nor her father's demand ringing in her ears. She had been sworn to secrecy. So, she was going to dissemble with every ounce of her being and pretend the incident with the robe never happened. Since she was as shocked and confused as he was, she had no answer to give him.

She blinked again. "My foot slipped. My mule balked. I nearly fell over the edge. Thank you for saving me."

His eyes narrowed. The corners of his mouth tightened. "What," he said very slowly, "happened to that robe?"

She innocently widened her eyes. "What robe?"

"The one that burst into flames and disappeared." He spoke as if to an imbecile.

"A robe burst into flames?" she squeaked. "Oh my! How awful! I didn't see that. Do you suppose Al Jabbar had something to do with it?" she said, cringing inwardly, because she lied and sounded like a simpleton.

"You are not featherbrained," he growled. "Do not lie to me."

Sydney swallowed. She had no idea why the robe had incinerated, but from the dangerous look in the Pirate's eyes, he would not believe that. If she lied again, would he push her over the edge of the cliff? He looked like he might. She didn't want to take that chance.

Quietly, she said, "It was my father's."

"Then you know what happened."

She shook her head and hoped a half-truth would satisfy him. "I—I don't. I brought it because it was his. It's the only thing I have to remember him." Appalled when her eyes filled with tears, she turned away.

He said nothing, then gently, he put his fingers against her jaw and turned her to face him. "Your father's," he mused. "He must have been a powerful wizard. Did he teach you to use your powers?"

The touch of his fingers distracted her, and she nearly blurted the truth about her father. At the last moment, she remembered her promise to tell no one about her father's secret. Her mother had reinforced that promise, instructing her that no one should know that she was a witch, and no one should know about her father's secret organization. Her mother had been the one to teach her about her special abilities, her mother who had brought her up with the manners of a lady despite owning a gaming hell. And her mother had taught her that men sometimes used gentle words and wooing to get what they wanted. The Pirate's tenderness was only a skillful way to get her to reveal information.

Guilelessly, she said, "He was my father, that's all."

A tiny line appeared between his brows. He didn't believe her. A pang of guilt at her dishonesty made her wish she could tell him the truth. She closed her eyes, shutting out the mistrust she saw in his golden gaze. The burden she carried was too heavy to carry alone. Tears of self-pity trickled from the corners of her eyes.

He muttered something in a foreign language. The pad of his thumb wiped away a tear.

Mesmerized by his tender touch, Sydney's eyes opened. She gazed up into those lion eyes, intense, burning. The need to keep her secrets floated away, dissipating into nothing. Her brain stopped functioning. He leaned in, those eyes coming closer. Her gaze landed on his mouth, sculpted perfection. Her lips parted as she drew a breath. Anticipation and heat shimmied through her. He was about to kiss her. Her eyes slipped closed again.

"You are blocking the path, Miss Whelton," he said, his words feathering against her cheek where his thumb had been. "The others are waiting."

Sydney's eyes snapped open, and her cheeks abruptly heated to a blaze. He indicated her mule standing docilely on their side of the boulder. A dimple teased his cheek. How could she have been so gullible?

"I'll move as soon as you stop looming over me," she snapped.

Amusement flared in his eyes. He straightened and fluidly stepped to the lead. "Looming?" he said. "I've never been accused of looming before." Laughter threaded through his words, barely loud enough for her to hear. Then he called to Zayed that the path was clear and began to lead his mule away.

Angry with herself, Sydney glared at the Pirate's mule in front of her and placed one foot solidly in front of the other as she followed him. How could she have been so silly to think he would kiss her? She must have looked ridiculous to him as she waited, compliant and eager for his kiss, like a naïve ninny. Besides, why ever would she want him to kiss her? Theirs was a business arrangement. He was the person she had hired to find the man with the Crystal Dagger, nothing more. His chest was broad and his shoulders wide, his golden eyes hypnotic, and his voice as smooth as honey, but that did not mean he should affect her. And just because her insides melted whenever he came close was no reason for her to entertain the notion that he would kiss her. *Why would I want him to kiss me?* she wondered. *He is insufferable. Arrogant. Smug.* The kiss they had shared after his nightmare was a mistake, one that she would never make again. He'd merely been caught in the dregs of his nightmare, and she had merely been trying to help him. Nothing more.

Now all she had to do was stop thinking about the feel of his lips every night before she fell asleep.

Raphael smiled to himself as he led his mule and watched for rock falls and treacherous drop-offs on the narrow path ahead. Behind him, Miss Whelton stomped along. Occasionally, she heaved an exasperated breath. Was she angry at him or herself? Whatever the reason, it made no difference. She was distracted enough that she paid no mind to the dizzying height. He didn't want her freezing in fear again.

He was surprised by her fright. She had obviously traveled far to find him, and no doubt encountered all sorts of challenges. Arriving whole and unharmed at his tent in the Tuareg village proved she was daring and dauntless. But not completely. She was afraid of heights.

His heart had stopped when he thought she might topple off the mountain and then it had erupted into a gallop as he grabbed her and the mule and hauled them to safety. When that robe had burst into flames and disappeared without a trace, he wanted to shake the answers out of her. His intention fled when tears had trickled down her cheeks.

A woman's tears were his weakness. He knew many women could turn them on and off at will, but something about her tears had punched his heart. They surprised him as much as her fear of heights. Since the moment she had walked into his tent, she had been determined and confident. Fearless. Self-assured. Exasperating. And he had learned she was kind. She had not hesitated to pick up the child who had fallen in the village. She had been concerned when he'd experienced the nightmare. And she had apologized after blasting him in the chest with her witchy power. When she started to cry, he wanted to soothe her, despite his discovery that she was a witch and despite watching that robe erupt into flames and vanish.

By the tears of Allah, he wanted to do more than soothe her.

He wanted to kiss her. More than kiss her.

He almost had. The near touch of her as he caged her against the wall had lured him in. The warmth of her. The possibility of her soft curves. Her scent, like lilies with a touch of spice, delicious. Those eyes, changeable and deep. And those lips, the bottom one pouty and full. Her body had loosened as he bent closer, prepared for his kiss. Expecting it. Wanting it.

Only at the last moment had he come to his senses, telling himself he was a fool, but regretting his decision at the same time. He would not kiss her. Again. The memory of that kiss when he was still partly in the thrall of the sorceress remained with him. It teased him nearly every night in his imagination.

Kissing her was dangerous. She was a witch. And he knew about witches. Sorceresses who could lure you with their wiles and then sink their claws into your chest. But she was hiding something else. Some knowledge about the robe that burst into flames, the same robe that had shown him a vision. A vision where he had seen a woman in terrible danger, a woman with eyes like his own.

He and Miss Whelton were connected.

With a deep breath, he gazed at the mountains and valleys. A long journey lay ahead, plenty of time to learn more about the woman who trailed behind him.

She tripped and regained her footing, muttering something under her breath, most likely a curse directed at him. He grinned. The farther they traveled, the more he enjoyed the adventure. With her. Discovering all of Miss Whelton's secrets along the way would be a pleasurable experience.

Chapter 8

Two days later, they made camp on a small plateau sheltered by an overhanging rock. Relief washed over Sydney when she realized they were finally heading out of the mountains. Steep drop-offs still kept her warily in the middle of the path, but the trails were wider, the slopes gentler, and the Pirate had allowed them to ride their mules instead of leading them.

They were rolled in blankets beneath a dark, cloudy sky. The black night was a vast void except for the embers of their dying fire. Sydney and Lucy lay close together on one side of the fire. The Pirate lay on the other. Zayed kept watch, perched on a rock somewhere above them.

Sydney remained awake for a long time, waiting until she was sure the man on the other side of the embers had fallen asleep. Then she poked her friend. "Lucy," she whispered. "Are you awake?"

Lucy groaned and rolled over.

Sydney shook her. "Lucy."

Lucy flopped back over to face her. "What?" she mumbled.

"Sh." Sydney took a peek at the sleeping mound of man on the other side of the fire. He hadn't moved. She turned back to her friend, who appeared to have drifted off to sleep again. "Lucy." She shook her again.

A sliver of light reflected in Lucy's eyes as she barely opened them. "You had better have a good reason for waking me," she grumbled.

Sydney clapped her hand over her friend's mouth. "Sh. Quiet. Please. I don't want him to hear." She motioned to the Pirate who seemed to be tightly wound in the arms of Morpheus.

Lucy's eyes were wide open now. "What's wrong?" she demanded, whispering as well. "Did he do something untoward? Was he less than a gentleman?"

"He's the furthest thing from a gentleman," Sydney scoffed and scooted closer to her friend. "No, it's Al Jabbar. He's been following us. Have you seen him?"

Lucy shook her head. "I thought we lost him after the village. I don't like him. He's not a nice man, Sydney. He frightens me."

Sydney scowled. "The one you should be frightened of is the Pirate. He kidnapped me and dragged me into the desert without you."

"Well, the Pirate is quite frightening, but Zayed said they took us to protect us from Al Jabbar," Lucy said.

Sydney tsked. "Yes, I know. The Pirate told me the same. Have you been able to see into him, sense his true nature?"

"No." Lucy's shoulders crept up around her ears. "He's too intimidating."

Sydney silently agreed with her, but she was not going to pursue any more thoughts about the man who slept on the other side of the embers. A man she almost kissed a couple of days ago. Instead, she said, "I'm going to try to contact Al Jabbar."

Lucy sucked in a breath. "Why? You know Mr. Pirate doesn't like him."

Sydney had a feeling that the Pirate's feelings about Al Jabbar were much stronger than dislike, but she had to discount that. "I need Al Jabbar to help me kill Nulkana."

"But I thought the man with the Crystal Dagger could do that," Lucy said.

"Yes, he can, but I need Al Jabbar, too." Sydney wasn't going to explain that her father had stressed that she needed a member of the Legion of Baal to help her slay the sorceress.

Lucy was silent for a moment, then asked, "How are you going to contact him?"

"I don't know yet." She had an idea, but she wasn't going to tell her friend until she knew it would work.

"Are you sure? You're taking a terrible risk. What if the Pirate catches you?"

"What if he does?" Sydney challenged. "What can he do?"

"He could — he could — " Lucy halted, her whisper trembling.

"Lucy," Sydney soothed. "I'll protect you."

"But I'm worried about you." Concern created a line between Lucy's brows.

"Remember what I can do," Sydney soothed. "Everything will work out. You'll see." *I hope,* she added silently.

Lucy clutched at Sydney's hand. "You're so brave. I'm glad you're my friend."

Sydney squeezed back. "Me, too. Now go back to sleep."

Lucy snuggled into her blanket but kept hold of Sydney's hand as she returned to her slumber. Sydney stared up at the stars. If she were going to contact Al Jabbar and let him know she wanted his help, she must do it across a distance. She had caught a glimpse of him with his men, tiny figures moving in a line, as they descended into a valley, then they had disappeared behind the hills that separated them. At least, she thought it was Al Jabbar. It had to be Al Jabbar. Who else could it be? She was convinced it had to be him.

She could only send a message when both she and Al Jabbar were within sight of each other. But even then, she couldn't be sure he would see it. Besides that, she had to make sure the Pirate didn't catch her.

She had hired the Pirate to help her find the man with the Crystal Dagger, but she had not anticipated that he would kidnap her and not allow her to have Al Jabbar as her bodyguard. The Pirate was being absurdly overbearing in that matter. He was insufferable, as she had first thought. She never should have hired him. Despite the fact that he had saved her from falling to her death. Despite the fact that her knees felt like aspic whenever he came close. Despite the fact that those lion eyes made her feel warm all over. That was being silly. That was only because he was exotic, with his lion eyes. That he was big and moved like a cat. That he was dangerous. Much too dangerous. To her person and her mind. To her senses. Especially her senses. He smelled too good when he was near. Like sandalwood and sun-warmed skin.

She wanted him to touch her, to kiss her again, but she couldn't allow that. The strange feelings she had when he was near her were merely the result of being too long in the desert with him. Her journey became longer and more arduous with each passing day, and she wanted to get back to England to regain her equilibrium. But first, she had to find the man with the Crystal Dagger. And she needed to contact Al Jabbar, because without him, a member of the Legion of Baal, Nulkana couldn't be killed. Not even the Pirate would be able to help her. And maybe, with Al Jabbar nearby, the Pirate would be too busy to tease her with his tantalizing dimple and those almost-kisses, and then she could banish unsettling thoughts about him. She hoped.

A few days later when they stopped to rest, Sydney and Lucy hid behind a group of boulders. On the other side of the rocks, the Pirate and Zayed were sitting close to a small fire and heating water for tea. She and Lucy had excused themselves to take care of their needs. But Sydney actually intended to contact Al Jabbar.

In front of her, a valley stretched from left to right. She didn't mind standing at the plateau's edge, for the ground sloped away gently to the bottom where a swath of green palm trees marked where a river flowed. On the other side, the land rose into hills and crags and then became the mountains they had crossed. Somewhere in those mountains was Al Jabbar.

She had seen him and his men again, tiny human specks, far, far away. Her only problem was how to contact him, to let him know where she was so they could meet again to plan Nulkana's demise. After giving the problem a great deal of thought, she realized that shiny objects reflected light. If she could catch the sun's rays in the right direction, she could signal him so he would know where she was. She had first tried Lucy's spectacles, but they were too small. Then she remembered she had a miniature portrait of her father in a gold case. It was about the size of half her palm. The outside of the case was engraved in an intricate pattern, but the inside of the cover was polished gold, which would be perfect for reflecting the sun.

She was absorbed in tilting the case the right way to catch the sun's rays when Lucy quickly stepped away. A hand reached around

Sydney from behind and snatched the case from her grasp. Startled, she spun to the culprit with a squeak of outrage.

"What are you doing?" the Pirate demanded through clenched teeth.

"Give that back!" She grabbed for the portrait.

He pulled it out of her reach. "No."

"How dare you!" She lunged for the case.

The Pirate held the portrait above his head, far beyond the tips of her fingers. His eyes turned hard as gold. "Do you have any idea what you are doing?"

"I know perfectly well what I'm doing." She made another grab for the case, which brought her up against his body, as unyielding as the boulders beside her. "I am trying to contact Al Jabbar." Jumping, she attempted to snag the case from his hand, still far above her head. And that brought her up against his chest again. Definitely the wrong thing to do.

"You will not contact Al Jabbar," he stated, anger riding beneath his flat tone.

"I will." Retreating a step, she gave up trying to retrieve the little case and planted her hands on her hips. "I hired him because...." Should she reveal why she really needed him, to help kill Nulkana? That he was a member of the Legion of Baal? No, she had promised her father to keep his secret. She decided she should give the Pirate a half-truth and perhaps that would convince him to return her portrait case. "I need him after we find the man with the Crystal Dagger. For protection."

"From what?" he snapped.

Frustrated beyond belief, she blurted, "From you. And, it turns out, with very good reason. You kidnap me and drag me into the desert with no thought of telling me where we're going. We are heading in the exact opposite direction from where I told you the man we seek could be found. For all I know, you may decide not to honor our agreement and murder us both."

His eyes narrowed. "Right now, that is a very attractive suggestion."

Lucy stepped forward, her fists raised as if she were entering a boxing ring. "You'll not harm my friend."

The Pirate glowered at her a moment, then sighed. "Don't worry, I won't throw her off the mountain. At least not at this moment."

Afraid that her friend might provoke him to violence, Sydney tried to calm her. "Lucy, don't fret. I'll be fine. Why don't you go have a nice glass of tea with Zayed?"

Lucy's mouth flattened, and she glanced from Sydney to the Pirate and back again. She stepped very close to him and shook her fist in his face. "If you hurt her, I'll hurt you back, Mr. Pirate."

He nodded solemnly. "I understand, Mrs. Foster. I promise not to lay a finger on her."

Lucy dropped her fist and huffed. "Well." She huffed again. "Well. A promise is a promise." She took two steps back. "I believe I will go have that tea now."

Sydney watched her friend scuttle beyond the boulders, then she turned back to the Pirate and held out her hand. "I'll have my portrait case now."

He held it clenched in his fist. "No, you won't. I'll keep this."

She sucked in an insulted breath. "You can't! That's my property!"

"I can and I will." He took an intimidating step forward. "You will not contact Al Jabbar while you are with me."

"You can't order me around," she said, pretending defiance while her knees shook, but she stood her ground. "I can contact whomever I wish. I paid him a very good price for his protection."

The Pirate barked a laugh. "His protection?" He stepped even closer, and his face darkened. "Weren't you paying attention when I told you what sort of villain he is?"

Sydney refused to yield, even though only inches separated them. She ignored the galloping rhythm of her heart and the flutter in her belly. "I found him to be the perfect gentleman. Perhaps your opinion of him is clouded by the disagreement between you."

"Disagreement?" His word sputtered into incredulity. He stared down at her and a muscle jumped beneath the scruff on his jaw. After several deep breaths, he said, "What is between us, Miss Whelton, is more than a *disagreement*. He is a thief and a murderer."

Sydney blinked. Obviously, he knew more about Al Jabbar than she did. The Pirate had warned her about the man before and had told her that Al Jabbar had given him the scar, but he had not told her how. It could have happened as the result of an accident. She rather doubted it, but that was beside the point. He would not win this argument.

Defiantly, she tipped up her chin. "I have heard the same about you, Mr. Pirate."

A corner of his mouth deepened. "Have you? Then you should be concerned about your safety. Especially after I saved you from falling off the mountain." His tone was rich with irony.

She ignored his surliness and blew out a breath, stymied, because obviously, if he were a murderer, he would not have saved her. "Well. Thank you for that. Again." And then she saw how she might win this argument. "But that only proves that one can't believe everything one hears, can one? Al Jabbar might not be as bad as you think he is." She held out her hand. "I would like my portrait case back, please, so I may contact him."

He held it out as if he would return it, then wrapped his fingers around the case tighter than before. "No."

"No? Why, that's stealing!" She nearly stomped her foot in frustration.

"You may have it back after we have found this man with the ridiculous dagger made of crystal," he said calmly.

Sydney's temper rose. "Perhaps I don't want you to help me find him any longer. Perhaps I will find him on my own."

He shrugged. "If that's what you would like."

His nonchalance at her veiled threat of canceling their agreement made her teeth clench. The man was infuriating. Insufferable. Why had she ever hired him in the first place?

"Yes," she snapped. "That is exactly what I would like." She held out her hand again. "I would also like my portrait case back."

"No, I don't think so." He pushed it into the folds of his kaftan. When his hand reappeared, it was empty. "I believe I'll keep it as a reminder not to agree to search for lost souls."

Sydney's eyes narrowed. "Then you are a thief."

He raised an unconcerned brow. "Your opinion, Miss Whelton. I prefer to think of it as a gift for my trouble."

Her mouth dropped open. Then she snapped it shut. "I will find some other way to contact Al Jabbar."

He shook his head. "Not while you're with me."

Sydney's temper flared beyond all rational thought. "Then Mrs. Foster and I will find our own way." She raised her chin in challenge.

He shrugged again. "Suit yourself."

"I will." She jerked a nod.

"Good," he snapped.

"Good," she snapped back.

She glared at him for two heartbeats.

He glared back.

With a groan of frustration, she spun on her heel and stomped around the boulder. "Lucy," she called. "Gather your things. We're leaving."

Lucy looked up from her tea in shock. "Leaving? But I haven't finished my tea."

Sydney stalked to her mule. "Please, Lucy. I'll make you some tea when we stop again."

Lucy scrambled to her feet and hurried to Sydney's side. "Why are we leaving?" she asked in an undertone. "Zayed said nothing about continuing yet."

"That's because he and Mr. Pirate aren't leaving with us." Sydney checked that everything was tied securely to her mule.

"But...But...How will we find our way?" Lucy's voice teetered on the edge of panic.

Sydney faced her. "Lucy, we're not traveling with that man any longer. I'll find someone who is more agreeable and polite who will help us."

Lucy glanced around as if looking for that someone. "But there's no one else."

Placing a comforting hand on her friend's arm, Sydney said, "Trust me. Please?"

Still looking uncertain, Lucy nodded. "All right. If you say so." She untied the lead of her mule.

Sydney shot a glance back at their small camp. Zayed still sat and drank his tea. The Pirate stood near the boulder and watched them with narrowed eyes and crossed arms. She could feel that gaze like a sharp weight. Telling herself she was doing the right thing, she smiled at Lucy and led her mule onto the path. How hard could it be to find their way out of the mountains and hire someone else to help them find the man with the Crystal Dagger? Besides, Al Jabbar was not that far behind them. He could help. He couldn't be as threatening as the Pirate said he was. He had been perfectly polite when she had hired him. He was a member of the Legion of Baal, and one of her father's associates. Surely, she could count on him. She hoped.

Putting all doubts out of her mind, she raised her chin, made sure that Lucy was following, and strode down the path.

Raphael ground his teeth and watched her go. Foolish woman. Her head was high and her back was ramrod straight. Her anger was evident. She was infuriating. Stubborn. Headstrong. Unruly. She made his blood seethe. He wanted to shake some sense into her.

He wanted to tangle his fingers in that fire-touched hair and kiss her senseless.

He must have desert madness.

She'd hired him to find that damned man with the dagger. Their relationship was purely business. Nothing more. He told himself he didn't care what she did. She had paid him half of the exorbitant amount he had requested. Their deal was done.

So why did he have this hollow ache in his chest?

"Your agreement with the woman is at an end," Zayed said from where he still sat drinking his tea.

His question draped in a statement dragged Raphael's attention from the woman who bravely, foolishly, unreasonably led her friend down the mountain. "It appears so," he said, forcing his voice to mildness, and plunked down across the fire from his friend.

Zayed handed him a glass of tea. "She wished to continue her agreement with Al Jabbar."

"Yes." Raphael took a sip of tea so he would stop grinding his teeth. "She was trying to signal him."

"A resourceful woman." Zayed stirred the fire with a nearby stick.

Raphael allowed his gaze to follow the trail to where he could see that wide-brimmed hat bobbing farther away. "Yes."

Zayed focused on the fire. "You desire her."

He swung back to his friend. "No."

Zayed said nothing, but his silence was loaded with disbelief.

Raphael sighed. "Yes."

"She is not like the other women you have desired," Zayed said with a penetrating gaze.

Raphael turned to look down the trail again. The hat was slowly disappearing below the curve of the slope. "She is not."

"You also think she may have a clue to your origin." Zayed paused. "Another desire."

"More than a desire," Raphael said. "She—" He stopped, loathe to admit what he truly felt about her leaving. "I have a sense. Here." He placed his hand against his chest, then pulled the talisman from beneath his kaftan. "This warms sometimes when she is near." He would not tell Zayed about the tingles that erupted on his skin when he touched her as darkness. "Why would that happen unless she is a connection to what I am?"

Zayed leveled a look at him across the fire. "Perhaps a connection to the evil that made you what you are."

Had his friend deduced that the woman was a witch? Remorse twinged at him for not having confided in him sooner. Raphael's gaze slipped away. "I don't believe she is evil. She isn't like the other who torments me in my dreams."

Zayed said nothing for a moment. Raphael could feel his searching look.

"You have not told me all," his friend finally said.

Raphael pressed his lips together. He should have told Zayed when he first learned what Miss Whelton was. He owed it to his friend for protecting him all these years. Now, he had kept it too long. He wanted to keep it to himself longer, afraid of hurting his friend with his omission, and for some reason, wanting to keep that bit of information all to himself. But the time had passed when he could hold on to that secret. He hoped Zayed could forgive him.

Looking across the fire, he said, "She is a witch."

Zayed's eyes flashed wide, then his expression turned stony. "When did you discover this?" He held up his hand. "No, do not tell me. This is a secret you should not have kept from me. Have I not watched over you when you become like the night? Have I not kept you from madness when you have returned to yourself? Do you think so little of me that you keep this from me?"

Raphael's guilt tore through him. Zayed had done all that and more. Through all the years, he had been father, mother, and brother. "I am sorry, my friend."

Zayed's hand sliced through the air, cutting off anything else that Raphael might have said. "It is done. Now I know. It is good she is gone."

Raphael nodded, but he did not agree with his friend. He looked down the trail again. All he could see was a sliver of the crown of that hat.

Zayed followed his gaze. "The women will meet with Al Jabbar. He will save them or murder them, as the whim takes him."

"Or they will meet a leopard, a viper, or a group of marauders," he said. The fate of the women worried him despite his anger.

Zayed turned back to the fire and thoughtfully took another sip of tea. "My tea is cold. We have rested long enough." He stood. "Only one trail leads down to the desert."

"So, the women will never be far from our sight," Raphael concluded. His dark thoughts lifted.

His friend sent him a calculating glance. "A curse or a blessing."

As Zayed kicked dirt and pebbles over the fire to kill it, Raphael wondered the same thing. Which would Miss Whelton be?

Chapter 9

Three nights later, Sydney stirred the millet porridge over their pitiful fire. She had tossed in the last of the pounded goat cheese to give the bland dish flavor, but so far, she hadn't been able to match Zayed's cooking. This was her turn to cook since Lucy had cooked the night before. Sydney tried her best, but the first night she had cooked, the results were barely edible. Lucy's attempts with the few ingredients they had were much better.

The fire hardly warmed their chilly fingers and toes, and she was regretting her impetuous declaration of independence from the Pirate. She hadn't tried magic yet, but she was leaving that for the very last resort. She never forgot her mother's warning about using it too often. It could reveal her to a dangerous and evil element. She didn't want to find out what that element was.

Had her mother done a kind of magic that drew evil to her? Had something evil caused the strange disease that killed her? The question nagged at Sydney. The magical energy she shot at the Pirate had been a mistake, pure reflex after being startled. She hoped nothing evil had sensed it.

Lucy huddled next to their small fire and looked miserable and frightened, even though she tried to hide it. Sydney sympathized, for she felt a bit miserable and frightened herself. They had navigated safely down the trail so far, but it had been quite visible. What if she couldn't find the trail and they became lost? What if they ran out of food or water? She didn't want to think about that. She would solve that problem when — and if — it happened. She stirred the millet again.

She should ask the Pirate for help, but her pride got in the way. She was still angry. He had stolen the portrait case. He'd most likely sell it once he reached a city. After all, he was a brigand. Why did she think he was honorable?

If she turned her head, she could see their fire a bit farther down the mountain. The two men had passed them earlier in the afternoon when she and Lucy had stopped to rest. During the last few days, they had passed each other several times, sometimes with the men going by as she and Lucy rested, sometimes the other way around. Each time, she had pointedly ignored them in this strange game of tag. The Pirate and Zayed were never out of sight, at least not for long, and she could sense the Pirate's eyes on her. That annoyed her. She had terminated their agreement. He was no longer obligated to help her find the man with the Crystal Dagger, so he could hurry away to his next nefarious task. But he didn't. In fact, sometimes when they passed, he would send her a look that both set her teeth on edge and made her skin tingle. And that made her even more annoyed. Sometimes, she even heard his voice in her head.

You need more kindling to start your fire, Miss Whelton.

Conserve your water, Miss Whelton.

We killed a nice, fat rabbit, Miss Whelton. We'll be glad to share if you are hungry.

She ignored that voice. Or tried to. But it was his voice, sometimes rough-edged, sometimes smooth as black velvet that invaded her mind. She'd heard his words in her head when she had been in his tent in the Tuareg village. At that time, she thought she had imagined the deep, fluid voice inside her brain. Now she knew she hadn't. That ability intrigued her. But now his suggestions, made in the most reasonable tone, infuriated her. She was perfectly aware of the need for more kindling on her fire, or the need to conserve their water. And she wouldn't take his offer of rabbit meat even if she were starving. Although the idea of feasting on a succulent rabbit made her mouth water and stomach rumble embarrassingly. But she did feel guilty for depriving Lucy of that rabbit.

Yet secretly, deep in a part of herself that she did not want to acknowledge, she felt his presence reassuring. She would bite her tongue off before she asked him for help, but the mountains were lonely, and having him in sight made her less apprehensive.

She checked the millet. It was almost ready.

"Sydney?" Lucy said, her tone apprehensive. "You know I think that you are very brave and wise—"

Sydney interrupted with a shake of her head. "I'm not very wise at all."

"Yes, you are." Her friend gave a decisive nod.

Sydney's lips twisted wryly. "Look at where we are, Lucy." She indicated the empty expanse of mountains, hills and brush that surrounded them. "And we're on our own."

"Well, that's what I wanted to talk to you about." Lucy shifted closer. "Do you think...I mean to say...Perhaps we were a bit hasty in parting from the Pirate?"

Sydney's insides twisted in guilt again at her friend's question. Perhaps she had been a bit hasty in severing their agreement. After all, up until then, they had always had a guide to show them the way, to light their fires and protect them from wild animals or marauding tribes, even though they had met neither.

Her shoulders slumped. "I'm so sorry, Lucy," she said. "I never should have dragged you away. It was wrong of me." Her gaze met Lucy's. "But the Pirate forbade me to contact Al Jabbar, and when he took away my gold box with my father's picture—I snapped. I was so angry. I need Al Jabbar to help me kill Nulkana. Besides, the Pirate was leading us in the exact opposite direction we need to go."

Lucy blinked at her from behind her spectacles. "That is true," she said slowly. "But the Pirate did save you from a terrible fall. Maybe he has his reasons for taking this path."

She had to agree with her friend and cast a surreptitious glance at the two men sitting complacently around their blazing fire a bit farther down the mountain. For some reason, their easy attitude made her temper flare.

"He saved me because if I had fallen, the supplies on my mule would have been lost, not to mention the rest of the fee I owed him. I doubt his motive had anything to do with honor or concern for my welfare." She tried very hard to shut out the memory of his large body blocking her in and protecting her. And she certainly was not going to think about that almost-kiss.

A line of doubt creased Lucy's brow. "Well, perhaps you are right."

"Of course, I am." She used the declaration to convince herself as well as Lucy and removed the pot of millet from the fire to end the discussion. "Dinner is served, Mrs. Foster," she said, mimicking the tone of a very proper butler.

Lucy giggled. "Oh, Sydney, you are so droll."

Relieved her friend had dropped the subject of reconnecting with the Pirate, Sydney grinned and dished out their meager meal. She would not think about the dangers and disasters that might lie ahead. She would not think about confronting the evil Nulkana if she could not contact Al Jabbar.

And she certainly would not think about the man with the eyes of gold who lounged at his fire farther down the mountain. No, she definitely would not think of him.

With determination, ignoring the faint aroma of roasting rabbit that wafted up the hill, she plunged a spoon into her bowl of millet.

Raphael lounged back on one elbow beside the fire. He was alone, for Zayed had gone off to meditate on the stars. He held the portrait case he had taken from Miss Whelton and absently rubbed his thumb across the engraved surface. If he looked up across the top of the flames in front of him, he could see the small fire the women had lit farther up the slope. Mrs. Foster appeared to have retired, for he could see her form stretched out on the ground, but Miss Whelton's dark silhouette remained sitting upright. She was obviously awake. Occasionally, the flames lit her face, teasing him with a peek at her mouth and chin, or her cheek and one shadowed eye. He found himself wanting to follow that touch of light with a brush of his thumb across her lips or a trail of his fingers down her cheek. Dragging his thoughts away from that dangerous territory, he focused instead on their situation. The women seemed to be doing all right on their own. Miss Whelton appeared to be a resourceful woman.

He glanced down at the case in his hand. His conscience pricked him for taking away the portrait of her father. It must mean a great deal to her if she carried it on this very long journey. Perhaps he would return it before they finally parted.

He flicked it open and turned it toward the light of the fire. The man in the portrait was middle-aged with regular features. Ordinary, not a bad-looking man. He was elegantly dressed in coat, waistcoat, and shirt tied off with an elaborate neckcloth. Raphael could see a family resemblance to Miss Whelton around the mouth and shape of the chin. But where Miss Whelton's eyes were warm and expressive, the man's eyes were hard and cold. Raphael could not understand how that could come across in a miniature portrait. A chill chased through him. He glanced around, thinking the wind had changed and heralded a storm. But the air was still. The night animals rustled in the underbrush. Nothing disturbed them. He shrugged off the sensation.

Turning the case over, he held it closer to the fire to see if any inscription was engraved on the back. A strange series of lines was barely visible. A design of some sort, but he couldn't figure out what it was. He ran his thumb over the design, and it seemed to warm beneath his touch. A faint glow appeared along the lines. Frowning, he examined it closer. The glow disappeared. A reflection from the fire? Or his imagination?

Had Miss Whelton somehow magicked it? He sent a piercing glare to her slender form huddled beside her own fire. If the portrait case contained a special spell, then of course she wanted it back, not only because it contained a likeness of her father.

He did not feel quite so guilty now about snatching the case away. In fact, his chagrin disappeared. What took its place was a need to discover exactly what the design on the back was and what it meant. What was the purpose of the case and what spell had Miss Whelton placed on it?

He closed his fingers around it and glanced once more up the hill. She was too wily to reveal its secret if he asked. Somehow, he would learn the truth about the portrait and the secret of its case. He would keep the women in his sight, even if it meant he would have to dog Miss Whelton's every step. Getting the truth from her could prove a very intriguing, delightful task.

With a sly tip of his lips, he slid the case back into his pocket and settled down to wait for Zayed's return.

Chapter 10

When they finally reached the foothills, Sydney released a sigh of relief. She hadn't been aware that she'd actually been holding her breath until that moment. While the hills were not exactly flat, she didn't feel as though she might fly off into the air at any moment.

The last several days had been uneventful, and they had left the Pirate and Zayed behind. She wondered at that. Had the two men gone a different way? Had they turned back to the Tuareg camp where she had first found them? Or had something terrible happened to them? She tried not to think about the Pirate ravaged by a wild beast or falling to his death on jagged rocks. And she tried to ignore the fact that she missed his reassuring presence in front of her on the trail, or not so far behind her, when she could sometimes sense the tickle of his gaze as if it were something solid.

She had other things to think about, worrisome things, like how they were going to find their way through the desolate scrubland that stretched out before them. How she was going to find someone she could trust to guide them. How she was going to find the man with the Crystal Dagger and complete her task. Because the Pirate had taken them in the opposite direction from his location, if the information she'd been given were true.

She knew cities existed to the north near the coast. And she knew the sun rose in the east and set in the west, so she hoped if they traveled north, they would happen upon a town or village. But she wasn't sure how far away those were, and they were running out of food. The magnitude of what she had done in separating from the Pirate weighed heavily on her. This journey might kill her. That frightened her. But she felt even worse for dragging Lucy into this and possibly killing her, too. Every day, she struggled to tamp down her rising anxiety.

She had not caught a glimpse of Al Jabbar since the day she had tried to signal him. Part of the reason she had rashly severed her agreement with the Pirate was because she had thought Al Jabbar would help her. Now he appeared to have abandoned her. That infuriated her. He was supposed to be loyal to her father and the Legion of Baal. He was supposed to want to help her kill Nulkana. Now, he had disappeared. Besides that, she had paid him a large fee. But the fee was the least of her worries. She had seen Nulkana's magic in the battle at Stonehenge. The power of the sorceress frightened her. Without the assassin and Al Jabbar to help her, how could she accomplish what she had set out to do? She was truly on her own. She sighed. She couldn't dwell on that now. She had more pressing problems to solve. She had to get herself and Lucy to safety.

Lucy had become very quiet. Her friend's head was bowed, and she seemed to be a bit wobbly on her mule.

"Lucy? Lucy, are you all right?"

Lucy's head came up. Her eyes were distressed behind her spectacles, and her face was pale.

"I'm feeling unwell. Perhaps we could rest for a moment?"

Before Sydney had a chance to respond, Lucy toppled off her mule.

Panicking, Sydney slid from her mule and rushed to her friend's side.

"Lucy! Lucy!"

She patted her cheek to try to rouse her. But Lucy didn't awaken. Her skin was cold and clammy. Spotting Lucy's water bag hanging from the saddle, she grabbed it, noticing how much heavier it was than hers. She trickled water into Lucy's mouth. At first, the water merely ran down Lucy's cheek, but after a few tries, her friend finally swallowed some. Moments later, Lucy's eyes finally fluttered open. She blinked up at Sydney.

"Oh, dear," she said. "Did I faint?"

Sydney nodded. "How are you feeling?"

"Silly. For fainting and falling off my mule." She sat up and clutched her head. "Oh, oh, the world is spinning."

Sydney supported her and held out the water bag. "I think you need to drink more water."

Wrinkling her nose, Lucy shook her head. "I couldn't possibly. It tastes vile. Like hairy goat."

Sydney shook Lucy's nearly full water bag. "You haven't been drinking water at all, have you?"

Lucy glanced away, but Sydney caught the guilty look in her eye.

Patiently, Sydney said, "Lucy, dear, you have to drink more water or more mint tea."

Her guilt at involving her friend in her argument with the Pirate tore through her. Lucy was not an adventurous soul. She would have been quite content to remain in the kitchen of the gaming hell and create delicious meals and pastries. But when Sydney had closed the establishment, Lucy had come with her on this treacherous journey.

Sydney glanced around. They were in a *wadi*, a dry streambed that could suddenly flood during a very heavy rainstorm. Since this was not the rainy season, Sydney thought there was little chance of a flood. Low, scrubby bushes sprouted here and there, a sign that no rain had fallen in some time. She had felt relatively safe traveling the path the water had carved between the hills. The going was easier than traipsing up and down the slopes, and the *wadi* meandered in the direction she wished to travel. A large swath of shade darkened one side of the *wadi* where its bank rose up to block the sun.

"Lucy," she said, "do you think you can stand and walk to that shade?"

Lucy squinted in the general direction where Sydney indicated. "Yes, of course."

But when Lucy finally stood with Sydney's help, her knees gave out. Sydney caught her before she collapsed and propped her up. Concern for Lucy turned to panic. What if Lucy were seriously ill? They were far from any help. What would she do? Regret and guilt at leaving the Pirate's protection stabbed her. No, she couldn't think about that. Right now, she had to get Lucy into the shade.

With halting steps, they finally reached the bank of the *wadi*. Sydney eased her friend down, so she was leaning against the dirt slope. She handed Lucy the water bag with a strict direction to drink, but she was distracted by the mules' braying. When she turned around, she froze. The mules were gone, and in their place stood a large lion. Instead of chasing after the pack animals, the predator focused on her. Its bones poked beneath its skin and its mane was mangy and thin. As it slunk forward a step, saliva dripped from its mouth. It licked its chops. If she didn't do something, she and Lucy would be its next meal.

"Lucy," she said very quietly. "Don't move."

She heard Lucy emit a sound halfway between a whimper and a muffled scream. The lion's eyes reminded her of the Pirate, beautiful but deadly. She should never have separated from him.

The lion crouched, getting ready to pounce. She dared not move, not even to pull the little knife from her boot. She would have to use magic. The threat of an evil force finding her loomed large in the back of her mind, but she had to protect Lucy, which meant more at that moment than the possibility that evil might sense her.

The lion sprang forward.

She threw up her arm, preparing to hurl magic.

A spear pierced the animal's side.

It dropped to the ground, jerked once, then lay still.

She stared at the dead beast. Where had that spear come from?

"Sydney," Lucy said with a tremor in her voice. "There are men on that hill."

Glancing up, she saw them. Six men on camels. They must have been tracking the lion. The camels appeared scruffy, not well-groomed like the camels in the Tuareg camp. The men looked dangerous and threatening, each holding either a sword or a spear. Clenching her fist, she felt her magic, already gathered to defend from the lion. If she had to use it to save herself and Lucy, she would.

The camels plodded down the hill. As the men came closer, Sydney backed up to stand beside Lucy. The men might be willing to help them. Or they might be ruffians. Whatever they were, she would defend her friend.

The men stopped before them in a semi-circle, blocking them in against the sand bank, leaving her and Lucy no way of escape. Besides the weapons in the men's hands, knives and swords swung at their hips. Her knees were already shaking from the threat of the lion. Even though one of the men had killed the animal, she couldn't be sure if their next victim might be her or Lucy. Despite the trepidation that made her hands and knees quiver, she decided she would be polite and charming.

She took a deep breath and smiled. "Thank you for killing the lion. My friend isn't well, and the lion chased away our mules. Could you help us, please?"

The man in the center of the semi-circle grinned, exposing several gold teeth. He said something in his language, none of which Sydney could understand except the word "English." His friends laughed.

Sydney clenched her fist, preparing to throw her magic.

The men edged their camels closer, tightening the circle around them.

"Sydney." Lucy's tone held both warning and fear.

"Don't worry, Lucy," she said. "I'll take care of this." She took a small step closer to the men and tried to look very frightened and helpless. Not a difficult thing to do. "Please, can you help us?"

The camels moved nearer.

"We mean no harm," she said, holding out one hand, palm up, to show she wasn't holding a weapon. She kept her other fisted by her side.

The man in the middle said something else and nodded. He pointed at his friends, who grinned and chuckled. Sydney didn't like the sound of that laughter. Once again, they edged nearer, close enough that she could feel the camels' hot breath.

One of the men leaned down and flipped off her hat with his knife. The others chortled. A few made comments. Their eyes reflected their lewd intent. Terror shot through her. These men wouldn't help them. Without another thought, her arm snapped up and she let her magic fly. It hit one of the camels, which let out a bellow and ran off with its rider.

Anger twisted the leader's face, and he snarled some words. His men closed in around her, their camels bumping her. When she tried to avoid an animal on one side, she bumped into another. The men plucked at her, grabbing and tearing at her clothes. They pulled her one way, then another as they yelled and laughed. She spun and squirmed as she tried to avoid them, but she was surrounded.

Desperately, she shot magic at one, then another, but they had the advantage, riding high on their camels. And she was outnumbered.

She heard Lucy scream. Out of the corner of her eye, she saw one of the men ride past with Lucy in his grasp. No! She wouldn't let them take her friend.

Yanking out of the grasp of a ruffian who had grabbed her arm, she shot a stream of magic at the man riding away with Lucy. It hit him squarely in the back. He released Lucy, who tumbled to the ground, and he slumped sideways on his camel. But she had no time to rejoice that her friend was free. Two of the men, one on each side, grabbed her arms. They lifted her off the ground between them, dangling her like a rag doll. She wriggled and struggled, but they held fast. She thought her arms might pop out of their sockets.

Suddenly, one of the men holding her grunted, released her arm, and tumbled off his camel. A dagger stuck out of his back. The other man still held her, dragging her along. Pain ripped through her shoulder.

The second man reeled, and he slumped over his camel's neck. Another dagger had found its mark. His grip loosened. She landed with a jolt, sprawled on the dirt and stones. The wind whooshed out of her.

As she fought to draw air into her lungs, she saw two riders on mules approach. Two more bandits to fight off. She had no time to tend to scrapes or bruises. Scrambling to her feet, she blinked away her blurry vision. She fisted her hand and tried to find her magic. It barely sparked. The two men came closer.

The Pirate and Zayed.

She nearly wept with relief. But of course, she didn't. She was supposed to be strong. Self-sufficient. Determined. Not weak and weepy.

The Pirate halted before her and slid from his mule. Zayed turned to help Lucy. All the bandits had either fled or lay dead or wounded.

The Pirate stalked toward her and halted mere inches away. "Are you hurt?"

Sydney's throat closed up and she couldn't speak. She shook her head.

"Your animals ran away," he said.

She nodded.

He glanced beyond her. "They haven't gone far. I can see them down the *wadi*."

Sydney nodded again. She felt foolish for being mute. Swallowing several times against the lump in her throat, she was finally able to croak, "Thank you."

The corners of his eyes crinkled. "I couldn't let you get taken by outlaws," he said, his tone solemn. "After all, you still owe me the rest of my fee."

Sydney opened her mouth to say something, but she had no words. Her relief at his appearance overwhelmed her. The gleam in his eyes and his teasing helped to relieve her fear.

Feeling the sting of tears, she glanced away. She couldn't let him see her cry. She blinked them away, swallowed, and searched for something to say. "You followed us." That sounded accusatory, and she didn't mean it like that at all. But for some reason, her brain wasn't working the way it should.

The corner of his mouth hitched up. "There is only one way out of the mountains, Miss Whelton, and this *wadi* is the easiest route."

She nodded and glanced down, searching for the courage to say what was careening around the inside of her head. Her gaze landed on the scuffed toes of her boots. She should get them shined when she reached a city. But that was irrelevant and wasn't what she wanted to say at all.

After taking a breath, she said, "I am very grateful for your help." She took another breath. "Perhaps I was a bit hasty in separating from you."

She glanced up into his eyes and wished she hadn't. Those eyes drew her in until she felt she could lose herself in them. She wanted to cuddle against him. She wanted him to wrap her in his arms and hold her. But she couldn't allow that. She had to be strong. After all, she was safe now. And so was Lucy. No need to be weak and weepy.

"The desert and the mountains deceive with their beauty," he said. "You are not the first to yield to them." He cupped her cheek. "You are safe now." His thumb caught an errant tear.

Appalled that she'd been crying, she swiped at the tears, and his hand fell away. She missed the warmth of his touch. She wanted to revel in it, sink into it. For a moment or two. But she shoved that thought away and glanced around for Lucy. Her friend sat in the shade where she had been before the attack, and Zayed stood guard over her.

"I should go to Mrs. Foster," she said to distract herself and avoid any further touching from the Pirate.

Before he could disagree, she turned and walked to where Lucy sat huddled, shivering and crying softly. She had to walk away from the Pirate and his gentle touch. Away from her weakness.

As she sat beside Lucy and comforted her with an arm around her shoulders, she wondered how she was going to be able to endure the rest of the long journey with the Pirate.

Who had saved her twice.

Who teased and tantalized.

Who turned her world topsy-turvy.

Who made her so angry she wanted to pummel him.

Who made her want to kiss him.

Raphael set a rapid pace as they left the carnage behind. He felt extremely lucky that he and Zayed had happened upon the women's tracks. He hadn't exactly been following Miss Whelton and her companion, but only one path led through the mountains, so he couldn't help but have the women in his sights. But once they had left the foothills, he had lost them, which wasn't what he had told Miss Whelton because he hadn't wanted to frighten her any more than she already was. He had watched her try to hide her fear and had wanted to tell her to let the tears fall. She would feel better for it. But he hadn't. Instead, he had refrained from gathering her against his chest to comfort her. He ignored the need to reassure himself that she was safe and all in a piece. When he had lost sight of her, he had tried to tell himself that he didn't care, that Miss Whelton had severed their agreement and he had no responsibility to her. But a definite unease settled in his gut when he could no longer see them.

He had finally found their trail again when he and Zayed entered the *wadi*, and relief poured through him. As much as she annoyed him, he didn't want harm to come to her. If it did, it would haunt him. He had told Zayed they would follow her but keep out of sight. Although his friend shook his head in exasperation, he said nothing.

When Raphael saw the six sets of camel tracks in the sand, a warning niggled at the back of his brain. When he saw the men attacking the women, rage replaced his unease. These were renegades, marauders, outlaws, who preyed on any hapless traveler who wandered through the territory they controlled. The two women would have been dragged back to their camp and turned into slaves after they had been defiled in turn by each of the men. The thought made his stomach clench. He had to force himself not to race after the sons of scorpions who had escaped and cut them to pieces. He consoled himself with the fact that two of them lay dead where they had fallen and two others lay wounded, baking in the sun. He and Zayed had left them there, taken their camels and their water, and set off as soon as they could get the women back on their mules.

The two women rode behind him now. He wondered what they were thinking. They had been in a subdued mood ever since they set out a couple of hours ago. Mrs. Foster sniffled occasionally, then dissolved into tears. Miss Whelton murmured comforting words, but that was the only conversation between them.

After another hour had passed, he heard Miss Whelton's mule quicken its pace, and she appeared beside him. His curiosity at what she had to say curbed his desire to point out succinctly and in detail the idiotic naivete that made her think that two women traveling alone in the mountains and desert would be safe simply because she was a witch. He didn't look at her, but he could sense her unease. Good. She should squirm for being so stubborn and obstinate. And foolish.

She cleared her throat. "Mr. Pirate." She stopped, took a breath, then started again. "Mr. Pirate, I want to thank you again for your help."

He noticed she did not mention that he and Zayed had *rescued* them. He kept his gaze on the vista before him and his tone casual as he said, "You hired me to guide you, Miss Whelton. I was only fulfilling my obligation."

She cleared her throat again. "Yes, well." Her unease was palpable.

This time, he looked at her. Her wide-brimmed hat was bent and torn in several places. It ruined her image of the perfect lady. Dirt smudged her skirt, and a three-corner tear near her knee flapped open. Her vulnerability peeked out from beneath her cool exterior. But he would not soften, not yet. He was still seething at everything and everyone, despite not knowing why.

He quirked up an eyebrow. "Are you trying to thank me for *rescuing* you, Miss Whelton?"

Her eyes widened as if she had never had that idea at all. "Um, well, ah, yes. I believe I am."

"Hm." He turned to face front again.

Silence came from beside him. Then in a quietly controlled voice, she said, "I believe the proper response is, 'You are welcome, Miss Whelton,' or 'My pleasure, Miss Whelton.'"

He whipped to face her. "It was not a pleasure at all," he growled. "I had to kill to save you."

She blinked, owl-like. "Oh, my. Of course, you did." Her cheeks paled. "I'm sorry for that."

He ground his teeth, not trusting himself to speak. What made his temper heat was her complete folly in the matter. How could a woman who had navigated her way across two continents be so foolish?

"I will add to your fee." Her chin lifted.

"You will not."

Her brows snapped together, and she turned away. Catching her bottom lip between her teeth, she gnawed on it for a moment. Finally, she said quietly, "I hope I haven't discouraged you from guiding us."

He took a moment to digest her round-about request. "Are you asking me to continue to help you find the man with that silly dagger of crystal?"

"Yes." She did not look at him.

His anger still rode him hard. Clenching his teeth, he fought it back until he could speak without roaring at her. "You might want to ask me nicely, Miss Whelton. Especially since I saved your life and that of your friend," he said.

Her mouth flattened and she turned away. Her cheek paled. When she faced him again after a moment, she said evenly, "Please, Mr. Pirate, will you help me find the man with the Crystal Dagger?"

"My price has gone up," he said, wanting to see her reaction.

"But…but you said…" That pale cheek bloomed with color. Her lips clamped together, then she huffed, "You still have my portrait case. It's made of gold."

"So, it is." He turned to face front again.

"All right," she muttered.

"What was that?" He leaned toward her as if he could not hear.

"Yes," she snapped. "I'll meet your price."

He hid his smile as his anger leaked away. He remained silent a moment. Finally, he said, "I'll continue to guide you on one condition."

"What condition?" she ground out.

"That you tell me your full name."

She sputtered and he nearly laughed aloud. He already knew her name from that night when he had snooped in her journal, but he wanted to hear it from her. He was curious why a woman would carry a man's name, and he intended to question her about it in the future. Besides, having her reveal her given name gave him a tiny weapon in this war of wills they waged. He waited patiently for her answer.

Finally, quietly, he heard her say, "Sydney. Sydney Charlotte Whelton."

"Thank you, Miss Whelton," he said. "I accept your commission."

"You must tell me yours," she countered.

"My what?" Of course, he knew precisely what she wanted to know.

"Your given name." She spoke as if he were a child with no understanding.

He raised a brow at her. "Are you sure I have one?" With that question, he was not only putting her off, but asking himself the same thing. Did he have a given name? What parents had bestowed it on him? Where were they? Why had they abandoned him?

She scowled. Then with a huff of exasperation, she turned back to ride next to Mrs. Foster without answering his question.

Raphael let her go. He was pleased their arrangement had been renegotiated. Now he could keep track of the delightful, exasperating Sydney Whelton. As he contemplated the possibility that she might hold answers to his curse, the amulet that hung beneath his clothes felt warm against his skin. That dark spot in his heart opened again. A prickle of something shadowy and furtive touched his mind. Something seductive but evil, like his nightmares. Like the nightmare Miss Whelton had chased away. He wrapped his fingers around the amulet and let his thoughts rest on the woman who had dragged him from the pit of agony. The evil sensation receded.

He shook it off. But the questions swirled in his head. Where did that evil sensation originate? Why did it haunt him? Was it from the same sorceress who tortured him in his dreams? Who was she? Was she connected to the amulet he wore around his neck? Why did he have to wear the amulet to remain human? Why was he cursed? What were his origins? And what connection did Miss Whelton have to all of it?

Out of habit, he pushed the questions away. They would be answered in their own time. Or not. He could not worry about them. As Zayed kept reminding him: *Inshallah.*

He turned his thoughts to a much more pleasant subject: Miss Whelton—Sydney—and the many chances he would have to tease and spar with her. The time he would spend in her company on the journey to find the man with the dagger of crystal would not be wasted. With a smile, he started to sing.

Chapter 11

Sydney shifted in the saddle. Her bottom was sore. She felt as if they hadn't rested for days, even though they had started out from their midday break only a few hours ago. She had recovered her composure after the attack by those horrible men the day before. Lucy seemed to be better as well. By the time they had settled down for the night, she felt as if the attack had been a horrible nightmare. But she startled at every noise made by a night animal. Lucy did the same.

Shifting again, she wanted to ask the Pirate when they would be stopping, but that would make her appear weak. He had saved her and Lucy from those horrible men. And he had saved her from falling off a mountain. She would be dead if not for him. Perhaps she *was* weak. With a silent sigh, she acknowledged that she was quite grateful that he was her guide.

From beside her, Lucy called to the two men riding ahead of them. "Excuse me, Mr. Pirate, sir. Would you mind stopping for a few moments?"

Sydney glanced at her friend in surprise. Lucy had become much surer of herself since they had joined the Pirate in their travels. Before, she had barely spoken in the presence of their guides.

The Pirate glanced back at them, held a short conversation with Zayed, then dropped back to ride beside them.

"Zayed will stay with you while you rest, Mrs. Foster, and accompany you while you walk for a time," he said. "Miss Whelton and I will ride ahead to a search out a place to take our ease for the night. Is that acceptable to you, Miss Whelton?"

His gaze landed on Sydney as if daring her to object. She wanted to rest as much as Lucy, but she wasn't about to admit that. Instead, she straightened her spine.

"Whatever you think best, Mr. Pirate," she said primly, then gritted her teeth. She would travel on with him even if she couldn't walk for a week.

With a nod, he faced front again, but she saw a tiny twitch at the corner of his lips.

Lucy and Zayed dropped back, and Sydney waved a farewell to her friend, confident that Lucy would be safe with Zayed.

They rode for a while, then the Pirate said, "Sydney is an unusual name for a woman."

Surprised at his observation, she was silent for a heartbeat. Then she said, "The Pirate is an unusual name for anyone."

He smiled. "Tell me about yours and I'll give you a name."

She studied him. "Your true name, or another that you fabricate?"

His eyes remained fixed on the desert before him. "I will tell you what those who know me call me."

His evasive answer intrigued her. Her own name embarrassed her. It was a boy's name, after all. She cleared her throat. "My father wanted a boy."

"But he got a girl instead." His glance slid to her.

"Yes. I was taught many things that any other girl would not have learned." She kept her gaze front, for in the world of London society, her upbringing shamed her. Young ladies did not learn to shoot a pistol with accuracy, nor learn to wield a knife with deadly skill. Nor could they summon magic with a thought and blast an enemy. Besides that, she was illegitimate. Being the daughter of a powerful man did not change that, and she lived in a gaming hell on the shadowy side of London society. Despite the tutors her mother hired to teach her etiquette, dancing and the other proper behaviors of a young lady of society, she couldn't erase who she was.

"If you had not been taught those things, you would never have come on this journey," he observed.

Heat rose in her cheeks. "But I cannot play the pianoforte, and my embroidery is atrocious. No proper gentleman will have me for a wife." Then she added very quietly, "Not that I wish to be someone's wife."

"I don't know what a peeno-fortay is, but it sounds rather useless," he said. "If all you knew was embroidery and this peeno-fortay, we would never have met. I would have been forced to amuse myself with raiding caravans or thieving from a fat, wealthy pasha."

She swung to face him. Her eyes snapped. "So, I amuse you?"

He grinned. "More than you know." Then after a tiny pause, "Sydney."

With a narrow gaze, she huffed in exasperation. But her name on his lips warmed her.

"Your turn, Mr. Pirate."

"You may call me Raphael." He said the words as if his name did not matter.

Her eyes widened in surprise. She did not expect such a European name. But then, she knew nothing about his background except the rumors and stories of his ruthlessness and cunning. "A beautiful name. Like the angel," she murmured.

"That is what Zayed said when he called me that," he said with a diffident shrug.

"Zayed?" Intrigued, she sensed a story behind that offhand remark.

He glanced at her, then away, as if embarrassed. "I was quite ill when I was very young. He said I kept mumbling 'angel' in my fever. So, he started calling me by the only angelic name he knew."

"But is Raphael your true name?" she asked.

"It's the only name I know. I can't remember what my parents called me." His golden gaze landed on her with a look that warned her she shouldn't probe further.

Empathy for the young orphan welled in her. She wanted to know his story. What happened to his parents? Why couldn't he remember them? Curbing her curiosity, she said, "I'm sorry."

"You don't need to be sorry. It was a long time ago," he said with another shrug.

She sensed his discomfort and marveled that he had shared that much with her. To change the mood, her lips curved in a teasing smile. "You are not like an angel. Except that you have saved me."

"Perhaps I am more like a fallen angel." An inquiring brow arched up. "How many angels have you met?"

She smothered a laugh. "You are the first."

"Then I will teach you what angels are like. Fallen or otherwise. Another thing that so-called young English ladies would never learn." Those lion eyes landed on her. "Are you interested?"

She gasped. "What are you suggesting?"

A corner of his mouth tipped up and his golden eyes turned warm. "Whatever you would like to learn, Sydney-Who-Is-Not-A-Boy."

She should not have been shocked, for he had been teasing and provoking her since she had first walked into his tent. She remembered that kiss when he had just awakened from his terrible nightmare. The heat that had flamed through her, the wild throb of desire that had erupted deep within her. She had never imagined kissing a man could be so exciting. The sensations had made her giddy with wanting more. They had frightened her with their intensity. But he fascinated her, and his offer tempted. What would it be like to experience what he could teach her?

She looked demurely down at her fingers clutching the reins of the mule's halter. "That is quite improper."

His smile turned into a grin. "I think we have already scandalized the scorpions and snakes."

"But…" She tried to come up with another excuse but failed.

"We are in the desert, with no one around to see or judge," he said with a wave of his hand at the expanse around them. "No one will know unless you reveal what we do. Would you tell anyone?"

"Of course not!" The thought took her breath.

"Then?"

His prompt hung in the air between them. She looked away, unwilling to face him or the highly inappropriate thoughts running through her head. Like kissing him. Touching him. Tasting him.

"I will think about it," she said, forcing a stiff, cool tone.

He huffed a laugh. "Whenever you're ready, Miss Whelton."

His assumption that she would give in to his offer made her fingers tighten on the reins. He might have the name of an angel, actually an archangel, but he certainly was not one. More like the fallen angel he described, for he enticed like one of Lucifer's own. No, she definitely would not accept his offer. They still had too far to travel. Besides, how could she face Lucy if she succumbed to the Pirate's wiles? She would be mortified.

With her decision made, she straightened her spine. But she did wonder how many more of those delicious sensations he could make her feel. Perhaps... one more kiss.

"I found him!" Deep in her lair beneath Venice's lagoon, Nulkana exulted. "Kek, I found him!" she crowed.

The skeletal form of Kek emerged from the shadows. "That is a great achievement, mistress." A faint smile, resembling the grimace of a gargoyle, crossed his face. "You must celebrate, perhaps with a special meal."

"Yes, yes." Nulkana waved away his suggestion as she gazed down at the red crystal on the table before her. In its center was a hazy scene of two people—a man and a woman—riding on mules through the desert. "I went into his head. I saw through his eyes for a moment. He is awake this time." She caressed the crystal and peered closer. "He has that woman with him." Her lips twisted with hatred. "*She* was the creature that pushed me away the last time I visited him in his sleep. Who is she? There is something about her..."

"I am sure you will eliminate her, mistress," Kek murmured.

Nulkana swung away from the crystal. "She thwarts me, Kek!" she screamed. "Like the others!" She paced the length of the table and back again. "First, I had to deal with the two descendants of my self-righteous bitch sister, Halima, who saved those Auriano twin whelps. Then the Druid priest interfered and protected their sister. Now, I find a witch who has powers so ancient even I don't know where they come from. And I am wounded! Stonehenge was supposed to protect me! But that foolish, stupid leader of that group attacked me. They called themselves the Legion of Baal. Ha! As if Baal could help them. He was vanquished eons ago." She turned back to the red crystal. "Something about that woman reminds me of their leader." Abruptly, she bent over, clutched at her chest, and screamed in agony. "I am dying, Kek!"

"No, no, mistress, you are healing, getting stronger every day." Kek bowed, his words unctuous.

"I am not!" Her screech bounced off the black walls, then turned to a wail. She pressed a bony hand against the green, putrid stain on her gown. "I am never going to heal!"

"Mistress, you need to feed." Kek snapped his fingers at the cowled figure standing at the edge of the shadows. "Get your mistress her meal."

The figure did not move immediately. Then after a long moment, it turned and disappeared into the shadows.

Kek gazed after him into the gloom. "He still resists," he mused as the wail of young women from deep in the bowels of the lair grew louder.

Nulkana nodded absently and rubbed the seeping wound on her chest. She stared deeply into the red crystal. "I see a way to get what I want," she said. "Yes-s-s. I know a way. I will contact the one who swims in the river. She owes me. All I want is the piece of the Sphere. She can have the rest of him. I'm sure he will delight her palette."

With a pleased cackle, she turned expectantly toward the shadows as she waited for her meal.

Late that afternoon, Raphael and Sydney rode into a gorge that took Sydney's breath away. The rust-orange rock walls reached hundreds of feet on either side, leaving only a narrow *wadi* between. Beside the dry wadi, a shallow river surged and bubbled its way across stones and around sand bars. While the path they traversed and the river were shaded, the setting sun left a band of bright orange across the cliff tops.

"Spectacular," she said as she twisted to look up at the towering cliffs.

"We are in the Todgha Gorge, and this is the Todgha River." Raphael indicated the wide stream rushing beside them. "The land can be harsh, but it can also be beautiful. It fascinates me."

His gaze settled on her with a warmth that caused the blood to rush to her cheeks and a throb to pulse between her thighs. Was he speaking of the land? Or her? She quickly looked away. What was happening to her? Just a glance from him, and she wanted his kiss. His touch.

Foolishness, she thought. The long journey, the threat of the lion, the attack by the outlaws, the expanse of the desert—the hardships made her think in ways she normally would not. Why, in her mother's gaming hell, she had seen handsome men every evening, and she never wanted them to kiss her. She shifted in her saddle and focused on the cliffs rising hundreds of feet beside her. But before she looked away from him, she caught the tiniest lift at the corner of his mouth. She ignored it.

They made camp at the foot of the cliffs, and Lucy and Zayed rode in not long after. Sydney had missed having her friend near, especially after all they had been through on this journey. Besides, with Lucy's arrival, Sydney could distract herself from those wayward, tantalizing, naughty thoughts that the Pirate—Raphael—had stirred up in her brain.

After they had eaten Zayed's cooking, once again a miraculous concoction of millet with herbs and spices and pounded goat cheese, they all retired. The sun had set quickly, leaving the gorge in thick darkness. Sydney fell asleep to the soothing sound of rushing water.

She was in a dreamless sleep when she woke with a start. She lay very still, wondering what had awakened her. The moon had risen and sent a sharp slant of silvery light onto the cliff face opposite. It reflected into the canyon of the gorge so that she could make out the forms of the others sleeping nearby. But one was missing. Where the shape of a body should have been, only a tangled blanket remained. Who was missing? As she peered around, she saw no one walking about, but she thought she heard voices. Sound carried strangely between the gorge's walls, and the rushing water distorted it more. She felt a *wrongness* to the scene.

Scrambling to her feet, she wiped sleep from her eyes and stared further into the darkness. Along the bank of the river, she saw the shape of Raphael, and beyond him, hovering above the water, a shimmer about the size of a person. Again, she thought she heard voices, but who could he be talking to? The shimmer?

As she crept closer, the center of the shimmer revealed a woman, one of the most beautiful, exotic creatures Sydney had ever seen.

Her long, dark, curly hair floated on a non-existent breeze. She was dressed in a diaphanous kaftan trimmed in glittery jewels, inappropriate attire for the middle of the desert. Her clothing flowed and hugged her voluptuous body as it hid and revealed.

Sydney could hear her speaking, indistinct but musical words lost in the rush of the river. Raphael appeared spellbound. He stepped toward the woman, toward the water, as if he were in a trance. This was magic, dark magic. A chill swept through Sydney. Who was this creature? With slow, languid movements, she reached out, enticing Raphael closer. He took another step.

The woman kept luring him nearer, as if she could not leave the river, but needed him in the water. In a flash, Sydney knew Raphael shouldn't get even his little toe wet. She sensed that if he did, she would never see him again. That frightened her. A heavy ache of loss gathered in her chest. He had saved her life. Twice. He had offered to teach her about kisses and other things that sent a thrill through her. She was not about to lose that opportunity.

Raphael stepped forward again. He was nearly at the water's edge. Another half step would get his toes wet. Sydney hurried closer.

"Stop!" she yelled.

The woman swung to her with a hiss.

"Get away from him!" Sydney allowed a globe of power to spark in her palm.

The woman turned back to Raphael and beckoned him, her gesture seductive. Sydney would not allow that *creature* to win this battle. She threw her globe of magic, so it landed at the woman's feet. With a screech of frustration, the seductress reared back. Her glowing luminescence dulled, and her form began to change. Sydney watched, astounded, as the beautiful woman turned into a gigantic monster with tentacles and scaly, gray skin.

"Who are you?" Sydney demanded. "What do you want?"

The fiend slipped lower into the water.

"Answer my questions," Sydney ordered, "or I'll throw this." She bounced another ball of power in her hand. "I won't miss this time."

The monster whined. "She asked me to come. She said I could have him if I brought her what she wanted."

"Who did? What did she want?" Sydney demanded.

"N-n-n-n-o-o-o!" With a final wail, the monster slipped into the river and disappeared. A dark blob remained where the creature had been, then flowed away with the current. The river bubbled and gurgled as if nothing had disturbed it.

As soon as the monster had gone, Raphael dropped to his hands and knees as if cut loose from a tether. Sydney rushed to him. Kneeling beside him, she placed her hand on his shoulder. She ignored the feel of the warm, firm muscle beneath her palm. And the faint tingle through the cloth of his shirt.

"Are you all right? Did she hurt you?" she asked.

He turned his head to look at her. His eyes were glazed.

"You saved me," he said. As he spoke, his eyes cleared. "You saved me from that monster." A thread of admiration ran beneath his words.

Relief made her giddy as she realized he was unhurt. "Well, yes, I suppose I did." Half-teasing, half-serious, she added, "I didn't want to lose my guide."

He stared a moment, then his eyes lit with humor. "You thought you might miss your lesson in kisses." His words murmured warmly.

Embarrassed that he had guessed her thoughts, Sydney straightened her spine. "I merely wished to save myself the trouble of finding a new guide."

He sniggered.

Zayed and Lucy arrived in a breathless run. While Lucy exclaimed over Sydney's well-being, Raphael exchanged a glance with Zayed. Sydney saw that look.

"Who—what was that?" she asked.

Zayed turned his solemn gaze on her. "It is Aicha Kandida. She is an *afrit*, a water demon. She lures with beauty. When she has her victim, she turns into her true form. Then she drags him to her lair to consume him."

Lucy gasped in horror and clapped a hand to her mouth as if she might be sick. Sydney's stomach churned in revulsion. She had witnessed horrible things before, like the strange sickness that had killed her mother and the night of her father's death, but the thought of what that fiend might have done to Raphael seemed even worse. Why would such a demon attack him?

A line of confusion appeared between Raphael's brows. "But she stays in the River Sebu in the city of Marrakesh. What would she be doing out here in the desert?"

"She said someone sent her," Sydney said. "Someone who wants something from you."

Raphael's hand went to his chest as if protecting a precious object.

"What is it?" she asked. "What did she want?"

His eyes turned suddenly hard and belligerent as if they had never shared that teasing moment. "You will never get it," he growled.

Sydney fell back a step, hurt by his sudden aggression. But she would not let him see that. Instead, summoning up exasperation, she exclaimed, "Dash it all! Whatever it is, I don't want it. I only wish to know what I must guard against."

He stared at her, his gaze suspicious and unrelenting.

Zayed said quietly, "It is only fair, *akhi*."

Raphael swung to him. "You don't know what it is to—" His words halted abruptly.

With a nod of acknowledgment, Zayed said, "You have not been so close to death in a long time. Miss Whelton chased away the *afrit*."

The Pirate turned those lion eyes on her and stared as if trying to read her soul. After a moment, he took hold of a cord around his neck and pulled an amulet from beneath his clothes. He looked at it as if seeing it for the first time.

"This," he said, hostility threading his word. "But no one will take it from me."

Sydney saw a carved piece of amber dangling from the cord. It was an attractive bauble, about the length of her forefinger, shaped in a zigzag, decorated with swirls and ending in a dull point, but it appeared worthless.

"May I see it?" She held out her hand.

"I'm not taking it off," he said, his tone combative and aggressive.

Sydney blinked at his surliness and dropped her hand. This was the side of him that was the Pirate, steely, dangerous, ruthless. Something about the amulet made him anxious. And he seemed to be protecting it with his life. Why was it so important? A connection to his past, perhaps? But his hostility chafed. All she was trying to do was help him, and she was still reeling from the encounter with the *afrit*, and. Her temper cracked at his attitude.

"Fine," she snapped. "You can fight the next monster on your own."

She spun away, but before she had stalked two steps, he stopped her with a hand on her arm.

"Miss Whelton. Sydney. Wait. Please."

She hesitated a moment, then turned back to him. His words sounded desperate, but that had not been the only thing that had stopped her. His fingers, curled around the sleeve of her jacket, sent a tingly jolt through the cloth to her skin. Why did that happen? Why did she feel a tingle every time he touched her? But this had been stronger than any she had felt before. Did he feel it as well?

She met his eyes. Something flashed through them, an awareness, a surprise, and then it was gone. Only his steady gaze remained, waiting, as if nothing unusual had happened. His hand fell away from her arm.

"I never take it off," he said, more calmly. "But you may look if you wish."

Despite his explanation, his attitude annoyed her. "I'm not going to steal it."

He sighed, as if beleaguered by her request. "I know. But I don't… Please, look if you wish, but I cannot remove it." He held it out to her at the length of the cord.

Something in his words and his tone made questions pop in her brain. Why couldn't he remove it? Why was he so protective of it? What would happen if he took it off? But those were questions for another time. He was offering an examination of something that was obviously very dear to him, so she would take the opportunity. It was possible the water demon attacked him to get the item he wore. Examining it might give her some insight into the enigma of the man who called himself the Pirate.

She slipped her palm beneath the amulet, held it up in the moonlight, and turned it this way and that. A vague memory nagged her, but the recollection was as wispy as fog and about as clear. The amulet seemed to pulse and warm in her palm. Startled, she dropped it, where it fell against his chest.

"What is it?" he demanded. "What did you see?"

"Nothing." She shook her head. "Nothing, I'm sorry." She would not tell him about the heat she'd felt, nor that prick of memory, not until she could decipher it. "It's a very unusual piece."

Suspicion darkened his eyes as he studied her a moment. Then he gave a single nod. With a glance toward the river, he said, "The *afrit* won't bother us again tonight, but we should move on."

Sydney agreed. She needed to think, and she doubted she'd be able to close her eyes for fear some other monster might rise up out of the desert. The confrontation with the demon had been unnerving and frightening. The Pirate's harsh words still burned. His strange reaction to her examination of the amulet had roused her curiosity. Turning back to their camp, she saw that Lucy and Zayed had already begun to gather their belongings. She looked forward to the monotony of travel, for she would have time to process her thoughts and perhaps dredge that memory from the recesses of her mind.

And she would have a chance to ponder the Pirate—Raphael—and wonder why such a strong, powerful man was so protective of what appeared to be a simple amulet.

Chapter 12

They rode in polite companionship for the next several days. No teasing or taunting came from the Pirate. Instead, he was back to calling her Miss Whelton, and she called him Mr. Pirate. She and Lucy rode side by side behind the two men. When they stopped to rest during the day or for the night, conversation was limited to how far they had gone, who would collect fuel for the fire, when they next expected to see a village or reach an oasis or well. After each excruciatingly polite exchange, Lucy sent her a perplexed glance, as if Sydney had suddenly become another person. Sydney ignored the looks. Her last exchange with the Pirate was too complicated and fraught for her to explain.

They had passed through one small village and had exchanged their mules for camels once more. Sydney could not decide which was more uncomfortable. But the uncomfortable ride was not what occupied her thoughts. The Pirate's reaction to her request to look at his amulet and his refusal to remove it made her think it was much more than an unusual bauble. If she added in his nightmares and the attack of the *afrit*, she arrived at a conclusion that made her wary. The Pirate must be something beyond human, but she had no idea what. He sounded human when he teased and provoked her, and he certainly felt human when he had kissed her, except for that unusual tingle. Unable to decide what he might be, she put all of that aside.

What bothered her most of all was that she had been insulted and hurt by his suspicious and hostile response to her request. He obviously didn't trust her. But her reaction to his mistrust confused and angered her. She shouldn't care what he thought of her. But she did. Nor could she deny the painful twinge in her chest at his attitude.

After one long day of traveling, they came upon a series of mounds that stretched far into the distance. They were spaced apart about the length of a very fine ballroom, and about the height of a very tall man. The Pirate told her they were called *khetteras* and were part of an irrigation system that fed water into the city of Marrakesh. The mounds consisted of desert debris left from digging out the underground waterways. On top of one, a complicated wooden structure resembled the framework of a church steeple. He explained that it provided the means to draw water from the current below.

They made camp in the shadow of a mound. After they had eaten, the Pirate offered to take them into the underground tunnels. Lucy declined, but Sydney followed him along the line of mounds to a small stone structure. Carved steps led down into the earth. A shaft of light from the setting sun fell on the descending wall and lit the interior. He preceded her down the steps.

"What will we see at the bottom, Mr. Pirate?" she asked, trying to dispel the awkwardness between them. She'd pushed aside the hurt feelings after his harsh words at the river. "Monsters? Ghosts? A dragon?"

"Something that will astonish you," he said, his tone light and teasing.

Intrigued, Sydney followed him. At the bottom of the steps, the narrow stairway widened into a small chamber, barely high enough to accommodate his height. On one side, a channel disappeared into the darkness, and directly opposite was another channel leading away in the other direction. A continuous small stream of water ran through the channel from one side of the chamber to the other.

Sydney bent, dipped her finger in the flow and found it was only deep enough to cover the second knuckle of her forefinger. "This doesn't seem like enough water to supply a city," she observed.

"It runs faster and deeper during the rainy season. The water is collected in reservoirs near Marrakesh," he said.

Absently, she watched the water flow past her feet as she asked, "Will we be stopping in Marrakesh? I've heard it is a marvelous city."

"No," he said. "Marrakesh is west. We're heading north."

"Why?" He had led them west since they began this journey. Disappointed they wouldn't be visiting the exotic city and curious about their change in direction, she turned to him. What she saw made her gasp, cover her eyes, and spin away. He had completely shed his clothes!

"What are you doing?!" she demanded, keeping her back turned. "I don't know what you think of me, Mr. Pirate, but I am not some hussy who will couple with any man who beckons."

"I think that you are brave but daft for coming on such a journey," he said. "I think I insulted you when you wanted to look at my amulet. I want to explain."

"By taking off your clothes?" she squeaked.

"No, by showing you."

"I think you have shown me quite enough," she huffed angrily.

Sydney, he said silently, *please turn around.*

She heard the voice in her head. Like the voice she had heard when she left his tent in the Tuareg village. Like those teasing, taunting comments he had annoyed her with when they were traveling separately. Then she remembered the shadow man who had visited her that first night. He had also spoken in her head, but she assumed he was something other than human. But the man at her back was solid, flesh and bone. Human. How could he have such a skill?

She'd thought it was merely a parlor trick, but now she suspected he held more power than he'd admitted. But what sort of power? She had no answer. She didn't want an answer. She didn't want to discover he was something beyond human. And she did not want to turn around. But something compelled her, whether it was the use of her name, or the touch of desperation behind his words. Bracing herself, she turned, pasting her eyes on his face, and hiding her confusion and embarrassment with false bravado.

"Well?" she demanded, pretending an indifference she didn't feel. The glimpse she'd had of his body took her breath away. He was magnificent, all tight muscles and smooth skin. "I have seen naked men before. You have shown me nothing new," she lied.

A small smile touched his lips. "I'm sure I haven't," he said aloud, "but I thought you might like to see why I refused to remove the amulet."

His turn of phrase confused her. He needed to *show* her why he didn't take it off? But she was gratified he wished to make amends for his rudeness.

"There is a price," he added.

"Of course, there is," she scoffed, castigating herself for thinking he might have manners, that he might offer something for nothing. "How much more should I add to your fee?"

"Not that." He shook his head. "A kiss."

"A kiss?! You presume too much, Mr. Pirate." She crossed her arms and glared at him.

"Very well." He shrugged and bent to retrieve his clothes. "I take back my offer."

Curiosity gnawed at her. From what he'd said, she deduced that taking off the amulet did…something. But what? "Wait."

He straightened, his baggy pantaloons dangling from his hand. "Yes?"

"I agree." She raised her chin, challenging him to taunt her for changing her mind.

He didn't. Instead, he gave a solemn nod and allowed his pantaloons to fall to the stony floor. Wrapping his fingers around the amulet, he pulled the cord over his head and let the piece fall. It landed on his clothes with a soft plop. Nothing happened for a heartbeat. Then, very slowly, his outline became blurry. The blur moved across his skin, covering him, and in its wake she saw a shadowy form. He became darker than the night, as if absorbing all the light, but with the faint outline of muscle and sinew. A man, but not a man. A shadow man. With eyes like molten gold, and the shadowy physique of an Adonis. Beautiful. Frightening. Seductive.

Her breath left her in a rush. "You're…." She fought for air. "You visited me at my tent that first night." She frowned. "You suggested that we might become lovers."

His laugh huffed through her head. *I did. We might, you know.*

She reared back in outrage, "Not—"

His step forward halted her words. *Don't turn away from something you know nothing about.*

She glared. "I know everything I need to know." She didn't. But she ignored the little voice in the back of her head that reminded her of the delicious sensations he made her feel.

Do you? Truly, Sydney?

Her glance slid away. "Everything I want to know," she said, her words mulish, knowing she lied.

He stepped closer. *I think you don't want to know because you don't have all the information.* He softly ran his fingers across her cheek. *I think you might change your mind if you learned more.*

She gasped as his touch left a trail of tingles behind, more intense than when he was human. The sensation sent a shivery thrill through her. She was enthralled. And instantly regretted turning down his suggestion.

Abruptly, he stepped back. With a twist of his hand, the amulet rose into the air from where it had fallen and landed in his palm. Sydney watched in amazement. As if nothing unusual had happened, he slipped it over his head. Gradually, his shadowy form grew blurry and then solid. He turned back into flesh and bone and stood before her as he had only moments before. But his eyes, those glorious golden, lion eyes, had become dark and predatory.

Shocked at what he had shown her, she fell back a step. "Are you ill? Your eyes...."

He closed the distance between them and cupped her face in his hands. "I could become quite ill. A kiss will cure me. You agreed, Sydney."

She ignored the faint tingle of his touch, his seductive scent of sandalwood and sun-kissed skin. "Well, yes, but —" Before she had a chance to finish, his mouth was on hers.

He kissed her as if his life depended on it. As if he might die without it. She was surprised at his intensity, but the feel of his lips against hers raised the most delicious sensations. She throbbed deep in her center. Her skin came alive. Her breasts strained against her clothes. Oh, my, she never knew a kiss could be so invigorating, so exciting, so compelling. So delicious. This was so much more than that stolen kiss in the desert after his nightmare. She inched forward, pressed against him, and wrapped her arms around him, the feel of his skin warm beneath her hands. He sighed as if she relieved his pain.

His tongue traced her lips, asking for entry, and without thought, she gave it. This was more enthralling, more intimate than she ever dreamed. When his hand cupped her breast and massaged it, a tiny sound of pleasure escaped her. She wanted more. The sensations evoked by his touch transported her. If Raphael could make her insides quiver by that gentle touch, what else could he make her feel?

Raphael exulted in the feel of the woman in his embrace. Her touch soothed him. Something within her sang to him. The deep craving that always overcame him after he returned to flesh and bone from the darkness dissipated. He felt human again. Since he had been darkness for a short while, that need to touch, to satisfy the appetite that overwhelmed him had been brief. Less intense than when he had been darkness for longer periods. He should have ended the kiss then. She had given what he'd asked for, what he had needed. But he couldn't let her go. The woman in his arms was glorious. She returned his kiss with a fervor that astounded him. Her curves fit perfectly against him. And her touch was exquisite.

He wanted her more than he had ever wanted any other woman. He cupped her bottom and pulled her tight against him. A tiny sound escaped her, halfway between a moan and a sigh. He knew then. She wanted him as much as he wanted her. But he had to stop. He couldn't go any further.

He felt relief that she now knew the truth of who he was—cursed, part human, part something else. He'd wanted to make amends after his boorish behavior when she had asked to see the amulet. After she had saved him from Aicha Kandida. He'd wanted to apologize, and the only way he could think of was to show her his shadowy self. His true self, with no amulet to keep him human. But more than that, he felt they had a connection. A connection that went beyond what he felt now in her supple body beneath his hands. Why else would the amulet warm on occasion when she came near? Why else would he be able to feel her when he transformed into his dark, shadowy form? Why else would his skin tingle whenever they touched? She had seen another like him. Where and when? Who was this other shadowy person who turned from flesh and bone to a shadowy form?

That vision he had seen when he had touched the black satin robe with purple embroidery had shown him a woman with eyes like his. Who was she? What was her connection to him? Did she turn to darkness as well?

But all the questions singed away in the heated kiss with the woman who felt like paradise in his arms.

Reluctantly, slowly, he pulled away, back from the woman who riled him more than any other, who challenged him, who made his blood sing in his veins. He fought down his arousal and that other, more intangible need to touch, to hold, to make her his. His arms felt empty, bereft. But he needed to give her time. To give himself time. Too many unanswered questions lay between them.

She gazed up at him, her eyes dazed. She looked vulnerable and thoroughly kissed. He wanted to do more than kiss her. The desire to see her spread out beneath him with that same look in her eyes flashed through his brain. He immediately quashed it. This was not the time. Perhaps he would never see that time. She was a witch and held too many secrets that needed unraveling. She might turn out to be a dangerous enemy. But deep down, he knew that couldn't be true.

He retrieved her hat from the cavern floor and placed it on her head, covering that splendid hair. "A woman should keep her head covered in the desert," he said, repeating words he had said to her in his tent in the Tuareg village.

She blinked and her eyes cleared. Color suffused her cheeks. "Of course." She put her fingers to her cheeks. Her lashes swept down, and when she looked up again, her gaze was cool and impersonal. "Thank you for showing me." She seemed to fumble for words. "It must be a terrible burden. How long—?" She shook her head. "I'm sorry. I shouldn't pry."

"Almost all my life," he said, watching her try to make sense of his transformation. And perhaps make sense of the kiss they had shared as well. "You said you had seen another."

"Yes." Her tone turned muted, and she lowered her gaze. "On the night my father was killed. There was a terrible battle, and she killed almost everyone."

Her answer raised many questions. He could see she was still disturbed by the event, so he only voiced one. "Who killed everyone, Sydney? The other shadow person?" he asked gently, fearing her answer. What if he were as cruel and soulless as this other person?

She shook her head, and her eyes turned hard with hate. "No, not the Shadow. Nulkana, the sorceress. She destroyed them, incinerated them."

At the name, something frightful stirred within him. He had never heard that name before, but for some reason, it turned his blood cold.

He needed to ask one more question. "Did Nulkana kill this other Shadow?"

"No. At least, I don't think so." Her gaze slipped away. "I ran away, and when I came back, the Shadow was gone. I should have stayed. I might have saved my father."

"You did the right thing," he said. "You might have been killed as well." The idea of never meeting her, of her existence wiped from the face of the earth created a heavy feeling in his chest.

She looked at him again, determination a spark in her eyes. "I want to destroy Nulkana for what she did. That's the reason I want to find the man with the Crystal Dagger," she declared. "I want him to kill her."

Her need for revenge against the sorceress sparked something in him. His blood had chilled at the mention of the name of the sorceress. Could Nulkana be the evil presence who haunted his dreams and tortured him? If she was, then he wanted her dead as well.

Sydney tipped her head thoughtfully. "Perhaps Nulkana is the one who sent the *afrit* after you."

Not wanting to darken the bright moment they had just shared, he shrugged off her suggestion as he turned to don his clothes. "Perhaps. But you vanquished the *afrit*. It won't bother us again." He had no idea why Nulkana had an interest in him, nor did he want to pursue that possibility at the moment. After experiencing the nightmares, he was convinced the sorceress had sent Aicha Kandida to kill him, but he didn't want to confirm that to Sydney and frighten her. He needed to think about everything he had just learned and the danger that threatened, but that could wait for the moment. Right now, he wanted to savor the fleeting feeling of freedom he had felt and the sense of rightness that had settled in him during their kiss.

"Come, Miss Whelton," he said, holding out his hand to her.

Hesitantly, she placed her fingers on his palm. As she did, a flash of gold around her forefinger caught his attention. A ring. He'd seen it before, of course, but this time, he felt the urge to ask about it.

He looked closer. "That is an unusual ring. It looks like a dragon swallowing its own tail."

"It is an ouroboros. It represents the circle of life." She paused and tears filled her eyes. "It was my mother's. She died a month before my father."

"I'm sorry," he said gently. "First your mother and then your father." He raised her hand to his lips and kissed her palm. "Poor Miss Whelton." He watched her lips part and her eyes widen at his soft caress.

One tear spilled over, and she swiped it away. "Thank you," she said.

"Come." He gave her hand a tiny tug. "The sun has set. Zayed and Mrs. Foster will wonder if we got swept away to Marrakesh." He motioned for her to precede him up the stone steps.

Sympathy rose in his chest for her loss of both parents, but if they had not died, he never would have met the beguiling, fascinating Sydney Whelton. Her ring intrigued him. He wondered if it had some connection to her magical power.

The warming of his amulet when she had first entered his tent and the other times it had warmed when she was near made him question again if they were connected on a very deep level. He needed to discover what that connection was. In the meantime, he planned to keep her very close and get as much information from her as he could. And perhaps coax another kiss.

Because he very much enjoyed her kisses.

When they emerged into the short twilight after the sun set, Sydney was careful to act as if nothing unusual had happened in the cavern, but Lucy kept asking if she felt well. Sydney answered that she felt perfectly fine. She felt more than fine, despite the reminder of her mother's death. Her heart still raced, and those exciting sensations deep in her center confused her. She had thought that kissing a man was boring at best, disgusting at worse. What she had discovered was that kissing a man, kissing Raphael, was the most exciting thing she had ever experienced.

That first kiss out in the desert when he had come out of his nightmare had been pleasant, but she had been taken by surprise. The kiss she had shared with him in the *khettera* had shaken her, turned her world upside-down, evoked sensations she hadn't known she could feel. How could a kiss make her body react in such a way?

She felt a thrill, a joy, a frisson of deliciousness. Wanting to stay exactly where she was. In his arms.

She wanted more of those kisses. She wanted more of him. He had been so sympathetic when she told him about her mother. And that tiny kiss on her palm had comforted her, besides sending a thrill up her arm. But at the same time, she was afraid. He was different. Part human, part Shadow. What would happen if she gave herself to him? Would it change her? No one need know, only Lucy, and she would never breathe a word. But something held Sydney back. Fear of the unknown. Fear of never having experienced anything or anyone quite like Raphael.

But she did so enjoy his kisses.

Chapter 13

Several days later, right before sunset, they wound their way through the scattered tombs of a cemetery marked by crumbling mausoleums and the ruins of a palace. They halted at the edge of a cliff, and the city of Fès spread out below them, a jumble of flat-roofed buildings, dotted with domes and minarets. To Sydney, it looked like a child's wooden blocks spread out in a nonsensical design. She was relieved they had finally reached a city where she might bathe, but more important, where Raphael might learn the whereabouts of the man with the Crystal Dagger.

A well-trodden path led down into the city. She and Lucy followed Raphael, and Zayed brought up the rear. They stopped first at the *fonduq*, where the caravans halted to unload goods, take on supplies, and exchange or refresh the animals. Leaving their camels, they took only their personal items and set out on foot. Raphael led them through an arched gate into the *medina*, the ancient, walled part of Fès. As soon as they had passed through the gate, they were forced to turn to the right to follow the street. Raphael explained that the gate had been built that way for protection and to control access into the city. The wide street before them disappeared into a confusion of people and walls. Coffee shops and vendors selling food lined both sides. Raphael didn't follow it far. He paused to warn them to stay close so they wouldn't get lost, and he soon turned off into a smaller alley. This appeared more like a tunnel with the buildings connected overhead. Here, more people crowded the narrow space between the walls. Some were haggling with the shop owners, some were strolling, others hurried along to their destinations. Brightly colored and intricately patterned rugs for sale covered every available inch of space, some of the carpets hanging four or five deep. They turned again into another alley, open to the sky, which snaked between stalls where camel and goat meat was sold. Painted signs with pictures of the animals hung above the large, open windows with wide counters where the meat was butchered. Sydney and Lucy pulled scarves across their mouths and noses to keep out the flies and the smell. Farther along, baskets were mounded with dates, nuts, fruits, and vegetables. Colorful spices and herbs were displayed in wooden bowls.

Another turn and they entered an even narrower alley, this time covered over with lattice to diffuse the rays of the sun. As they wove their way through the throng, Sydney and Lucy gawked at the wares. Here was the *souk* that sold everything one might need to make clothing—rainbow-hued spools of thread displayed on a rack that looked like a fanciful porcupine, sacks of dye in vivid shades, bolts of cloth—from inexpensive, roughly woven wools and linens to smooth silks in vibrant jewel tones.

The alley opened suddenly into a square, bright and hot with sunshine. A fountain, built into one wall and decorated with a blue and green mosaic, flowed with water. Three other alleys branched off in different directions. One of them was the metal *souk*, where large, round serving trays, intricately etched teapots with long spouts, cooking pots topped by tall conical lids, knives, and utensils could be found. Another led into the leather *souk*. Sydney caught a glimpse of delicate slippers decorated with beads or painted with gold, studded and plain harnesses, saddles, pouches, and various other leather goods. The third branch was even narrower than the one they had just traversed and seemed to disappear into darkness. No goods were displayed, but rather bare walls and closed doors characterized this alley. The Pirate led them down that one.

"Mr. Pirate," Sydney called, a bit apprehensive about the gloomy alley. "Where are you taking us?"

Lucy edged closer and gripped Sydney's hand.

"To civilization, Miss Whelton," he called back over his shoulder.

Sydney exchanged a glance with Lucy as they hurried after him. They didn't want to get lost.

After a few minutes, he stopped and knocked on a nondescript door, wooden with a simple, curved design carved around its perimeter. Sydney realized the entrance was actually two narrow doors that met in the middle of the opening. The doors swung wide, and a wizened little man appeared. His eyes widened and he exclaimed, "*Sidi* Raphael!" then bowed deeply. He and Raphael exchanged some words, and then the old man ushered them inside.

Sydney had learned enough on her travels to know that the term *sidi* was an appellation of respect in Morocco. Bemused at the greeting, she exchanged a glance with Lucy, who also seemed surprised, then followed Raphael across the threshold. Zayed brought up the rear.

Like the gate into the city, a blank wall faced them as soon as they stepped across the threshold. With a turn to the right, they walked through a short, dark hallway to emerge into a high-ceilinged reception room at least two stories high. A giant, open metalwork lamp hung on a long chain from the ceiling that was decorated with deep blue mosaic tiles. Platforms covered in lush pillows and cushions ran around the perimeter for seating. The floor was an intricate mosaic of flowers and swirls of color. Archways made up one wall, and beyond it was a courtyard garden overflowing with flowers and fruit trees. In the center, a small fountain splashed. The beauty of the interior took her breath, especially compared with the dark, congested alleys they had followed to get here.

After a short conversation with the old man, the Pirate said, "A rug merchant named Abd Al-Karim lives here. He is away on a trip to buy merchandise. We will stay here while I make inquiries about the man you seek with the dagger made of crystal." He indicated the wizened little man. "Hamza will show you to the women's quarters and provide anything you might need. He speaks some English, so will help you with introductions to the wife of Abd Al-Karim and her daughters."

Awed by the opulence of the house, Sydney murmured, "Thank you." She couldn't find anything else to say.

Hamza bowed and led Sydney and Lucy up a set of stairs that was hidden behind one of the walls. They emerged onto a balcony that ran around the four walls surrounding the courtyard. They climbed to the third floor with its own balcony, but this one had screens of carved wood across the archways that looked down on the courtyard. Standing behind it, Sydney could see the flowers, bushes, and mosaic paths below, but no one looking up would see her.

A middle-aged woman appeared at the end of the gallery. She wore the traditional kaftan, but it was of an expensive silk and beaded down the front. Her salt-and-pepper hair was covered by a gauzy veil.

She bowed, touching her fingers to her heart, her lips, and her forehead, and murmured a few words.

Hamza translated. "The wife of Abd Al-Karim bids you welcome, mistresses, and invites you to refresh yourselves in the bath below. She regrets her husband is not here to greet you but knows that *Sidi* Raphael will supply all that you need. He is most generous."

Confused by the woman's reference to Raphael, Sydney watched the wife of Abd Al-Karim bow and retreat back behind a closed door. She caught a glimpse of two girls, both perhaps in their mid-teens. Hamza gave a clap and a sharp command, and another woman appeared. She was dressed in a simpler kaftan of plain linen.

Hamza said, "This is Anisah. She will see to your needs." With another bow, he withdrew.

Anisah led Sydney and Lucy to a room with sleeping pallets, each in its own alcove. She motioned for them to leave their belongings and beckoned them to follow her. They went downstairs and out a small door to the back of the house. A short path paved with flat stones ended at a small building. Anisah pushed open the door to a bathhouse, where a sunken tile pool beckoned. The sun shone through an opening in the roof and sparkled on the water. With hand gestures, she indicated they should undress and sit on one of the benches that lined the walls, then she withdrew.

Sydney and Lucy stared at each other in surprise.

"A bath, Syd," Lucy said, and gleefully tossed off her clothes.

As Sydney followed more slowly, she said, "I wonder how the Pirate became acquainted with the man who owns this house. He seems to be well-known here."

With a shrug, Lucy kicked off her unmentionables and stepped down into the pool.

"Didn't she want us to sit on a bench?" Sydney asked.

Anisah came back in, and with angry words, motioned for Lucy to get out of the pool. Another woman, dressed in the same plain kaftan, entered after her. Both women carried a bucket and a basket overflowing with sponges, brushes, pots of soap and other bathing supplies. With abrupt motions, Anisah pointed to two of the benches and indicated they were to lie down. Sydney and Lucy complied. The two women proceeded to massage oil into their hair, then scrubbed them all over with a black soap that had a fresh scent, a bit like olives. They sluiced off the soap with buckets of water. When they were done, Anisah indicated they were to go into the pool.

Sydney stepped into the luxuriously warm water. As she floated about, she watched Anisah lay out two kaftans in soft, white linen and beautifully decorated with elaborate, multi-colored embroidery at the hem, cuffs and neckline. After placing thick linen towels at the pool edge, the two servants left.

Sydney had never felt more relaxed. All the strain of traveling leached from her muscles. Glancing over at Lucy, she saw her friend leaning against the side of the pool with her eyes closed and a small smile on her lips. They were being treated like special guests. Sidney glanced at the kaftans, beautiful, costly garments. Were all guests treated in such a fashion? While she certainly appreciated the hospitality, she wondered at the generosity of the lady of the house. The manner in which Raphael had been greeted and the remark the wife of Abd Al-Karim made about Raphael's generosity kept popping into her head, as if the household were somehow subservient to him. But she couldn't get her brain to grasp it. Perhaps later, when she didn't feel like a limp rag.

The following morning, Sydney searched through the house for Raphael. After their amazing bath the previous afternoon, she and Lucy had napped, then eaten a delicious meal by themselves on the roof of the house. They had watched the sun go down and torches lit, looking like fireflies within the dark alleys, then had retired. Sleeping in a house on a comfortable pallet felt like a luxury after spending weeks sleeping on the hard ground under the stars. Sydney had been awakened by the delicious smell of a pancake-like pastry and mint tea, which had been left on a table by her bed.

After dressing in the lovely kaftan she'd been given after the bath, she set out to find Raphael. She hadn't seen him since they had arrived, and she wanted to be sure he was making inquiries about the man with the Crystal Dagger. She found him in deep conversation with Hamza in a small room off the courtyard. The two men sat on cushions on the floor around a low table strewn with papers.

"Miss Whelton," Raphael greeted her. "Is there something that you need?"

As she stepped across the threshold, Hamza rose quickly, and a chilly look of disapproval crossed his face that was quickly replaced with stoic blandness. Sydney sensed she was intruding where she should not, but her need to find the man she was seeking outweighed the trespass of any rule of etiquette.

"I wish to speak to you," she said, "but I haven't seen you since we arrived."

Raphael spoke a few words to Hamza, who bowed and left. Leaning back on an elbow, he gazed up at her with those golden eyes. He looked like a contented jungle cat.

"I am at your disposal, Miss Whelton. What would you like to speak about?"

His gaze, direct and cool, disconcerted her. Something about his manner was different from when he was out in the desert. In the wilderness, he seemed more approachable, despite the aura of danger that surrounded him. Here, within the city, in the confines of the house, during his interactions with Hamza, he reminded her of an English lord on his estate. What had been nagging her since their arrival suddenly struck her. The words that the wife of Abd Al-Karim had spoken made sense.

"This is your house!" Her exclamation sounded more like an accusation.

He raised a single, cool brow. "Does that matter?"

"Well, no." Her thoughts were in turmoil. "But—but you're the Pirate!"

His lips twitched. "I am. A scoundrel's name, don't you think? I rather like it."

Suspicion that she had been duped edged through her. "Are you truly the Pirate?"

A chill entered his gaze. "Do not think because this house is comfortable that I am anything but what I say I am."

At that moment, he *was* the Pirate, all steel and hard edges. Embarrassed at doubting him, she turned defensive. "You didn't have to hide it." Her words gained momentum as she spoke. "Did you think that if I knew you were wealthy, my opinion of you would change?"

Heat entered his eyes. "And what is your opinion, Miss Whelton?" He rose in a single fluid motion and stepped around the table.

Sydney's eyes widened at his approach. His manner wasn't threatening exactly, but something about him made her wary. She fell back a step. What *was* her opinion? He was the handsomest man she had ever met. He smelled divine. His kisses made her toes curl and her insides throb. But she couldn't say that. Instead, she faltered, "I think…I think…you are quite…um…quite able to defend yourself."

"I have been known to defend myself on occasion," he said, his tone solemn. "Do I have to defend myself from you, Miss Whelton?"

She shook her head vehemently. "Oh, no. You are safe with me."

He stepped closer. "Would you like to know my opinion of you, Sydney-Who-Is-Not-A-Boy?"

She shook her head in the negative, then hesitated and gave a wordless nod.

"I think…" His words trailed off as he brushed a stray strand of hair from her cheek. "I think…" His fingers traced along her jaw. "I think…" His thumb landed at the corner of her mouth. "I think you are the most kissable woman I have ever met."

Sydney's lips parted in a tiny gasp.

His mouth replaced his thumb with a tiny butterfly kiss. Then he did the same to the opposite corner of her lips. Her eyes slipped closed.

"I find your mouth fascinating, Sydney Charlotte Whelton," he whispered. "Do you mind if I kiss it?"

She drew in a breath. "Um…" Her mind went blank.

"*Choukran*," he murmured. "That means *thank you*."

"Oh."

"Perfect," he said against her lips.

His hand slipped around to the back of her head, while his tongue traced the outline of her mouth.

Sydney was captured. All her concentration centered around what he was doing. He nibbled at her bottom lip, placed other kisses at the corners of her mouth, then he took complete possession. She swayed against him, her equilibrium gone in the dizzying heat of his kiss and wrapped her arms around him. She needed to hold on. Flattening her hands against the hard muscles of his back, she marveled at the perfection of him — the flat planes, the ridges of his spine, the smooth slope to his waist. But that was a delectable backdrop to what he was doing to her mouth. When his tongue probed between her lips, she welcomed him in.

His arms wrapped around her, drawing her closer. But not close enough. She wriggled to get even closer. His hardness pressed against her belly. She throbbed, wanting more. A whimper of need escaped her.

His hand dipped between them and covered her breast, kneading, pinching, eliciting an answering pulse deep within her. Sydney had never felt anything so exciting. This was so much better than the surprise kiss out in the desert, or even the agreed upon kiss inside the *kheterra,* which had been quite marvelous. How had she never known that kissing a man could be so delicious?

Raphael lost himself. Sydney's supple body pressed against him, teasing, tantalizing with her soft curves. Beneath the kaftan, she wore almost nothing, and he could feel every delightful swoop and dip of her body. She kissed him back with an ardor that fired his blood. What he had told her was true. She had the most kissable mouth of any woman he had ever had the pleasure of kissing. Her curves fit him perfectly. Her breast beneath his palm responded readily to his touch, its pert tip coiling into a tight bud. Standing thigh to thigh, the emptiness between her thighs begged to be filled. His hand slid down her back to her sweet bottom and tucked her closer. He wanted to explore all of her, touching, tasting, inhaling the scent of her until he could fill that empty space.

He left her mouth and trailed kisses across her jaw, down her neck, nuzzling the sensitive spot beneath her ear. A moan escaped her. Smiling at her passionate response, he licked at her pulse, once, twice, again, and a fourth time.

Lost in the moment, in the taste of her, he wasn't aware when the change happened. He suddenly felt himself falling for the space of a breath. And then he was someplace else. Somewhere he had never been, yet somehow familiar.

Abruptly, he knew. He was inside her head.

He froze, paralyzed by shock. This had never happened before.

Sydney gasped and stiffened.

"What are you doing?" she demanded, her tone taut with fear.

He floundered for a moment, trying to get his bearings. Her lovely body in his arms grounded him. In that instant, he felt as though they were nearly one entity, yet at the same time separate. The experience was astonishing, awe-inspiring. Her mind was a sublime place, filled with sparkly lights and gossamer wisps. Warmth spread over him, as if he had been welcomed and enveloped in a soft blanket.

I've touched your mind, he said silently. *It is beautiful.*

He sensed her pleasure at his compliment, but at the same time, felt her discomfort at his intrusion. He wanted to stay where he was, in comfort and peace, but he shouldn't. He invaded where he had not been invited.

"Please, don't," she said.

With a final light kiss against her pulse, he slowly withdrew. He missed the connection as soon as it was broken. He wanted more of that—knowing her mind, her desires and her fears. He wanted it as much as possessing her body, although the feel of her lovely curves in his arms was luscious.

She stared up at him with wide eyes. "What are you, that you can enter my mind?"

With a wry twist to his lips, he said, "Merely a man with a curse."

As she slipped from his embrace, she shook her head. "More than that." Fear turned her cheeks pale.

His arms felt bereft when she stepped away, and he missed the touch of her mind, even though it had been brief. But the power to do that befuddled him. This was an ability he hadn't known he possessed. He needed to ponder it, talk to Zayed about it before he admitted to the woman before him that what he had done was an accident. Even though he had shared his curse with her, he wasn't ready to open himself up completely. He'd lived too long protecting his secret and hiding his innermost feelings.

"I am neither more nor less than what you know of me, Miss Whelton," he said, using the formal mode of address to put some distance between them. Invading her mind had brought them too close too soon.

Her eyes narrowed at his cool tone, and a bit of color returned to her cheeks. "I believe you are much more than what you appear, Mr. Pirate."

He was not about to share anything else. He'd already revealed too much. With a forced smile, he returned to his cushions. "Was there something in particular you wanted to ask me, or did you come to visit merely for a kiss?"

High color spread across her cheeks. She glanced away, licked her lips, then turned back to him. After taking a breath, she said, "I would like to explore and see the sights of the city, and I was wondering if you could give me directions to interesting places."

"No." His abrupt response came from an overwhelming desire not to see her in any danger. The *medina* was a maze, and she could easily become lost. While people crowded the *souks*, many alleys within the city were empty and dark, perfect places for evil to attack her. After seeing her assaulted by the outlaws in the desert, he did not want to feel that terrible fear in his gut again.

"I beg your pardon?" The color in her cheeks darkened.

"You will not be roaming the *medina* on your own, Miss Whelton." He shuffled a few of the papers on the table before him, pretending to be busy.

"May I ask why?" Her voice wavered as if her temper were about to fly out of control.

He glanced up. She appeared recovered from his entry into her mind. Her eyes sparked and her chin was at a rebellious angle. She was magnificent in her anger. What would she be like in the throes of passion? Already aroused from their kiss, he found he could barely suppress the desire to spring from his seat and drag her onto the cushions, where he could make glorious, wild love to her.

He forced his gaze back to the papers, but he didn't see them. Only those changeable eyes, now a dark green.

He kept his tone even and impersonal despite wanting to shout that he didn't want any harm to come to her. "Because you will get lost in the maze of the city, and it is not the custom here for women to wander about by themselves. They rarely leave their houses, and when they do, they are accompanied by a servant."

A heartbeat of silence came from her. "Oh, I see." Her words were muted, as if she were very disappointed.

Without looking up, he said, "I will speak with Zayed. Perhaps he might be inclined to show you about."

"That would be very kind of you," she said coolly. "Thank you." She paused, then added, "I'm sorry I disturbed you."

Without another word, she turned and left. Raphael glanced up in time to see the hem of her kaftan as she disappeared out the door. The room, which he had always found so comfortable and inviting, seemed cold and formal without her presence. He sighed.

What was he going to do about her? She was becoming much too important to him. After he found the man with the dagger of crystal, she would leave to complete the task she had set for herself — to assassinate the sorceress who had killed her father. He would be left behind to wonder if she accomplished it, if she were safe, if she returned to her home in England. And then he would wonder if she found a man to wed who would be her partner for life.

He pushed around the papers before him without seeing them. He had to stop kissing her. She was much too dangerous to his existence. He'd worked very hard to become the Pirate, a man with few vulnerabilities, and certainly no emotional ties to anyone except Zayed, especially no woman.

One beautiful, stubborn, brave woman would not disrupt his life. He would keep his distance from her. No more teasing to see the color rise in her cheeks, no more touching to feel her silky skin beneath his fingers or that intriguing tingle, and certainly no more kissing that most delicious mouth and falling into her astonishing mind.

As he had agreed, he would make inquiries about the man with the dagger of crystal. Zayed could guide the women through the city, and his friend could deal with any other requests they might have. With his decision made, Raphael finally focused on the reports and tallies Hamza had put before him.

But the memory of her beautiful mind and her luscious mouth remained with him.

Chapter 14

The next day, Sydney hurried through the *medina*. The sun was going down and soon the maze of alleys would be in inky darkness. Only a lamp here and there from a merchant who was late shutting his shop, or a torch lighting the entrance to a house, flickered in the gloom. Far above her head, the thin strip of visible sky between the flat roofs of the houses was fast turning from pale blue to indigo. The cramped, dim passages that twisted off to the sides were nearly pitch black. Everyone was at home behind the plain wooden doors of their houses, so the narrow alleys were deserted.

Zayed had taken her and Lucy and the two daughters of the house out into the *medina* to explore and shop. The two girls, around fourteen or fifteen years of age, were quiet young ladies except when they saw something they wished to buy. Then they haggled and bargained until both they and the shopkeeper were satisfied with the price. They strolled through the *souks*, each selling various wares. Extravagant gold jewelry was sold in one that blended into another that sold metal objects of silver and brass. Women selling cloth and slippers of colored felt stood next to another *souk* selling *djellabas,* which were long robes with pointed hoods, and kaftans, some plain wool or linen, others of brightly colored silk with intricate decoration of embroidery and even jewels. The pottery *souk* was lined with plates hanging from its walls and tables chock full of jars and bowls in a multi-colored array.

Somehow, Sydney had become separated from the others in the henna *souk* where she had become fascinated by the tiny painted pots, scented candles and other implements needed for the beautiful swirling designs with which women decorated their hands and feet. She had called to Lucy that she wanted to look more closely, but evidently Lucy hadn't heard. By the time she had seen her fill and stepped from the *souk*, Zayed and Lucy and the two girls had disappeared. She doubted that Zayed or Lucy had noticed she was missing until some time had passed because the streets were crowded with shoppers and people stopping to chat or wandering from here to there.

Everyone would be worried. Well, perhaps not the Pirate. He would be annoyed. She had avoided him since their kiss the day before, both because of the kiss, which was the most arousing thing she had ever experienced, and because of his connection to her mind, which was rather unsettling. While she would like him to kiss her again, she did not want him in her head, seeing her thoughts and secrets. That ability frightened her. Why, he might discover how she yearned for his kisses, and perhaps for something more than kisses. That would never do. But she would confront that fear when she returned to his house. The trip through the *medina* with Lucy and the others had been a welcome distraction from sorting out her feelings about him.

Now, apprehension filled her as she tried to find her way through the twisting alleys. Would she ever find her way back? She felt as if she were going around in circles. She had seen that apothecary shop before. She had asked directions to the house of the Pirate — Al Qarsan — but no one seemed to know him, or they responded in their own language which she didn't understand. Adding to her trepidation was a sense that she was being followed. When she threw glances over her shoulder, she saw that the crowd that had clogged the streets earlier had thinned, but no one seemed focused on her. Still, the skin between her shoulder blades tickled, as if someone dragged a feather across her back.

She came to a small square where three alleys met. She remembered walking through the square, but from which street? A small water fountain against one wall trickled water. Across from her, the large bronze door of a mosque shone dully in the dwindling light. This was the *souk* where anything made of metal could be purchased. When she had passed through earlier, copper, brass, and silver plates and trays had been hung on open doors, multi-tiered serving dishes and bowls with conical covers had been displayed in a jumble on the tile-covered ground, and intricate metal-work lamps dangled from the ceiling. In other shops, knives of different lengths and shapes hung in rows on the walls and doors, and the sound of the grind-stone sharpening blades provided a background noise to merchants and buyers haggling over the price of goods. But now, the wares were taken in, and the doors shut and locked. No one was around to ask directions.

Sydney scanned the square as she tried to get her bearings. Had the fountain been on her right or left? She did not remember the bronze door of the mosque, for it was recessed in the wall and she hadn't seen it when she passed through before. A sliver of panic slid through her. Which way?

Coming to a decision, she headed down the left alley. It seemed a bit brighter, since no covering had been placed across the top between the buildings for protection from the heat. But as she hurried between the closed shops, the sun dipped below the horizon and dark settled into the alley. The sense of being followed lifted, and she breathed a bit easier.

Abruptly, a robed figure appeared in front of her, a heavy cowl dipping low across its brow, shadowing its face. A dull, eerie, green glow surrounded the figure, chilling and menacing. Sydney froze. Her heart raced. She dared not move. Summoning her magic, she slipped her hand behind her back to hide it. She wasn't about to reveal her power unless she needed it.

"Are you lost, little one?" a woman's voice asked. The question sounded sincere, but a hint of threat wound through the words.

"I'm on my way home," Sydney declared with more certainty than she felt.

"Ah," the woman said, and stepped closer. "I won't keep you, then, but I did want to meet you."

The woman pushed back her cowl, and within the glow surrounding her, Sydney saw she was beautiful with creamy skin and ruby lips. An abundance of dark, curly hair tumbled about her shoulders. Sydney had never encountered anyone so perfect, but a shiver of fear ran down her spine. Despite the woman's beauty, she sensed a *wrongness* about her, as if she were slightly out of focus.

"Were you following me?" Sydney asked. The woman seemed familiar, but she couldn't remember where or when she might have met her. Besides, in the twilight, with the glow emanating from the woman, it was difficult to see her clearly.

The woman gave a light laugh. "No, of course not. I knew where you were."

Sydney frowned, that shiver of fear turning into an urge to run. But something compelled her to remain. "I don't understand. How could you know where I was?"

The woman waved away the question. "That does not matter. I wished to meet you because I think we might work well together."

Even more sure that she should flee, Sydney shook her head. "I don't—"

Before she could finish, another figure suddenly stepped between them and faced the woman. This person was dressed in a full-length, light-colored *djellaba* with the pointed hood pulled up, a red tassel swinging from its point. The garment was worn and stained.

"Get away from her, you hag," a man's voice said.

Stunned, Sydney watched the woman's face contort in hatred.

"You can do nothing to me," the woman sneered. "You're nothing more than an insect I can crush beneath my foot."

He pulled something from beneath his *djellaba* that seemed to glow in different colors. The woman reared back with a growl.

"You know what this dagger will do to you," he said. "I'm not going to waste my time on an apparition, but I'll use it if I have to. You'll still feel its pain."

"We're not finished, whelp," the woman spat. Then she disappeared in a snap of air.

The spot in the alley where she had stood dropped into blackness, except for the dull pulse of light from the man's weapon.

Sydney felt as if she had been released from a thousand strings. She reached for the wall next to her to keep herself upright. Questions swirled through her head, but she couldn't pull even one from the maelstrom to voice it.

The man turned to her and pushed back his hood. "Did she harm you?"

She saw a man with dirty, tangled, shoulder-length, blond hair. A scruffy beard covered his jaw. The rest of his face was darkened by the sun. But his eyes, even in the dim glow reflected from his weapon, were arresting — the color of turquoise. His accent was French.

"No, I'm unhurt. Thank you," Sydney forced from a tight throat. Still trying to slow her racing pulse, she asked, "Who was that?"

The man's voice dropped to a deep growl, filled with loathing. "An evil sorceress. Nulkana."

The name nearly sent her to her knees. She was glad she still leaned against the wall. Nulkana, she thought, the creature from Stonehenge who had killed her father. The memory of that battle fought between the sorceress and her father and the man who called on the elements still made her squeeze her eyes shut and cover her ears. But the sorceress had looked different during that battle, larger than life, horrific in her fury and evil, less than human. The malevolence that Nulkana had unleashed that night made Sydney tremble. In contrast, the woman who had stood before her in the alley had been alluring and beautiful.

Sydney's gaze dropped to the glowing weapon still in the man's hand. A dagger of crystal that pulsed slowly in different colors.

She gasped. "You're the man with the Crystal Dagger!" She had found him!

He glanced down as if he had forgotten he still held it. "Yes, I am." His hand dropped to his side, and he nestled the dagger within a fold of his *djellaba*. Its light shifted and dimmed.

Bemused at finding the very man for whom she'd been searching standing before her, she said, "But you were supposed to be in Egypt with Napoleon's army."

Suspicion narrowed his eyes. "Was I?" He gave a shrug. "Evidently, I'm not."

"Why are you in Morocco?" Even as she asked the question, she knew he would not answer.

He studied her a moment. "Why are *you* in Morocco?"

She sighed. "That's a long story."

He said nothing, allowing her answer to be his.

"I've been searching for you," she said.

His gaze became even more suspicious. "Have you? Why is that?"

"I want to hire you," she said.

He shook his head. "Sorry, I'm not for hire."

Disappointment plunged through her. She had traveled far to find this man, and now he refused her. "Please. You're the only one who can help me." She took a step forward in her desperation.

He stepped back. "Surely not."

"The Crystal Dagger is the only weapon that will kill her," she said, trying to convince him.

"You want me to murder someone?" Disbelief and affront crossed his face, as if he didn't know whom she spoke about. "I'm not an assassin." To prove his point, he slid the dagger into a sheath that hung at the end of a braided red cord that crossed his body from shoulder to hip.

Despite his denial, Sydney saw something dark flash through his eyes. He was lying, hiding something.

"Not just anyone," she said. "I want you to use your Crystal Dagger to kill Nulkana."

He stared for a moment. The corner of his mouth twitched, as if he found something mildly humorous in her statement, then he glanced away. "No."

Taken aback by his abrupt retort, she pleaded, "Please, she killed my father."

"You have my condolences," he said, "but I'm not killing anyone."

She knew something about the Crystal Dagger. It was created long ago by the Legion of Baal to put an end to Nulkana, but it had a flaw. Only a descendant of Halima, Nulkana's good sister, could endow it with the power to terminate the evil sorceress. But by taking possession of the Dagger, that descendant was filled with an overwhelming desire to kill. The man standing before her was that descendant, most likely a good man, but he must have been tortured by holding the Dagger.

In a flash of insight, she said, "You've killed before."

He remained silent. His mouth flattened and his eyes turned stony.

"You want to kill Nulkana, don't you?" she pressed.

Anger twisted his features. "You know nothing about me."

"I know more than you think," she said, gentling her tone. "You saved me from Nulkana a moment ago. You hate her."

He took a menacing step forward. "Don't—" Stopping abruptly, he shook his head as if to clear it. His jaw clenched and he glanced away. His hand closed around the hilt of the Dagger. When he looked at her again, his expression had become placid, as if they had only been discussing the weather. "You shouldn't be out alone. Where do you live? I'll take you home."

Should she trust him? He had gripped the Dagger like he would pull it from its sheath and stab her, but he had fought down whatever demonic thrall had gripped him. He could have easily ended her life at that moment, especially since the alley in which they stood was deserted. Instead, he offered to guide her to safety. She knew nothing about him except that he carried the Crystal Dagger. He could be the worst sort of brigand. His disreputable appearance certainly suggested that he lived a hard life. He could be leading her into terrible danger. But something about him made her think that he would, indeed, see her to the house of Abd Al-Karim. Besides, now that she had found him, she was not about to let him disappear.

She told him where she was headed.

In the time they had been talking, twilight had given way to night. He sent a stream of energy at a dark torch stuck in a wall bracket, and it burst into a flame. That feat of magic convinced her more strongly that her search had not been in vain. Of course, the man had power that went beyond what the Crystal Dagger brought. He was a descendant of Halima, so he had magic of his own, perfect for bringing down Nulkana and finding revenge for her father's death. She still had the time on their walk back to the rug merchant's *riad* to gain his trust and convince him to fall in with her plan. As soon as she had a plan.

He turned back toward the small square and the metal *souk*. He knew the way or seemed to. She had no idea how. Having taken the wrong alley, she probably would have been wandering the *medina* all night. Relieved, she fell in beside him.

Despite her success at finding the man with the Crystal Dagger, she felt a sense of impending loss. The task for which she had hired Raphael was complete. He would most likely leave to return to the Tuareg camp. The thought caused a painful wrench in the vicinity of her heart.

No more teasing.

No more tingles when he touched her.

No more kisses.

She would miss those kisses. She had wanted to learn more about them.

But most of all, she would miss *him*.

The sight of him. The sound of his voice. The scent of him when he was near.

But she had a task to complete.

And their paths diverged now.

She swallowed down the lump in her throat and followed the man with the Crystal Dagger.

They walked through the alleys in silence. Sydney tried to question the man about how long he had been in Fès, or why he had left Napoleon, but his answers were evasive and terse, so Sydney gave up despite her curiosity about him. When they arrived at the rug merchant's house and Hamza opened the door, he gave her a look filled with both relief and reprimand, and denied entrance to her rescuer, but Sydney finally convinced Hamza to let him in. With a stiff bow, Hamza relented, ushering them to the courtyard. The house was unnaturally silent, and Sydney suspected it had something to do with her disappearance. When she entered the courtyard, Lucy rushed to her.

"Oh, Sydney! Thank the Lord you're safe!" Tears streamed down Lucy's cheeks as she wrapped Sydney in a hug.

"Of course, I'm safe," Sydney said as she patted Lucy's back. "I got turned around a bit."

"He's in a rage," Lucy whispered as she stepped back.

Sydney knew exactly who *he* was. Glancing beyond Lucy, she saw the Pirate standing at the far end of the courtyard with his arms crossed at his chest and glowering at her. Zayed, with a worried crease between his brows, stood beside him. At Sydney's appearance,

Zayed's worried frown disappeared, he gave a short nod, and melted into the shadows. So. She was to be left alone with Raphael.

She gulped. "It's all right, Lucy. I'll speak with him."

Concern crossed her friend's face. "I'll come with you."

Sydney took another peek at the other end of the courtyard. "No, I'll be fine." At least, she hoped she'd be fine. The Pirate looked ready to devour her.

Lucy, looking beyond Sydney's shoulder, whispered, "Who is that man with you?"

Sydney smiled. "It's the man with the Crystal Dagger, Luce," she whispered back. "I found him! Or rather, he found me." She glanced back to where he stood, hanging back beyond the entrance to the courtyard. "Would you stay with him while I..." She silently indicated Raphael.

At Lucy's nod, Sydney straightened her shoulders and walked across the courtyard. Raphael didn't budge an inch as she approached. When she stood before him, he glared, and a muscle jumped in his jaw.

"I'm sorry I caused an upset," she said.

"Where have you been?" he growled. "Zayed and I have been out searching for you. We have just come back to see if you had returned."

"I got separated from Zayed and the others," she said, contrite. "I was in the henna *souk*, and when I turned to leave, everyone had gone. I couldn't find them."

A vein pulsed in his temple. "Zayed blames himself for losing you. He thought you might have been taken by Al Jabbar."

"Al Jabbar?" She thought he had disappeared into the desert.

"He has been seen in the city." Raphael's flat tone indicated he wasn't pleased.

"Has he?" Sydney wanted to confront Al Jabbar. She had hired him for protection against Nulkana, but he had abandoned her in the desert. If he were here, perhaps he hadn't abandoned her after all.

Raphael's eyes narrowed, as if he suspected she was already plotting something. "Did he contact you?"

Something about the way he asked made her think that he had been very concerned about her getting lost. "No, of course not." She was very glad she could be truthful, at least about that. "I was perfectly safe," she lied, ignoring the danger of coming face to face with Nulkana.

He stared for a moment, studying her, as if trying to decide something. Without warning, he stepped closer, cupped her face and kissed her. Shock paralyzed her. But his mouth sent waves of delicious turmoil washing through her. One part of her wondered how he could be so angry and still want to kiss her. The other part didn't care. She leaned into him. His hands, his lips, his tongue made tingles skitter across her skin. Her nipples strained against her clothes. This man's kisses created the most magnificent sensations she had ever experienced.

A tittering laugh from behind the wooden-screened gallery above the courtyard reached her ears. The girls of the household. Abruptly, Raphael stepped back, leaving Sydney dazzled and swaying off balance. His eyes closed for a second and he swallowed. When he opened them again, his gaze was as cool as if they had merely exchanged pleasantries about the weather.

"I am relieved you are back," he said, his tone as impassive as his gaze.

Reeling from the kiss and his detached observation, as well as her own tangled emotions, Sydney blinked as she attempted to dampen her arousal. A twinge of something painful shot through her at his sudden reserve. She stiffened her spine. If he could be unaffected by such a kiss, then so could she.

"This gentleman helped me find my way." She indicated the man who had chased away Nulkana.

He was standing unobtrusively beneath an orange tree and looking like he wished to disappear into the foliage. When Sydney waved him forward, he glanced first at Lucy who hovered nearby. After her friend nodded encouragement, he approached. Stopping before Raphael, he bowed elegantly, as if he were at a French salon.

"Gide Delacroix, *monsieur*," he said. "At your service."

Sydney announced, "This is the man with the Crystal Dagger."

Dumbfounded by her announcement, Raphael studied the man before him. A hundred thoughts raced through his brain. Uppermost was the kiss he had just bestowed on the most aggravating, bewitching woman he had ever had the misfortune to meet. He had no idea why he had kissed her except he was so damned relieved to see her alive and in one piece that he needed to feel her mouth against his. That had been a mistake. His arousal raged, and he fought to control it and keep his hands off her.

He had envisioned all sorts of terrible things happening to her. But she had turned up looking as cool as if she was returning from an afternoon stroll. His concern had been unfounded. He was angry with himself for worrying and angry that his body had responded immediately to the sight of her, the feel of her, the scent of her. As soon as his mouth covered her lips, he wanted to drag her off to one of the upstairs chambers and make love to her for the rest of the night. Fortunately, one of the girls up on the gallery saw them kissing. That titter had slammed him back to reality. And made him angrier that he had lost himself in her.

Besides that, she had found the man whom she had hired *him* to find. That meant she no longer needed him. Both of those things annoyed him for a number of reasons, which he was not about to examine. Instead, he turned his attention to the man before him.

Gide Delacroix. The man looked as if he had seen better days. His cheeks were hollow from hunger, and his *djellaba* was filthy and ragged. From his poor condition, Raphael would have expected him to be dispirited, but instead, he met Raphael's gaze squarely. His eyes were like twin stones, hard and hiding deep secrets despite their unusual color. From his bow, he revealed he had obviously been familiar with European society. Sydney said the man could be found in the east with the French general, Napoleon. Why, then, was he in Morocco and looking like a beggar? Other questions rose in his mind, but he sensed the man would reveal only what he wished others to know and only in his own time. Raphael understood that reticence. He kept his own secrets.

"Miss Whelton has been searching for you," Raphael said. "I have been helping in her search. We came to Fès to make inquiries, since it was the closest city. She told me you would be found in the east."

A tiny smile curved Delacroix's lips. "*Oui.* She said as much. I was in the east at one time. I am no longer." He made a small bow in her direction. "Miss Whelton, I am happy to make your acquaintance." Turning back to Raphael, he explained, "We did not exchange names when we met. We were—ah—distracted."

Raphael did not like the sound of that at all. If she were kissing other men—this man … He scowled at Sydney. "Distracted?"

Delacroix huffed a laugh and sent a sideways glance at Sydney. "Not what you think, *monsieur.* The sorceress, Nulkana, paid Miss Whelton a visit. It was fortunate that I was nearby and able to help."

At the name of the sorceress, the amulet hanging against Raphael's chest pulsed hot, then returned to normal. The jolt nearly rocked him back, and he pressed his hand against it. Not wanting to reveal anything to the man before him, he pretended nothing was amiss and forced himself to concentrate on the conversation.

"You were the one following me," Sydney burst out.

Delacroix gave an amused shrug. "For one such as myself with unusual abilities, your magic shines from you like a beacon, *mademoiselle.* I could not help myself. I had to meet the lady who carried such power."

Raphael was having trouble processing everything. The man with the Crystal Dagger standing before him. Nulkana, the sorceress. The reaction of his amulet. And Sydney's magic shining from her? He glanced at her and saw nothing more than the woman who made his blood race through his veins. He had never seen her magic shining from her. Perhaps the man before him did have special abilities.

In order to give himself time, he said, "Perhaps you would care for refreshment? The evening meal is about to be served now that Miss Whelton has returned."

"That would be most welcome," Delacroix said with a small bow. "Thank you."

Raphael waved Delacroix toward one of the arches that led inside. As he passed Sydney, he murmured, "We will speak later."

He heard her huff of exasperation as she spun on her heel and went with Mrs. Foster to eat with the women. Smiling to himself that he had disconcerted her in return for disconcerting him, he escorted the man with the Crystal Dagger to the evening meal and to see if he could glean any information.

Late that night, unable to sleep, Raphael strolled through the garden as his thoughts churned. He had discovered some interesting details about the man with the Crystal Dagger—Gide Delacroix. After gaining the Dagger, an event which Delacroix refrained from describing, he had joined Napoleon, who took him to Egypt on his campaign there. Delacroix had become disenchanted with the general and had deserted, making his way across Northern Africa to end up in the city of Fès. Now, he was trying to return to France to find his sister. Besides the desire to return to his home, a dark desperation lay beneath every word he spoke, as if he had a great need that demanded fulfillment. It was a shadowy thing, like a monster that hid behind a thin veil. Raphael was not sure the man could be trusted, nor even that he was completely sane. When he inquired about the Crystal Dagger, Delacroix became secretive and defensive. And when Raphael wasn't looking at the man, he felt the Frenchman's gaze on him as if he were being studied.

He was not comfortable leaving Sydney with Delacroix. But now that she had found the man, his task was complete. He could return to his tent in the desert, to his life of raiding, smuggling, and guarding caravans. The idea did not sit well. Neither did the thought of remaining in his house in the *medina* of Fès.

Before he could come to a decision about the next phase of his life, he saw a small, slight figure sitting on a stone bench tucked into the foliage. Apparently, Sydney had not been able to sleep as well. He felt a leap of anticipation at the sight of her. She was dressed as a woman of Morocco in a loose kaftan of pale green silk and a veil of some filmy, white material draped over her head. She appeared deep in thought. He approached slowly, so as not to startle her.

"Miss Whelton," he said when he stood before her.

She raised her head, and the hint of a smile touched her lips. "Mr. Pirate," she greeted. "You are walking late."

"You are sitting late," he retorted.

She nodded in agreement. "Is this the 'later' that you mentioned when we would speak?"

"Not as late as this." Without asking permission, he sat beside her.

They were both silent. He could sense her waiting for him to say something. He was trying to find the words for what he wanted to say. His fumbling confused him, made him angry. He'd never had difficulty speaking his mind. This woman turned him into someone he didn't know, flustered, fumbling, uncertain.

"You've found the man with the Crystal Dagger," he finally said.

"Yes."

Her single word told him nothing. He forged on. "What will you do now?"

"I will find Nulkana and kill her." The words were defiant, but something doubtful ran beneath them.

"Will you? How will you do that?" He needed to challenge her, to discover what she had planned. For some reason, he wanted to be sure the odds of success were in her favor. Then he wondered why he cared, because he had never given a thought to others who had hired him after he had completed their tasks.

"The man with the Crystal Dagger will help me." She spoke as if there were no alternative.

After sharing a meal with Delacroix, Raphael was not sure the man would fall in so easily with Sydney's plan. "Have you asked him?"

She glanced away, and with that, Raphael knew she had been turned down.

When she turned back to him, she said, "I will convince him. He chased away the sorceress for me. I know he hates her."

"I think he is a dangerous man," he said, stating the obvious, but not saying what he really wished to say, that he did not want to leave her alone with Delacroix. He didn't want to leave her alone at all.

"Of course, he is," she said. "But you are a dangerous man, as well."

Startled at her observation, his brows rose. "Am I?" A trickle of pride squirmed through him that she should think such of him.

She gave a definitive nod. "Yes. So, I thought that I should have two dangerous men with me on my search for the sorceress."

Not sure he had heard correctly, he asked, "Are you extending our agreement, Miss Whelton?"

"Yes, I am." She looked down at her hands folded in her lap, then peeked at him from the corner of her eyes. "Will you come with me?"

Delighted that she wanted him to travel on with her, he smiled. He brushed a stray strand of hair away from her cheek and tucked it under her veil. Allowing his fingers to linger along her jaw, he murmured, "My price has gone up."

She stared into his eyes and swallowed, but her tone was business-like as she answered, "I will pay whatever it is."

By the tears of Allah, he wanted to kiss her into oblivion. Instead, he dropped his fingers. "I will think on it."

"A kiss?" she asked. "Like the last time?"

At her question, his insides jumped to respond. "Hm. Your kisses are delicious, Sydney-Who-Is-Not-A-Boy, but we are doing more this time than searching for someone. We are going to kill an evil sorceress. Perhaps you will offer a price that I might accept."

Confusion and apprehension entered her eyes. "I don't—"

He placed a finger across her lips. "Sh. We will discuss it later. Now, I think it is time to sleep, for tomorrow you must convince the man with the Crystal Dagger to travel with us."

She bowed her head and nodded. Then she looked up at him, her gaze defiant. "I will not go to your bed," she declared. "That is not a proper payment."

He nearly laughed in delight at the challenge presented by that declaration. Instead, he raised an innocent brow. "Did I mention such a thing? Ours is a business arrangement, Miss Whelton. You may offer what you wish, and I will decide if the price is enough."

Uncertainty crossed her face, and she looked like she might respond. Instead, with a tiny nod, she rose. "I bid you good night, Mr. Pirate," she said coolly.

"Pleasant dreams, Miss Whelton."

He watched her walk through the courtyard and disappear into the shadows of the interior of the house. Smiling, he gazed up at the moon. Miss Sydney Whelton could offer a copper penny and he would accept it, because no matter what, he would accompany her on this next leg of her journey. If Nulkana were truly the sorceress who haunted his dreams, then he wanted her gone. And so, his goal was Sydney's goal. Along the way, he would have the delightful Miss Whelton to tease and kiss. And perhaps change her mind about coming to his bed.

Feeling much more settled than when he entered the courtyard, he left to find his own sleep.

Chapter 15

The next morning, Sydney went to wake Lucy so they could breakfast together, but when she entered the alcove where Lucy slept, her
pallet was empty. Thinking her friend might be in the courtyard or
someplace else in the house, she searched for her. After looking all
over and asking the servants if they had seen her, Sydney became
concerned. Where could Lucy be? When she returned to the sleep
alcove, she realized Lucy's clothes were still folded neatly in a pile.
And her spectacles were placed on top.

Lucy was gone!

Panicking, Sydney grabbed Lucy's spectacles and raced down
the stairs to find Raphael. One of the servants told her he was in the
hammam, the bathhouse. Without thinking, she pushed through the
door, checked in the empty steam room, and stepped into the room
with the pool. He was lounging against the side with his head back,
his eyes closed, and his arms stretched out along the edge. At her
noisy entrance, he lazily opened one eye.

A smile curved his lips. "Miss Whelton! This is a surprise. Have
you come to join me?"

Sydney tried not to stare at his muscular chest, visible above the
water. Nor at the long, lean, naked length of him submerged beneath.
She clapped a hand over her eyes.

"I'm sorry to disturb you," she said, breathless, "but Lucy is missing."

She heard the splash of water as he stood.

"Missing?" he asked, all teasing gone from his voice. "What do
you mean *missing*?"

She peeked between her fingers. Yes, he was standing, thigh-
deep, the water sluicing off him. And nearly every glorious inch

of him was visible, including his man parts, which seemed, to her inexperienced gaze, very robust. She closed her eyes and gulped. This wasn't the time for such a distraction.

With a throat tight with emotion, she said, "I've looked all over for her. She left her spectacles."

She heard more splashing and his footsteps approaching.

"Are you sure you searched everywhere?" His voice rumbled from right in front of her.

She nodded, then said emphatically, "Yes. She wouldn't go anywhere without her spectacles. She can barely see without them."

He sighed. "Speaking of seeing...Miss Whelton—Sydney—I can't hold a conversation with you if you won't look at me."

Reluctantly, she dropped her hand and slowly opened her eyes. He had wrapped a towel around his waist, but his bare chest drew her gaze. All she wanted to do was run her fingers over those wet muscles and that dark mat of hair. No, no. Lucy was missing, and she must focus on finding her.

Raphael was speaking again, and she caught the last few words. " — search. Please meet me in the courtyard."

With a jerky nod, she turned and fled.

She rushed into the courtyard and paced down one path and up another as she tried to cool her heated cheeks. Her mind churned with the vision of Raphael, naked in the pool, and her frightened concern over Lucy's disappearance. What could have happened to her?

Raphael, completely dressed in a calf-length open kaftan with belted tunic and loose pantaloons beneath, soon joined her along with Zayed. Mr. Delacroix arrived not long after. Raphael had offered him a place to sleep for the night when he admitted he had been sleeping in the *fonduq* since arriving in the city. She was surprised to see him included, especially because Raphael seemed suspicious of him, but she supposed if they were going to look for Lucy, they could use his help.

The three men murmured among themselves about how the kidnappers snuck in and out of the house without anyone hearing and how to search and where to go, leaving Sydney out of the discussion. She didn't care how the kidnappers got in and out, and she didn't mind being left out of the discussion, because she had no idea how to begin looking for her friend. She only wanted Lucy found. The men finally decided to go out into the *medina* and split up.

Raphael turned to her. "You will wait here, Miss Whelton, on the chance that Mrs. Foster might return."

While that decision made sense, Sydney wanted to search for Lucy as well. When she was about to argue, Hamza appeared at the end of the path and cleared his throat.

Bowing, he said, "A thousand pardons, *Sidi* Raphael. This was delivered for the English lady." He held out a folded bit of parchment.

Sydney took the note and opened it. Inside was scrawled:

> *I have your friend.*
> *Come get her.*
> *Come alone.*

The signature was in Arabic, swirls and curvy lines and dots, which Sydney couldn't read. A terrible, empty space opened in her chest.

"Someone has taken Lucy," she said.

Mr. Delacroix, who was standing next to her, supplied the information. "Al Jabbar," he said, indicating the signature.

Angry, confused, and shocked at hearing the name of the man who was supposed to protect her from Nulkana, she blurted, "Why? Why did he take her?"

Raphael's face was dark with fury as he exchanged a look with Zayed.

"The man is without scruples," Zayed said.

"But where is she?" Sydney cried, as she stared at the flowing script that she couldn't decipher.

"The Street of the Fig Tree," Mr. Delacroix said, glancing at the note. He indicated another line of script below the signature.

"Where is that?" she asked, determined to retrieve Lucy.

"You are not going." Raphael's flat pronouncement fell into the air like a slap.

Sydney's temper flared. "Of course, I'm going. Al Jabbar sent the note to me. Lucy is my friend, so I will go and bring her back."

"He is a ruthless blackguard," Raphael snapped. "I warned you about him. He wants to lure you away from here. Most likely for some evil reason."

She couldn't fathom why he would kidnap Lucy. "I'm sure he only wants to speak with me," she said, falling back on her initial impression that he would help her.

"If he only wished to speak with you, why did he kidnap your friend?" he growled.

Flummoxed and feeling silly, because that was a perfectly logical argument, Sydney glanced down at the note while she tried to think of a rebuttal. Why did Al Jabbar take Lucy? If he were going to kidnap anyone, why didn't he take her? Why kidnap anyone? He could have merely sent a note asking to meet with her. Raphael had been right about him all along. If Al Jabbar was not to be trusted, who would help protect her from Nulkana?

Leaving that question for another time, she said, "I don't know why he kidnapped Lucy, but I have to get her back. How am I supposed to do that unless I do as he asks?"

"We'll think of another way," Raphael said with a tight jaw.

"I know Al Jabbar," Mr. Delacroix volunteered. "I know his house."

Raphael's gaze cut to Delacroix. After studying him a moment, he said, "I'm not going to ask how you came to know him or where his house is."

"Perhaps a wise decision would be to allow Mr. Delacroix to take Miss Whelton there," Zayed suggested.

Sydney saw the thunderclouds gathering in Raphael's eyes. Before his frustration could explode, she intervened. "I think that's a wonderful idea!"

"No, it's not," Raphael barked.

Zayed turned to the Frenchman. "Will you show Miss Whelton to the house of Al Jabbar?"

"Of course." Mr. Delacroix gave a decisive nod. "I will keep her safe."

The corners of Raphael's eyes tightened, and a muscle jumped in his jaw. He sent an angry glance to Zayed, who merely gazed back with equanimity. Raphael's gaze swung back to Delacroix.

"See that you do," he snapped. "Zayed and I will follow at a distance. We'll be watching."

Sydney escaped from the uncomfortable atmosphere as fast as she could to retrieve her hat and veil. Relieved that a plan had been made to rescue Lucy, she decided that along the way, she might learn a bit more about the mysterious man with the Crystal Dagger.

Sydney and Mr. Delacroix wound their way through the *souks*, now crowded with people shopping and haggling over prices. Hundreds of people filled the alleys. The noise of their chatter, the calls of the merchants, the sound of thousands of feet treading over the stones filled her ears. At one point, he pulled her out of the way of a man driving a donkey laden with several large, unwieldy bundles. The driver called out, "*Balak, balak, balak!*" as he went, the universal warning in the city to move aside or be run over. The crowd parted before him as if Moses were parting the Red Sea, then closed again behind him.

After the man and his donkey had squeezed past, Sydney glanced down the alley behind her. As the crowd ebbed and flowed, she could see the tall forms of Zayed and Raphael. A sense of safety wrapped around her. While she was sure Mr. Delacroix would guide her to the house of Al Jabbar, he had been so reticent in providing any information about himself, she wasn't sure he was trustworthy. The crowd in the *medina* was too dense to hold any sort of conversation with him to discover more about him.

Finally, he indicated a narrow alley off to the side where no one seemed to be walking. "Down here," he said.

Sydney peered down the dim passageway, then she glanced behind her looking for Raphael. He hadn't appeared yet. Would he see where they went?

"Perhaps we should wait for Raphael," she suggested.

Mr. Delacroix looked beyond her. "I see him." He gave a quick wave, then taking her by the arm to avoid bumping into two men who had stopped to talk, steered her down the narrow alley.

At the sudden quiet and isolation from the crowd, Sydney decided this might be a good time to question him. "I wish to speak with you about that matter we discussed last evening."

He scowled. "I refused then. I haven't changed my mind."

"But—"

Before she had a chance to say anything more, they stopped before a plain wooden door. He knocked in a short series of raps. After a moment, the door opened.

Al Jabbar appeared in the opening. "Miss Whelton, I'm so glad you accepted my invitation. And Delacroix! This is a surprise." He touched his hand to his heart, his lips, and his forehead and bowed. "*As-salamu aleikum.*" Peace be upon you. Smiling, his blue eyes twinkling, he opened the door wider and beckoned them inside. "Please, come in. This is quite lovely. We shall have a pleasant visit."

Sydney was incensed at his suggestion that this was a social call. She had come to free Lucy, whom he had kidnapped. But she refrained from commenting and stepped into the house followed by Delacroix, who glowered. That made her even more uneasy. Did the two men have some disagreement? Would that put both her and Lucy in danger?

Al Jabbar ushered them into a receiving room like the one at Raphael's house with very high ceilings and seating platforms around the walls. Plump cushions in vibrant colors covered the platforms and spilled onto the floor. With a clap and a short command, he sent hovering servants scurrying, then urged Sydney and Mr. Delacroix to be seated.

She perched on the edge of one of the cushions. "Where's Mrs. Foster?" she demanded.

After making himself comfortable, he said, "She is safe, Miss Whelton, have no fear of that."

Her anger overcame any misgivings she might have about being in this man's house. "Why did you kidnap her? Why did you disappear in the desert? I hired you to protect me." She spit out her angry words at his blithe unconcern at what he had done. "You abandoned me, sir! I had hired you for protection, and you abandoned me and my companion! And then you kidnapped her!"

"Ah, well, in the desert it seemed the Pirate wanted you all to himself." He beamed a smile. "But here you are, all in a piece, and in Fès, no less. How fortuitous!"

"I would like to see Lucy and have her returned to my care," she declared.

Annoyance crossed his features. "As you wish." He snapped his fingers at one of the servants and spoke to him in a low voice.

As they waited, servants brought tea and pastries. Al Jabbar chatted about inconsequential things, like a caravan newly arrived from the east, another that had arrived from the south, but Sydney paid no attention, too anxious about Lucy. Finally, several pairs of footsteps approached, and Lucy appeared, accompanied by one of Al Jabbar's men. Still in her nightshift and wrapped in a large, colorful shawl edged in fringe, she gazed around her with a myopic squint. With a cry of relief, Sydney ran to her, and they hugged tightly.

When Sydney made certain that Lucy was unharmed and returned her spectacles, she turned on Al Jabbar. "Why did you kidnap my friend?"

With an amused gleam in his eyes, he shrugged. "My men made a mistake. They were supposed to fetch you."

"If you wanted to speak with me, you could have sent a note," Sydney huffed.

"That would not have been as enjoyable." He casually took a bite from one of the delicacies on the large tray before him.

Sydney was infuriated at his dismissive attitude. "I'm not some bauble to steal off a merchant's table, sir."

He swarmed to his feet. "Then explain to me why you stole away in the middle of the night with Al Qarsan and left me."

She fell back a step at his threatening stance. Something about this man made her want to protect Raphael. She was not going to admit that Raphael had kidnapped her. Raising her chin, she countered, "You did not adhere to our bargain to protect me. I would like my payment returned."

His eyes went cold. "I'm afraid that's impossible."

At that, she sputtered, "Why that's—that's—thievery!"

Those eyes turned dangerous. "An unfortunate word, Miss Whelton."

Lucy leaned close. "Let it go, Sydney," she whispered.

"He stole from me, Lucy," Sydney returned in an angry whisper. "And he kidnapped you."

Before she could pursue the matter further, Delacroix demanded, "Why did you want this meeting with Miss Whelton, Thurgood?"

Surprised that Mr. Delacroix knew Al Jabbar's true name was Robert Thurgood, Sydney wondered about the acquaintance between the two men, one from the desert and the other from France. Even though they were connected by the Legion of Baal, they did not seem to be on the best of terms.

"The members of the Legion of Baal have been wondering when she will reveal who will be the next Lord High," Al Jabbar said and turned cold blue eyes on her.

Shocked, Sydney's mouth dropped open. "I know nothing about that."

Al Jabbar's eyes narrowed. "I don't believe you. There is a document that the Lord High left with someone he trusted that named his successor."

"I have no document," she said, and wondered about the rolled parchment she had found in her mother's safe. Tied with a red cord, the document had been written in some strange code that she couldn't decipher, so she had stuck it in the back corner of her armoire. It had been stolen shortly before her father was killed.

"I don't believe you," he snarled.

"Why would Miss Whelton have such a document?" Mr. Delacroix asked on a sigh, as if he were bored with Al Jabbar's surly manner and accusations.

Al Jabbar rounded on him. "Because she's the Lord High's daughter, you fool!"

If Delacroix's eyes had been weapons, they would have pierced through Al Jabbar's chest. He turned a suspicious glare on Sydney. But his tone was mild as he said, "Perhaps the Lord High left the document with someone else."

"Like you?" Al Jabbar sneered. "Why haven't you killed Nulkana yet? The bitch is still weak from the battle with the Lord High. She's vulnerable."

At the reminder of that battle, a pang twitched Sydney's heart. But she hung on Delacroix's answer.

He shrugged. "The Legion doesn't control me any longer. I'll take care of the sorceress when I want."

At that moment, a commotion erupted at the entrance to the house. Raised voices and a crash echoed through the room. Within seconds, Raphael and Zayed appeared at the entrance.

"Miss Whelton, Mrs. Foster," Raphael said, "this visit has been going on too long. It is over. We are leaving now."

Al Jabbar swarmed to his feet. "You trespass, Raphael," he growled.

Raphael glared. "I've come to protect the women from a treacherous viper."

"They are unharmed." Al Jabbar indicated Sydney and Lucy with a wave of his arm.

"At the moment," Raphael growled, "but I'm sure you'll find some excuse." He turned to Sydney. "Miss Whelton, please step outside and take Mrs. Foster with you."

Al Jabbar stepped in front of her. "The ladies have not finished their visit with me."

A finger of fear slid up Sydney's back. Why wouldn't he allow her and Lucy to leave? She grabbed Lucy's hand and sidled toward the door.

"Um, we'll be going now," she said. "Thank you for your hospitality."

Al Jabbar's hand landed on her arm. "You'll stay."

Frightened at the coldness in those blue eyes, Sydney tried to shake him off. "Unhand me, sir."

Raphael's fist snapped out and landed with a crack on Al Jabbar's jaw. As he reeled away from Raphael's blow, Sydney pulled Lucy out the door and into the alley. Confusion erupted behind them. Mr. Delacroix followed on their heels, and then Raphael and Zayed, straightening his turban, a moment later.

Raphael took her by the arm as he hurried her away from the house. "I knew letting you come here was a bad idea."

Still skittish from having Al Jabbar grab her, Sydney pulled loose from his hold and halted. "Why did you break in? Why didn't you wait?"

He glowered. "You were inside too long, as I said."

"I was perfectly safe," she huffed.

"Were you?" He glared.

"Of course, I was," she bluffed, not believing her own words. A strange tension had permeated the atmosphere of that house. And then Al Jabbar wouldn't let her leave.

He grunted his disagreement.

Annoyed by his overprotective attitude, she said, "If I hadn't come, I wouldn't have discovered —" She clamped her lips closed before she revealed anything about the document Al Jabbar had mentioned. It was a secret she felt compelled to keep.

"What did you discover?" His brows snapped together.

Before she had a chance to fabricate an answer, Zayed grabbed a fistful of Mr. Delacroix's *djellaba* as the man inched away down the alley.

"You will stay," Zayed said.

Mr. Delacroix stared daggers at Zayed.

Lucy stepped closer to them. "Please, Zayed, release Mr. Delacroix. I'm sure he will return with us." She sent the Frenchman a sweet smile. "Won't you, Mr. Delacroix?"

After a slight hesitation, Zayed let go of the Frenchman, but Delacroix did not wait for Zayed's arm to fall away before he shook him off. He glared at Zayed, then turned to Lucy and in a gentle tone, he said, "I will return with you because you ask. My name is Gide. I'm sorry I did not introduce myself properly last night."

Lucy smiled, blushed, and dipped a small curtsey. "A pleasure to meet you, Gide. I am Lucy Foster." Then she glanced away and pushed her spectacles up her nose.

Sydney was struck speechless at her friend's response to the man with the Crystal Dagger — Gide. She had expected Lucy to be afraid and intimidated by him. She certainly found him intimidating. Instead, Lucy appeared rather taken with him. This was not a situation that Sydney had envisioned. She would have to warn Lucy to be very careful. The man carrying that awful weapon might be terribly damaged by its magic. Despite Lucy's ability to tell a person's nature, good or bad, the magic of the Crystal Dagger might hide his true intent.

Before she could think on that anymore, Raphael led them out of the alley. Zayed sent a warning glare to Gide not to try to run. As she followed along, she worked on the problem of how to convince Gide to go with her to Nulkana's lair and kill the sorceress. He was obviously reluctant to fulfill the command of the weapon he carried. She wondered why, then cast a speculative glance at Lucy. Perhaps her friend could persuade him to reveal his reasons. While she dodged shoppers and merchants with laden donkeys, she smiled at her perfect idea. All she had to do was convince Lucy to convince him.

Chapter 16

When they arrived at Raphael's house, he led them into the *bâyt*, the salon. After speaking with Hamza, he sat and invited everyone to join him, but the invitation sounded more like a command. Although he appeared calm, Sydney sensed he was seething. As he lounged back among the cushions, he turned to Sydney. "Miss Whelton, please, sit here by me." He patted a plump pile of cushions.

The last place she wanted to be was next to him, but she thought it best to accede to his invitation. Apprehensive, she perched uneasily on the edge of a cushion he had indicated. Zayed and Lucy also sat, but Gide remained standing, looking angry and sullen.

Two servants appeared, carrying a huge silver tray, which they placed on a low table in the middle of the room. It held an array of sweets, *ghoriba*, which were Moroccan sugar cookies, *fekkas*, crunchy sweet biscuits, and *baghrir*, a type of pancake sweetened with honey, the same thing Sydney had for breakfast that morning. Hamza arrived carrying a large, ornate, silver teapot with a very long spout. With a flourish, he poured everyone a glass of mint tea, then he and the other servants left.

"These sweets look delicious," Lucy exclaimed as she reached for one, then stopped with her hand extended. "Mr. Delacroix, Gide, won't you join us?"

After a moment's hesitation, and with a short nod, he settled between Lucy and the Pirate, the only place available around the low table. Lucy smiled at him, then took one of the *ghoribas* and happily munched on it.

Sydney felt Raphael's gaze as she took a sip of tea. She tried to ignore him.

"I think we need some explanations, Miss Whelton," he said. "Why did Al Jabbar kidnap Mrs. Foster?"

Lucy was about to take another bite of her *ghoriba,* but halted and exclaimed, "Oh, his men took me by mistake. He really wished to speak with Sydney." At Sydney's pained expression, she mumbled, "I wasn't supposed to say that, was I?"

Sydney wanted to melt into the cushions. She really didn't want to have to explain her complicated connection to Al Jabbar, nor did she wish to reveal the secrets of the Legion of Baal. She took another sip of tea to delay.

Raphael's gaze felt like a physical pressure. He wouldn't relent until she gave him an answer. Carefully, she placed her glass on the table as she tried to devise an explanation.

"Well, he—" she began.

"Mr. Al Jabbar is not a very nice person at all," Lucy interrupted with a tiny shiver.

"He is not," Gide agreed and pushed back the hood on his *djellaba.*

As he did, his sleeve fell away, revealing a tattoo on his wrist, mangled by a scar. Like a hawk pouncing on its prey, Raphael's hand snaked out, grabbed Gide's arm, and captured it, wrist up, against the table. Raphael stared at the other man's wrist, then raised his gaze to glare at Gide. The two men stared at each other, like two predators assessing each other's strengths, as if they had each discovered something amazing about the other.

"What is that mark?" Raphael demanded with narrowed gaze.

Gide snarled something unintelligible and tried to yank his arm back. Raphael held it tightly. With his other hand, he reached into his pocket and pulled out the portrait case he had taken from Sydney. He placed it next to Gide's wrist with the etching of the frog glyph face-up. If Gide's tattoo had not had a scar running through it, the etching on the case would have matched it exactly.

"What is that mark?" Raphael repeated in a growl. Then he turned those lion's eyes on Sydney.

Sydney opened her mouth to tell him, then closed it again. Her father had made her promise never to reveal this secret.

"*Mon Dieu,*" Gide muttered. "You have no idea."

The Pirate's hard gaze swung from Sydney then back to Gide. "No idea of what?"

Instead of answering, the Frenchman asked, "Do you know why *Mademoiselle* Whelton was searching for me?"

"Of course," he snapped. "To kill a sorceress named Nulkana."

"But that is all?" Gide challenged.

Raphael's brow furrowed and his eyes narrowed on Sydney.

Gide's gaze cut to her as well. "Tell him, *mademoiselle*. Tell him everything." Then he wrenched his arm from Raphael's grasp and sank back into the cushions as if preparing for some sort of entertainment.

Sydney's fingers twisted in her lap. She couldn't look at Raphael, who had saved her on the mountain path, who had worried about her safety in the city, who had kissed her and made her insides come alive with exquisite sensations. She had put him in danger by coming on this journey, something she had never expected. For that, she was very sorry.

She had not imagined it would be so treacherous. And she never thought she would develop any sort of connection to him. When she had first set out, she had believed she would pay for his guidance through the desert to find the man with the Crystal Dagger — Gide — and then they would each go their separate ways. But that was before. Now, she felt terrible about misleading Raphael, who had become much more to her than Al Qarsan, the Pirate.

What Gide urged her to do was betray her father's trust. Yet her father was dead, which was the reason for traveling so far and contracting the Pirate's help. If she didn't reveal the truth, then Gide would, and she did not want that. This had to come from her. She would tell something, but not all.

Straightening her shoulders, she met Raphael's gaze. "The frog glyph is a symbol of the Legion of Baal, an international organization of powerful men. They have sworn to kill Nulkana because she is evil. My father was their leader before the sorceress killed him."

"So, you are seeking revenge against her for your father's death," Raphael concluded. "You have told me that. Will killing her fulfill the purpose of the Legion of Baal?"

"Only in part," Gide interjected.

Sydney sent him an angry glance. He was forcing her to reveal more secrets.

"What else?" Raphael demanded.

She shrugged with a nonchalance she did not feel, and then lied, "I am only a woman, so I do not know. I was not privy to their secrets." She felt Gide's penetrating gaze at her deception.

Raphael was more direct. "I don't believe you."

Sydney worried her bottom lip. She glanced at Lucy, but her friend couldn't help her because she didn't know. Gide would tell him if she didn't, and she wanted Raphael to hear it from her. Turning back to him, she said, "They are also searching for an ancient artifact called the Sphere of Astarte."

Raphael stared at Sydney as a wisp of memory floated through his head. It was from his very early childhood. Someone—a woman—placed something around his neck. The talisman he wore now on a cord. It felt heavy back then and seemed much bigger. He had wrapped his tiny fingers around it and saw the ends poking out both sides of his fist. Now, it was not heavy at all, and his fist encompassed the whole piece. But he remembered a name, too, which his child's brain had transmuted to Circle of a Star. He never understood what it meant. The words he had heard could have been *Sphere of Astarte.* Could that be the name of the talisman that kept him human? But the piece which hung on a cord around his neck was not a sphere at all.

He was drawn back to the present by the Frenchman's voice. "The name of the artifact means something to you, *oui?*"

Raphael, still caught in the cloud of the memory, couldn't answer.

"Others also search for this Sphere," Delacroix continued. "A Venetian family. They have very distinctive eyes. Like yours."

Raphael blinked. Like the woman he had seen in that vision. "What are you saying?"

Gide shrugged. "All I am saying is that there is a resemblance. A family resemblance."

"Impossible," Raphael snapped.

Gide took up his glass of tea. "Perhaps. This family is also cursed. It is said that the Sphere will break the curse." Casually, he took a sip.

Speechless, Raphael felt the tips of Sydney's fingers against his arm, as if she wanted to comfort him.

"Raphael," she said quietly.

He noticed she used his name.

"Raphael," she said again, this time close to a whisper. "They turn to Shadow. That is their curse."

He blinked at the revelation, then snapped, "I cannot be part of this family. That is impossible."

Yet, not so impossible. His early memories were of a man and woman whom he called aunt and uncle, not mother and father. They told him that one day, when he was older, he would know his true origins. But before that could happen, before they were able to reveal who he was, they had been slaughtered by marauders, and he had been ripped from his home while still a very young boy and taken to the slave market in Tripoli. What the Frenchman and Sydney implied could be true. But his denial had revealed his secret to the Frenchman, whom he did not know or completely trust, and, it seemed, to Mrs. Foster. That lady had her hand to her mouth in amazement or shock or fear or all three. Delacroix did not seem at all disturbed by the revelation.

"So," the Frenchman said with a calculating glance. "You are cursed as well, *oui*? Perhaps, also a member of the House of Auriano."

The House of Auriano? That sounded very grand. And part of a family? Raphael couldn't imagine such a thing. Since those agonizing, frightening days when he had first arrived in Tripoli as a child, when he had been sold like cattle and forced to do menial, degrading chores from before sunup to well after sundown, the only family he'd had was Zayed, until Darwish al-Rafiq bought them and treated them as sons. At the memory, his gaze settled on his friend. Zayed's brow was creased, an unusual expression for him, and indicated that he was greatly disturbed. Raphael was disturbed as well. So much so, that he had no words. His thoughts whirled inside his head like a sandstorm, obliterating everything else. He couldn't focus. He needed to sort this out.

He sensed Sydney's shock beside him. But he was too stunned, too confused, and too disconcerted at having his secret revealed even to look in her direction. Standing abruptly, he strode out of the room to the stairs that led to the roof. There, above the city, he could feel as if he were in the open desert, where, if he wished, he could let his thoughts fly to disappear into the expanse. And there, he could decide if he believed what he had been told and what to do.

Sydney stared after him, bemused at his abrupt departure. She glanced at Lucy, who looked as surprised as she felt. Then she glanced at Zayed, who gazed after his friend with a line of concern between his brows, an expression she couldn't ever remember seeing on the man's face, except on the day she had become lost. On the other side of the space where Raphael had been sitting, Gide helped himself to one of the sweets on the tray.

As he examined the pastry, he said, "*Monsieur* Qarsan seems perturbed. Perhaps he does not know he is a member of the Auriano family. Perhaps he does not wish to know." Then he took a bite out of the sweet.

His words goaded Sydney into action. She bolted from her seat and threw one word at Zayed: "Where?"

"The roof," he answered.

She found Raphael with his legs braced apart, his arms folded at his chest, and staring out over the city. He did not turn when she approached. She stood silently next to him for a long moment.

Understanding that his thoughts were most likely in turmoil, she decided to distract him with something other than what he had just learned.

"I never expected this journey to be quite so complicated," she said. The journey was more than complicated, but it was the only word she could think of to describe it.

He responded with a grunt, sent her a sardonic glance, then turned back to the vista of the city.

She forged on. "My business with Al Jabbar is finished."

At that, he swung to her. "Did you think I was telling tales when I said he was not to be trusted?"

Sydney's eyes widened at his sudden vehemence. "Well, no, but—"

He ignored her denial. "He is the only one who has ever left a scar on me, but that's not why I hate him. He killed a man, slit his throat, a man who did not beat me or treat me like a slave after he bought me when I was a child. Because Al Jabbar was jealous." He gave a sarcastic twist to the name.

Speechless, she stared, her mouth hanging open, disconcerted by his outburst, appalled by what he had revealed. He had never before shared anything about his past. She had no idea his childhood had been so tragic. Her heart swelled in compassion.

Raphael saw her horrified expression and turned away, hiding the sharp pain of rejection. Why had he disclosed his past? He never revealed anything about himself, which was why he perpetrated the sham that the house belonged to Abd Al-Karim, who was merely the caretaker. But that was a minor revelation compared to what he had told the woman beside him. Now that she knew what he had been, she despised him. How could she not? He had been a slave. He turned into darkness if he removed his talisman. He could barely be called human.

"Go ask Delacroix to help you find the sorceress," he snarled.

She gasped. "I beg your pardon?"

"Wasn't he the one you wanted to find? Now you've found him, the man with the Crystal Dagger. You don't need me any longer." He refused to look at her. He did not need to see the pity in her eyes, nor the revulsion.

Despite the need to rid himself of the sorceress's torment, despite wanting to accompany Sydney in her search, despite wanting to kiss her very kissable lips, he was not going to be reminded of his shameful past every time he looked into those changeable eyes of hers, filled with sad sympathy. With pity. He needed no one's sympathy, and certainly no one's pity. The past was over. He had become more than someone's slave. He had stolen and raided and bargained his way into wealth and reputation. He had become Al Qarsan—the Pirate. His jaw clenched.

She took a breath and let it out. "Mr. Pirate," she said in an imperious tone that could rival a queen's. "I paid you a handsome sum to guide me."

"To find the man with the Crystal Dagger," he growled. "You've done that."

"We entered into another agreement last night," she said. "You have not fulfilled that."

"And you have not offered anything in payment," he bit out and turned to look at her.

That was a mistake. Her eyes weren't filled with the pity he had expected. Instead, they snapped a heated green. Her nose stuck obstinately in the air. Two spots of color decorated her cheeks. Her lips were compressed in anger. In spite of his resolve to distance himself from her, he wanted to kiss those lips into softness, compliance, surrender. Then her lips parted, as if she'd had some sort of revelation, as if she could read his thoughts, and doubt flashed through her eyes before her lashes swept down, hiding them.

That doubt made up his mind. He couldn't let himself become involved with this woman. She was a danger, both to his physical well-being and his heart. He had allowed himself to be enticed by her beauty, by her innocence, by her core of steel wrapped in sweet naivete. What he thought at first was an uncomplicated quest to find the man with the Crystal Dagger had turned into a tangle of revelations and ghosts from his past. His life had been simple before this woman stepped inside his tent. He didn't need to find this family who carried the same curse as he did. He didn't need to find the magical Sphere of Astarte. He didn't want to know about the powerful Legion of Baal. And he certainly did not want Robert Thurgood dogging his steps.

Turning back to the city laid out before him, he said, "It doesn't matter. Our arrangement ends here."

"No. It does not."

At her adamant rebuttal, he slid a glance in her direction. She was vibrating in her anger. Wary of such fury, knowing she could snap her magic at him, he calmly asked, "Why not?"

"Because I have traveled all this way so that I could kill Nulkana. So that I could find the man with the Crystal Dagger to help me do that. So that I could find *you*." Tears brimmed in her eyes.

Unsettled by her tears and her declaration, he could find no words.

"Nulkana killed my father, and I did nothing," she went on. "I should have helped him. I should have added my magic to his. He might be alive today if I had. So, I need to get my revenge on the evil sorceress."

Her tears finally spilled down her cheeks. He reached out to wipe them away, but she stepped back with a firm shake of her head.

After swiping at her cheeks, she raised her chin. "Now we find that you might be a member of the House of Auriano. They also want Nulkana's death. If you continue with me, you might free yourself from her torment. You may discover you have a family. Perhaps you don't want that, and it's your choice. But please, whatever you decide, I would like you to finish this journey with me." She sniffed. "Last night, you agreed to stay with me for an acceptable fee. I will pay anything you want. *Anything*."

An unfamiliar turmoil at her proposal erupted in his chest. She was offering herself in return for his guidance through the rest of her journey. But that offer didn't sit well. He wanted her because she wanted him, not in payment for anything he did.

"No," he said, unable to find the words to explain.

Hurt flashed through her eyes, then the heat of anger replaced it. "Don't you want to kill Nulkana?" she demanded. "Doesn't she invade your dreams? She sent that river demon to devour you. If I — we — don't do away with her, she'll keep trying until she has destroyed you."

"Yes. No." In confusion, he walked away three steps, then walked back. His refusal to accompany her had nothing to do with Nulkana and everything to do with the fear that if he was a part of this grand Auriano family, they would reject him because of his past as a slave and what he had become — Al Qarsan, the Pirate. Then Sydney would leave him because she had completed what she had set out to do.

Her brows drew together in bewilderment. "Please…" She swallowed, as if the next words were difficult to say. "I need you to come with me."

Why was he being such a coward? This proud, stubborn woman was pleading with him. He didn't understand why she needed him, but the fact that she did warmed his heart. It made no difference if the Auriano family rejected him. He didn't need them. He had lived without them for most of his life, perhaps all of it if the memory of his childhood were true. After Sydney destroyed the sorceress and returned to her own life, he would return to the desert alone with only Zayed as company. Where he belonged. But by the tears of Allah, before that, he would take whatever time he had left with this woman and treasure it.

He drew a breath. "Yes. I will go with you to kill Nulkana. No, you will not offer me anything in return for my help." He brushed his fingers across her cheek. "Whatever you give me will be because you wish it, not because of any debt or because I demand it in payment."

Her eyes widened, then in a rush, she hugged him around the waist. "Oh, thank you! Thank you!"

Gently, he enfolded her in his arms. The feel of her against him was delightful, beautiful, luscious, a sensation that he wished he could savor forever. But forever was not part of his destiny. When she stepped back, he let her go.

Color painted her cheeks. "I'm sorry. That was quite forward of me."

His lips twitched. "That was quite pleasant."

Her blush spread across her face and down her neck.

Even if nothing else were accomplished on this quest, he would be able to enjoy Sydney Whelton's company for a while longer. With a sweep of his arm, he indicated the stairs leading down where the others waited. They would make a plan.

Despite his misgivings about the outcome of this journey, he discovered that anticipation settled in his middle.

When Sydney and Raphael returned to the *bâyt*, Lucy was deep in conversation with Delacroix. Zayed sat quietly, listening.

Lucy glanced up and said, "Gide has a sister in France, but he hasn't seen her in several years."

Sydney murmured her sympathy at the long separation. Lucy seemed about to say more, but Raphael interrupted.

"We're traveling on," he announced, his resolve radiating from him. He turned to Delacroix. "Where is Nulkana's lair?"

Gide assessed him with a steady gaze. "Venice."

"Venice?" Sydney said. "But I saw her in the *medina*."

She felt Raphael's aggravated gaze at that reminder of coming so close to danger.

Gide's lips turned up in a grim smile. "What you saw, *mademoiselle*, was a projection. I do not think she is here in Fès at all."

Sydney sank to a cushion, suddenly exhausted. She had thought that once she found the man with the Crystal Dagger, Nulkana would be close. Now, she would have to make arrangements to travel to Venice.

"Then we will go to Venice," Raphael announced.

"*Bon chance, mon ami,*" Gide said dismissively, as if he were finished with the problem of Nulkana. "Do you suppose I could have more tea?"

Sydney stared at him as his words settled in her brain. "Won't you be coming with us?"

"No, I am done with killing." He sipped the tea which Zayed poured for him. "I did enough of that in Egypt with General Napoleon."

"But the Crystal Dagger," she argued. "It's meant to kill Nulkana. What will you do with it?"

"Do?" he repeated as something dark veiled his eyes. "I will carry it and keep it from other hands."

"An excellent sentiment," Raphael said, as he placed his hand on Sydney's shoulder, warning her to allow him to direct the conversation. "A tragedy that it keeps you from your sister. Perhaps you would like to travel with us to Venice and then make your way to France to see her."

Gide's eyes narrowed in suspicion. "I'll not kill anyone, not even Nulkana."

"It's an invitation, Delacroix," Raphael said with a touch of heat. "*We* will kill Nulkana." He indicated Sydney and himself and the others around the table. "Don't concern yourself with her. Once we get to Venice, you are free to continue to France."

Sydney bowed her head to hide her smile. Raphael had subtly challenged the Frenchman who held the weapon that would kill the sorceress. Would Gide feel that because he owned the Crystal Dagger, he might be compelled to take up the challenge?

Gide took another sip of tea. After placing his glass on the table, he stood. "I accept your invitation. I will travel with you to Venice."

Lucy clapped her hands. "That's wonderful! We have so much to talk about."

With a smile and a bow, Gide said, "I look forward to more conversations with you, *madame*."

"Oh, I'm not a *madame* at all," she said. "That was all make-believe so that Sydney would have a chaperone."

The three men in the room stared at her. Zayed appeared nonplussed. Raphael chuckled and sent Sydney an approving glance. A pleased grin crossed Gide's face.

"Then I look forward to many, many more conversations, *mademoiselle*," the Frenchman said, then turned to Raphael. "When you have made preparations, you may find me in the *fonduq*." With another little bow, he left.

Lucy gazed around at everyone, and a blush rose in her cheeks as she pushed her spectacles up her nose. "Well, I couldn't let him go on believing I was married, could I? He's such a nice man once you get to know him."

Sydney laughed and hugged her. "Oh, Lucy! I am so glad we're friends!"

With a startled blink and then a smile, Lucy hugged her back. "Me, too, Sydney."

Chapter 17

Three days later, they left the city of Fès. They had collected Gide at the *fonduq* along with camels for the trek to the city of Tangier on the coast where Raphael said they could board a ship for Venice. Along the way, Sydney watched Lucy and Gide become better acquainted as they chatted and laughed together. Gide's smile transformed him into a handsome man, erasing the hard lines of his face. Sydney wondered what hardships he had endured to turn him so sullen and suspicious. Perhaps the Crystal Dagger he carried was a burden too heavy for a man to bear.

The time passed peacefully. Zayed had said the trip to Tangier would take about ten days. They saw no sign of Al Jabbar. While Sydney was relieved that she didn't have to deal with him again, she was also apprehensive about confronting the sorceress without his support. Several members of the Legion of Baal had emphasized the importance of having him present at the confrontation. She wasn't sure why he was such an important factor in killing Nulkana, but she put that out of her mind for now. She would deal with that problem when she found Nulkana's location in Venice.

Lucy and Gide chatted frequently, and occasionally Lucy giggled at something he said. She seemed thoroughly entranced. While Sydney was glad her friend was enjoying herself, she was also apprehensive about the friendship blooming into an affair that might bring heartache to Lucy. Gide Delacroix was a man who had revealed little about himself or how he had acquired the very dangerous weapon he carried.

Two days before they were to arrive in Tangier, Sydney's camel broke free in the middle of the night and wandered away, disappearing into the desert. Zayed observed that it most likely would end up back at the *fonduq*. They were eight days from Fès and nearly at Tangier. Raphael decided that Sydney should ride the rest of the way with him. Even as she protested and grumbled, all she could think about was that ride through the desert when they were alone, when she had fallen asleep on her camel, and he had caught her before she toppled to the ground. He'd put her on his camel, and she had slept cradled against him. His arms had been strong and firm, and she had felt secure...and comforted.

Now, as he settled behind her on the camel, she argued with herself that she shouldn't want him this close, despite liking the feel of him at her back. Primly, she sat up as straight as she could, leaving a minuscule distance between them. She sensed his amusement, but he said nothing. In fact, he was the perfect gentleman, helping her on and off the camel, attempting not to touch her when they were snugged against each other on the beast. Despite that, she was keenly aware of him at her back, his breath, his heat, his scent, all quite distracting.

The first day passed without incident, or without his teasing, for which Sydney was grateful. The tension of being so near him frayed her nerves. When they stopped for the night, she couldn't get off the camel fast enough. Only one more day remained before they reached Tangier. Surely, she could endure that short amount of time.

The next morning was a repeat of the day before. She mounted the camel, then Raphael swung on behind her. Several hours passed with some conversation interspersed with silence. Sydney was feeling a bit more at ease sitting in front of Raphael on his camel when his arm came around her and he dangled something in front of her. It was her portrait case. And it swung from a gold chain.

"I thought I'd return this," he said.

Relieved at seeing it again, she took it in her palm. "Thank you. And you put it on a chain."

"Since it is your father, I thought you might want to have him close." He took hold of the chain and slipped it over her head. The case settled at the crease between her breasts. "Perfect," he murmured.

As she glanced down at it, she felt him lean closer, brushing against her.

"I want to kiss you, Miss Whelton." His whisper caressed her ear.

With a tiny indrawn breath, she sat up straighter, pretending to the others that she had heard nothing. But a frisson of excitement spun through her. Every night before she fell asleep, the memory of his kisses warmed her. She wanted to kiss him, too.

"I want to taste your mouth," he went on. "I want to press your body against mine and feel your lovely curves."

Yes, she wanted to press back against him. But she didn't. All she could do was blink. And stare straight ahead.

"I want to touch your breasts. I want to kiss them, lick them and suck on them." He demonstrated by dipping his head, nuzzling her neck, circling the spot with his tongue, and then sucking gently.

A shot of pure pleasure arrowed through her. "Mr. Pirate," she whispered a bit breathlessly, "the others will see."

"No, they won't." His denial held a hint of amusement. "No one is paying attention to us."

Sydney saw that he was right. Zayed rode at the front of their small group. Lucy and Gide were to one side a bit in front, and deep in conversation.

"Do you know what I would like to do then?" he asked, then blew on the damp spot he had left on her neck.

She shivered and shook her head. What more could he possibly do? Anticipation swirled through her.

"I want to take down your hair and let it fall down your back. I want to run my fingers through it and feel it in the palm of my hand." His voice dropped to a whisper. "I want to undress you, slowly, so I can see every beautiful inch of you."

Undress her? Flustered at the very idea, she heated all over. No, that was quite improper. Then she had the very opposite reaction. She *wanted* him to see her. What was she thinking? The idea made her squirm, even as her insides melted. But she wanted to see him, too. All of him. Every glorious inch.

"I want to look upon your breasts." His hand brushed across one of them as if by accident, and his voice dropped even lower. "I want to see the thatch between your thighs."

Sydney caught her bottom lip in her teeth as that very thatch he spoke of became embarrassingly damp. She shifted to find some release from the pressure building between her thighs. What had he done to her?

"And then I want to kiss you all over." He demonstrated by lifting the veil that trailed from her hat and placed a soft kiss at her nape, then the curve where her neck met her shoulder. He finished with a nip of his teeth.

She let out a squeak. When Lucy turned at the noise, Sydney forced a calm smile and waved. She was feeling anything but calm. The temperature of the desert seemed to have risen. Her insides throbbed. She had the most extraordinary need to tear off her clothes. Instead, she shifted in her seat. As she squirmed, she felt something press against her. It was something large and quite firm. Oh, dear Lord, that was *him*! She closed her eyes and gulped as she had the wicked, naughty desire to see it, touch it. And she wanted him to see her, touch her. Especially down there, where she throbbed. She squirmed again.

His hand landed on her thigh. "If you move like that, I won't be accountable for my actions, Miss Whelton."

"I'm sorry," she whispered.

"No, don't be sorry." His words fanned her neck. "You are doing exactly right." His fingers crept closer to the space between her thighs.

For some reason, she wanted those fingers to move closer, and at the same time, she was appalled at the thought. Without realizing what she was doing, her thighs relaxed and fell open even more.

"Are you uncomfortable, Miss Whelton?"

His question was perfectly proper, but she knew he wasn't speaking of her seat on the camel.

"No. Yes." She fell back against his chest.

"I can help with that," he offered.

"Yes, please." She agreed without knowing exactly what she was agreeing to. Whatever it was, she had the feeling it would be wonderful, like his kisses.

"Later," he whispered. "Not here." His hand slipped up her ribs and cupped her breast. With a gentle squeeze and a light kiss on her ear, he straightened.

Her gaze focused on their little group spread out before them. Of course, not here. What had she been thinking? Whatever he would do to relieve the throbbing and pressure could not be done out in the middle of the desert in front of everyone.

He halted the camel and made it kneel. "Miss Whelton and I will walk for a while," he announced to the others.

He helped her slide from the camel's back, then he dismounted. Sydney was relieved to put some distance between them, even if it was only a few feet. She felt jittery and wanting, wishing for Raphael's hands all over her. She wanted to kiss him. How could that be? Only a few weeks before, she had thought he was the most insufferable man she had ever met.

"Shall I tell you a story, Miss Whelton?" His question interrupted her thoughts.

"Could you sing something instead?" she asked.

With a wicked smile, he obliged.

While Sydney listened, she tried to imagine what he might do *later*.

Minutes before sunset, Lucy glanced behind her and said, "Do you know, I believe someone else is traveling to Tangier as well."

"It is a port, *mademoiselle*," Gide said. "Caravans stop there to sell their wares to the ship masters who take them to other countries."

"Yes, of course." she looked over her shoulder. "But these people seem familiar. Don't you agree, Sydney?"

Sydney peered around Raphael's broad shoulders to see who was behind them. She gasped. "It's Al Jabbar!"

Raphael tensed. "Why would he be following us?" His tone sounded merely curious, but beneath ran a thread of rage.

"I don't know." Sydney said the first thing that came to mind. She really didn't know exactly why he followed, but she could think of several reasons, none of which she wanted to admit to the man at her back. She had kept too many secrets from him. Revealing them now would destroy the tenuous spark between them.

Gide sent her a shrewd glance. "Perhaps he wishes to find the Sphere of Astarte for himself."

"Of course!" Sydney pounced on that explanation. She was not about to explain that he also wanted her to reveal whom her father had chosen as the next Lord High of the Legion of Baal, another reason he could be following. "It has great power."

"Then it is quite valuable."

Raphael's dry tone made Sydney wince. Of course, it was valuable, especially to Raphael. It was the only thing that kept him human. If the amulet he wore was a piece of the Sphere, then Al Jabbar wanted it. But did he know about Raphael's piece? With Gide so close, she was not about to ask, revealing that Raphael wore it around his neck. Although Lucy said he was a good man, he made Sydney uncomfortable.

Raphael and Zayed exchanged a look. Without a word spoken between them, they both urged their camels to a faster pace. Sydney held on and tried not to feel guilty about keeping yet another secret from Raphael. Soon, when her quest ended, she would reveal everything to him. She hoped after that, he would not despise her.

They arrived in Tangier the next day. The night before, they had seen Al Jabbar's campfire across the desert. In the desert dawn, he and his men had been dark shapes behind them, closer than they had been the day before. Sydney was anxious to keep ahead of him, especially when she had learned for herself what sort of man he was.

After traveling on the flat desert for days, they huffed their way up to the gate of the city that had been built on low, rolling hills. They left their camels and supplies at the *fonduq*, then Raphael hurried them through the city. The *medina* bustled like the one in Fès, and each *souk* sold its own type of wares. But unlike the other city, where everything was sold from tiny shops, farmers here spread rugs on the ground on street corners or in a small space where they mounded their fruits and vegetables for sale.

Sydney and Lucy stopped briefly to buy a few dates and figs and munched on the fruit as they wound through the maze of alleys until they reached the wall facing the sea. A set of stairs leading to the rampart hugged the wall, and they climbed up. Sydney could smell the ocean, and she was impatient to look at something besides flat desert or steep mountains.

At the top, she caught her breath. Spread out before her was the harbor and the bay beyond with ships from many nations anchored in its calm waters. At the foot of the wall, a wide stretch of sandy beach extended around the edge of the bay. Excitement made her shiver. She was coming closer to the end of her journey. If what Gide said was true, then across that water was Nulkana, the creature who had killed her father.

Raphael held a brief conversation with Zayed in the language of the desert, then peered out to the harbor. He pointed at one of the larger ships anchored not far offshore. Activity on deck indicated that it was preparing to sail soon.

"That is our ship," Raphael said. "I sent ahead, so her master is waiting for us."

Sydney was grateful for his thoughtfulness, but at the same time, she wondered at a ship's captain who would sail at the request of a man of the desert. Did Raphael know him? How could that be?

They made their way down to the strand where several small boats were beached. One was being loaded with supplies. Raphael spoke to the men loading it, then he waved everyone forward and onto the boat.

As they approached the ship, Sydney was able to see its name: *Desert Star*. After clambering aboard, a stocky man of middle years with a great mustache stepped forward. He wore a motley combination of clothing from various lands—a formal velvet frock coat over an embroidered red silk tunic from the Far East and loose white linen pantaloons like those that desert-dwellers wore. On his head was a huge, wide-brimmed hat decorated with a peacock feather. His feet were bare.

"*Señoritas* and *Señors*," he said grandly as he swept a bow. "Welcome to the *Desert Star*. I am Don Quixote, the master of this ship. My first mate, Iago, will show you to your quarters." He indicated a tall, thin man who seemed to have no hair anywhere that was visible. His bald head shone in the sun. Don Quixote turned to Raphael. "*Señor* Al Qarsan, please, a word."

The two men stepped aside and held a short conversation. Sydney held back from the group following Iago below. Something about the interaction between the ship's master and Raphael made her curious, and she shamelessly wanted to eavesdrop. She didn't hear much, only a few words, but she heard Don Quixote remark that Raphael's regular quarters had been made ready.

When the two men separated, she confronted Raphael. The ship's name, its availability to sail them to Venice, and the master's remark about Raphael's quarters all added up to something more than finding a random ship to take them on as passengers.

She stepped in front of Raphael before he disappeared below deck. "Is this your ship?"

He answered with a question of his own. "Does that create a problem, Miss Whelton?"

He was back to being formal, and he obviously did own the ship. But he lived in the desert. And he owned the *riad* in Fès. Sydney blinked as her impression of the man rearranged itself yet again.

"I thought you wished to travel to Venice as quickly as possible," he said. "This ship happened to be in port."

"Of course. Thank you." Flustered, grateful for his consideration, she couldn't find anything else to say.

"I don't own the ship," he explained. "I have a share with Don Quixote."

She blinked again. So, he didn't own the ship outright, but having a share in it implied he was much more than a brigand of the desert. But she had already surmised that. The knowledge hadn't congealed in her head until now.

Instead of revealing her thoughts, she changed the direction of the conversation. "Don Quixote is an unusual name," she said. "Like the Cervantes' character."

He grinned. "Not his real name, of course. But he has told me he spent much of his youth jousting at windmills. You'll find that many of the crew have unusual names as well."

"Like Iago?" she asked.

"Yes, but he is not treacherous like Shakespeare's character."

Sydney's thoughts reeled. The man before her was also well-read. What other surprises was he hiding? Then she remembered a much earlier conversation with him.

"You said you didn't know what a pianoforte was," she said, a touch of accusation in her tone.

His lips twitched and he shrugged. He had been teasing. Again.

"The name Al Qarsan is also unusual for a man who lives in the desert," she observed.

He chuckled. "Just so, Sydney-Who-Is-Not-A-Boy."

She laughed.

Gesturing at the bulkhead that led below, he said, "Shall I show you to your quarters, Miss Whelton? We will be raising anchor soon, for the tide is beginning to turn."

She followed him to the deck below, where she shared a cabin with Lucy. But as she listened to Lucy's chatter about the ship and its unusual master, she tried to reconcile what she was learning about Raphael and his reputation as a ruthless brigand. She realized he was more than what she had first thought, the man called the Pirate.

Much, much more.

Sydney stood at the rail of the *Desert Star* next to Zayed and craned her neck to peer high up into the rigging. They were about to sail for Venice and the sailors were scrambling about the ropes far above her head. She watched one man in particular, her breath stuck in her throat. He stood, stripped to the waist, with his bare feet braced on a line and leaning over a spar as he worked with several others to unfurl one of the sails. Raphael. As if he had been a sailor all his life. But what if he fell? The deck of the ship was far below him, and landing there would surely injure him badly, perhaps even kill him. Sydney didn't want to think about that.

Forcing a calm she didn't feel, she said, "That looks very dangerous."

"It is so." Zayed watched Raphael for a moment. "He has a love of the sea and the ships that sail on it."

Surprised at learning one more thing about the man called the Pirate, Sydney said, "But he lives in the desert!"

Zayed met her gaze. "Not always. At one time, when he was very young, he lived near the sea. He remembers running along a beach and playing in the surf. But that is one of only a few memories he has of the time before he was taken from his home. When he was older, Darwish al-Rafiq, our beloved master, saw his love of the sea and sent my brother on ships to other lands to act in his place." He indicated Raphael high in the rigging. "He learned much on those voyages."

"Didn't you go on those voyages, too?" she asked.

"Sometimes. But I am not of the sea," he said. "I am of the desert. I was a slave, so I performed the tasks put to me by our master. I stayed behind, worked in our master's warehouses, and waited for my brother to return."

"You are very loyal," she observed.

"He has saved my life, as I have saved his." He glanced away across the harbor as if his words meant nothing.

Intrigued by his modest statement, she said, "I would very much like to hear those stories. That is, if you would care to tell them."

He said nothing for a very long time, staring across the harbor. Sydney thought he wouldn't answer, and she was about to move away to leave him with his thoughts when he began to speak in a low voice.

"Our first master, Abd al-Aziz Arif, was hard and cruel. One day I came upon him as he was using one of the female slaves. She was young, barely a woman, and he was hurting her. The woman was my friend and in my young, foolish mind, I thought she might be my wife one day. I struck Abd al-Aziz Arif many times. He was enraged and would have had me beheaded, but my brother convinced him to sell me instead, for instead of losing a slave, Abd al-Aziz Arif would make a profit. And then my brother convinced Abd al-Aziz Arif to sell him as well, for we were both useless slaves and should be sold together — two useless slaves who together made one barely useful slave. Abd al-Aziz Arif would gain coin and rid himself of us."

Sydney smiled at Raphael's cleverness at the same time that she wanted to beat Abd al-Aziz Arif herself. "What happened to the young woman?"

"I do not know," he said, his tone muted. "I never saw her again."

Swallowing down her anger at the injustice that allowed those cruel men to treat others like objects, she asked, "How did you save Raphael's life?"

"He was a small child when he was bought by our first master. On the first day in the house of Abd al-Aziz Arif, my brother dropped a pitcher of milk that spilled on our master. Abd al-Aziz Arif became enraged and beat my brother until he lost his senses. He became very ill for a very long time. Abd al-Aziz Arif would have let him die. My young brother was fevered and slept for many days, sometimes crying out. I cared for him the best I could, making him drink tea and sharing my food with him. When he returned to this world from his sleep, he remembered little of his life before, not even his name, only the beach and the sea. That is when I named him Raphael, for he would call out 'angel' in his fever."

"That was very kind of you," she said, her voice thick with emotion, "to care for him like that."

"Only what one soul should do for another. He is my brother." He paused. Then as if he hadn't shared painful memories from the past, he asked, "Once you have found this sorceress and killed her, what will you do then?"

Sydney's gaze traveled to where Raphael was climbing down the rigging to the deck, where he landed, lithe and agile. He sent her a cocky little smile, then turned to speak to one of the sailors. She released a breath of relief that he was again on solid footing and turned over Zayed's question. What *would* she do? She had come to expect to see Raphael every day. Now that she knew more about his hard, tragic childhood, she admired him even more for becoming the complex man he was. When she had accomplished her task, she would return to England, and he would return to the desert. What would her life be like without him? She didn't want to answer that question. She had the sudden insight that her feelings for Raphael had changed and deepened since the day she entered his tent in the Tuareg village. When he had bargained with her. When he'd had her take down her hair. When she thought he was the most insufferable man she had ever met.

Her breath stopped.

She had come to love him.

Chapter 18

In the dead of night, two days into their voyage to Venice, Sydney wandered the deck of the *Desert Star*. She couldn't sleep, so she had thrown a large shawl over her night rail, crept out of the cabin, and left Lucy slumbering peacefully. She should have dressed, but anxious thoughts about what they would find in Venice and the inevitable confrontation with Nulkana roiled through her head. She wondered what would happen when — if — they met the members of the House of Auriano. Was Raphael related to them? Was that why he was cursed?

As if her thoughts had conjured him, she saw him standing at the rail and staring across the sea. She went to stand beside him. He pointed at a spot near the horizon.

"Al Jabbar follows us," he said.

Sydney strained to see. As the *Desert Star* rose and fell on the waves, she saw a tiny light at the horizon against the night sky that appeared to blink in and out. It was the running light of another ship, dipping up and down as it rode the sea.

He spoke again in a low voice. "When this is over, one of us will be dead."

She gasped. "No, please don't say that."

He turned to her. "He and I have a complicated past together. He was my friend once when we were young."

"Why does he hate you?" she asked. "Why is he so jealous?"

He let out a breath and gazed at the other ship a moment. When he turned back to her, his eyes glittered with anger. "He wanted this." He pulled his amulet from beneath his shirt. "He saw me once as darkness when the cord had broken, and it had fallen off. He thought the piece had magical powers to free him from slavery and make him rich. So, when Darwish al-Rafiq began to send me on his ships as his envoy, Robert — Al Jabbar — believed it was my amulet that gave me such power. He wanted it and he wanted our master to notice him. But Robert became a liar and thief, and our master knew that. One night he whipped Robert for stealing things from the warehouse and selling them for his own gain. The next night, Robert cut our master's throat. Zayed and I were afraid that we would be sold again, or worse, accused of helping him, so we escaped into the desert. Robert blames me for telling Darwish al-Rafiq about his thievery. I hate him for murdering a man who was kind to me."

Guilt tightened Sydney's chest. She had brought Al Jabbar to Raphael and resurrected the enmity between them.

"I'm sorry," she said. "I didn't know what sort of man he was when I hired him."

After a moment, he asked, "Did you know what sort of man I was when you hired me?" His question was half-challenge, half-teasing, dismissing the heaviness of his difficult past.

Taking up his challenge, Sydney tipped her head and studied him. "I had heard that you were ruthless, a fierce fighter, and audacious."

His brow quirked up. "Audacious?"

"Oh, yes. Fearless and daring." She gave a decisive nod.

"Hm. I had heard nothing about you before you stepped into my tent," he mused. "You were audacious that day. How fearless and daring are you now, Sydney Whelton?" His voice had dropped nearly to a whisper.

He brushed a strand of hair from her cheek, then placed a soft kiss where his fingers had been. With a smile and a challenge in his eyes, he turned and sauntered away to the bulkhead that led below.

Sydney stared after him. His question swirled in her head. His tingly touch awakened all the feelings he had aroused when she sat before him on his camel, and he had murmured those delicious things he wanted to do. Was this the *later* he meant? How fearless and daring was she?

She had crossed continents to reach him and journeyed many miles since then in his company. She had climbed mountains and fought bandits in the desert. Surely, she could travel the few feet across a ship's deck and down a ladder to follow him. She loved him.

Before she lost her nerve, she took one step, then another. Excitement fluttered in her middle.

The door to the master's cabin was open, but the cabin was dark, lit only by dim moonlight. His dark silhouette was outlined by the luminescence of the wake of the ship that she could see through the stern window.

"I knew you would come, daring and fearless Sydney." His voice reached out to her, drawing her closer.

She closed the door behind her and swallowed. What she was about to do seemed more daring than crossing continents and deserts and mountains.

"I want—" Her voice broke, and she cleared her throat. "I want to learn about kisses. Is this *later*?"

He chuckled. "Yes."

She took a step closer. "Will you teach me?"

"It would be my pleasure."

Something froze her. She couldn't make her feet move. She was afraid. But of what?

"Sydney," he murmured.

Her name on his lips freed her. His voice, soft and deep, drew her forward. Another two steps and she was directly before him, nearly touching.

"I would like you to kiss me, please," she said.

"Why don't you kiss me instead?" he suggested.

"Oh!" Her eyes widened and she fell back a half step. Ducking her head, she thought over his suggestion. "Well, I suppose I could," she mused. Rising on tiptoe, she placed a light peck on his lips.

He sighed dramatically. "Miss Whelton, have you learned nothing about kissing? That was not a kiss."

He was right. It certainly was nothing like the kisses he had bestowed on her. She could do better. Cupping his cheeks, she placed her lips against his. He stood very still. What she was doing felt very nice, but not nearly as exciting as when he had kissed her. Perhaps she could persuade him to help out. She ran her tongue around the contour of his mouth. That felt very nice as well. The whiskers from his beard tickled. She kissed one corner of his mouth and then the other. She kissed his chin. And his jaw. Then she moved lower to his neck. His shirt was open, so she kissed the hollow of his throat. She was so involved in what she was doing that she barely noticed that his hands came to rest on her hips. He urged her forward until their bodies brushed together.

The movement distracted her enough to stop what she was doing and ask, "Am I doing this correctly?"

"Perfectly," he murmured. "But I think you should put this —" He touched his finger to her mouth. "Here." He indicated his own lips.

"Mm. Yes, of course." She followed his suggestion.

His arms came around her, pulling her close. Her thin night rail was no protection against the solid mass of his body. But she didn't care. His kisses made her feel deliciously wanton and tingly. They made her body throb. She wanted more.

His hands curved around her bottom and eased her closer. They were thigh to thigh, and she could feel his hard length against her belly. One of his hands crept up her ribs and cupped her breast. Was that part of kissing, too? When his thumb stroked her nipple, pleasure streaked through her. A tiny moan escaped. Embarrassed at her wanton reaction, she gasped and jerked away.

"I'm sorry," she said. "I didn't mean to do that."

He cupped her cheek. "It only means you like what I do to you. I want to hear more."

"Oh." She thought that over.

"Don't be afraid," he whispered, as he pulled her shawl from her shoulders. "I want to feel how beautiful you are."

He thought she was beautiful! She hadn't believed him before, when he had used that as an excuse to spirit her away from Al Jabbar in the desert.

She felt his lips touch her jaw, then that sensitive spot below her ear, then the curve of her neck. Oh, yes. Without thought, she tugged at the ribbon that kept the neckline of her night rail closed and loosened it. His gentle fingers brushed the garment from her shoulder, then trailed down to caress the swell of her breast. He pushed the night rail from her other shoulder, and it slipped to her waist. She didn't care that she was partially exposed to him as his fingers tweaked her nipple. And then his mouth was there. A current of pure pleasure shot through her. Her eyes slipped closed. Another moan escaped.

She didn't notice.

Because his mouth was on her other breast.

He didn't abandon the first, for his fingers circled and pinched. Her head fell back as she savored the delicious sensations running through her. She never imagined a man could make her feel such glorious things. And then he stopped. Her eyes opened.

"Do you want me to go on?" he asked.

She gazed up at him. With the rise and fall of the ship, the moonlight streaming through the stern window first lit, then shadowed his face. Hiding, then revealing. Like the man who had her in such thrall. When she first met him, he was a dangerous enigma. But as she had come to know him, she had learned that he carried a light inside him, despite his grim background, despite his curse. And she had realized that one other, very important thing.

She loved him.

She wanted very much for him to continue.

"Yes," she said, as she pushed the night rail from her hips and let it pool on the deck. "Make love to me."

Raphael stared down at her in awe. This woman had the courage of a lion. She had crossed continents and endured the desert and mountains. Now she stood before him, naked, without the armor of her serviceable clothes and that wide-brimmed hat, without the armor of her prim demeanor. She was open and thoroughly vulnerable. Giving herself to him.

He swallowed. Something in the vicinity of his heart shifted. Making love to this woman would be nothing like when he had lain with other women. Sydney was different. He would worship her, cherish her, cradle her in pleasure.

Sweeping her up in his arms, he laid her on the bed. Her hair fanned out around her, framing her with its luxurious curls. He picked up one of those curls and allowed it to slip across his palm.

It was soft, silky, but seemed alive in his hand. It appeared nearly black against the white linen, but he knew it hid fire. Like the woman spread out before him. Enticing. Delicious.

He bent over her, about to kiss those delectable lips, when she stopped him with a hand on his chest.

"I want to see you," she said. "All of you." She caught her bottom lip between her teeth. "Am I too brazen?"

Even in the dim moonlight, he could see the dark stain on her cheeks. He chuckled. "No, *ya helo*. You are wonderful."

"What does *ya helo* mean?" she asked.

"My beautiful one," he said and pulled his shirt over his head.

Her gaze landed on his chest, then she smiled. "You are beautiful, too."

He grinned as he stripped off his breeches. No one had ever considered him beautiful.

She stared at his manhood, engorged with need for her. "Oh! You are quite…um…beautiful there as well."

Laughing, he crawled onto the bed and propped himself above her. This woman warmed his insides where he had been dark and cold for a long time. "I will make you feel like the most beautiful woman in the world."

She shook her head. "But I'm not."

He placed a soft kiss on one cheek, then the other. She had no idea how beautiful she was, but he would change that. "Wait and see," he whispered.

Sydney was not about to argue with him, so she lay quietly while he kissed her jaw, the hollow of her throat, and her shoulder. Those kisses were all very nice, but she wanted his mouth at her breast again. She wriggled, trying to get him to kiss lower, but he obstinately refused to go where she wanted. Instead, he kissed the side of her breast, the inside of her arm, her elbow down to her wrist, where his tongue danced across her pulse, then her palm. He proceeded to suck on every finger.

When he had finished, he kissed his way back up her arm, then, once more, the side of her breast. While his kisses were quite lovely, she wanted his mouth on her nipple. But she was distracted from that thought when he kissed down her ribs, to her belly. He swirled his tongue inside her bellybutton and that made her giggle. Then he moved lower.

Sitting up, he trailed his fingers down the inside of both thighs. She shivered. He ran his thumbs back up her thighs, and then he touched her *there*, where no man had ever touched before. She sucked in a breath, surprised, shocked, but loving his touch. It felt so good. Her legs fell apart, her eyes slipped closed, and she moaned.

"You are wet and delicious," he whispered. "I want to kiss you."

"Um-hm." Of course, he could kiss her.

But instead of kissing her mouth, she felt his tongue down there, where he had touched. Embarrassed at the incredibly intimate touch, she squirmed, but she didn't want him to stop. She had never expected making love could feel so wonderful.

One of his hands crept up and cupped her breast. His talented fingers rubbed and tugged at her nipple. She throbbed. She burned. She felt sensations she had never experienced before. She thought she might die. Her body was like a taut rope, ready to snap at any moment.

And then it did, releasing in a spasm of pleasure that made colors explode before her eyes.

Raphael watched her come apart in wonder. The prim, courageous woman who had stepped into his desert tent was the most sensuous woman he had ever known. And she tasted like heaven.

Slowly, her eyes opened. With a satisfied sigh, she said, "That was marvelous." Her fingers drifted across his shoulder and down his arm. "I want to touch you. All over."

He smiled. "You may touch all you like, *ya helo*."

When she gave him a little push, he obliged by rolling to his back. She sat up, leaned over, and placed a gentle kiss on his lips.

"Thank you for that wonderful experience," she murmured.

He chuckled. "It was my pleasure." And it was. Making love to Sydney gave him more joy than he'd ever known.

She ran her hand over his chest with a light touch, causing delightful tingles to erupt on his skin. Then her hand crept down across his ribs, his stomach, lower, and stopped.

"May I touch you there?" she whispered.

"Of course." He wanted that touch very much.

She wrapped her fingers around his shaft. And then she kissed and licked it. He was already aroused more than he'd ever been, and he nearly lost control at the touch of her tongue. But he closed his eyes, gritted his teeth, and endured the exquisite pleasure.

Sydney was surprised at the feel of him. Silky skin over steel. And he tasted divine. She licked and sucked and was surprised that her insides began to throb again with pleasure. Then she had the most marvelous idea.

"I want you inside of me," she said.

His eyes snapped open. They gleamed with a predatory light. A corner of his mouth tipped up.

"Are you sure?" he asked, as he brushed a strand of hair from her cheek.

Sydney didn't have to think about her answer. She loved him, and even if they never saw each other again when her quest was over, she would have this memory to cherish.

"Yes. I'm sure."

He rose, and in a single motion, she found herself on her back and him above her. She was trapped beneath him, but she didn't feel intimidated. Instead, she felt safe, protected. And excited. His head dipped and his mouth fastened on her breast. All those exquisite sensations deep within her jumped to life again.

She felt him nudge against her where he had kissed before. She opened her thighs and invited him in. She was throbbing with need.

Then he slipped inside her. But not quite far enough.

"I'm sorry," he whispered next to her ear.

At his single thrust, a sliver of pain cut through her. She gasped and froze.

"It won't ever hurt again," he murmured. "I promise. And I'll make the pain go away." Then he kissed her. His talented fingers played with her breast.

She loved his kisses. And his tugs at her nipple sent pleasurable pulses through her. He thrust once. She wanted more. She thrust back.

And then all she wanted was this. Him inside her, above her, giving her exquisite pleasure.

Until she spiraled up to the stars and exploded into a million sparks.

Raphael was lost in the feel of her. Her sensuous response amazed him. All he wanted was this woman. When she reached her peak, he barely had enough sense to pull out and swallow her scream in a kiss, for his pleasure peaked at nearly the same instant. Collapsing, he rolled to his side and took her with him, cuddling her against his chest. He had the insane thought that he would like to do this again and again, perhaps for the rest of his life.

But that could never happen. She would return to England, and he would return to the desert. But he had the feeling that separation would leave a hole in his heart.

"That was marvelous," she murmured. "Thank you."

He smiled and kissed her temple. "Perhaps we can do that again."

"Mm, yes, wonderful." Then she yawned and snuggled closer.

He kissed her temple as he hugged her against his chest. And the most amazing sensation curled around his heart.

I love you, Sydney Whelton, he said silently.

But she was already asleep.

Sydney awoke to Raphael's mumblings and thrashing. She had fallen asleep in his arms after their lovemaking, for once not thinking about her journey, her need for revenge, or how she was going to accomplish it. She had cuddled against him, secure from the demons that drove her. As the cobweb of sleep evaporated, she realized he was experiencing another nightmare like the one in the desert. In the dawn light coming through the stern window, she could see he was drenched in sweat and appeared to be in pain.

She tried to shake him awake, but that didn't work. So, she kissed him. His thrashing stopped and he kissed her back. His fingers tangled in her hair, his thumbs caressing her neck below her ears. It was a kiss like nothing she had ever experienced, desperate and searching. Then abruptly she was someplace else. Not in bed with the man who had made love to her but standing next to him in a dark cavern.

She was inside his nightmare.

And before her stood Nulkana in all her evil beauty.

"You!" the sorceress sneered at her. Then she crooned to Raphael, "So you have brought your little witch to protect you." She sashayed closer. "You know she cannot help." She drew a finger down his bare chest. "Only I can help you." Hooking a finger around the cord that held his amulet, she let it dangle. "If you give this to me, I can free you from your curse."

Raphael attempted to step back, but he appeared frozen.

"Leave him alone!" Sydney summoned her magic, but nothing happened. Of course. She was in a dream.

Nulkana turned to her. "Do you think you can save him with your puny power?" She studied Sydney with narrowed eyes and pursed her ruby lips. "You seem familiar to me. Who are you?"

Sydney raised her chin. "You killed my father. And I'm going to kill you."

Nulkana laughed. "Yes, of course. Now I know. He was an annoying insect beneath my heel." She tipped her head, once again studying Sydney. "But something else... Something else about you I should know..." She waved her hand in dismissal. "It does not matter." Placing her finger against Sydney's chest, she smiled an evil smile. "I will destroy you in the end."

Cold so intense it hurt radiated out from Nulkana's touch. Sydney gasped and tried to duck away, but she was held in place by some invisible force.

"Let her be!" Raphael yelled.

His fingers brushed hers, and their little fingers entwined.

Abruptly, Sydney was back in Raphael's bed in the master's cabin of the ship and being thoroughly kissed. In shock, she jerked back and stared down into Raphael's face. Bemused, he stared back.

"What was that?" she demanded.

"Another visit from the sorceress," he said, as he brushed back her hair.

Her brow creased in confusion. "But..." She glanced around the cabin. "We weren't here."

"I think we were in Nulkana's lair," he said.

She gasped at the implication of that statement. "I was in your nightmare with you."

"Yes. It seems our minds can connect when I touch you here." He traced a circle on the sensitive spot beneath her ear where a tiny pulse beat.

Sydney wanted to nestle into the gentle sensation, but instead, she waited, alert, to see if she would fall into his mind again. "Nothing happened this time."

"I'm not sure how it happens. Perhaps Zayed might be able to explain it. Or perhaps the man with the Crystal Dagger." Sympathy clouded his eyes. "I'm sorry the sorceress hurt you."

Sydney shook her head. "It doesn't matter. But don't ever give in to her. Whatever she promises, don't give up your amulet."

As soon as she said the words, the vague memory that had nagged her when she first saw the piece came into focus. Her father had owned a similar piece made of the same amber and with the same carvings, but a different shape. By the time she had returned to the stone circle and found him dead, it had disappeared, perhaps taken by the shadow creature. Or perhaps Nulkana. What would Nulkana do with two pieces? Sydney didn't want to think about that consequence.

"Promise me," she said.

"I will not," he promised solemnly. "I have my fierce Sydney to protect me." He listened a moment to the ship coming awake, the murmurs of the sailors below, the banging of pots from the cook, the tread of feet on the deck above. A teasing light entered his eyes. "I think I was kissing you a moment ago. I think I would like to kiss you again if that pleases you."

She smiled as her insides throbbed in anticipation and the fear of Nulkana dissipated. "That would please me very much."

Lucy would no doubt wonder where she had spent the night. Sydney didn't care. Whatever embarrassment she might feel was worth having Raphael kiss her and touch her, be inside her, and make her feel all those glorious sensations all over again.

Chapter 19

Sydney waited anxiously, along with Raphael, Zayed, Lucy, and Gide, in the *andron,* the entry hall, of the Ca' d'Este, the Venetian *palazzo* of the House of Auriano. The setting sun, shining through the wall of windows surrounding the water gate, bathed the room in an orange-gold glow. It was an impressive space despite its sparse furnishings and wall decorations and implied the huge size of the *palazzo* above. Intimidated, Sydney wondered for perhaps the third or fourth time if she had made a mistake coming here. After all, she was about to ask this powerful family for help to kill an evil sorceress. She gazed around the room again, absorbing its stark grandeur, and tried to tamp down her anxiety.

The floor of alternating red and white stone squares stretched from the water gate where they had arrived by gondola to another door at the opposite side. A huge wrought iron chandelier hung from the ceiling two floors above, and a gallery ringed the upper floor. The family coat of arms was carved into the paneling and painted on the each of the walls above benches placed at intervals around the room. The heraldic device was unusual — a broken circle of three arcs, stabbed through the center with a lightning bolt.

Raphael, looking every bit like a pirate in black leather breeches tucked into jack boots, white linen shirt open at the neck, and gold brocade waistcoat, stood with his arms folded before one of the carvings and stared at it. His turban was gone, and his shoulder-length, chestnut hair was pulled back into a tight queue highlighted with golden streaks as if the sun hid within its depths. He had trimmed and partially shaved his beard, leaving only a thin line along his jaw and above his lip.

Sydney thought he had to be the most attractive, dangerous, daring, gallant man she had ever met. He appeared entranced by the carving, for he had been gazing at it since they first stepped inside. She watched him with concern wrinkling her brow. Something about those carvings troubled him.

She glanced at the others. Zayed, dressed in desert splendor of white turban and white kaftan over white tunic and pantaloons, stood inside the water gate. At his hip, a dagger hung from a red braided cord that ran across his chest from his shoulder. Lucy and Gide stood together, appearing to gain comfort from each other. Gide was in his raggedy *djellaba* with its hood pulled low, and Lucy wore the only frock she had brought, a yellow muslin that washed out her features. She had lost weight on their journey, and the dress drooped in places that she used to fill out. Sydney distractedly decided that when they returned to England, she would buy her friend a new frock, maybe several, and ones that would bring out Lucy's lovely brown eyes and pink cheeks.

Sydney smoothed the skirt of her green muslin frock. It was a serviceable garment, but not one she would have wished to wear meeting a member of the House of Auriano for the first time. She and Lucy had brought only a meager, serviceable wardrobe when they had left England. She had never expected to come face-to-face with one of the most powerful families in Venice.

When they had arrived in the lagoon where the ship anchored the day before, she had sent a message to the Auriano *palazzo*, asking to meet with one of the family. She had received a terse response agreeing to a meeting, and signed cryptically with an ornate letter *A*. Who would be receiving them? She knew little about the family, and Gide had been less than forthcoming. He said he knew of three siblings, two brothers and a sister, but refused to say more.

The man who let them in, dressed simply in brown woolen breeches, white shirt, and brown woolen vest — unlike the formally dressed butlers of London — gave no indication of which family members were in residence. His gaze had stuttered when he saw Raphael, but his expression remained impassive. He had asked them to wait, and then had disappeared up the staircase leading to the mezzanine and other floors above.

Several minutes passed, then servants began to appear carrying chairs and a small table, followed by others with a basket of fruit, a tray of meats, cheeses and olives, and several bottles of wine. The man who had allowed them in followed.

"Make yourselves comfortable, *per favore*," he said. "I am Piero. If you require anything else, you will let me know, *si*? *La duchessa* will be with you shortly." He bowed and retreated behind a door beneath the stairs that led to the mezzanine.

Sydney looked around at the others who appeared just as nonplussed as she was. No one moved for a moment. Then Lucy sat in one of the chairs placed around the table overflowing with refreshments.

"I'm famished," she said, "and this looks delicious." She cut a small piece of cheese and popped it into her mouth. "Mm. Very tasty."

Sydney took a step toward one of the chairs but stopped when she heard footsteps descending. A beautiful blonde woman appeared on the stairs. Her fashionable, simple, high-waisted gown of blue-green wool set off eyes of an amazing turquoise color. As she stepped to the floor, she smiled coolly.

"*Bonjour*," she said. "I am la Duchesse d'Auriano. Welcome to the Ca' d'Este." Her encompassing glance faltered when it fell on Raphael, but she continued smoothly, "I am sorry that my husband cannot be here to greet you, but he is unavailable at the moment."

Lucy rose from her seat, and both she and Sydney bobbed a curtsy. Raphael and Zayed bowed. Gide remained unmoving, as if struck to stone. Puzzled at his impolite behavior, Sydney sent him a quick glare.

"Thank you for agreeing to meet with us so quickly, duchess," she said, hiding her surprise that the duchess first greeted them in French. She thought the family was Venetian.

"Please, call me Solange," the woman said.

Sydney made the introductions and was about to introduce Gide, when he made a strange choking noise.

"You are the *duchessa*?" he blurted. "How can that be? I saw you kill him!"

Solange stared at him, then gasped and the color drained from her face. "Oh, *mon dieu*! Gide! Is that you?"

Gide looked as if he wanted to take back his words, then he pushed back the hood of his *djellaba*. "*Salut*, Solange."

Solange rushed to him with a cry and enfolded him in a great hug. As she sobbed on his shoulder, his arms slowly encircled her. Sydney saw the sheen of tears on his cheeks. Touched by the sweet reunion, she motioned everyone to the chairs, so Solange and Gide could have a private moment. The two joined them not long after with Solange dabbing at her eyes with a frilly handkerchief and Gide surreptitiously swiping his cheeks.

"*Pardonnez-moi*," Solange said. "I have not seen my brother for two years."

Gide continued to stare at her. "The Duke of Auriano is dead. I saw it with my own eyes. What happened? Did you wed another brother?"

She smiled. "No, I did not wed another. The duke, Antonio, my husband, is not dead. It is a long story that I will tell another time." She took his hand, then glanced around at everyone. Her gaze stopped at Raphael.

"*Pardonnez-moi, monsieur*, but have we met? You look quite familiar," she said.

"Unfortunately, no, duchess," he said. "But I am glad to make the acquaintance of such a lovely lady."

She laughed lightly at his gallantry, then sobered. "If my brother is here, I have the suspicion that you have not come with good news."

Sydney took a breath. She had practiced what she would say many times, but now, sitting before this woman who had been reunited with her brother, she was reluctant to reveal her purpose in arriving at the *palazzo*. Moreover, she had a suspicion that the duchess, despite her calm words, most likely would not welcome what Sydney was about to ask her.

She took a sip of the wine one of the servants had poured to gain some time and fortify herself. Absently, she noted the wine was delicious. As she placed the glass on the table, she said, "I am trying to find someone, and I was informed that the House of Auriano might be able to help."

Solange slid a glance at her brother, who stared back. The corners of her mouth tightened, but her tone was level when she asked, "Who are you trying to find?"

Sydney swallowed. "A sorceress named Nulkana."

Everything seemed to go very still, as if the house and all its occupants held their breath. Solange stared at Sydney, then turned to Gide, who gave a small nod.

Casually, the duchess picked up her glass of wine, but her hand shook. "I have not heard that name spoken in almost two years." She took a sip, and when she placed the glass on the table, it wobbled and spilled. Servants rushed forward to clean the mess, but she waved them away. "She is very dangerous. Malevolent. Why do you wish to find her?"

"Because she killed my father." Sydney's hand clenched in her lap. The ring on her forefinger dug into her, reminding her of her mother's horrific death. A tiny, suspicious connection began to form in her brain, so wispy and shapeless that she couldn't grab it.

Solange took a moment before she murmured, "You have my condolences. But I am not sure I can help you. I would have to discuss this with the rest of the family. They are in seclusion at the Castello d'Auriano in the north. My husband and I will return there tomorrow."

Disappointed, Sydney watched the spilled wine drip to one of the white squares on the floor, staining it like blood. Then her glance fell on Raphael, who sat brooding and gripping the arms of his chair with white knuckles. Something disturbed him.

"The carvings on the walls are very interesting," he said. "Can you tell us something about them?"

Solange tipped her head as if thinking over her answer, or as if she were listening to something. Then she said, "It is the family crest. It's supposed to represent an ancient artifact with powerful magic, but that is nonsense, a mere legend. Magic is part of fairy tales, *oui*?" Her smile seemed a bit forced.

"The artifact appears broken," he observed.

"*Oui*, very sad." Solange nodded. "The legend says that the artifact was broken apart and the pieces scattered."

Raphael pulled his amulet from beneath his shirt. "Like this piece?" The amulet appeared to glow, looking like a streak of lightning dangling from the cord, then it went dark.

Solange's eyes widened and she sucked in a breath.

"The ancient magical artifact isn't nonsense, is it?" he demanded. "This is one of the pieces, isn't it?"

"How did you get that?" Solange whispered, as if afraid to speak aloud.

"I've owned it most of my life." Raphael tucked it back inside his shirt.

Solange watched him hide it. "Who are you?"

"I don't know." Raphael's statement landed like a stone in the room.

Uneasy, startled silence filled the space.

Sydney felt the need to explain. She cleared her throat, reluctant to insult the duchess if what she was about to suggest were untrue. "Gide believes that Raphael might be related to the House of Auriano."

Solange looked to her brother, who shifted uncomfortably in his chair, but nodded. She glanced up at the mezzanine, dim now with the setting of the sun, then she turned back to Raphael.

"Do you wear it all the time?" she asked.

"Is that important?" His eyes narrowed with suspicion.

"*Oui*, I believe it is," she said, her gaze level.

"Why?" he challenged.

"Because if it is a piece of the magical artifact, it could have harmful effects on a member of the House of Auriano," she said.

"It does nothing." His jaw clenched obstinately.

You are lying, si?

The voice sounded in Sydney's head, not aloud, and not from anyone sitting around her. It was not Raphael who had spoken. She glanced first at him, but he was frowning at Solange. Then Sydney looked around the room as she searched for the source. Lucy and Zayed appeared shocked. Gide looked angry. Movement near the rail of the mezzanine above drew her attention. A shadowy figure floated down and landed beside Solange's chair.

Raphael shot to his feet, knocking his chair backwards.

Another! Like him!

Solange smiled up at the shadowy figure. "May I present my husband, Antonio, Duke of Auriano. It is unfortunate that he is in his Shadow form when you arrived, but these things happen, *oui*?" She ended with a fatalistic shrug.

The Shadow executed a formal bow. *Buona sera, signores e signorinas.*

"Oh, my!" Lucy, looking very pale, fanned herself.

Gide took her hand. "Don't worry, *mademoiselle*," he said, shooting a hostile look at the Shadow. "He's quite harmless."

Only with the ladies. The duke cast an annoyed glance at Gide, then turned to Raphael. *Would you mind if I examine your piece?*

Stunned, Raphael stared. The figure was about his size, well-formed, dark, as if cancelling all light within its outline, with the faint definition of muscle visible. His eyes looked like molten gold. Was this how he appeared when he turned to darkness?

Still in shock, Raphael could only manage to shake his head.

Per favore, Sior Raphael. I will return it, the shadow figure said.

Raphael's thoughts raced. If this man — the Duke of Auriano — turned to the same type of darkness he experienced, could he truly be part of this family? Did they share the same curse? Could he trust them? They were searching for the Sphere of Astarte, but to what end? Good or evil? If he handed over his piece, would they return it? If he removed the piece from around his neck, he would become like the man before him — a Shadow, the duchess had called him. Should he reveal that?

Sydney said she had seen another Shadow on the night Nulkana killed her father. Could this be the same one?

Raphael couldn't get his thoughts to settle. He was relieved that he was not the only soul who became something else, who turned to Shadow. At the same time, his uniqueness had given him a sense of identity that he lacked, not knowing who his family was. He wanted very much to be part of a family. He had longed for it his whole life. He had tried to remember his origins, but he only remembered snatches, not enough to help. But he had also learned that a man who was a friend could turn to enemy. Was this man friend or enemy?

Unsure where the duke's principles lay, Raphael came up with an answer to his request.

223

"I will remove it, but I will require privacy," he said. He didn't want to shock the ladies when he shed his clothes.

The duke sent him a shrewd look as if he were aware of the path of Raphael's thoughts. *In there.* He indicated one of the closed doors.

With a nod of thanks, Raphael glanced at Sydney, who smiled her encouragement, then stepped into a small room. A few crates were stacked against one wall, but otherwise, the room was empty, perfect for his needs. After undressing quickly, he wrapped his hand around the amulet. It felt a bit warmer than the heat it gained from his body. A bad omen or a good sign? Only one way to discover that answer.

He pulled the cord over his head. Then he let the amulet drop to his pile of clothes. The chill he experienced whenever he turned to darkness slipped through his body and took his solid form with it. He glanced down at his hand. Dark, shadowy. Clenching his fist, he felt nothing. No skin against skin, no pressure of moving muscle or sinew. His sense of touch was gone. He was—as the Auriano family called it—Shadow.

With a flick of his fingers, he raised the amulet from his pile of clothes. It hovered beyond his hand. Another tiny flick and the cord appeared to twist around his palm, an illusion that looked like he held it. In reality, the hold he had on it was mental, not physical. He would allow the duke to examine the amulet, but he was not about to release it into his custody.

With a breath, he walked out to reveal himself.

Lucy was the first to see him. "Merciful Heavens! Oh, my!" She looked about to faint.

Sydney patted her hand. "It's only Mr. Pirate. He won't hurt you, Lucy. Here, take a sip of wine." She handed her friend a glass.

Raphael's attention centered on the duke, who scrutinized him head to toe. The man said nothing for several long moments, and Raphael forced himself to endure his examination.

Piero emerged from the door beneath the stairs and stopped dead. "*Madre di Dio!*" He muttered something else and made the sign of the cross. "It is him!" Fixated on Raphael, he crept forward until he stood next to the duke.

Do you know this man, Piero? the duke asked.

"*Sior* Tonio," Piero began, then stopped and swallowed as he stared at Raphael. "*Sior* Tonio…the curse…It is only on the House of Auriano."

Si, that I know, the duke said, his tone dry.

Piero continued to stare at Raphael. "*Sior* Tonio, this man belongs to the House of Auriano."

Is he a cousin? the duke asked, then answered his own question. *Impossible. Piero, my father was an only son, no siblings.*

Piero finally looked at the duke. "*Sior* Tonio, I believe this man is your brother."

Silence dropped into the room.

Raphael felt everyone's shocked gaze, but the heaviest was from the man — the Shadow — standing across from him. That molten gaze looked upon him with suspicion and a bit of hostility. Antagonized by the man's reaction, Raphael stiffened. He hadn't traveled to Venice to be insulted. He had come to help Sydney in her quest. Despite his desire to find his roots, he didn't need to be accepted by this duke or his family. He had Zayed and his own life. When Sydney had accomplished what she had set out to do, he would return to the desert.

My brother, my twin, is in Auriano, the duke finally said, his silent words chilly.

Piero ducked his head. "There was another."

Che cosa? The duke swung to Piero.

"Your parents," Piero said with another gulp, "had another child, a boy, before you were born."

Si, I had heard of this. The babe was born dead. The duke's words challenged.

"No, *Sior* Tonio, he was not." Piero shook his head, then sent a sympathetic glance in Raphael's direction before continuing. "Nulkana was menacing the people in the *castello* and the village, and she threatened to steal the babe. To keep him safe, your parents sent him to your mother's sister and her husband, who had no children of their own. Several years passed before the sorceress retreated to Venice. When your parents were finally able to retrieve the child, they learned that your mother's sister and her husband and everyone in the town where they lived had been either killed by raiders or taken as slaves. No one was left. They searched and sent letters everywhere, but no one knew what had become of the child, whether he had been killed or taken by the raiders. Your mother was devastated." He paused and looked at Raphael. "The child's name was Angelo. Angelo Felice Lucio D'Este."

Stunned at hearing the name, Raphael stared at Zayed, who stared back. *Angel. Angelo,* he mused. *Could that have been what I was trying to say when I was sick?*

"It is possible," Zayed said.

Raphael turned back to the duke and explained about being ill, calling out in his fever, and losing most of his early memories.

The duke was not convinced. *That could have merely been a sick child's rantings.*

The duchess covered the duke's hand resting on her shoulder. "But, *mon amor,* there is a resemblance about the eyes, *oui?*"

"Gide noticed that, too," Sydney said. "He was the one to suggest that Raphael might be related to the House of Auriano."

Raphael watched the duke send an aggrieved glance at Gide, who shrugged an insolent shoulder and smiled derisively. These men shared a complicated history, but Raphael wasn't interested in that. He sensed that Auriano resented his sudden appearance and the possibility that he might be a long-lost brother — an older brother who could usurp his title and wealth. Raphael wanted neither. He only wanted to know his origins. And perhaps break the curse.

Auriano turned back to him. *May I see your amulet?* He held out his hand.

Raphael noticed a tug on the cord wrapped around his palm. It was a signal that the duke would use his power to examine the piece if Raphael refused. With a wry tip to his lips, he held up the amulet, allowing it to dangle freely, but kept a firm hold on the cord. Two could play at this game.

Auriano wrapped his fingers around the amulet. He immediately froze. His eyes widened. Then he grimaced. A silent bellow of pain pounded into Raphael's head. And Auriano's hand, once dark and shadowy, slowly began to turn to flesh and bone. But the duke was doubled over in agony.

"Tonio!" The duchess tried to pry open Auriano's fingers. "*Mon amor,* let it go!"

226

Auriano finally dropped it and fell back a step. With a muttered *"Scusi,"* he turned and strode away, stopping before one of the carvings on the wall. Cradling the hand transmuting back to its shadowy form, he stared up at the heraldic device for several moments.

Raphael watched him closely as he wondered at the duke's violent reaction to touching the amulet. Unlike the duke, he had never experienced anything like that. The piece had always been a comfort to him, a security against the darkness, the otherness, the loss of touch, smell, and taste that he suffered when he removed it.

When Auriano turned around, he said, *Piero, what was that?* But he stared at Raphael.

"It is a reaction to touching a piece of the Sphere of Astarte, *Sior* Tonio," he said, looking nervously from Auriano to Raphael.

But he wears it about his neck, and it doesn't affect him. Auriano jerked his chin in Raphael's direction. His molten gaze landed on Raphael. *Why doesn't it affect you?*

Affronted at the rudeness of the duke, who was also Shadow, Raphael gave an insolent shrug. *Perhaps I am stronger than you.*

Auriano took an angry, threatening step forward. Solange jumped to her feet and planted herself before him.

"You will not challenge him," she declared. "He is a guest in our house. He could be your brother."

Auriano's chin went up aggressively as if he might attack. Then his shoulders dropped.

Of course, he said and executed a bow in Raphael's direction. *Mi scusi. This is a mystery that we must solve. You will come with us to Auriano tomorrow.* His gaze encompassed the others seated around the little table. *Per favore, you will be our guests at our castello.*

Raphael glanced at Sydney, who chewed her bottom lip. A line of uncertainty appeared between her brows. He wanted to travel to Auriano to find the answers to the mystery of his family. But he had committed to Sydney's quest, and he would follow her lead, for during this journey, she had become very dear to him. He loved her.

Signorina, Auriano added, bowing again, this time toward Sydney. *I believe you will find help in what you seek to do at our castello. Your desire for the sorceress's death is also our desire.*

227

Sydney's face cleared. "Of course, Excellency. Thank you for your kind invitation." She smiled, then turned to Raphael with a warm glance.

Solange clapped. "Excellent! You will be our guests for dinner. Piero will show you where you may freshen up."

Apprehension assailed Raphael. Once he replaced the amulet around his neck, he would need to feed the cravings that came when he returned to human.

Solange smiled at him. "We will bring anything you might need when you return to flesh and bone."

With a silent sigh of relief, Raphael bowed his thanks. The only thing he would need was Sydney's kiss to feed the craving. Perhaps more than a kiss, for he had been Shadow for quite some time.

He hid his smile of anticipation.

Raphael paced in the opulent room he had been given. The sun had set, and glorious pinks and oranges reflected off the water of the canal below his window. They created colored patches on the coffered ceiling and the walls covered in gilt-edged panels of green silk. But he wasn't interested in the room's decoration. He needed to satisfy the cravings after he transmuted from Shadow to flesh and bone. The duchess had assured him that he would be given anything he needed. A large tray on a table beneath one window held the scattered remnants of the food he had consumed. But he needed something else.

The touch of a woman.

Any woman would do.

No, not any woman.

What he truly craved was Sydney's touch.

That was not going to happen. He didn't want her to see him like this, half-mad with wanting. Desperate. Feeling as if he might crawl out of his skin. He ran his fingers through his hair and halted before a window. A single gondola floated past, its occupants hidden inside a small cabin. He wondered who they were and where they were going, a tiny distraction from the need that rode him.

A knock sounded at the door. He strode across the room and flung the door wide. He had expected to see someone who had been sent to alleviate his pain. Instead, Sydney stood there with a hesitant smile on her lips, her glorious hair flowing down her back, and her bare toes peeking from beneath the hem of her dress.

"I thought you might need some help," she said.

Oh, yes, he needed help, but not hers, not like this.

"Go away," he growled. "Come back later."

Her smile slipped. A crease appeared between her brows. "I always knew you were an insufferable cad."

At the insult, his eyes widened. She had called him insufferable before. Then, he had found it amusing. Now, it pierced his heart. As she started to turn away, he knew he couldn't let her go.

"No," he croaked.

He caught her before she slipped away. Threading his fingers through her hair, he pulled her close and kissed her. The feel of her lips caused something to unclench deep inside him. This was what he wanted. What he needed.

Backing into the room, he dragged Sydney with him, never breaking contact, and kicked the door shut. *Stay,* he said silently. *Please.*

Her response was to wrap her arms tighter around him and press against him. The heat between them sizzled. His hands wandered over her, feeling her curves, delighting in her softness. Swinging her around, he backed her toward the bed, where they fell together.

He couldn't get enough of her.

He wanted.

Needed.

Craved.

He had no thought except to satisfy the compelling desire of his body. She was the first sip of water after days of thirst. She was the cool shade after the burning sun. He pulled up her skirt, fumbled with his clothes. All the while, he kept his mouth glued to hers.

And then—Allah be praised!—he was inside her. She was tight and slick, and she felt like heaven. Her legs wrapped around his waist. And he was gone.

His climax hit him like a tidal wave. It dragged him under, pounded through him, and sent pleasure surging through him again and again and again. Mindless, he rode it, letting it take him to heights he had never experienced. Stars exploded. Galaxies swirled. The sun kissed the earth. When it was done, when it had wrung every last bit of sensation from him, he collapsed on top of her.

The gnawing, hungry craving was gone. In its place was sanity, and a realization of where he was.

What had he done?

Sydney.

Remorse and guilt stabbed through him. He had taken her, used her without thinking. This was Sydney, brave and unselfish, who had given herself to him. He groaned and rolled off her.

"Forgive me," he said.

"For what?" She propped herself up on an elbow.

"For acting like an animal. For being an insufferable cad, as you said." He couldn't look at her and threw his arm across his eyes. "You should go on to Auriano without me."

"Why?"

Surging to his feet, he paced to the window, straightening his clothes. "Because I'm cursed. Because you deserve better."

"Better than what?" A touch of annoyance edged her question.

"Better than someone like me." He ran his fingers through his hair in frustration.

"Why would I want someone else?" This time, anger traced through her words.

He swung to her and ground out, "Because I took you like a dog in heat. Thoughtlessly. Because I've been a slave. I'm an adventurer with no roots, no family."

"You may have found your family." With a wave of her hand, she indicated the *palazzo* around them and the people in it. She seemed to ignore the rest of his bad qualities.

He snapped, "I've been a thief. I've killed people."

She rose to her feet and approached. "Did you thieve to live? Did you kill to protect yourself?"

He had. But that did not dull the guilt that clouded his heart.

Stopping before him, she did not wait for his answer. "I believe you are a good man in here." She touched his chest where his heart resided. Her hand dropped to her side, and she bowed her head. "I am not from a great family," she said quietly. "I am not even from a respectable family. My parents were not married. I am illegitimate. I'm a nobody. My mother ran a gaming house, and my father — " Her words choked off. She shrugged and started to turn away.

He caught her by the arm. "Sydney...." When she turned back to him, doubt shadowed her eyes. He brushed a strand of hair from her cheek. "Sydney, that does not matter to me."

She said nothing for a moment as she gazed at him. "Then why should what you were in the past matter to me?"

Stunned into speechlessness at her logic, he merely stared at her.

A tiny smile curved her lips. "I am concerned with what you are now. I think I should very much like to learn more. You've taught me about kisses and such, and that night on the ship was lovely." A hot blush colored her cheeks. "But just now...um...." She gestured at the bed. "Um...You seemed to...well...enjoy yourself immensely." That blush seeped down her throat and across her chest.

He was entranced. And awed. And humbled. And determined to make amends for his selfish oversight.

He cupped her cheeks. "Sydney," he whispered. "Sydney-Who-Is-Not-A-Boy, will you make love with me?"

Her tiny smile grew into a grin. "Oh, yes, please."

Sydney had not quite known what to expect when she knocked on his door. She had experienced his desperation behind the kiss in the *kheterra* after he had shown himself to her as Shadow. But his distress this time wrung her heart, so she forgave his rough and quick coupling. Now, as his hands glided down her arms and he drew her to the bed, she knew her gentle lover was back.

His touch sent tingles down to her fingertips. She wanted those fingertips all over him. And she wanted his fingertips all over her. When he sat on the bed, she stood before him and trailed her finger from the hollow of his throat down the vee of the open neck of his shirt.

His gaze turned mischievous. "Would you like to see more?"

231

Oh, yes, she would very much. But she was still shy and a bit embarrassed about seeing him unclothed. Even though dusk had fallen, a strip of sunset at the horizon still lit the room with color. The last time they had made love, the cabin on the ship had been dark with only the moon for light. Swallowing, she nodded.

He tipped his head. "If I show you more, you will have to show me something in return. One body part for another, Miss Whelton."

Sydney hid her grin at the reminder of their bargain in the desert when he had revealed his face. But two could play at this game. "That depends on what you show me," she said coolly, feeling anything but cool.

A dimple deepened in his cheek. Without taking his gaze from her, he toed off one of his boots.

She glanced down at his stocking-covered foot. "Oh, Mr. Pirate, you are hardly showing me anything."

With a grin, he toed off his other boot.

Crossing her arms, she sniffed her disdain. "Really, Mr. Pirate, I believe you can do much better."

"Perhaps you could suggest something, Miss Whelton," he said, with a perplexed crease between his brows.

Oh, my, what could she suggest? She wanted to see all of him. But embarrassment tied her tongue. At the same time, she remembered the feel of his muscular chest beneath her hands. She very much wanted to see that.

"This," she said, pointing at his shirt.

A sly smile curved his lips. "If I remove my shirt, what will you show me in return?"

The prospect of undressing before him heated her down to her toes. The memory of being naked with him, skin to skin, created a delicious throb between her thighs. Without saying a word, she untied the bow at the neckline of her frock. The dangling ribbons teased with promise.

"Ah," he said. Then in one fluid motion, he pulled his shirt over his head and flung it aside.

He was magnificent, all golden skin over the planes and ridges of his muscles. She couldn't keep her hands away. Without thinking, she reached out, but he ducked away.

"No touching until you keep your side of the bargain, Miss Whelton," he said.

Sydney caught her lip between her teeth. The last time she was undressed before him, they had been in his dark cabin. The prospect of being naked and in full view both embarrassed and excited her. Beneath her shift, her breasts seemed to press against the material, wanting escape. Slowly, she slid her frock from her shoulders and let it slide down her arms.

He leaned back on his hands, his gaze warm with sly appreciation. "Very nice," he said. "But our bargain isn't quite equal."

Of course not. She had purposely not worn stays, but her shift covered her, although barely, while he was gloriously exposed. And she did so want to touch that golden skin. Before she lost her courage, she slid her arms out of her frock and shift. Her frock slipped to the floor, and her shift fell to her waist.

"Magnificent," he murmured.

He pulled her between his knees, wrapped his arms around her waist, and sucked on first one breast, then the other. An arrow of pure pleasure shot through her. She gasped and her head fell back. His tongue and lips worked magic, and before she realized it, her shift joined her frock on the floor at her feet. She stood before him, naked.

He fell back on the bed, taking her with him. The feel of his hard chest beneath her felt wonderful, but he still wore his breeches. As he continued his caresses, she pushed herself away.

"Not quite a fair bargain, Mr. Pirate," she said, straddling him.

He grinned. "You're right, Miss Whelton, but you'll have to help me. My hands are full." To demonstrate, he cupped each of her breasts and tweaked the nipples.

Sydney sucked in a breath at his touch. While that felt amazing, she wanted more. The only way to get that was to undress him. She'd never, ever undressed a man before. But if she were going to do that, the man she wanted to start with was the one who lay beneath her. She unbuttoned one of the buttons on his breeches. Then another. And another. And another. Each time, the arrow of hair that pointed downward across his taut belly became more visible. She knew what was at the end. Her prize.

She pulled down his breeches, stripped them off, and flung them away. His erection stood proud and large. She stared. Raphael had caressed her private parts and created the most magnificent sensations inside her. She wanted to do the same for him. Tentatively, she ran a finger down the shaft. The silkiness of the skin always surprised her. Wrapping her hand around it, she squeezed. Raphael went very still.

She snatched back her hand. "Did I hurt you?" she asked.

His eyes gleamed in the near darkness. "Not at all. Just the opposite." He took her hand and placed it back where it had been.

Fascinated, Sydney ran her hand up and down his shaft. This was his most intimate part, his maleness. It was him. Bending closer, she kissed the tip, then swirled her tongue around it.

A half moan, half sigh escaped him.

Encouraged, she took him into her mouth. She found that kissing him like this was nearly as pleasurable as having him kiss her. And as she kissed him, his hands trailed over her, leaving tingly warmth wherever he touched.

"Sydney," he murmured, as his hands landed on her hips. "I need to be inside you."

Oh, yes, she wanted him there. Before she had another thought, he lifted her and impaled her on his shaft. She gasped in surprise and pleasure.

"Ride me," he whispered.

Her eyes widened. She'd never imagined that she could do such a thing. But he felt so good snugged deep inside her. She remembered his sensuous words as they rode together on his camel. His breath fanning her ear. His suggestions swirling in her head like sumptuous smoke. Her muscles clenched with desire.

She experimented by wriggling a bit. That felt very nice. And then one of his very talented thumbs dipped between her thighs and caressed her nub. A hard throb of pleasure pulsed through her. She needed to feel more. With her gaze locked on his, she rode him as he wanted. As she needed.

Her world shrank down to where they were joined. To where her need met his desire. To where nothing mattered but the passion between them. Hotter and higher. Until she reached the peak and exploded into space. With him. Together.

Then she collapsed on top of him. And fell asleep, still connected to the man she loved.

Chapter 20

They left for Auriano the next morning. To Raphael's surprise, the duke was flesh and bone when they gathered in the *andron* of the Venetian *palazzo*. He was a handsome man of the same height and build as Raphael. His dark brown hair had gold streaks through it, and his eyes were the color of old gold, resembling his own in color and shape, and like those he had seen in the vision from the satin cloak. The similarities between himself and the duke were beginning to convince him more and more that he was the child Piero had described.

Solange explained that since finding a piece of the magical Sphere of Astarte, her husband became Shadow only at night when the curse came upon him. Before that, he had transformed into Shadow at the full moon and not returned to flesh and bone until the new moon. Raphael felt some sympathy for the man who was unable to control his curse.

Placing his hand over his amulet, he thanked Allah, God, Yahweh, and any other name of the Almighty for its presence. His first master had taken it from him once when he was a youth, and only returned it after being frightened by his shadowy form. But the helplessness Raphael had felt upon losing it had sent him into deep despair.

They headed to the mainland and crossed the lagoon in a flotilla of gondolas and small boats loaded with their possessions. As they passed the *Desert Star*, Don Quixote and the sailors lined the rails and rigging and cheered them on. When they reached the mainland, two coaches awaited. Gide rode with the duke and duchess because Solange wanted to reacquaint herself with her brother. Sydney, Lucy, Raphael and Zayed rode in the other. But after one stop to refresh themselves, Zayed opted to ride up beside Piero, who drove one of the coaches, and Lucy rode with Gide in the duke's coach. That left Raphael alone with Sydney.

As soon as they set out, Sydney felt his warm gaze. Despite having traveled for weeks through the desert with Raphael and having made glorious love with him the night before and on the ship, she shyly refused to look at him and kept her gaze on the forest they were passing through. She couldn't believe how wanton she had acted at the *palazzo*. Why, she had knocked on his door and offered herself. And then when they had made love, why, she had been so…forward. It was much too embarrassing.

His presence seemed to overwhelm the space inside the coach. She pulled her shawl tighter around her shoulders and tried to ignore the tickly sense of his gaze on her.

"Do you find the trees interesting?" he asked, as he ran his fingers up her arm beneath her shawl.

A shiver ran through her at his touch, distracting her from the endless wall of trees outside the coach. Without turning, she said, "I have never been to this country, and I wish to see everything."

"One tree is like another." His fingers trailed back down her arm.

That made her turn. "I should think that you would find them fascinating, since you live in the desert."

"I find you fascinating, lovely Sydney," he said. "I want to kiss you."

Without warning, he circled her waist, plucked her from her seat and sat her on his knees. She straddled him, and in order not to slip to the floor, she grabbed his shoulders.

"This is quite inappropriate," she said, both embarrassed and excited at her seductive position. Visions from the night before flashed through her head. But they weren't in any private place. They were in a coach, for heaven's sake. "What if the coach stops?"

"It won't. We just set out." His fingers slid up her arm again, creating those delicious tingles and raising goosebumps.

"But what if we are stopped by bandits?" she asked, her words breathless.

His hand cupped the back of her neck. "Do you care what bandits think?"

"Only this one," she said.

He chuckled as the coach lurched. She would have toppled off his lap if he had not wrapped his arms tightly around her. As she slipped closer, his erection pressed against her where she was soft and damp and aching for him. She gasped.

"I'm going to kiss you, Sydney-Who-Is-Very-Much-Not-A-Boy," he murmured. "Would you mind if I did that?"

She did not mind. In fact, she wanted him to kiss her. Quite a bit. Staring into those golden eyes, all she could do was nod.

One corner of his mouth tipped up in a sly smile. "I did not think you would mind."

With a bit of pressure at her nape, he drew her closer until their lips barely touched. He brushed her mouth once, twice, and again. Sydney thought that was very nice, but she wanted one of those kisses that made her drown in him. That made her toes curl. That turned her brainless. Cupping his face, she kissed him back, but he drew away.

"Tsk, beautiful Sydney," he whispered. "Slowly. We don't want to scare the horses."

"No, of course not," she said, but she could not understand how what they were doing inside the coach would matter to the horses.

He drew away her shawl, then tugged the ribbon that tied the neckline of her dress. With a sweep of his fingers, he pushed both her dress and her chemise off her shoulders. One breast popped free. Before she had time to protest, he bent his head and covered it with his mouth. He sucked and licked, twirled the nipple with his tongue. She breathed a moan.

Releasing her breast, he touched a finger to her lips. "Sh. Remember the horses."

"I'll try," she solemnly agreed. Then she swirled her tongue around his finger and sucked it in.

"Mm," he said.

She giggled. "Sh. Remember the horses."

"I'll try," he murmured as he kissed her jaw and covered her breast with his hand. Then he captured her lips once more. Hungrily, she kissed him back, opening to him, inviting him in. Heat pulsed through her, centering between her thighs. She undulated against him, pressing against his hardness where she was soft and wanting.

His fingers slipped up her leg and his hand splayed across her thigh. She wanted to feel those magnificent sensations that he could create inside her. With a little whimper, she wriggled closer, her thighs falling wider to give him access. His thumb dipped down and touched that magic nub. He pressed and stroked. Soft and slow. Then harder, faster.

And with a burst of exploding stars, she came apart, screaming into his kiss.

When her world righted itself, she was a limp doll with her head on his shoulder. She felt languid and cherished. She wanted to stay snuggled against him forever. Slowly, her eyes opened. She blinked. The forest outside the windows had become fields. They were in a coach on their way to the Castello d'Auriano.

"Oh my!" Her eyes widened at the realization of where they were and what they had done. Heat rose in her cheeks. The bodice of her dress was around her waist and her skirt was bunched at her hips. One of his warm hands was on her bare back. The other was still between her thighs, cupping her secret parts. "Oh, my!" she exclaimed again.

His pleased little smile turned into a grin. "Shush, dearest Sydney. You don't want to frighten the horses."

Appalled at herself, she gasped. "Did I scream?" She clapped a hand to her mouth. "Oh, my goodness! I did scream." She scowled at him. "You made me scream."

"It was a very nice scream. Quiet and ladylike." His thumb caressed her little nub. "I could make you scream again."

"You will not." She pushed his hand off her thigh and tried to wrestle the top of her dress back into place. "I cannot believe I allowed you to kiss me."

He helped to straighten the top of her dress. "It was more than a kiss." His fingers tangled in her hair and drew her toward him.

"This is a kiss." He demonstrated by covering her mouth with his. By the time he finished, she was dazed.

She blinked, drew a breath, and straightened. "Yes, well."

"You like my kisses." Those golden eyes challenged.

She released a defeated breath. "Well, yes." She loved his kisses. She loved his hands, and his fingers. She loved his body. She loved him. "But we're not kissing again in the coach."

He chuckled. "No, we're not. I don't want you to frighten the horses."

With his hands about her waist, he stood her up, allowed the skirt of her dress to fall into place, then sat her on the seat. He snuggled her against him and placed a kiss on her temple.

"You have stolen my heart, Sydney Whelton," he whispered.

His words barely entered her consciousness. Comfortable in his embrace, drowsy from their lovemaking, Sydney smiled.

They arrived in Auriano the next day, having stopped at a charming inn for the night. Only the sleeping arrangements had made it less than perfect, for propriety demanded that Raphael and Sydney sleep separately. But he was entranced with the beauty of the country. After making their way through the charming village with its stucco and stone houses and tile roofs, they climbed the road to the *castello*, sitting in magnificent complacency atop a rugged hill. Vineyards on one side of the road and fields of lavender on the other stretched away to meadows and woods. From the top of the hill, he could see olive groves and farms scattered in the valley below. It was an idyllic scene that belied the danger that threatened.

The coaches rumbled through an archway guarded by heavy wooden gates reinforced with large iron hinges, then stopped in a grand courtyard surrounded by a tall, stone wall. The rampart along the top of the wall had crumbled in one corner, and the rubble lay in a dusty pile. The *castello* was hundreds of years old.

After Raphael helped Sydney climb down from the coach, they followed the duke and duchess up a short flight of marble steps and entered the *castello* through wooden doors carved with bucolic scenes. The entry hall was impressive with a high ceiling and terra cotta tile floor. The Auriano heraldic device of a circle broken into three parts with a lightning bolt through its center was molded into the middle tiles. Tooled leather with a dyed and gilded floral design covered the walls.

As soon as everyone was inside, a boy of about seven or eight years came barreling into the room. "Uncle Tonio!" Sliding to a stop, he gave a short bow to the duchess and grinned. "Hello, Aunt Solange."

"*Bonjour, cheri*," she replied with a warm smile.

Then he turned to the duke. "Uncle Tonio! Papa and I are going hunting for rabbit tomorrow. Will you come? Uncle Sebastian is coming, too." His eyes widened when he saw Zayed in his desert robes and Gide, looking like an exotic beggar. Then his gaze landed on Raphael. A puzzled frown crossed his face and he looked about to say something, but he was distracted when a lovely, dark-haired woman followed him into the room.

"Evan, where are your manners?" she chided gently. "We have guests."

"Sorry, Mama," Evan muttered, then bowed formally to Raphael, Sydney, Zayed, Lucy, and Gide. "I am very pleased to greet you."

The woman stepped forward and smiled. "Welcome to the Castello Auriano. I am Sabrina, Princess of Auriano. And this is my son, Evan." She smoothed a shock of dark hair away from his forehead. A man, obviously Antonio's twin, entered behind her. "This is my husband, Alessandro, Prince of Auriano." She rested her hand in the crook of his arm.

Raphael and Gide bowed, Sydney and Lucy curtsied, and Zayed salaamed, touching his hand to his heart, lips, and forehead. Solange introduced them to the prince and princess, and then pulled Gide forward.

"This is my brother, whom I have not seen in two years," she announced, her voice wavering with tears.

In the middle of the stir created by the appearance of Gide, Evan crept closer to Raphael and stared up at him. The boy's eyes had darkened. He seemed to be in a trance.

"You are the one," he intoned. "You have come."

All conversation stopped.

Raphael blinked in surprise. What did the boy mean?

"Evan—" Sabrina began.

But Evan turned to Sydney. He seemed perplexed. "You are…" He tipped his head as if trying to puzzle out something. "You are good, but there is a darkness…." He frowned and shook his head as if he couldn't figure it out. Then he looked at Gide. "You have the weapon."

Everyone stared at the boy in stunned silence. Gide shifted from one foot to the other.

As if he hadn't disrupted the gathering, he turned to Sabrina. "Mama, my tutor is waiting for me. May I be excused?"

"Of course, darling," Sabrina murmured as she smiled at him and smoothed his hair again.

But Raphael noted that her hand shook a bit. She had been shaken by what the boy said. He glanced at Sydney, who appeared taken aback by the boy's declaration. Even he felt a bit unnerved.

Evan bowed and then walked calmly to the stairs. As soon as his foot landed on the first step, he scampered up and disappeared down a hallway at the top.

The boy's pronouncements hung in the air. No one spoke for several long moments. The atmosphere in the great hall was tense, charged with an unnamed danger.

He is the one? Alessandro said silently to his brother. *What does that mean?*

Si, Antonio answered. *Piero says that he could be a long-lost brother. Do you remember the story about the babe that died?*

Si.

The babe didn't die. He was sent away to our mother's sister and her husband. This man might be him. He wears a piece of the Sphere of Astarte.

Raphael noticed that the others appeared uneasy in the long silence, and then realized he was the only one aware of their conversation.

He looked from one twin to the other. *I can hear you,* he announced silently.

The prince and the duke exchanged a surprised glance.

Abashed, Alessandro made a small bow. "Please forgive us."

Antonio chuckled. "Perhaps we will have to be more careful in the future when we converse silently. Or perhaps we will have to include you…*beh*, we shall see." He sent Raphael a calculating gaze.

Alessandro turned to Sydney and the others. "Please excuse our son. He is prescient and sometimes sees things that others do not." He exchanged a look with a man standing back from the gathering and waved him forward. "This is Gasparo. He will show you to your rooms. Please call on him or Piero if there is anything you require. Luisa, their sister, is also available to help the ladies."

Gasparo led them up the grand stairway to the floor above. They followed the servant through winding hallways as he stopped at one door, then the next as he showed them to their rooms, first Gide, then Lucy, then Sydney. As she closed the door to her room, she sent Raphael a shy little smile. He noted which door was hers. The possibility of a late-night visit enticed.

Zayed was given the next room, and across the hall was Raphael's, a huge space on a corner with windows on two adjoining walls. Gasparo waved him through the door, then fussed about one of the windows, unlatching it and throwing it open. The late summer air wafted through, filled with the scent of lavender and grapes. But Gasparo seemed to be delaying, as if waiting for Raphael to question him. Like Piero, something about him made Raphael believe he knew a great deal about the curse and was much more important to the family than a mere servant.

"Gasparo, have you been with the House of Auriano a long time?" he asked.

"*Si, Sior* Raphael." Gasparo nodded. "All my life. And my father and mother before me. My family has served the House of Auriano for many generations."

"So, you also know the story of the lost child," Raphael surmised.

"*Si*, I do."

"Do you think I could be that lost brother?" Raphael asked.

Gasparo studied him a moment. "You certainly have the look of the family." He shook his head. "But that is not for me to decide." As if he had said too much, he bowed and quickly left.

Raphael, left alone, surveyed the room. A large bed with ornate carved posts and red brocade hangings and coverlet sat against one wall. Comfortable chairs flanked the fireplace, and a writing desk was tucked into an alcove. Various colorful rugs were scattered across the terrazzo floor. The space was impressive, quite a bit larger than his tent in the desert, even his bed chamber in Fès, and he surmised, was one of the better rooms, allocated to those the family liked or wished to impress. Perhaps the family had begun to accept him.

Unsure how he felt about that, he wandered to the window. The view was breathtaking with the village nestled below the *castello* and the rolling hills beyond, covered in olive groves and rows of grapevines that dissolved into pastures and woods. The sights and sounds and scents of the country overwhelmed him. He had been to foreign places before, traveling for his master, Darwish al-Rafiq, but never to this country, nor on his own journey of discovery. Did he want to discover more about his origins? Did he want to learn more about this family? Did he want them to accept him? He wasn't sure about any of it.

He had learned that the House of Auriano was old and powerful. The twins, prince and duke, were wary of his arrival. He would be wary as well if a stranger suddenly appeared at his tent, claiming to be a lost brother. What if the twins decided they didn't want him as part of their family? If he were truly their elder brother, he was a threat to their titles and everything that went with them. While he sensed he was in no immediate danger from them, he had the feeling that they could make him disappear without a trace if they wished. If he detected any menace from either of them, he would make himself disappear, back to his tent in the desert.

A scream pierced his reverie. It came from outside. And it sounded like a woman.

Sydney!

He raced out of his room, through the winding hallways and down the stairs before he burst out between the huge wooden doors. Others had heard it as well, and they ran out the gate and beyond the *castello* wall. A crowd had begun to gather in the middle of the field of lavender. When he pushed his way through, he found the prince and duke, along with their wives, standing over Sydney, who clasped a hysterical Lucy in her arms. The two women huddled together on the ground. Sydney looked up at him, her face tight with worry, but she appeared unharmed. It was not her scream he had heard, but Lucy's. The unfamiliar panic that had tightened his gut relaxed slightly despite his concern over what had frightened Lucy.

Lucy was babbling between her tears and hiccups. "She — she — she —"

"She's gone now, Lucy," Sydney said calmly. "Take a breath and tell us what happened."

"I s-s-saw her from my window," Lucy sniffled. "She was in the middle of the lavender, and she wanted me to come out and see how beautiful it was. She was so lovely. When I got out to the field, she started asking questions about who was in the castle." She glanced at everyone standing around her.

"I'm sorry," she said, tears streaming down her cheeks. "I shouldn't have told her. That was a mistake. But when I tried to run away, I couldn't move, and she laughed. It was horrible. I was so frightened. And then she became a horrid old crone, and she had a terrible wound. Here." Lucy pointed to her chest. "It oozed green pus." Her mouth pinched in disgust, then she turned watery eyes on Raphael. "She said she was going to rip it away from you — whatever *it* is. Did she mean your amulet? Oh, Mr. Pirate!" she wailed. "You can't lose that! I'm so sorry!" She broke down into sobs.

Nonplussed at Lucy's distress, Raphael assured her, "She's not going to get the amulet, Miss Foster."

"*Si*, she is not," Alessandro said. "Now, everyone back inside the *castello* walls, *per favore*. The walls are warded with magic, and the evil one cannot get in."

Sydney helped Lucy to her feet, and with an arm around her friend's shoulders, guided her back inside. The others trailed behind, the women gathered in a sympathetic group around Lucy, the men appearing vigilant and ready for danger. Raphael took a moment to glance around the field of lavender, not sure exactly what he expected to see. Surely, the sorceress was gone. A man had hung back as if waiting for him. As Raphael made his way toward the gates of the *castello*, the man fell into step beside him.

"I heard you might be a long-lost son of the family," he said, his accent indicating he was English.

"Your name, sir?" Raphael, unsure who this man was or where his loyalties lay, was not about to reveal anything.

The man smiled and stopped. "Forgive me. That was quite rude. I was in the stables when you arrived. I am Sebastian, Earl of

Hawksmoor." He bowed. "I am wed to Princess Allegra, sister to Prince Alessandro and Duke Antonio."

Raphael introduced himself, touching his hand to his heart, his lips, his forehead. When he straightened, he felt the other man studying him.

"Yes, I believe you are the one who was missing," Hawksmoor said, and continued to stroll toward the *castello* gates.

What did the man mean by that? But Raphael kept his curiosity in check and fell into step beside him.

Hawksmoor chuckled at Raphael's stony expression. "Let me explain. I have a gift. I can see the essence of people. When Alessandro, Antonio, and Allegra were gathered together, I saw that one essence was missing. Yours, I believe. And it seems the sorceress isn't happy that you have arrived to join your essence to theirs."

"I'm not sure I want to join with anyone," Raphael said. "The Auriano twins don't seem too eager about that either."

Hawksmoor's lips tipped up in a wry smile. "They are a close family, and protective of what is theirs, but if you prove worthy, they will stand at your back."

They stepped through the gates into the courtyard, and Raphael felt the slight sizzle across his skin that marked the magical wards that the prince had mentioned. Before they reached the entrance, a young woman came racing out and stopped in a flurry before Hawksmoor.

"Oh, *amore mio*! Are you unhurt?" she exclaimed. "I was with our babe when I heard the sorceress was about. Tell me you did not fight with her." She patted Hawksmoor's chest and arms as if checking for wounds.

The Englishman caught her hand and placed a gentle kiss on her palm. "No, dearest Alli, I am not hurt, as you can see. Nulkana was gone before we could confront her." He turned to Raphael. "May I present my wife, Princess Allegra?"

Raphael was struck dumb. He barely heard Hawksmoor introduce him to Allegra. He stared. This was the woman he had seen in the vision when he picked up the satin robe in the desert. He glanced at Hawksmoor. And he realized this man had also been in that vision.

"I have heard *Sior* Pirate is charming, but he seems to have no manners," the princess said with a sniff.

Her words broke through Raphael's daze. The lady appeared very displeased. "My apologies, princess. A pleasure to meet you," he said with a bow. "I believe I have seen you before."

Her displeasure turned to confusion. "*Che cosa*? How is this possible? We have never met, *Sior* Raphael."

"I saw you in a vision," he said, then realized that sounded ludicrous, or at the least, a bit odd.

The princess stared at him.

He tried to explain. "You must think me mad." He smiled. "When I picked up a garment belonging to Sydney—Miss Whelton—I saw you, looking quite distressed, in the middle of a circle of robed figures. You were in a place I had never seen before, with huge stones all around." He turned to Hawksmoor. "And I believe I saw you, as well, sir."

Allegra and Hawksmoor exchanged a surprised but perceptive glance. With a nod, the earl turned back to Raphael.

"I think we should discuss this inside," Hawksmoor said and motioned to the doors of the *castello*.

As they headed inside, the princess said, "You look very familiar, *Sior* Raphael, but I know we have never met."

Before Raphael could respond, they were met inside the door by Gasparo. With a small bow, he said, "*Sior* Sandro would like everyone to gather in the red salon, *per favore*." His glance took in Raphael as well as Hawksmoor and Allegra.

"A family gathering," Hawksmoor mused. "It must be something important. The red salon is this way." He indicated a door at the far end of the entry hall.

As Raphael followed along, he wondered at being included in the gathering. Did Hawksmoor's reference to it being a family meeting indicate that he had been accepted as a member of the House of Auriano? Unsure how he felt about that, unsure if he wanted to be accepted, he kept silent. But one thing he did know. He would not give up his amulet.

Chapter 21

Sydney checked her appearance in the glass and adjusted a few loose pins in her hair. Behind her in the reflection was the bed chamber she had been given, the most opulent space she had ever seen. The large room was certainly a sharp contrast to the accommodations she'd had while traveling, except for the few nights spent in Fès in Raphael's house. White-washed walls reflected the sunlight, and the wooden coffered ceiling above her head had intricate carvings within each of its squares. The bed was elegant and large, with its grand four posters and brocade hangings. The other pieces of furniture — a few chairs, a desk, a couple of small tables — were graceful and inviting. Small rugs were scattered about the terrazzo floor. She wondered what Raphael's chamber looked like. Perhaps she might knock on his door later to find out. The idea intrigued her.

The woman the prince had mentioned, Luisa, had knocked on the door only a few minutes previously and issued the invitation to join everyone in the red salon. Sydney had the impression that Luisa was more than a mere servant. While the middle-aged woman was perfectly polite, something about her demeanor indicated that she should not be ignored, that her position within the household was important, similar to both Gasparo and Piero. And the keen look she had given Sydney before she extended the invitation implied that she could see beyond the ordinary.

With a sigh, Sydney turned away from the glass. She couldn't do much with her hair after being in the desert for such a long period. And her frock, well, nothing could help that after the long time it had spent in her valise. She tugged up the bodice, a bit loose since she had lost weight in the desert. No wonder Raphael had so easily disrobed her in the coach. Her cheeks burned at the memory, while at the same time a throb of desire pulsed through her. Those devilish hands could turn her to a wanton with only a few strokes. But she could not think of that at the moment. She was about to gather with the members of the House of Auriano, and she must be on her best behavior. While her frock might be merely a serviceable garment, at least her gold portrait case on the chain around her neck dressed it up a bit. She patted her hair into place one last time.

As she left her room, she met Lucy in the hallway. They linked arms as they descended the ornate marble staircase with spiral spindles and newel post topped by a filigree sphere.

"Are you recovered from your fright, dear Lucy?" she asked.

"Oh, my heavens!" Lucy glanced at her with wide eyes. "That sorceress is horrible! Even from a distance, I could feel her evil. How are you ever going to kill her?"

"I was hoping Gide would help." She slid a peek at her friend and saw the color rise in Lucy's cheeks at his name. "Do you suppose you could convince him to help me?"

Lucy's cheeks turned pinker. "I could try." They descended two more steps, and then Lucy whispered, "What do you suppose this gathering is about?"

"I don't know," Sydney whispered back, "but I think it's important. Maybe the family will help me kill Nulkana."

"Oh, that would be wonderful," Lucy said with relief. "Then you will be done with this quest, and we can return home." She pushed her spectacles up her nose. "I hope they have food at this gathering."

Sydney chuckled. "I hope they have food, too."

They were the last to enter the red salon. Solange chatted with Gide, who had discarded his *djellaba* in favor of frock coat and breeches. He had also shaved and cut his hair. Lucy gasped at his changed appearance, and Sydney hid her smile when her friend continued to gape. He was an extraordinarily handsome man. But then, every man in the room was exceptionally attractive, and each of the women was quite beautiful. Sydney felt frumpy and awkward in their midst.

Raphael and Zayed were in conversation with two new people. The Englishman and his wife seemed familiar. Then she swallowed a gasp as she realized why. She had seen him at Stonehenge during the battle with Nulkana. And his wife…why, she had been the Shadow who had warned her away from the danger.

Sydney scanned the rest of the room. Alessandro and Antonio had their heads together in what seemed to be an intense discussion. Sabrina sat on the floor playing with a pair of toddlers, a boy and girl who looked like twins. Another boy baby crawled around, and a baby girl sat on a blanket and chewed the foot of a rag doll. Evan sat near his mother and hungrily devoured tidbits from a plate. Gasparo, Piero, and Luisa stood along a wall.

The red salon was aptly named, for red brocade covered the walls, and an enormous Chinese rug with a red background to its complex center design covered the terrazzo floor. Portraits and paintings by the old masters hung on the walls. Comfortable chairs and side tables were scattered about. Along one wall, trays of cheeses, meats, olives, and fruit were laid out, along with bottles of wine and a very large silver tea service.

"Oh, look, Sydney," Lucy whispered. "They are serving tea!"

A handsome man turned to her with a smile and introduced himself as Sebastian, Earl of Hawksmoor. "Yes," he said, "Princess Sabrina insists on having tea every afternoon, despite the grumbles of her husband, Alessandro, who despises the brew. We're very fortunate that the princess is English, like us."

"Oh, I couldn't agree more," Lucy said, and headed for the table and a teacup.

When Sydney didn't follow her, Sebastian asked, "Aren't you a tea drinker, Miss Whelton?"

Feeling comfortable with him, someone from her own country, someone she had watched try to defeat Nulkana, she smiled. He might have even visited her mother's gaming hell at one time. "Yes, but my appetite has fled since the appearance of the sorceress."

"She is a foul presence," he agreed. "But I think you might have some power yourself. Raphael related a story about a black robe you own and a vision he had when he touched it."

A vision? Raphael had never told her about that.

"The robe wasn't mine," she said. "It was my father's. It—" She halted. How could she explain that it burst into flame and disintegrated into nothing? She didn't understand that herself. Besides, it was part of her father's secret. "I lost it when we crossed the mountains."

"How unfortunate," he murmured sympathetically, but the penetrating look in his eyes made her think she had revealed information she shouldn't have.

Raphael overheard the conversation between Sydney and the Englishman. While the man appeared perfectly civil, he had an air that made Raphael think he hid a deep, dangerous power. Raphael felt the need to protect Sydney from it. He stepped up beside her.

Nearly everyone in the room seemed to exude a powerful force. The combined energy made his ears buzz, and he wanted to cover them to shut it out. Besides the intense energy, he sensed he was under examination, making him edgy. He had a feeling this gathering related to his appearance in their midst and the possibility of being a member of their family. He wanted to escape but that would be cowardly. So, he forced a pleasant expression onto his face and waited to see what would happen.

Beside him, Sydney's fingers twined with his and she smiled up at him. That little smile bolstered his confidence and warmed his heart. He could endure anything when she smiled like that. The touch of her fingers made him want to kiss her senseless. When he smiled back, her cheeks tinged a delightful pink. And that made his mind run with all the delicious things he could do with her if they were alone.

Later, he said to her silently.

The pink in her cheeks flared to a deeper color and she ducked her head. But her lips still curved in a smile.

Alessandro ended his conversation with his twin and cleared his throat, gaining everyone's attention. "Tonio and I have been discussing the possibility that Raphael Al Qarsan is our lost brother." He nodded in Raphael's direction.

Raphael's teeth clenched. He didn't like the idea of being discussed.

"First," Alessandro said, "he has shared his memories of his early childhood at the edge of the sea, and the adults who raised him, whom he called aunt and uncle. Our mother's sister and her husband lived on a small island off the coast of Sicily, on the shore, and they would have been his aunt and uncle. We know that raiders attacked the island, and our mother's sister and her husband were killed. Second, Raphael has told us that he became a slave at a very young age, so he could have been taken from the village and sold." Alessandro sent him a sympathetic glance. "Then there is the curse, which is only upon the House of Auriano."

Raphael stiffened. "I didn't come here to be examined like a strange insect," he said, seething beneath his cool words. He didn't need this man's pity.

Alessandro met his gaze. "*Si*. If I have offended, then I offer my apologies." His head dipped in regret. "But allow me to continue, *per favore*. I found something interesting when I was in the library." He turned to an easel covered with a cloth, and in a dramatic swipe, revealed a painting beneath. "*Ecco!*" It was a portrait of a man dressed in the clothes of a past century.

Beside him, Sydney gasped. "He could be your twin," she said in awe.

Alessandro explained. "This is our great-great-grandfather, Angelo Baldassare Cesare D'Este, fifth Prince of Auriano. I think the resemblance is striking, *si*?"

Raphael forced himself not to shift under everyone's gaze. Silence hung in the room as they turned from the portrait to Raphael. But unlike the others, Sebastian barely glanced at the portrait, staring at Raphael instead.

Finally, Sebastian said, "You are the essence that was missing." He turned to the others, seeming to examine them. "His essence fits."

Allegra explained. "My husband can see a person's essence, and he saw that one was missing when he put my essence together with Sandro's and Tonio's." She smiled, showing delightful dimples. "I think we have found a brother." She stepped before Raphael, placed her hands on his shoulders, and kissed first his left cheek, then his right, then his left again. "I am sorry for everything you have lost and all the hardships you endured." Tears shone in her eyes. "But you are home now. Welcome to the House of Auriano."

A smattering of applause erupted. Raphael shifted, uneasy under such attention. His mind whirled. For nearly his whole life he had no one but Zayed. Now, he had two brothers, a sister, and their spouses.

And Sydney, for as long as she would have him. She squeezed his hand and smiled up at him.

"You've found your family," she whispered. "I'll let you get to know them." Her fingers slipped from his grasp, and she wandered away in the direction of the table with the food.

Warmed by her smile and touch, he watched her pour herself a cup of tea. He felt overwhelmed and cast around for a spot where he could be inconspicuous, but Antonio and Alessandro approached, joining Sebastian, who stood next to Raphael. He was cornered, forced to be polite.

The three men offered their hands, welcoming him to the family. Their grips were firm, and they seemed sincere. Their gazes were forthright. His defenses relaxed.

Antonio spoke first. "Solange is grateful to you for finding Gide. He has been missing more than two years."

Raphael waved away his gratitude. "I had very little to do with finding him. Miss Whelton searched and found him." He met her gaze across the room. Her smile steadied him.

"Why did she search for him?" Sebastian asked.

Distracted by the lovely blush that stole into Sydney's cheeks, he said, "She seeks the death of Nulkana in revenge for killing her father. Delacroix possesses the Dagger that she thinks will do away with the sorceress."

The three men shot glances at each other.

Alessandro remarked mildly, "An unusual objective for a young lady."

Raphael's attention focused fully on the three Auriano men. "Sydney Whelton is an unusual woman. She traveled across continents to contact me so I could help her find Delacroix, and we traveled far to seek you out."

Antonio cast a glance at Gide, who was in conversation with Lucy at the far end of the room. "We've heard of this Dagger," he said. "Do you know how Miss Whelton learned of it?"

Suspicion that the twins and the Englishman knew much more than they let on made Raphael wary. "I believe from her father." With a disarming smile he said, "A good bedtime tale told by a father to a daughter."

"Of course," Sebastian murmured. "If you will excuse me, I believe I will fetch a cup of tea."

As Raphael watched the man wander away, he knew that a cup of tea was the last thing on the Englishman's mind, because Sydney still stood near the tea service. Despite Hawksmoor's apparent nonchalance, he was heading straight for her. Raphael had said something that had caught the man's attention.

Undercurrents had swirled beneath the conversation with the men. He wished he knew what they were. As Hawksmoor approached Sydney, Raphael excused himself and strolled in their direction. Listening in on their conversation might provide a clue.

As Sydney sipped her tea, she watched Sebastian make his way in her direction. She had observed the men converse, and while they appeared perfectly civil, she had the feeling that Raphael was undergoing some sort of examination. Before she could decide whether he had passed it, whatever it was, Sebastian appeared at her elbow.

After pouring himself a cup of tea, he said, "Raphael speaks highly of your arduous journey to seek him out and then find Gide. You must have loved your father very much to go so far to avenge his death."

Had she loved him? She wasn't sure. He had been remote, only showing emotion when she had mastered a skill, like fencing or knife-throwing, or when she had exhibited her magical power. But he had opened her eyes to the power that a man could have—that she could have—and for that, she was grateful. Her guilt at his death seemed out of proportion with her feelings for him. Out of proportion with the grief she felt at her mother's passing. The compulsion to seek revenge on the sorceress who had killed him had driven away all her grief.

"He was an unusual man," she said, evading his probing words. "I should have helped to protect him."

"If you don't mind my asking, when did he die?" He took a sip of tea.

"Two years ago, at Stonehenge, in a horrific battle with Nulkana." The memory of that night still made her tremble. "I was there that night. I saw you."

"Were you?" Sebastian's words were mild, but his cup rattled as he placed it back in its saucer. "A terrible night. Many men died in that ring of stones," he murmured. "My condolences." He took another sip of tea, then remarked, "That is a beautiful locket."

"My father gave it to me. Would you like to see his portrait?" She slipped the chain over her head and held out the portrait case.

After putting down his teacup, he took the locket in his hand. Turning it over, he rubbed his thumb across the etching on the back. Sydney thought she saw tiny sparks erupt along the lines of the frog glyph, but they were so small and disappeared so fast, she couldn't be sure. Then he popped open the case. He stared down at the portrait for a very long time.

Slowly, he raised his head, his eyes cold. "This is your father?"

"Yes." She couldn't understand why he had suddenly changed from the polite Englishman to someone who made her wary.

"You are the daughter of Sir Cyril Foley, Lord High of the Legion of Baal." His statement, sounding more like an accusation, caused all conversation in the room to halt. Even the children became silent.

Perplexed at everyone's reaction, Sydney said, "Yes. Nulkana killed him. That's why I am seeking her death."

As Sabrina and Solange gathered up the children, Gasparo, Piero, and Luisa placed themselves between Sydney and the rest of the family. Everyone acted as if she were about to attack.

Alessandro snarled at Raphael, "You brought an enemy into our house."

"She's no enemy," Raphael snapped. "She protected me from Nulkana."

"A misdirection," Alessandro growled.

Antonio hauled Gide from his chair. "What were you thinking to bring her here?"

Gide's eyes narrowed. "She has powerful magic. She could help," he said, his words challenging.

"You've been gone for two years, and the help you bring is an enemy? Beh!" Antonio shoved Gide away.

Gide's face darkened and his hands curled into fists. Before he could attack Antonio, Solange stepped between them, and sent first one man, then the other a hard stare. With their faces set in angry lines, the two men turned away from each other.

Shocked at the sudden enmity, Sydney asked, "What is wrong? I've done nothing wrong."

Allegra stepped forward, her eyes like chilly stones. "You are the daughter of the Legion of Baal. That makes us enemies."

"But Gide is a member of the Legion of Baal," Sydney argued.

"Not anymore," he said, shaking off Antonio's grip. He pulled back his sleeve and showed the frog glyph tattoo on his arm with the jagged scar disfiguring the pattern.

"I don't understand," Sydney said. "The Legion of Baal wants to kill Nulkana. I thought the House of Auriano wanted that as well."

"They do," Gide said. "But the Legion of Baal has another goal, *mademoiselle*." A puzzled frown creased his forehead. "Don't you know what that is?"

Baffled, Sydney shook her head.

He sighed and focused on straightening his cuff. "They want to destroy the House of Auriano."

"I beg your pardon?" Sydney asked, not sure she understood.

"The House of Auriano is a rival in the race to find the pieces of the Sphere of Astarte," Gide explained. "If the Legion destroys all members of Auriano, then it wins the Sphere."

Appalled at the implication, she gasped and glanced around at everyone. Why had her father never mentioned this? "You think I came here to kill you? To steal the Sphere of Astarte?" Her fingers went lifeless, and the cup crashed to the floor. "No! No! I would never...!"

Her gaze met Raphael's. A scowl creased his brow. His mouth flattened. His eyes held no warmth as they had only moments before. Even he believed she wanted his death. She would never hurt him, nor any member of the House of Auriano. How could he think that? She had given herself to him, had opened herself to him. She loved him.

Bewildered, hurt, her heart a gaping wound, she turned and fled the room, out of the *castello*, through the gates and into the vineyard, where she finally collapsed, sobbing, beneath the vines.

Raphael watched her flee. And he did nothing. Confused, he was paralyzed, unable to think, move, or make a decision. Instead, his thoughts swirled like evil bats inside his head. Was she truly malevolent, seeking his death and those of the members of the House of Auriano? Was her shock and distress an act, calculated to allow her to remain close? Or had she truly not known that one of the reasons for the existence of the Legion of Baal was to destroy the Auriano family?

Unable to settle on an answer, he pushed his way out of the room into the entrance hall, where the huge front doors stood open. He stopped and stared out into the courtyard, seeing nothing but Sydney's distraught face. Seeing her bending over him as he awakened from his nightmare. Catching the determined look on her face as she chased away the *afrit*, Aicha Kandida. Watching her luscious mouth draw into a prim little line as he teased. Looking deeply into her beautiful, changeable eyes as she peaked in passion.

"Aren't you going after her?" Lucy demanded from right beside him.

His brain started working again as well as his feet. *Sydney*!

She was out there, vulnerable to discovery by Nulkana, who had already accosted Lucy. He didn't care if Sydney was the daughter of the Lord High of the Legion of Baal, whose purpose was to destroy the House of Auriano. He didn't believe she would murder innocent people. And he would not lose her to Nulkana.

With a leap, he sped out the door and across the courtyard, where the gates were wide open. Bellowing her name, he raced into the vineyard. When he found her, he would bring her back to the *castello*, to safety.

And he would tell her he loved her. Again.

Chapter 22

Sydney heard them calling for her, but she refused to show herself. She had hidden within a tangle of vines that had fallen from their supporting stakes at the very bottom of the vineyard. Eventually, the voices of Lucy, Gide and Raphael faded away, and she assumed they were looking for her elsewhere. It didn't matter. She needed to be alone. To think about what she had learned. She was the daughter of the Lord High, presumably deceptive and evil, intent on murder. But she wasn't. How could she convince Raphael and everyone else that she meant them no harm?

Her heart ached. How could she not know that the Legion of Baal wanted the death of the members of the House of Auriano? Her father had shared so many other secrets with her. About Nulkana's evil. About the Crystal Dagger. About the Sphere of Astarte. Why had he kept that one secret? Perhaps because his motives weren't as honorable as he wanted her to believe. Perhaps because he was not the encouraging, generous father he had appeared to be.

The realization caught at her heart, that organ already bleeding from Raphael's rejection. Curling into a tight ball, she hugged her knees to her chest, trying to protect herself from more hurt. Her tears were spent, and all she wanted to do was keen her pain. But she couldn't make a sound. She didn't want to be found and dragged back inside the *castello* to suspicion, outrage and loathing. So, she bit her lip until she tasted blood and wailed silently.

She didn't know how long she stayed in that position, but eventually, the sharp pain in her heart turned to a dull ache. Raising her head, she peeked through the vines. The sun had set, and in the falling twilight, lights began to twinkle in the village below. With the coming night, the air had grown chilly, and she shivered. She couldn't stay beneath the vines forever. Going back into the *castello* wasn't an option. Perhaps she could find a place to spend the night in a barn or outbuilding. Tomorrow, she would decide what she could do to convince everyone that she was not their enemy. Or perhaps she would leave Auriano and make her way back to England. Lucy would be fine. She had Gide.

She crawled out from beneath the vines and glanced up at the *castello*. Many of the windows were bright with lit lamps. Was anyone watching for her? That didn't matter now. Turning her back on food and shelter, staying low so she wouldn't be seen, she made her way down the hill toward the village.

The gibbous moon threw plenty of light so she could see where she was going. She quickly crossed the open meadow and grassland, and then small, planted fields beyond the houses. Slipping through an alley between two houses, she emerged onto a narrow street. The village appeared empty, but she could hear people inside, talking and laughing, children's voices, and two people having an argument. She passed a café where a few men congregated. Keeping her head down, she hurried along, trying to appear as if she knew where she was going. As she wound through the streets, she thought she heard footsteps behind her, but they turned off. She breathed a sigh of relief and hastened toward the far end of the village. She didn't want to explain her presence, and she wanted to be as far away from the *castello* as she could.

As she rounded the back corner of a house where she could see a small shed for animals, a perfect shelter for the night, a man stepped in front of her.

Startled, she gasped. Then gasped again when she recognized him.

"Al Jabbar!" She fell back a step.

He swept a bow. "At your service."

"How did you find me? What do you want?" she demanded, covering her apprehension with irritation.

He smirked. "I found you by following you, dear lady. And how fortuitous you have left the castle and come for a stroll through the village."

Sydney was not about to reveal why she was beyond the castle walls. Instead, she asked, "What do you want?"

"What I want is the bauble that hangs around your lover's neck." Despite his mild tone, his statement threatened.

Raphael's talisman. A piece of the magical Sphere of Astarte. Her chin went up. "You'll never get it."

"Oh, I disagree."

He motioned to someone behind her. Before she could turn around, something slammed against her head. A bright flash erupted before her eyes. Then darkness. And nothing.

Robert Thurgood, known as Al Jabbar, made his way through the olive grove that grew in the valley below the Castello Auriano. The moon, nearly full, was high in the sky, so he had no trouble seeing. His destination was an ancient tree deep in the middle of the large grove.

He felt like whistling, not because he was afraid in the dark and wanted to scare away ghosts and evil spirits, but because he was pleased with the unfolding events. He had Sydney Whelton as his prisoner, and he was about to meet the powerful sorceress, Nulkana. If everything went his way in the next day, Raphael would be dead, and a piece of the Sphere of Astarte would be in his possession. But he couldn't accomplish all that by himself, not even with his paid thugs.

When he arrived in the village of Auriano, he had seen Nulkana on the hillside in the field of lavender when she had confronted Miss Whelton's nervous companion. It had been an easy task to use his frog glyph tattoo to let the sorceress know a member of the Legion of Baal was close. She had responded by sending her creepy, skeletal man, Kek, to invite him to her temporary lair.

He found the tree where Nulkana would be waiting. Like all olive trees, it was not tall, but still must be hundreds of years old. The trunk was twisted and gnarly, and looked like it had melted then frozen with big, drippy, woody globs. It was as big as four or five men together, and the enormous roots left gaping spaces before they disappeared into the ground. A dull glow came from one of the black openings between the roots. The space didn't look nearly big enough for him to crawl through, but as he stepped closer, it expanded to reveal a wooden door. Before he could knock, it opened to reveal Kek, bowing him through.

"My mistress is waiting," Kek said in his sepulchral voice.

He waved Robert into a chamber that resembled the inside of a desert nomad's tent, a much larger space than a hollow beneath the tree. It was bare except for beautiful rugs woven in intricate designs laid across the floor. Colorful cushions were scattered about. A single open-work brass lantern hung from the junction where three tent poles met in the ceiling. Sitting on several cushions beneath the lantern was a figure robed in red silk and a hood pulled up far enough to cover the figure's face.

As he approached, Nulkana revealed herself, pushing back the hood with hands covered in red satin gloves to match her robe. She was beautiful, her black hair falling in heavy whorls across one shoulder. Thick lashes surrounded her dark eyes, and a luscious mouth, nearly as red as her robe, pouted with promise. Her alluring smile welcomed him.

"Please, sit beside me, Al Jabbar of the desert," she purred.

Robert was immediately aroused, not certain whether her smile or voice caused such a swift reaction. He didn't care. He had come here for one thing. If he left with something extra, that was only a bonus. When he sat near her on the rug, her delicious, musky scent filled his nose, but as he greedily breathed it in, he thought he caught a faint undertone of rot.

"Tell me, Robert Thurgood, why you have come," she said, as she slid one finger down his arm.

He shivered at her touch, but he forced himself to focus on her question. "I think we can work together to get what we both want."

"Why would I want to work with you?" she asked. "I can get what I want on my own." Humor at his presumption lit her eyes.

Her indulgence didn't fool him. He had to be careful. She could incinerate him at any moment if he said the wrong thing. Now was the time to lure her in.

"I can give you something you didn't think you wanted, mistress," he said.

Her nose tilted at a supercilious angle. "I know exactly what I want, and if you play games with me, I want you dead."

He smiled, not letting on that her declaration sent a chill through him. But he had her complete attention. "You want the piece of the Sphere of Astarte."

She said nothing, her silence speaking for her.

"I can give you something better." Now, it was his turn to seduce. As he trailed his fingers along her jaw, ignoring the slightly slimy feel of her skin, he dropped his voice to an enticing whisper. "What if I could give you the daughter of the Lord High of the Legion of Baal?"

She pushed his hand away, but he had seen her barely perceptible reaction to his touch. He doubted she'd had any man touch her in such a way for a very, very, very long time. And he had seen the flash of interest in her eyes at his offer.

"Why," she asked, "would I want her?"

"She is a powerful witch. You could feed off her magic for a millennium." He knew the tricks of a rug merchant. Entice with possibilities, true or not. Many times, he had observed his master, Darwish al-Rafiq, convince a customer to buy.

Her eyes narrowed with suspicion. "What do you get in return?"

He shrugged nonchalantly, hoping she wouldn't flame him to ash. "Merely the bauble that Raphael Al Qarsan wears around his neck."

She reared back, and he could see the fury building behind her eyes. Kek stepped forward and whispered in her ear. After listening to her minion, she gave Robert a calculating glance.

He didn't like the look in her eye, as if he might be a tidbit she was thinking about having for a snack, but he was distracted by a robed figure he hadn't noticed before standing in a dark corner, dressed in a deep cowl, and swaying back and forth. Robert thought he heard moans in his head that seemed to come from the figure. Nulkana snapped her fingers, and the figure froze. The moans ceased.

"How do you plan to get this bauble?" Nulkana asked, regaining his attention. "And when can you bring me the daughter of the Lord High?"

He smiled as he laid out his plan. He had successfully made a bargain with the powerful, ancient sorceress. The piece of the Sphere of Astarte would be his. Unfortunately, the lovely Miss Whelton had to be sacrificed, but no goal worth achieving was without some forfeit. He could then take the next step in becoming the Lord High of the Legion of Baal.

Sydney became aware of her surroundings very slowly. Her head pounded. She was lying on her side on hard-packed earth with something that smelled like goat beneath her head. Her ankles were bound, and her wrists tied behind her back. A fire crackled nearby, but she wasn't close enough to feel its heat. She shivered in her thin dress.

Trying to remember how she came to be in this vulnerable position, she lay quietly with her eyes closed. Someone had taken her prisoner. Then, a flash of memory brought everything crashing back. Al Jabbar. His betrayal. The whack on her head. The blackguard. She had been foolish to hire him in the first place, duped into doing so by members of the Legion of Baal—her father's apostles. And she had been foolish to run out of the *castello*. But the events that made her run ripped through her heart. The discovery that she was the daughter of the Lord High of the Legion of Baal. The revelation that the Legion wanted the destruction of the House of Auriano.

Raphael's rejection.

She nearly cried out at that painful memory, but caution made her bite it back. If she was tied up, then she was in danger. She needed to discover her situation to figure out how to escape. Slowly, she opened her eyes and glanced around. She was in a house of only a single room from what she could see. A simple bed sat against one wall, and opposite that was a hearth where a fire burned, the only light. An elderly woman dozed in a chair next to the hearth, a cat draped over her lap. The door to the house was directly across from where Sydney lay, but any thought of escaping was quashed by the hulk of man snoring in front of it.

She tried to summon some magic to burn through her bonds, but it merely sparked, then died. She couldn't concentrate. Tears of self-pity flooded her eyes. The man she loved hated her. She was cold and hungry and thirsty. Her head hurt. She was Al Jabbar's prisoner. And she was alone. So very alone. She sniffled.

Then she realized the woman was awake and watching her. The woman pushed the cat from her lap and put her finger to her lips. Sydney watched her quietly take a wooden bowl from a shelf and then ladle something from a pot over the fire into the bowl. Tiptoeing closer, she helped Sydney sit up and held the bowl to her lips.

Sydney tasted a delicious broth flavored with vegetables and herbs. It warmed and revived her, making the pain in her head retreat slightly. In the light from the fire, she saw a dark bruise on the woman's cheek. Al Jabbar or one of his thugs had mistreated the poor woman, most likely forcing her to cooperate. If — when — she got free, she would make him pay.

When she finished the broth, the woman took the blanket that smelled like goat and wrapped it around Sydney's shoulders. Before she stood, she touched Sydney's cheek, then returned to her chair. The cat settled in her lap again.

Through the single window, Sydney could see a streak of dawn lighting the sky. She'd been gone all night. Was anyone looking for her? Did Raphael care that she was gone? Tears—-threatened again, but she blinked them away. She couldn't think about that now. Somehow, she had to convince Al Jabbar to release her. Then she would make her way back to the *castello* and explain her relationship with her father and why she hadn't known about the Legion's objective to eliminate the House of Auriano.

She was distracted from her thoughts by a rattling at the door. The man sleeping before it instantly surged to his feet and flung it wide. Al Jabbar sauntered in. His eyes twinkled and a smile graced his face. If Sydney hadn't known that he was a black-hearted demon, she would have thought him handsome. He strolled over and crouched before her.

"I am so happy to see you awake, Miss Whelton," he said, sounding sincere. "I'm sorry about this." He lightly touched the bruise on the side of her head.

She winced and jerked away.

He tsked. "My apologies. That must be painful. But after tonight, I'm sure it won't bother you."

His smile was too smug. Now that she knew how devious he was, she suspected that whatever he had planned was malicious. "What will happen tonight?"

Those blue eyes twinkled merrily. "Oh, Miss Whelton, it wouldn't be a surprise if I told you." He tipped his head thoughtfully. "But I suppose I could give you a hint." Leaning closer, he whispered in her ear, "You'll get to see your lover."

What was he plotting? Obviously, it involved Raphael. But Raphael was protected inside the *castello*, and he had the men and women of Auriano at his back. She suspected that whatever Al Jabbar was planning included Raphael's death. But what would draw him out from the protection of the *castello*? Surely, not any threat to her. Raphael had made his feelings about her quite clear. The anger on his face was etched in her mind. He saw her as his enemy, like his newfound family did.

Robert Thurgood, the man known as Al Jabbar, stood. "There now. That's all I'm going to say. You'll have to wait for your surprise."

"Why are you doing this?" she asked.

"Why?" His brows went up in surprise. "Don't you know?" He tipped his head as he studied her. "Your father never told you the truth, did he?" He chuckled. "My dear naïve Miss Whelton, the members of the Legion of Baal want power and wealth. The Sphere of Astarte will bring them that, and the Lord High will get the most. I plan on being the next Lord High." Those twinkling blue eyes turned frosty. "No one, neither you nor Raphael Al Qarsan, will stop me." Turning away, he gestured to the elderly woman to bring him something to eat.

Appalled, stunned, Sydney sat frozen as the truth swept through her. Her father had led her to believe that the Legion of Baal only wanted Nulkana's death to protect the world from her evil. In truth, he and the men in the Legion were trying to eliminate the rivals in the race to find the Sphere of Astarte, which included the members of the House of Auriano. She had been deceived.

The guilt which had driven her to cross continents dropped away. In its place, anger at the scheming man who was her father swirled in her chest. She strained at her bonds. Somehow, she had to get free and warn Raphael. She didn't care how he felt about her, or that he didn't believe her. She desperately needed to keep him safe. And then she would return to England, where she could disappear and forget the Legion of Baal, the Sphere of Astarte, and the House of Auriano. And that a man named the Pirate ever existed.

Raphael stood on the ramparts of the *castello* and stared over the dark fields of lavender and the vineyards. The mingled scents of the plants filled his nose, and at any other time, he would have breathed them in with pleasure. But tonight, all he focused on was trying to glimpse Sydney's form. The moon had set, and a streak of dawn lit the horizon. He had been standing here all night, refusing to give up the watch. It was a foolish exercise. He doubted Sydney would allow herself to be seen.

They had searched for her until dark when the gibbous moon had risen, even the Auriano siblings and their spouses joining in, but she couldn't be found in the fields, and no one had seen her in the village. Finally, Alessandro made everyone retreat inside the warded walls. When Raphael belligerently refused to go, Sebastian and Antonio, who was about to transform to Shadow at any moment, had wrestled him to the ground. With a brotherly punch to the chin, they convinced him to give up the search for the night. But that didn't mean he couldn't keep watch.

Where could she be? He scanned the valley below for the hundredth time. She could be anywhere. Sydney was a resourceful woman. She could already be on her way to the coast where she might find a sympathetic fisherman to take her to Venice. The only reason he felt she might still be in the area was that Lucy was here.

Once more, he damned himself for not jumping to her defense when the family discovered who she was. How could he have been so slow-witted to allow her to run away? She was the courageous, beautiful, sensual woman he loved. His hands clenched on the stony battlement before him.

He heard footsteps climbing the stairs, but he ignored whoever had come to urge him to give up his vigil. Two men came to stand beside him, Gide on one side, and Sebastian on the other. If they tried to force him to leave his post, he would toss them back down the stairs.

Sebastian cleared his throat. "We've had a family meeting," he said.

"I don't want to hear about any more family meetings," Raphael growled. The last one had torn his heart apart.

"Yes, of course. I understand. We are truly sorry about what happened." Sebastian paused.

Raphael grunted at the man's apology.

"You see, Miss Whelton's father, Sir Cyril Foley, was my mentor," Sebastian went on. "I infiltrated the Legion of Baal for him as his spy. But then I realized how treacherous he was when I learned of his intentions toward the House of Auriano. He was a devious, controlling, vengeful man. It's quite possible that Miss Whelton was being truthful when she appeared to know nothing about the goal of the Legion of Baal to do away with the House of Auriano. I believe he might have been deceiving her and using her for her magic. The family agrees with me."

"Don't you think it's a little late to come to that conclusion?" Raphael snapped.

Sebastian sighed. "Yes, it is, and I'm truly sorry for that. But, you see, I didn't understand her magic at first. It was unlike anything I had sensed before. When Gide revealed she was the daughter of the Lord High of the Legion of Baal, I assumed she was like him. But her essence isn't dark like his. It's light and airy and looks like a rainbow. Her magic is very special."

Raphael turned on him. "Of course, it is. *She's* special. That is why—" He halted. He wasn't about to announce to these men that he was in love with her. He hadn't even said those words aloud to Sydney.

Gide jumped in. "You don't understand, *mon ami*. Solange and I and Sabrina inherited our magic from Halima, Nulkana's good sister, who lived long ago. But Evan, Sabrina's son, helped us puzzle this out. Sydney, *mon Dieu*, she doesn't get her magic from Halima. She gains her magic from the goddess Astarte herself!"

Raphael's brow creased. "Astarte? Like the Sphere?"

Gide nodded. "*Oui*. A wizard fell in love with the goddess and created the Sphere for her. They had a child together who inherited Astarte's power. Sydney is their descendent. Her power is quite formidable."

"How do you know this?" Raphael asked.

"Her magic shines from her," Sebastian explained. "It glows like the Sphere."

"I can't see her magic," Raphael said. "How can you?"

Gide and Sebastian shared a glance.

Raphael's eyes narrowed. "You might as well tell me. I seem to be part of the family."

"The Dagger I carry has given me extra abilities," Gide said.

A wry smile curved Sebastian's lips. "I'm a Druid priest." He shrugged. "Extra abilities as well."

Astounded by the revelations, Raphael looked from one man to the other. He had changed his thinking about the Crystal Dagger being useless, and he had heard of Druids, able to control the elements. Both men had extraordinary power.

"If Sydney's magic shines from her, why couldn't you find her?" he asked.

"Her distress might have hidden it," Sebastian said. "But we think it has drawn Nulkana here. She wasn't merely a projection when she appeared to Lucy."

Panic rose in Raphael's throat. "We have to search for her again!" He started for the stairs.

He was met by Alessandro and Antonio, who had turned to flesh and bone at dawn after spending the night as Shadow. Both men looked grim.

Alessandro held out a folded parchment. "I think someone has already found her."

Raphael stared at the note as if it were poison. His name was scrawled in Arabic across the front. A sense of dread slumped into his chest. Slowly, he took the parchment and unfolded it. The words shifted and blurred before he could focus.

My friend,

I have come into possession of something quite valuable to you. I'm willing to make an exchange for the bauble you wear. Meet me tonight at moonrise in the lavender field so we might discuss this like gentlemen.

As always,
Robert

Raphael crumpled the note in his fist. "Al Jabbar," he muttered. Fear for Sydney's safety closed off every other thought in his head.

"Who is Al Jabbar?" Antonio asked.

When Raphael didn't answer, Gide explained.

"What does he want?" Alessandro demanded.

In the short time between reading the note and Alessandro's question, Raphael had decided what he was going to do. He glanced at the four men standing before him.

"He wants my piece of the Sphere of Astarte in exchange for Sydney," he said.

"You can't give it to him," Gide said. "He's a member of the Legion of Baal. It will give him and the whole Legion tremendous power."

"And you will turn to Shadow, *si*?" Antonio added.

"I must give it to him," Raphael argued. "You don't know him like I do. He'll slit her throat with a smile on his face."

"Perhaps there's another way," Sebastian suggested.

"There is no other way." Raphael felt his temper rising. Didn't these men understand that he could not lose Sydney?

"If you don't mind," Sebastian said, "I would like to confer with Sabrina, Solange, and Gide here. After you have rested, perhaps we can decide what to do. We have all day to make a plan."

The men surrounded Raphael in an informal group, but he suspected that if he resisted, they would force him back to his room. With a last glance out across the fields and valleys, he allowed himself to be guided off the ramparts. But before he descended the stairs, he sent out a silent message.

I'm coming for you, ya helo.

Chapter 23

Once again, Raphael stood on the ramparts of the *castello* and gazed out over the vineyard and the field of lavender. Above the horizon, the moon hung huge and gold, bright as a coin in the sky. On any other night, the scene would have been beautiful, but tonight, menace lurked. A breeze wafted through the lavender, shifting the shadows. Nothing bigger than a mouse could hide there, but across the road in the vineyard, the men and women of Auriano waited, concealed by the vines. He strained to see them, but they were well-hidden. Only Antonio was visible as he crouched at the edge of the vineyards, but no one else would have seen him. He was Shadow, transforming as soon as the moon had peeked above the horizon.

Zayed, silent, faithful as ever, stood at Raphael's shoulder. He had argued in his stoic, unflappable way against this meeting. The arrangement did not make sense. The son of a scorpion was planning more than an exchange. Someone standing on the ramparts of the *castello* could easily do away with Al Jabbar, instead of Raphael meeting him face to face. Raphael had agreed with Zayed, along with the rest of the family. But he would still meet Al Jabbar in the field to make sure Sydney was safe.

So, for protection, Gasparo, Piero, and Luisa stood on the ramparts armed with crossbows and rifles. When he turned his head, he could see their dark shapes crouched below the walls. Lucy crouched there with them, for she refused to remain safely in her bedchamber.

Shifting his gaze to the road, he watched a group of figures approach. He saw Robert in the lead and two hulking men behind him, holding Sydney. Several other men trailed behind, bristling with scimitars and jambiyas, the curved swords and daggers worn by men of the desert. But he had his own scimitar hanging at his hip.

He wondered why Sydney hadn't used her magic to escape, then realized her hands were tied behind her back. She stumbled and was dragged along by the brutes who held her. His hand, resting on the stone of the rampart, curled into a fist. If they hurt her, he would make sure they felt double her pain, then kill them.

With a last glance at Sydney, drinking in every beautiful inch of her, he nodded to Zayed, indicating he was ready, then the two of them made their way down the stairs. Raphael sensed his prediction to her on the ship would come true. Either he or Robert would be dead before this night was done. He decided it wouldn't be him.

As he reached the wooden gates that led to the road, he heard Robert call out.

"Raphael! I've come with your gift! Come and get her!"

He pushed the gates wide and walked through, leaving Zayed, scimitar in one hand, jambiya in the other, guarding the entrance. Al Jabbar had left the road and waded into the lavender. Raphael followed, wondering why his enemy had gone into the field of flowers. The heavy footsteps of the men trampled the herbs, and the scent filled his nose. He heard Sydney sneeze twice. Was she ill? His anxiety for her intensified.

Robert stopped in the middle of the field. Raphael noted that Nulkana had appeared to Lucy in about the same spot, and he wondered if that was a coincidence, or if the area held some sort of magical menace. Sydney sneezed again. His gaze narrowed on her. She seemed to be in distress, not ill, but shaking her head as if to clear it and glancing around as if trying to find something.

When Raphael halted several feet away from Robert, he asked silently, *Sydney, what is wrong?*

All she managed was a confused shrug.

He wanted to enfold her in his arms and comfort her. Instead, he felt helpless, and his rage at the man before him bubbled in his veins. He snapped, "I'm here, as you asked. Release Miss Whelton."

Sadly, Robert shook his head. "Raphael, where are your manners? You might at least greet me civilly."

Raphael's fist tightened on the hilt of the scimitar hanging at his hip. "You're not worth it. Release her."

Al Jabbar's eyes went flat. "Where is the amulet?" He grabbed Sydney from his henchman and put the deadly point of a jambiya to her throat.

Terror at Sydney's precarious position and frustration, so intense Raphael thought he might choke, rose in his throat. He wanted to snatch Sydney out of Robert's grasp and slice him to pieces. But he couldn't. Not with that dagger threatening her death. Instead, he took hold of the cord around his neck that held his piece of the Sphere of Astarte, pulled it over his head, and let the amulet dangle.

"No!" Sydney struggled against Al Jabbar's hold. "Don't give it to him! You can't!"

"Stay still," Al Jabbar hissed, and tightened his hold.

She sneezed again. "There's something in the field. It's making me—"

Her words cut off as a pulse of energy thumped in the air, staggering everyone. And then Nulkana materialized nearby in the middle of the lavender. In a black robe and hood, she appeared menacing and frightful. Her dark eyes gleamed with unnatural light. The rest of her face was shadowed. This was not the seductress Raphael had seen in his nightmares, but the deadly sorceress in all her power. Behind her, barely visible in the dark, was a man with skeletal features, dressed in a dark garment. Another robed and cowled figure, emanating deep sorrow, stood beside him. Raphael had seen this figure before in one of his nightmares. It had seemed very distressed and in pain.

"Were you about to double-cross me, Robert?" Nulkana asked sweetly. "The little witch is no good to me behind the walls of the *castello*. Or dead."

Al Jabbar said smoothly, "I was drawing him out, mistress. After I get the amulet, you may have her."

Aghast, Raphael said, "You would give Sydney to that monster?"

With a charming smile, Al Jabbar said, "Merely a business deal. Darwish al-Rafiq would have done the same."

Raphael was so enraged he couldn't speak. While his former master could drive a hard bargain, he was an honorable man. The thought of Sydney in the clutches of the evil sorceress made his stomach churn. The only thing that kept him from wrapping his hands around the man's throat and squeezing the life from him was the dagger threatening Sydney's life.

"Enough!" Nulkana's voice boomed out. "Give her to me, Al Jabbar of the desert, or Robert Thurgood, or whatever you call yourself." She turned to Raphael. "And I'll take that bauble in your hand."

Defiantly, without a word, Raphael slipped the cord back over his head. When the piece of the Sphere landed against his chest, it sent a warm glow through his body. Determination flowed through his veins. Somehow, he would resist the sorceress and save Sydney from the murderer who held her, even if it meant giving up his own life.

Sydney's confusion cleared as soon as the sorceress appeared. Her sneezing stopped, and she realized Nulkana had used the field of lavender to block spells that might have prevented her appearance. While Sydney didn't need spells to use her magic, whatever the sorceress had done to the lavender had created disarray in her head.

With relief, she watched Raphael slip the cord around his neck. That amulet meant his life, and she didn't want him to give it up for her. But the stony look on his face frightened her. He was furious, enraged beyond all logic. Two deadly enemies confronted him. He would put himself in danger to fight them. She had to get free. To help him. To stop him. To save him.

As soon as she had seen him stride out of the *castello*, she had felt her magic begin to awaken again. He had come to get her. Even if they never saw each other after this night, at least he cared enough to try to save her. But when Al Jabbar had dragged her into the field of lavender, the constant hum of her magic had turned to a discordant confusion. But now her magic was back.

She focused on releasing her bonds and ignored Al Jabbar's dagger at her throat, the point digging into her skin. A drop of blood trickled down her neck. But Al Jabbar was distracted by Nulkana and Raphael. Twisting her hands, she separated them enough that she could send a small spark of magic onto her bonds. They gave a little. Another small burst, one more after that, and the ropes loosened a bit more. But before she could free herself from Al Jabbar, he swung her around to face Nulkana.

"If you want her, get me the amulet," he called to the sorceress.

Sydney snapped the ropes, but only a tiny jolt of magic jumped to her hands. Desperate to be free, she sent whatever she could muster back toward Al Jabbar, who held her as a shield. He jerked away, and the dagger point dug deeper into her neck. She froze at the sharp pain.

"That was not very sporting of you, Miss Whelton," he said.

Raphael lunged at him. "Let her go!"

Al Jabbar yanked her away. "Give me the amulet," he said, his voice icy with menace.

A clap of thunder shook the ground. "Enough!" Nulkana bellowed. "Give me the witch!"

Al Jabbar shook back his sleeve and revealed a tattoo of a frog glyph on his wrist. Then, with a flick, he sent out a stream of energy that landed near the sorceress's feet.

Shocked and frightened at his ability, Sydney shrank away from him. She thought only her father as the Lord High had such ability. Another secret he had held from her.

Al Jabbar tightened his grip on her, then called to Nulkana, "You'll have to come get her."

The sorceress glanced down at the charred spot where the magic stream had landed, then turned a smile on him, loaded with evil intent. "You'll regret that."

Focusing her attention on Raphael, she said, "Give me the piece, or I'll turn you to ash." She sent a ball of energy in Raphael's direction, forcing him to jump away.

"You'll have to catch me first," he taunted.

Sydney finally wrenched away from Al Jabbar. The drag of the dagger across her neck made her gasp. But her magic flowed through her, strong and steady. With a flick of her hand, she sent a ball of energy in Nulkana's direction.

"Leave him alone," she yelled.

The sorceress reared back. And then she smiled, a terrible, evil smile. "I know who you are, little witch, daughter of Astarte. I killed your mother."

Sydney froze at the revelation that confirmed her suspicions.

Nulkana chuckled. "Oh, yes, I killed her. I sent a man into her gaming hell with the poison. She was much too powerful to live. But you are an infant, barely aware of your power. And I'm going to destroy you by sucking your magic from you."

Shocked and furious, Sydney blasted pulses of energy, one after another, at Nulkana. But the sorceress batted them away as if they were annoying insects.

"So, you want a battle?" the sorceress called. Chortling with glee, she reached deep into a fold of her robe. When her hand appeared again, she clutched a small vial that churned with putrid yellows and greens. "Then let us battle!"

She flung the vial in Raphael's direction. It landed with a bang. Noxious smoke exploded that quickly coalesced into a viper — huge, yellow and green, with enormous fangs. Looming over everyone, it focused its slitted, hideous, yellow eyes on Raphael and released a menacing hiss.

Everyone froze.

Sydney recovered first. She was not about to let some monstrous creation attack Raphael. Nor was she going to allow Nulkana to scare her away. She had made the long, treacherous journey to kill this evil witch. First, to seek revenge for her father's death. But now, more than that, she needed revenge for her mother's murder. That was the truth of her journey. And she would save Raphael from the sorceress. No matter what it took.

Gathering her magic, she threw it at the snake. It ripped a gaping hole in the monster's side that quickly closed up. That venomous gaze landed on her. As the viper lunged, Raphael drew his scimitar and sliced off the snake's head. It disintegrated in a puff of disgusting smoke.

"I'm not done, little witch!" Nulkana yelled.

The sorceress threw vial after vial, scattering the potions around the field of lavender. Each one exploded into an unnatural beast. One was an ogre, its purple skin dotted with scabrous growths and fangs that dripped acid. Another was an enormous orange lizard whose slitted black tongue flicked out, shooting sparks. A third became a second snake, pale and ghostly, even larger than the first, towering

276

above everyone. And then there were tiny, human-like creatures looking as if they were made of slimy mud, too many to count, who could duck, unseen, among the stalks of lavender. These were even more fearsome, with long, sharp teeth and needle-like swords. One of them attacked one of Al Jabbar's men, who died a horrible death, screaming and writhing in agony. Horrid monsters — ghouls and fiends and demons — appeared everywhere.

Sydney edged closer to Raphael. She would not allow Nulkana to kill him, nor would she let the sorceress take possession of his amulet. If she died trying, she would at least prove that she would not harm anyone of the House of Auriano.

Raphael grinned at her. "We can do this. *You* can do this. Just like the *afrit*."

Her heart warmed at his words. But she knew, even with her magic and Raphael's brave expertise with his scimitar, they couldn't fight Nulkana, her monsters, Al Jabbar, and his thugs by themselves. Soon they would be overrun. But if she were going to die, she would die next to the man she loved, defending him.

A shout came from the vineyard on the other side of the road. The women and men of Auriano swarmed from the vines. They weren't alone! Alessandro and Allegra brandished rapiers and stilettos. Sabrina, Solange, Sebastian, and Gide threw great balls of energy at the creatures. Antonio was Shadow, and using his ability, picked up rocks with his mind and tossed them. Zayed rushed from the *castello* gates, and from the ramparts, magical arrows rained down where Gasparo, Piero, and Luisa stood. The field of lavender, once serene and beautiful, became a battlefield beneath the huge, golden moon.

Right before the creatures attacked, Raphael had a moment to gaze on the woman he loved. Her dress had a great tear at the knee, dirt smudged her cheek, her hair dangled in unkempt strands, and blood trickled down her neck where Robert's dagger had sliced. She was the most beautiful, bravest woman he had ever known. Doubt was in her eyes when she glanced at him, and he knew he had put that doubt there. He wanted to tell her that he didn't doubt her, that he believed her. That he loved her. But there was no time.

Nulkana's tiny men with their needle-like poisonous swords were upon them. Behind them were the huge monsters. Nulkana's vile magic exploded all around. As the Auriano men and women rushed from the vineyard, confusion erupted across the field. Rapiers flashed and magic boomed. One of the tiny men lunged at Raphael's leg. He swatted it away with his scimitar. It landed near one of Al Jabbar's men, who squashed it beneath his foot.

Across the field, Alessandro and Sabrina fought the ghostly snake. While the prince jabbed with his rapier, Sabrina launched energy balls as the viper hissed and lunged with its fangs. Meanwhile, Antonio and Solange fought the ogre. They dodged in, evading its acidic poison and grasping claws, as they attacked again and again. To combat the tiny creatures wielding toxic swords, Sebastian created a vortex that sucked them in, spun them around, and spit them out to be cut down by Allegra's sword. One after another exploded into a noxious vapor. Arrows rained down from the ramparts, attacking Al Jabbar's men and Nulkana's tiny monsters.

In the middle of the chaos, Gide, locked in a standoff with Nulkana, held the Crystal Dagger in one hand and blasted deadly energy toward the sorceress with the other. She returned her own lethal fire as she evaded the deadly blade.

A maelstrom of screams, howls, grunts, and growls echoed around them. A cloud of gas from the destruction of the creatures floated above the field. Flashing steel, snapping jaws, swiping claws, and the sizzle of magic created mayhem. Above it all, Nulkana's cackle reverberated.

In the confusion, Raphael and Sydney became separated. As he stomped on a tiny man and sliced through a ghoul, he saw Sydney fighting two of Al Jabbar's men. Slicing with her dagger and throwing energy balls, she was magnificent.

Raphael turned and came face-to-face with Robert. His former childhood friend, now his enemy, held up his arm, revealing the frog glyph tattoo. His eyes twinkled as if he were thoroughly enjoying himself.

"I'll take that bauble," he said with a glance at the amulet.

"Why don't you fight me for it like a man?" Raphael swiped away one of the tiny creatures with his scimitar. "Or has joining the Legion of Baal turned you into a coward?"

The twinkle in Robert's eyes died. His arm dropped to his side. "You were always a righteous bugger. Darwish al-Rafiq's favorite, watching over the rest of us, tattling if we stepped out of line." With a nod, he pulled his scimitar from its sheath. "All right. We'll fight your way. To the death, then."

"To the death," Raphael agreed.

They circled each other. Raphael had not fought Robert for a long time, not since they had been child slaves together and had practiced with wooden swords. Back then, they had been friends, but each strove to win. Robert was a wily opponent, sometimes an unfair fighter. But Raphael knew his tricks. Besides, he had a few of his own.

In the middle of the lavender field, surrounded by battles against Nulkana's monsters, they came together, swords clashing. For Raphael, the noise and chaos around them faded away. His entire focus was on the man he fought. He would be the victor. He couldn't let this man steal his piece of the Sphere. It belonged to the House of Auriano. But more important, losing his life was not an option, for he needed to tell Sydney that he loved her.

Robert lunged at Raphael's mid-section. Raphael blocked him and countered with a slice to Robert's side. Robert jumped away. They continued to fight, evenly matched, lunging and blocking, attacking and retreating, the clash of steel on steel lost in the clamor of the other battles around them.

Then Robert raised his arm, and a flash of energy hit Raphael's right shoulder. It burned like nothing he had ever felt before. Nearly dropping his sword, Raphael held onto it by force of habit formed from years of training. He had been expecting Robert to try something devious. Well, he could be unscrupulous, too.

Pretending to be hurt more than he was, he sank to one knee. Robert moved in for a killing blow with his arm raised. The frog tattoo was exposed. Right before the twitch that signaled Robert's release of the stream of energy, Raphael's sword swooped up. The deadly blade sliced through flesh, muscle, sinew, and bone. Robert screamed as his forearm, cut from the rest of his body, fell to the ground, the frog tattoo on the severed arm now useless.

Blood spurted everywhere. Robert dropped to his knees, those blue eyes clouded with pain and tears.

"I only wanted to be like you," he gasped. "I only wanted our master to love me like he loved you."

A wave of sorrow came over Raphael. "He tried to love you, Robert, but you stole from him and betrayed him. You tried to place the blame on me."

Robert toppled sideways. "I'm sorry," he whispered. "Forgive me."

He held out his hand and Raphael gripped it. This man had once been his friend, a slave, like him. But he had taken a different path.

Robert smiled weakly. "Kill the witch for me." And then the light left those twinkling blue eyes.

Raphael climbed to his feet. He had no time to mourn, for monsters swarmed through the field. Their numbers had multiplied in the time he had been battling Robert.

He spotted Sydney fighting a ghostly figure that breathed out streams of sickly green vapor. Every time she threw a ball of magic at it, the figure seemed to absorb it with no ill effects and inched closer to her. Determined to protect her, he fought his way to her side.

Sydney caught a glimpse of Raphael out of the corner of her eye making his way in her direction. He was covered in blood, and she had a moment of panic when she thought he might be injured. But he wasn't limping, and he had no trouble fighting off an ogre. She threw an energy ball at a ghastly, ghostly figure that had suddenly appeared before her. Her magic felt weaker, and she was tiring. She threw more magic, but the monster didn't die. Raphael arrived at her side and with a single swipe of his scimitar, he lopped off the figure's head. The monster exploded in a puff of putrid green fumes.

She sent Raphael a grateful grin. He grinned back, then sliced at an enormous lizard that had slunk up behind her. But the lizard suddenly disappeared. Around her, all the other vile creatures dropped, lifeless, one by one. Streams of vile dust and smoke rose from them and floated through the air, coalescing at one point. Around Nulkana.

She was drawing the magic back from the monsters and erecting a supernatural shield that held Gide at bay. No matter how many times he sliced with the Crystal Dagger, he couldn't break through. The sorceress smiled a deadly smile and turned her attention to Raphael.

"You will give it to me," she said.

Nulkana flicked her hand and a rope of magic snaked out, wrapped around Raphael, pinned his arms, and dragged him toward her. He struggled against it, but the more he fought, the tighter it became.

Sydney grabbed Raphael's hand to try to pull him back. As soon as she touched him, her power surged. She shot magic at the rope, but it did nothing. Nulkana would not get Raphael. Sydney loved him. And if the sorceress got her hands on his piece of the Sphere, her power would be enormous.

Alessandro, who was closest to her, threw his arm around her waist to help her. Once more, she felt her power surge. She threw more magic at Nulkana. As she did, her mother's ring caught the light. It seemed to glow. The ouroboros. The infinite circle. Wholeness. She knew what they must do.

"Hold hands, everyone," she yelled. "Make a circle!"

Sabrina took Alessandro's hand. Then Sebastian, and Allegra, and Antonio, and Solange all joined hands, and Sabrina twined her arm through Raphael's. They encircled Nulkana and Gide, who was trying to cut through the shield with the Crystal Dagger. He swung around and sliced through the magical rope dragging at Raphael. It snapped, the sound reverberating across the field. Nulkana staggered back, and Gide lunged once more at the shield, but it was still too strong.

Sydney could feel everyone's magic surging through her. It pulsed, warm and strong, wanting to be used. As Gide stabbed again and again at Nulkana's shield with the Crystal Dagger, she had an idea.

"Throw your magic at the Dagger," she called out.

Sabrina and Solange threw out a stream of magic at the weapon. Sebastian created a small storm cloud that shot lightning bolts at the

Dagger. Their magic was stronger than anything Sydney had ever seen. The Dagger's pulsing light grew brighter. Gathering the surging power from everyone, Sydney sent a blast at the shield surrounding Nulkana. It exploded in a cascade of light and noise, of flames and shooting sparks. Gide leaped forward, and with a single thrust, stabbed Nulkana in the chest. She released an unearthly scream that pierced Sydney's ears. The ground shook. The air rumbled. Vile, putrid smoke streamed from Nulkana's mouth.

And then the ancient sorceress who had persecuted the House of Auriano for centuries dropped to the ground in a heap.

Nulkana was dead.

Chapter 24

Silence fell. No one moved. Raphael half-expected Nulkana to rise up in all her evilness and torture him again. But the sorceress remained dead, her cloak a dark blob of black on the charred field. Not even the shape of a body remained. She had disappeared into nothing.

His amulet warmed and pulsed softly against his chest. The sensation reassured him. Was the curse finally broken, now that Nulkana was destroyed? He hesitated to discover the answer.

A clatter distracted him. The skeletal man who had stood behind Nulkana, urging her on, crumpled into a pile of bones. A bare skull rolled from beneath his robe and came to rest against Sabrina's foot. In disgust, she kicked it away. It bounced its way across the field and onto the road where it landed in a muddy puddle.

Beside him, Sydney let out a sigh. As he turned to her, she swayed, her eyes slipped closed, and her knees buckled. Before he could catch her, she collapsed to the ground.

Panic gripped him as he dropped beside her and wrapped his arms around her. "Sydney!"

Slick blood covered her neck and stained her dress down one side. The wound at her neck that Robert had inflicted bled profusely. He had no idea it had cut so deep. She had fought bravely, despite bleeding from her wound. He tried to staunch the blood, but it seeped between his fingers. Someone handed him a cloth that he pressed against Sydney's neck, but it soon became saturated with her blood. In the glow of the golden moon, her face was pale, her lips colorless. She barely breathed.

No, no, no! She couldn't die. He loved her.

"Sydney," he whispered. "Sydney, Sydney…You can't die. I have so much more to teach you about kisses."

But she didn't respond. No shy smile curved her lips. No blushes bloomed in her cheeks.

He wouldn't let her die. She was the most courageous woman he had ever met. Despite her injury, she had fought on, helping to destroy the evil sorceress who had plagued him most of his life, who had placed a curse on his family. That family gathered around him now.

Use the Sphere.

Raphael heard the words in his head, but they didn't make sense. The weak voice didn't come from anyone standing around him. It sounded like an older man. He thought he had imagined it.

Use the Sphere, the voice said again.

Finally understanding, he gripped his amulet, pulled it over his head, and pressed it against the wound on Sydney's neck. Tiny lights danced around his hand and spun faster and faster. The amulet glowed golden, pulsing softly. Slowly, the bleeding stopped. Beneath his hand, he could feel the wound knit together. The dancing lights disappeared and the glow in the amulet faded away.

Sydney sucked in a breath. Her eyes fluttered opened, those magnificent changeable eyes. Relief, so strong that he had to blink away tears, swept through him. She wasn't going to die.

Her hand gently cupped his cheek. But her eyes filled with tears as she gazed up at him.

"I would never hurt you," she said, then looked beyond him to those standing around them. "I would never hurt anyone in your family."

Raphael glanced around at the members of his new family. No one appeared to dispute Sydney's declaration. In fact, they all looked very relieved that she was alive and talking.

Taking the hand at his cheek, he placed a soft kiss on her palm. "I don't think you have to worry about that, *ya helo*. You have more than proved to the Auriano family that you are not their enemy."

Her face relaxed into a smile. "That's good. I was quite worried, you see. I wanted to explain, but then I couldn't because Al Jabbar took me prisoner."

"Yes, I understand," he said solemnly. "But there is something else…" He took his time slipping the cord with his amulet back over his head.

Her eyes widened. "Oh! The curse! Is it gone?"

"There is something else besides the curse." He glanced away, then back. "I wanted to tell you—"

"You're returning to the desert," she said, sadness clouding her eyes. "I understand."

"No, *ya helo*." He shook his head, bent closer, and whispered, "I want to tell you…I love you."

Surprise crossed her face, and then her eyes glowed. "Oh, my dearest Pirate. I love you, too!" She threw her arms around his neck and kissed him.

He thought he heard applause, but it faded away as joy flooded him. After all these years of not knowing who he was, he finally knew. He was the man who loved Miss Sydney Charlotte Whelton. She had become his life. He held her close, losing himself in the feel of her, the scent of her, the taste of her.

Someone coughed. And coughed again. It was a horrendous, deep, rattling cough. Distracted, Raphael reluctantly ended the delicious kiss and raised his head. The figure in the black cowl who had stood silently behind Nulkana next to the skeletal man staggered toward them. As everyone backed away, Zayed stepped forward to steady him. He sent Raphael a look that conveyed this figure was somehow important. Raphael scrambled to his feet and pulled Sydney up with him. Swaying unsteadily, the figure stopped in front of him. He whispered something, dropped to one knee, and toppled sideways. As he did, his cowl fell off, revealing an old man, his face ravaged by pain.

Allegra screamed. "Papa!" She fell to her knees beside the man and cradled his head in her lap. "Oh, Papa," she crooned, as she stroked his head, "you've come back to us."

Alessandro and Antonio looked at each other in amazement.

"Armanno," Alessandro said.

"Our father," Antonio said.

As they knelt beside him, tears streamed down their cheeks.

"We thought you were dead," Antonio said, his voice wavering.

"*Si,* we thought the sorceress had killed you," Alessandro added. His words were thick with emotion.

"She took me prisoner and put me under a terrible spell," their father explained in a voice rusty from disuse. "I so longed to see you all once again." His affectionate gaze traveled over each of them, then landed on Raphael, and he beckoned him closer. As Raphael went down on one knee beside him, Armanno touched his cheek.

"My long-lost son," he murmured. "Angelo. You've come home."

Raphael held the man's hand. This was his father, the man he had searched for his whole life.

Armanno looked beyond Raphael to his other children and their spouses. "It is good to see my family once more. You have grown and become strong. And now you have families of your own." Armanno coughed long and hard. "It is time for me to go," he whispered. "The curse will be broken. Complete the Sphere."

"No, Papa!" Allegra cried. "Don't go! The Sphere will make you well."

Armanno shook his head and he smiled. "No, *cara.* Your mother waits for me." His gaze focused on something beyond the family who circled him. "I am coming, *amore mio…my beloved.*" With a great sigh, he closed his eyes and was gone.

Allegra sobbed as she kissed his forehead then rose to stand beside Sebastian. Raphael stood beside Sydney, and one by one, the family held hands, circling their father. A wispy figure appeared, a woman, hovering over him. Slowly, Armanno's spirit emerged from his body to join her. The two spirits clasped hands, rose up, and disappeared. No one spoke. Allegra sniffled.

The great wooden gate to the *castello* rattled and was flung open. Lucy came running out.

"Gide! Gide!" she called, worry lacing her words. Halting before him, she patted his arms and chest. "Oh, my dear, are you all right? Are you hurt?"

The Frenchman caught her hands and hugged them to his chest. "I am fine, *mon amour.*"

"Oh, thank heavens!" She wrapped her arms around his neck and kissed him.

Unaware of the love blossoming between the two, Raphael watched them in bemusement. Turning to Sydney, he murmured, "Miss Foster has inspired me."

Sydney raised a cool brow, but her lips twitched. "Has she?"

"Yes. I would like to kiss you again very much." He trailed his thumb across those kissable lips. "But I need to know something first."

"I have no more secrets," she said, then paused. "Well, perhaps one or two teeny, tiny ones."

"Mm, I love a woman with secrets." He cupped her cheeks and whispered against her mouth, "But I want to know if you will marry me."

She released a sigh and whispered back, "I thought you'd never ask." Then she closed the distance between their lips.

As Raphael wrapped his arms around her, he knew one thing — no matter where in the world he would be — as long as Sydney was with him, he was home.

Epilogue

Raphael followed his new family down the stone steps that led into the darkness beneath the *castello*. Alessandro, Antonio, and Sebastian lit the way with torches as they guided their wives. Beside him was Sydney, his new wife, looking like a fairy in her shimmery white gown and band of diamonds threaded through her hair, jewels that the twins told him were his legacy as a member of the family. The sunshine and the sound of the wedding celebration, still bright and noisy, filtered through the open door behind him. He felt like the luckiest man alive. Once a slave with no home, no family, and no name, he had gained all three, and won the most beautiful, courageous woman he had ever known. He glanced back at her as he guided her down the stairs. Her mischievous smile warmed him and hinted at the delights that awaited him later.

He felt confined in his wedding clothes — black velvet coat and breeches, silver embroidered waistcoat, and a high collar and neckcloth tied in an intricate knot. If he'd had his way, he would have worn his loose desert clothing, but the prince and duke and earl all convinced him that wouldn't have been appropriate for the eldest member of the House of Auriano. Sydney's appreciative expression upon first seeing him made him glad for the discomfort. But right now, all he wanted to do was strip them off, wishing for a loose *djellaba*. Or perhaps nothing at all so he could make love to his wife.

Two weeks had passed since they had defeated the evil sorceress, Nulkana. Two weeks of sadness and excited preparations for a wedding. Two weeks of allowing the full cycle of the curse to run through the family to be sure no one would be caught in its grip.

They had buried Armanno in the family crypt next to his beloved wife. The whole village had turned out to mourn him. After a few days of quiet seclusion, the family started planning the wedding. Raphael had been relieved when the three men took him out hunting, riding through the countryside, challenging him to freewheeling matches of rapier against scimitar, or games of chess, where he inevitably won most of the time.

He had observed the three siblings as they endured the curse, each in their own time during the phases of the moon—human by day, Shadow at night. They had questioned him incessantly about his own curse. But the curse was about to end. That was why they had descended into the bowels of the earth.

Apprehensive about what he was about to do, he slowed his steps. Sydney squeezed his hand.

"My brave Mr. Pirate," she whispered.

"*Ya helo*," he whispered back. "Brave Sydney."

Sebastian, who was in front of them on the steps, murmured, "You might want to wait on the sweet endearments until this is done. The twins will tease—"

Before he finished, Antonio complained, "Why can't we even get to the bottom of the steps before he starts to make love to his new wife?"

Sebastian raised a brow as if to say, *I told you.*

"I seem to remember you did the same, Tonio," Alessandro said.

Solange sent Antonio a sly little smile that he answered with a wink.

"I think you are all naughty," Allegra added, then laughed as Sebastian squeezed her about the waist and planted a kiss on her cheek.

Antonio sighed dramatically. "I suppose we'll have to keep him."

"*Si*, and he does resemble you, Tonio," Alessandro said.

Sabrina chuckled and touched her husband's cheek. "He resembles you, as well, Sandro."

Alessandro captured his wife's hand and kissed her palm.

Raphael listened to the playful teasing with awe. His life had been bereft of such easy familiarity. He'd only had Zayed, who was as close as a brother, but growing up, their primary focus had been on staying alive rather than merriment. His good fortune in finding this new family overwhelmed him.

He had worried that Zayed would leave, but his friend — his brother — had agreed to remain. He had told Raphael that he felt welcomed by Gasparo, Piero, and Luisa. The winds would tell him if he should leave. But the winds were telling him to stay. The music from the open door changed to the rhythms of the desert, and Raphael smiled. He had the feeling the winds would be telling Zayed to stay for a very long time.

They reached the bottom of the stairs, and the men placed their torches into brackets on the wall. Raphael found himself in a small chamber carved out of the bedrock, deep beneath the Castello Auriano. The walls were rough-hewn, but the floor had been paved with smooth stones. A large, flat, circular stone that would take many men to move decorated the center. Alessandro, Antonio, and Allegra stood around the edge of the circle, leaving a space for him. With a nod, Alessandro indicated Raphael should join them.

They had explained what they were going to do, so when they extended their hands over the circular stone, Raphael did the same. Closing his eyes as the others did, he concentrated on moving the stone. He could feel the others' forces flowing through him. He had never felt so strong, nearly invincible. His fingers twitched. The huge stone lifted, and with a mental nudge from the others, he floated it sideways and let it fall with a thud.

When he opened his eyes, he saw that the floor beneath looked no different than the rest, but he had been told what was below. Following the directions that Alessandro had given him, he held out his hand over the spot where the stone had lain and walked around it in a counterclockwise direction. A circular area in the floor moved with him. He sensed a click in his head, and with a flick of his fingers, opened the vault that lay beneath.

He caught his breath at the sight. The vault was lined with gold, and in its center was an intricately wrought golden pedestal that held an incomplete sphere made of carved amber — the magical Sphere of Astarte. It emitted a dull glow.

The amulet against his chest warmed and started to throb. He had a nearly uncontrollable urge to rip it off and add it to the Sphere.

291

But if he did that, he would turn to Shadow. Forever. He clutched the amulet through his shirt as he tried to block the urge.

"You have to complete the Sphere," Alessandro said.

Raphael shook his head.

"Trust us." Antonio's simple words tugged at him.

Allegra took a step forward. "Please. You are one of us now."

Raphael met Sydney's gaze. He saw love there, and encouragement. Gathering his courage, he took hold of the cord holding the amulet and pulled it over his head. As soon as it came free, the piece lifted and strained toward the rest of the Sphere. Reluctant to let it go, he held on, but the drag on his fingers was too strong. It slipped out of his grasp and flew to the Sphere where it settled into the open spot with a snap.

A chill ran through Raphael, the same chill he experienced when he turned to Shadow. Looking down at his hand, he watched as it became indistinct and dark, the phenomenon starting at his fingertips, flowing across his palm, and disappearing beneath the cuff of his shirt. Resigned to being Shadow for the rest of his existence, he glanced at Sydney to see her reaction. But she wasn't looking at him. She was staring at the Sphere, her eyes wide in amazement.

He turned to the Sphere. His piece had pierced the middle of the Sphere like a bolt of lightning, fusing with the other pieces and forming a beautiful, carved ball of translucent amber. It pulsed with light, each pulse growing brighter than the last. Around him, he could sense the anticipation of the others.

The pulses rippled out in waves of power. Raphael gasped as they surged through him, more potent than anything he had ever felt, nearly painful. The power spilled beyond him, beyond their circle, into the stone walls of the chamber, into the bedrock below his feet. The *castello* seemed to absorb it, embrace it like a long-lost lover.

Then he heard a low sound like a heartbeat reverberate in the stone, followed by another, and another and another. The heartbeats continued, soft and steady, like an old clock.

Sydney gasped. "Your hand," she said. "It's not Shadow. It's normal."

He looked down at his hand, now flesh and bone where before it had been Shadow.

"The curse is broken!" Allegra exclaimed. "Sandro! Tonio! The curse is broken!" She exuberantly hugged them both, then came to stand before Raphael. Shyly, she asked, "May I embrace you, as well, brother?"

Bemused at the request, he had no immediate answer. He'd never had a sister. The only women he had held in his arms had been bed-partners, and now, only his new wife. But he had seen the affection that her brothers had shown her. This woman was his sister, and he liked her. He wanted to get to know her better, as he did her two brothers and the rest of the family. With a nod, he opened his arms to her. Standing on tiptoe, she wrapped her arms around his neck and kissed him on the cheek.

"Thank you for bringing us the last piece of the Sphere," she said, as she stepped back. "Thank you for coming home."

Silence prevailed for a moment as everyone absorbed the significance of what had occurred.

Antonio pulled his wife close with an arm around her waist. "If no one objects, I would like to return to the celebration and dance with my wife."

Everyone agreed that sounded like an excellent idea. Raphael and Sydney were the last up the stairs. He stopped on the bottom step and looked back at the chamber. The large, round, flat stone was back in place covering the vault. The magical Sphere of Astarte was where it should be. And the heartbeat of Auriano continued to pulse gently through the stones. He was no longer a slave nor a renegade of the desert. And Sydney was his home.

As he was about to start up the stairs, she placed a gentle hand on his chest. Her eyes twinkled mischievously.

"I want you to know that no matter where we are, I always want to sit before you on a camel," she said.

He pretended confusion. "But there are no camels in Auriano."

She grinned. "You are the Pirate. *My* Pirate. I'm sure you'll think of something."

Oh, yes, he could envision many somethings. "Sydney-Who-Is-Not-A-Boy, I predict many enjoyable rides in your future." He smiled slyly. "I think there might be a ride tonight."

She giggled. "I can hardly wait."

With a grin, he took her hand, and together they climbed the stairs to their life together, enfolded by their family.

THE END

PATRICIA BARLETTA'S BOOK LIST

On His Majesty's Secret Service
The Duke Who Loved Me
Book 1

The Duke's Dangerous Kiss
Book 2

Confessions of a Dangerous Duke
Book 3

Auriano Curse Series
Moon Dark
Book 1

Moon Shadow
Book 2

Moon Bright
Book 3

Moon Gold
Book 4

Sign up for Patricia's newsletter at
PATRICIABARLETTA.COM

Follow Patricia Barletta on BookBub

Follow Patricia Barletta on Amazon

Like Patricia Barletta's Facebook Page

About Patricia Barletta

Patricia Barletta is an award-winning author of historical and para-normal romance fiction. After a fulfilling career teaching English Literature at a private high school, she decided to go back to school herself, and obtained a Master of Fine Arts in Creative Writing at Stonecoast (University of Southern Maine). When she's not at a yoga class doing her best downward dog, Patricia is usually tending her hydrangeas or hosting a brunch for her writing group. Patricia loves to travel, and often finds the inspiration for her dark heroes, feisty heroines, and romantic settings while on a research trip. At the end of each journey she loves going home to her cozy, historical old house outside of Boston where she weaves her magical tales.

Find out more about Patricia and her books on her website: patriciabarletta.com where you can also sign up for her newsletter. You can also find Patricia on Facebook @patriciabarlettaauthor and Instagram.